The Wanderer Trilogy
Book One: Purpose
Brittany Hanson

Dedication:
To the ones who left scars. This was cheaper than therapy.

For information, contact:
www.BrittanyHansonWrites.com

ISBN: 978-1-970323-00-9
Printed in the United States of America
First Edition

Chapter 1

Dim, hazy lanterns flickered against the steel walls of the massive, single room building. Smoke billowed and stuck to its high ceilings, brimming over until the cloud reached the windows where it crawled out into the night sky. The source, small fires underneath boiling pots of food. That is, if you could call perpetual stew made from scraps of meat and vegetables, food. At the door in the front of the building, a line of men, women, and children waited to be served their second and final meal of the day. Both the cooks and their hungry patrons were clad in mismatched ragged clothing. Dust and mud-caked figures carrying small knives and blades grabbed their stomachs and licked their lips as they grabbed their bowl and scattered to various wooden tables inside the hall. These people, who called themselves Rovers, were farmers who worked tirelessly to grow enough crops so that their small colony of a few hundred could survive. With only a handful of skilled craftsmen among them, they had little to trade with the other peaceful peoples of the region. So they mostly stayed to themselves, working in the fields close to their homes and growing just enough to share amongst themselves.

Next to the queue stood a few pieces of rounded metal topped with wet-warped wood that resembled a bar. Glass vessels of varying shapes and sizes brimming with both clear and cloudy alcohols lined the table in a neat row. At one corner, a few of the patrons laughed loudly in a slurred, drunken stupor. Their kin ignored them. A dozen or so merchants and traders from other settlements outside the region bartered with each other for clothing, weapons, armor, and supplies around the edge of the room.

It was hard to believe that only a few years ago, this was once a much larger, more boisterous town. Today, the population barely filled the hall. Kidnapping and enslavement, murder, and famine had plagued the colony for over a decade. Now, the survivors spent their days living in fear of the next time the Gangs would strike.

These Gangs were massive settlements with two types of inhabitants - the Gang members themselves, and the tortured souls that served them. Seven compounds dotted the region between the crumbling city to the South, the towering bluffs to the North and East, and the endless miles of impassable woodlands to the West. Each one adopted the name of some animal that they felt embodied their people: Rats, Wolves, Leopards, Foxes,

Badgers, Tigers, and the Serpents. The two largest Gangs, the Serpents and the Tigers, commanded massive settlements in the East, while the remaining Gangs were scattered across the Western region, divided by a dense forest line.

Over the last few years, the Gangs' insatiable hunger for power had only intensified. No one was safe from their raids or kidnappings anymore. Certainly not a group of simple farmers like the Rovers.

In an intentionally unoccupied corner of the hall, at a lone table, sat a young woman. Her back, facing away from the rest of the crowd as it always was. She was silent. A hood concealed her face as she ate. Those around her paid little attention. The wide berth they gave her was intentional, not out of fear, but respect. She preferred to be alone. It was safer that way. *No one to weigh you down.* Although it appeared that she was ignoring everyone, she was always listening. Always alert.

The Rovers' voices fell silent when two loud men came bursting through the front door. Two gunshots rang through the hall, followed by the pained scream of a woman, and again, silence. A couple small children whimpered. Each bullet had met its mark in the body of two innocent Rovers, killing one instantly, and leaving the other writhing in pain for mere moments before falling limp,

Still, the woman in the corner did not stir.

"Bow or we will take more lives!" one of the assailants commanded, chuckling to himself. "The Rats demand it."

The woman in the corner mouthed the word "Rats" to herself. She knew that this Gang was smaller, but loud and merciless. Their compound lay West of the forest. They were notorious for their recklessness - almost an excitement - about ending the lives of others. Everyone in the food hall was now on their knees with their foreheads pressed against the floor.

Except for the woman in the corner.

One of the Rats noticed her defiance. "Hey, bitch!" He stomped across the room toward her, kicking and stepping on the Rovers that were in his path.

She lifted her head but did not turn to them.

"You *deaf*?" said the other man, nudging her shoulder with his gun, hard. "We told you useless pieces of shit to *bow down*."

The woman rose slowly to her feet with her back still turned to them. "And why… would I bow to you?"

"Because we shoot if you don't," the Rat scoffed. "You'll end up like your friends over there." He pointed at the bodies near the door. She could make out two motionless figures out of the corner of her eye.

"I have a better idea. Leave. Or I will return the favor," she demanded, back still facing them.

Lives are owed.

The Rats' laughter was cut short. Without pause, the young woman revealed a hidden knife in her sleeve and buried it deep into the eye socket of one of the Gang members. As his body came crashing to the floor, she snatched a handgun from his holster and pointed it at the survivor while he fumbled to reload his own weapon. Ammunition slipped from his trembling hands, scattering across his friend's lifeless body.

A half-smile crept across her mouth, barrel pointed at his chest. "Did you kill anything else before coming here? Shouldn't leave only two bullets in your weapon," she mocked. "I could have killed you ten times over by now."

"I… I - um," stuttered the Rat.

"Shame," said the woman melodically. "You are such a long way from home."

Her face was still obscured by her hood and the low lighting, but the man seemed to know of her.

"You're the one they talk about, aren't you?" he stammered. "You *must be her*. I've never seen anyone move so fast."

"I am the protector for those who cannot protect themselves," she replied. "And you take innocent lives with reckless disregard. Now, I am your justice."

She squeezed the trigger. The bullet burst through the man's rib cage. He doubled back, desperately clutching his wound. A few moments later, the color faded from his eyes and his body relaxed. Everything was silent. Once the Rovers were certain both Rats were dead and no others were coming, they slipped into the streets with quiet cries. Parents clutched their little ones and disappeared into the darkness. All around, heavy locks slammed, and barriers dropped over shack doors.

The families of the fallen remained behind, mourning as volunteers carried the bodies away for burial.

Just as it always was.

A man walked up and shook the hooded woman's hand. "Thank you for stopping two more of them. At this rate, there isn't much hope of us surviving even a few more years, but maybe it is possible. My wife believes your presence scares some of them from coming here."

"I am not so sure about that. They will return looking for their comrades," she spoke shortly. "Return their bodies to the edge of the forest. Perhaps the Rats will believe their members were killed by another Gang. Doubtful… but who knows."

After the Rovers had left with the corpses of their loved ones, the woman beckoned the bartender for help with the Rats. She looked around at those who chose to stay behind. Most of them had been with the colony for years, watching it dwindle in size as the Gangs continued to butcher and oppress their people. No one here was a warrior. Their weary faces bore the quiet acceptance that death at the hands of the Gangs was inevitable. Those that they called the Elders were no longer phased by bloodshed. She, too, had grown calloused to death itself.

The bartender addressed their champion. "Eva. We are always grateful for your protection. Though I must ask, do you really think that more will return for revenge? It's been so long since a Gang attacked us."

"As they always have." Eva removed her hood to reveal shoulder length burgundy hair and piercing aqua-colored eyes. "However, your kin just gained two more firearms tonight. Maybe this time, some of you should learn how to use it…"

The bartender nodded. Eva continued.

"If it isn't the Rats, it will be the Serpents or the Tigers. And if it's not them, it will be some other Gang. We must stand to fight or die. That is always the choice."

Even though I'm the only one fighting, she thought to herself.

She walked with the bartender over to the pale bodies of the assailants, knelt down, and began rummaging through their pockets, handing the contents to him. Two pistols, some ammunition, and a small loaf of bread wrapped in linen. He pocketed them. With help from a few others to carry the bodies, Eva led them out of the colony and towards the forest. She paid little attention to the setting sun as she trudged towards the purple twilight.

"Why not take them to the outskirts of the city instead?" one of the female Rovers asked Eva. "Or inside the forest."

She nodded towards the woods. "No one ventures through that tree line without a guide... especially at night. Plus, do you *really* want to drag them all the way to the city? I'm not risking being caught with

Rovers that can't fend for themselves against more Gang members. And if the Rats don't come looking for their 'friends' in a day or so, animals will take care of the mess."

The two lifeless bodies were soon discarded at the edge of the foliage, and the Rovers had returned to their shacks, locking them tight with wedges of metal and wood. Eva also had her own home near the center of town. Her shack, like the others, was constructed from pieces of large metal sheets riveted together decades before. In between these walls were small cracks and holes where the sunlight could seep in and illuminate her house in a dim, hazy glow. The front door was secured with a metal bar, which always shrieked with the grating sound of rust when she locked it from the inside.

With the last few rays of daylight piercing through her room, Eva slumped into bed. She laid there for a few moments, admiring her knickknacks. Shelves at her feet were lined with countless treasures from the Old Times, scavenged from the city over the last five years. She knew the names of these objects, but did not understand their purpose. Still, she displayed them as trophies and echoes of a life long past.

She often found herself asking questions and reminiscing about what life was like two hundred and fifty years ago, before the bombs fell. Before the War of Rebirth. Before the world descended into chaos and millions were killed. *What was life like before? What were these things used for? How did they get power for their lights?*

But her most treasured discovery was a journal, preserved to near perfection. Years ago, she came across it in a fireproof box under a wardrobe in the city. She could still recall the tingle of excitement when she realized the passages were still legible. As she carefully flipped through the entries, Eva noticed that the journal was only half-full, so she decided to continue the writings with her own adventures.

Stories of survival, both past and present, filled the pages, written by an anonymous author and Eva Calloway, spanning over hundreds of years. During every evening meal, she would read a new entry and add her own.

Two hundred and fifty years later, would they know I can still hear the echoes of their voices?

Tonight was the first night I heard those words on the radio... "World War." I never believed I would be living it. Bombs have been dropping all over the United States along with the rest of the world. The government is preparing us for the worst. Some are calling it the War of Rebirth. Rebirth of what? The human race? Is that supposed to make me feel better?

How much longer do we have? Not everyone can afford to build a bomb shelter and I don't believe the nonsense rumors of government-built vaults to house so-called the important people of this damned country. Or maybe I don't want to believe it. Leaving people out here to die when the morons we elected are safe and sound during all of this.

All the radio said is that America is no longer safe. It's only a matter of time before the end of the world. So many world leaders are at war with each other, and the rest of us are just innocent victims. Millions of people dying for the ideals of the few? How did it come to this... But it's too late now. Our fates are decided.... I guess it's a good thing I have the money to build a bomb shelter for me and my family. It's all the hope we have to survive this.

I just hope I built this thing right.

Eva flipped to the next available page and grabbed her pen, scrawling her evening into the leaf.

ANOTHER NIGHT OF BLOODSHED. TWO RATS KILLED TWO ROVERS WHILE EVERYONE WAS GATHERED FOR THE EVENING MEAL. THE RATS WERE EASY TO DISPOSE OF, THOUGH. WE TOOK THEIR BODIES TO THE FOREST. I HOPE THE ANIMALS TEAR THEM APART.

I KEEP ASKING THE ROVERS WHY THEY DON'T JUST ABANDON THEIR TOWN FOR THE CITY OR THE WESTERN ROVERS, BUT THEY ARE TOO AFRAID. THEY DON'T EVEN BOTHER LEARNING TO DEFEND THEMSELVES. WHAT'S THE POINT OF ME BEING HERE? WHY DO I EVEN BOTHER? THEY WOULD RATHER DIE A SLOW, PAINFUL DEATH THAN FIGHT FOR A CHANCE AT LIVING.

BUT I HAVE TO STAY. THEY LOOK UP TO ME. AFTER EVERYTHING I'VE DONE.

With that short entry, Eva was out of sunlight to continue. For a while, she laid in bed with her arm hanging over her gear, contemplating what to do the following day. Staring up at the rippled, riveted ceiling, her fingertips fell over the hilts of her blades. She caressed them, deep in thought. Soon, a wave of exhaustion finally overtook her, and she drifted into a deep sleep.

* * *

The sound of chirping birds roused Eva from sleep the next morning. Faint rays of light danced up the wall near her feet, and a cool breeze brushed the delicate hairs on her head as it floated through the room. Each day began with scavenging in the city while the Rovers slept. She tucked the journal beneath her pillow and swung her feet over the edge of the bed. Yawning and stretching, Eva laced up her boots and rolled onto her stomach to peek through one of the slits in her wall. Rustling of trees and the twitter of birds were the only sounds in the dew-covered town. A small herd of deer trotted almost noiselessly down the rocky path in the middle of town, disappearing in the morning haze. Rabbits that were feeding on the weeds noticed them and scuttled out of the way. If the thought of inherent danger had not been ingrained in her mind, Eva would have savored the calmness of dawn.

Instead, she lifted herself out of bed and rummaged through a cabinet of assorted fruits, vegetables, bread, and potatoes in her back room. The Rovers each had gardens right outside their homes, where they would plant various types of foods. Whatever crops managed to bloom during harvest seasons would be shared throughout the colony, which was mostly fruits, vegetables, and herbs. Other delicacies, such as wild game, chickens, and wheat for bread, were brought in through trade. The Nomads, a large group of nature-worshippers from the city, would travel to the colony to offer goods.

Eva choked down a quick meal while holstering a handgun, various knives, and her most prized possessions - two curved short blades. When she was much younger, she took them from the first person she ever killed.

The leather sheaths wrapped around her shoulders like a small backpack and crossed the weapons like an X over her shoulder blades. Each hilt felt as though they were constructed from a special type of hide that never thinned with use. Over the years, they had molded perfectly to her grip yet never needed replacing. And the blades themselves were cast from metal that never seemed to dull or tarnish. Part of her believed that these swords held supernatural abilities, somehow making her lighter and more agile with each life they took.

After taking a few drinks from a water canteen and finishing her meal, Eva cautiously made her way outside of the shack. *The first step is always the most dangerous.* Many Gangs traveled through the area during the day, terrorizing her people en route to the city. Many times, she had awoken to the sound of pounding on doors and the shouting of Gang members, but they never managed to break into the homes and wouldn't waste ammunition trying to shoot through the shacks. As long as the Rovers remained quiet, they would eventually give up and leave. Most of the time.

Even though the closest compounds were a two-day journey from the colony, there was always a chance of an attack. Many Gangs used the roads to bypass the forest on their way to the city to search for supplies.

When she was sure it was safe, Eva began her three-mile hike south towards the ever-crumbling city. Only the tops of these massive, misshapen buildings were visible from the town on a clear day. It would take about an hour to reach her destination.

Eva glanced up at the sky. Shadows crept across the land as dark clouds gathered on the horizon, swallowing the last of the morning sun. She pulled her hood over her head, bracing for what was coming. Distant thunder rolled through the ruined city and into the valley.

Eva Calloway had been on her own for as long as she could remember. This solitude had shaped her, sharpened her, and taught her what it meant to survive. Over time, she had learned to read the land, to feel it shift. She knew when to hide and when to move. But bad weather always made everything more difficult. The noise of a thunderstorm masked the sounds she relied on. The wind carried unfamiliar scents and scattered her focus. Out here, a single mistake could cost her everything. So she moved slower. Listened deeper.

Trusted less. Now was not the time for comfort. It was the time for caution.

The land between the Rover colony and the crumbling metropolis was scattered with remnants of the Old Times, consumed by centuries of neglect. Ancient, collapsed homes lined streets dotted with vehicles, while the tops of trees sprouted through overgrown buildings and pushed away the wreckage. The blackening sky seemed to echo the war's long shadow, a haunting reminder of all that had been lost. Eva often wondered what life was like before. From time to time, she had discovered papers that detailed the war. However, there was very little literature about her ancestors' daily lives. Much of it was barely legible after so long in the elements. Even so, the objects left behind could only ever tell part of the story. These strange trinkets, crafted from unfamiliar materials, fascinated her.

After nearly an hour, the cityscape came to meet her. The pitter patter of raindrops danced over her hood and slid down her shoulders in beads. She inhaled and closed her eyes for a moment of peaceful bliss as a welcoming shiver crawled up her spine. Then she stopped and shook her head.

Gotta stay alert.

Upon entering the city, Eva followed along a road she had not traveled in some time. Buildings in this area had largely been scarred by The Old Time War. There was jagged metal and loose rubble everywhere. It was dangerous to say the least. Thunder crashed above her. Nomads left no mark in this part of the metropolis. It made sense that they would stay away from the outskirts for fear of running into a Gang. Not to mention that these buildings were far more hazardous than the deeper parts of the city. At any moment, they could collapse. In fact, some of the towers looked as though they had fallen to rubble recently.

It was a particularly cool day as Eva continued her trek to a part of the city that was significantly less deteriorated. Towering storm clouds accompanied by a soft drizzle and the occasional flash of lightning and rumble of thunder. Despite all this, scavenging was never easy work. Even on her most successful adventures, Eva would gather maybe a handful of semi-valuable items after spending an entire day in the city.

Eva's boots crunched over broken glass as she stepped into the ruins of an old shop, one hand gripping the hilt of her blade. She moved carefully, eyes scanning the floor and shelves with practiced precision. Most of the food had long since rotted or been picked clean by animals. But she wasn't here for food. What she hunted were medical supplies, weapon parts, or rare items. Pieces of the past worth keeping, trading, or adding to her private collection. Unfortunately, not much was left on the shelves except a few open cans of molded lima beans and peaches. Two hundred years of scavenging and many obvious places were picked clean centuries ago.

Eva had almost given up until something caught her eye near the cash counter.

Passing a quick glance into the street, she hopped over to the desk. Against the wall in the corner, there was a palm-sized coin purse almost completely obscured by a piece of wood. When Eva opened it, she couldn't believe her eyes. *Jackpot.* Twinkling gems filled this clasp to the brim. Even though she did not know what type of jewels they were, she guessed they would fetch a high price with traders. And if nothing else, she could keep them in her home. Her eyes moved to a small box behind a fallen shelf next to the coin purse. It had a red cross painted on it. She opened it and smiled.

Bingo.

Inside the rusted box was a small first aid kit with some bandages, a small bottle of alcohol, and a few other items that had expired a century before. The bandages and alcohol would be useful, but Eva simply tossed the medications aside and stuffed the rest in her pockets.

Until midday, she rummaged through countless other shops and homes. She even traveled back to the more dangerous parts of the city and searched there as well. Unfortunately, the storms were making it difficult to traverse deeper into the city like she had hoped. Fallen metal sheets from the skyscrapers were now slick and the river that ran through the city streets flooded many of the buildings at the center of the metropolis. So, Eva decided to return to the colony early.

"Well, I guess I'm done for the day," she sighed. "Nothing but a few bandages and some gems… but no use in wasting any more energy."

The rain had softened by the time Eva reached the edges of the colony, but she kept her hood up to block some of the mist. From afar, it seemed as though the Rovers were still sleeping peacefully as she entered the ghost town in the afternoon. *Odd. Normally they are tending to their gardens by now.* Just as she reached the outermost ring of shacks, she heard a child's scream. Without a second thought, she sprinted towards the source of the noise, unsheathing her blades.

Not again. I hope I'm not too late.

Closing in on the source of the noise, more voices rose above the sound of her own breath. They were calling to the little girl, whose back was pressed against a tree in the center of the town. Eva slunk between two shacks and peered out down the main road to find a group of Gang members surrounding a small child.

Shit kid, she thought. *Why would you leave your house alone?*

"Come on little girl," one of them beckoned. "We will take you somewhere nice. You will never have to be scared again."

The girl dashed from the tree and backed up to a nearby shack.

Eva heard the faint click of a gun.

They'll only shoot her if she runs off, she thought.

She had one chance to keep this kid alive. If she was too loud, one of them would grab the girl while the others stayed to fight. And if she tried to attack them from afar, they may take the girl's life during the scuffle. She had to come between them, forcing a barrier, and fast. With one steadying breath, she crept around the circle of shacks.

Time dragged endlessly, each second seemed to stretch thin, before Eva finally reached the home behind the child. She stepped out quickly, blocking the predators from their prey, weapons at the ready. They took a step back in shock. Something shifted in Eva's mind. *Go.* Two strikes and two Gang members were dead at her feet with their throats slit. She replaced a blade with her handgun. Another blink and two more, dead. A single trickle of blood between their eyes. Every motion that she made had been meticulously practiced a thousand times before. A dance of execution. Completely natural. Until finally, only one Gang Member was left standing.

"*W-w-what* are you?" he stammered.

"I should ask you the same question," she answered, face still obscured by her hood.

"You're the one," he gasped and pointed at one of her curved blades. "There is a price on your head. A nice one."

She laughed. "And it seems that even *five* of you could not claim the bounty."

"Someone will put a stop to you," he gulped, his hand shaking to his pistol. "Someone will *end* you."

"I have yet to meet anyone skilled enough to kill me. Until then, I will hold that pleasure for myself."

The final ear-shattering gunshot echoed around the metal walls of the town. The man collapsed to his knees and slumped over one of the other corpses. Eva could feel the eyes of the Rovers on her, watching from the safety of their homes. She turned to the little girl who was trembling with fear. When Eva tried to reach out for her, the child bolted towards her home. The door opened just enough for her to vanish inside. Her father, standing at the threshold, thanked Eva with tears in his eyes.

"I am so sorry ma'am. She must've gotten out when I was resting. A few of the kids were out playing when we heard the commotion coming from up the road. The other kids scattered, but she wasn't quick enough… I… I feared she would be taken like her mother," he admitted. He wiped his face. "Thank you, Eva."

Eva nodded. "Don't let it happen again."

The Rover bowed deeply and thanked her once more before shutting the door again.

Eva holstered her pistol and slid her blade back into its sheath, then looked down at the bodies. She knelt beside them and began rummaging through their pockets, searching for anything of value.

The one thing Eva could never comprehend was how these Rovers lived with no desire to protect themselves against the Gangs. Instead, they hid. Parents would not dare chase after their children if they were kidnapped. The few who did never returned. Self-preservation was their sad truth.

In the last five years, Eva witnessed this colony shrink by half. And no matter how hard she tried to protect those who remained, it was never enough. Many who had been captured and forced into the compounds were just children or young adults. The other victims were killed on the spot.

She pulled out a handful of ammunition that matched her pistol. *Perfect*. Eva reloaded swiftly and continued searching. As she rolled one of the bodies over, her eyes caught the Gang's symbol stitched into his clothing. *Tigers*. They were the second-largest Gang in the region, known for trading metal weaponry and tools. At night, the glow of their ever-burning fires illuminated the clouds for miles. The demand for their craftsmanship was high, and their slaves paid the price, forced to work long hours with little food or water. In fact, horrendous labor conditions were common across all the Gangs.

Four of the fallen Tigers had nothing much of value. However, the one that Eva guessed was the leader carried two crumpled, bloodstained pieces of paper. One, a letter. The other, a map. Both had the same handwriting. From what she gathered by briefly scanning the note, it appeared to be a stolen note from the Tiger's only rival, The Serpents.

Bad news. The project hit a snag. Those damned traders are so tight-lipped about their paths through the mountains, everyone we've sent hasn't returned. Going through the cliffs is the only option. If we could get a tunnel through The Blooded Row, we could charge the other Gangs and enslave anyone coming in from the North. The workers moved the last few pieces of rubble covering that metal wall we found. Turns out it's a door. And we finally know what it is. Something from the Old Times. An entire town sealed away from the world with <u>hundreds</u> of people or more. Idiots thought we were going to help them. Their hands are being callused from work as we speak. They will make great Bondsmen and Doxies. First we gotta beat them into submission, though. Shouldn't take long. I want to make sure we go back before the Tigers. I don't want them stealing anything that could take us over. And they - sure as shit - don't deserve any more servants. The tunneling project will be put on hold until further notice. I've included the map to the location. Go back tomorrow to get anyone who got left behind. That is an <u>order</u>.

       -Chief Dalkin

Eva scanned through the letter twice. She couldn't believe what she was reading. People living in solitude for two hundred and fifty years? Not a single day of exposure to the outside world for two centuries? *That's not possible... is it?* If they had fought back against the Serpents or Tigers, they would have been executed. According to the note, those who surrendered had already been forced into slavery. Eva turned to the second piece of parchment and carefully unfolded the map. Her heart sank. She had intended to search for survivors before the Gangs returned, but as her eyes traced the location of the vault, doubt crept in, followed by a flicker of fear.

The two largest and strongest Gangs, the Serpents and Tigers, shared a border to their compounds north of the Rover colony. Between rows of colossal metal and brick walls crowned with barbed wire and dotted with watchtowers, stretched an old road that led up into the bluffs. It was used, although rarely, for the transportation of supplies, slaves, and weapons to other civilizations north of the region. The road itself was treacherous, but the only way out of the region from that direction. Aside from the Gangs, certain traders were permitted to travel through, but at the price of half their own goods. Anyone who refused would be caught, captured, and tortured by the Serpents or Tigers. Sometimes that would happen regardless. The X on this map happened to be right in between these two compounds at the base of one cliff. It was the most infamous part of this road. Rovers and Nomads came to appropriately name this straight The Blooded Row.

Eva struggled with the urge to ignore this letter and leave any potential survivors at the mercy of the Gangs. Her own survival was a priority, but these people were helpless and unarmed. *I can't just leave them there.*

But what if... Before she had a moment to reconsider, she punched the ground and rushed into her house. Gathering an empty pack along with some food and water, she sprinted back to the corpses, removed their jackets, and stuffed them in her sack. She noticed Rovers making their way towards the food hall from their homes. Some of the Elders stopped to question her.

She handed one of them the map. "I'm going through The Blooded Row," she explained. "The Serpents discovered some sort of civilization that's been cut off from the real world since the Old Times. There may still be survivors."

"Have you ever heard of this hidden place?" one of the Elders asked.

She took the map back and slid it in her pocket. "No. I don't remember seeing it in my lifetime."

"Watch yourself Eva," an Elder woman warned. "You may be able to pass as one of the Gangs, but they watch that Row day and night."

"Yeah, but they're blind at night." Eva threw the Tiger's oversized leather jacket over her own. "I'm leaving now."

"It's a two-day journey," another Elder added. "Make sure you eat with us tonight at the very least."

Eva decided not to protest. While many of the Rovers rarely spoke to her out of fear, the Elders cared about her safety and well-being. She followed them to the food hall, taking a bowl of stew and a haunch of bread. Just as she sat down to eat, she felt a tug on her shirt.

It was the little girl from earlier. She looked much more cheerful than before.

"Thank you for saving me today." Her high pitched voice was soft and sweet. Matted red hair hung in her face and dirt caked her cheeks. Thin valleys from old tears stuck to her puffy face. "I won't be going out anymore during the day. My friends won't either."

"That is a very good idea." Eva's heart softened a little. "Be sure to remember that promise."

The little girl nodded and scampered off to her father who was sitting at the far end of the building. Eva finished her meal without another interruption. She stood up and weaved through the crowd of people, dropping off her dishes. Closing the steel door behind her, she looked up at the sky and noticed the full moon overhead.

Her journey to the compounds began at a cobblestone street. Eva imagined that the road was once flat and paved with vehicles zipping past on either side. The slow decay of time had cracked and crumbled the stone to make room for grasses and wildflowers. There were days when Eva would have stopped to savor the few moments of calm she was given.

But not today. Every moment Eva hesitated, the chances grew that another Gang would find more survivors from the mysterious vault. Her pace quickened into a jog as she followed the road, the forest stretching to her left and a grassy land rising to her right, just beyond the hill. Hours passed as she pressed on, until the crumbling remnants of an ancient town finally came into view.

Old Time homes splayed out for miles in each direction with streets connecting each one in square blocks. Large oak trees, overgrown bushes, and ivy veiled what was left of this neighborhood. Several of the buildings were unsafe to enter after the war, but there were still a handful of homes that remained sturdy enough to take refuge at night. Eva knew that many of the Gangs used this area for trade as it was considered neutral territory. It was too far from any compound and too cumbersome to build a separate settlement, so many of the Gangs would meet here to exchange goods.

Night had settled over the region by the time Eva reached the abandoned homes. Knowing she needed rest for the day ahead, she searched for an intact structure near the center of town and found a dry room to sleep in.

She managed only a few hours of sleep. As dawn broke, Eva knew she had no time to waste if she was going to reach the compounds by nightfall. She snatched up her weapons and pressed on. When the dilapidated homes were far behind her, she began the trek up a large hill. At the top, Eva was met with a long stretch of highway. Smaller streets branched off on either side, leading to homes and shops from a forgotten era. Burnt-out and abandoned vehicles were clustered over the six-lane road, their rusted shells a testament to time. What metal had survived the elements had been scavenged long ago, stripped during the Gangs' early raids as they reinforced their compounds from the bones of the old world.

Eva slowed her pace as midday approached, becoming more hesitant as she neared her destination. The compounds' watchtowers were still concealed by the horizon, but she was only a few short hours from their outskirts. The land that separated the Rover Colony from the Tiger and Serpent's compounds was called No Man's Land. And many of the homes here were used as Posts— designated spots over the land for trade. Most were specific buildings or landmarks, unowned by a single Gang or other peoples. It was the only place where a truce had been exercised.

Usually.

Soon the old homes were replaced by a grassy clearing, sparse with trees. Eva took refuge near a sizable boulder for a short meal. A cool breeze and gray sky kept the region in a mild Summer's embrace. Four hours until it would be dark enough to enter The Blooded Row. Luckily, with the compound walls now perched atop the skyline, she was making good enough time to slow down a bit more. As soon as she finished a short nap, she continued on her way. The weather was so hypnotic, it lulled her mind into a haze, dulling her concentration.

I hope this is worth it, she thought. *What if I risk my life for a waste of time. Or what if I walk right into a trap? Those people have never had to deal with this shitty outside world. I would bet they walked right up to*

Serpents with their arms wide open. And even if I do find any survivors, I'm going to have to teach them how to survive out here… shit.

Eva's stomach dropped. The realization and doubt hit her hard. Up to this point, Eva had cherished her solitude. She had never been responsible for another life unless she chose to save it. Her own survival always came first. That mindset had kept her alive for so many years. After witnessing countless men, women, and children tortured and killed in horrific ways, she made a vow to never travel in a group.

Before Eva realized it, evening was upon her. She would reach her destination in perfect time. The sky grew dark as another heavy storm materialized over the region. A full day of sunshine was rare in the region, but she liked it that way. Especially today. The rain combined with her dark clothing would allow her to pass through The Blooded Row, unseen. But she also considered the potential strength of the storm brewing overhead. Unusually powerful weather was known to simply appear without explanation.

And this storm was no exception.

The heavens soon opened and waves of water fell to earth. Lighting ignited the sky and careened down to the watchtowers nearby in deafening explosions. Eva was motionless at the boundary into Gang territory. Over the torrential downpour, she still heard the occasional yelling from the slave masters to *'keep working'*. Thunder crashed overhead. *Now or never.* It was time to go. And with buckling knees, she took her first steps in between the two deadliest Gangs in the region.

Eva could instantly feel the presence of people in the compounds around her. In the towers above, she saw dark figures with guns marching back and forth as lightning lit up the sky, but their attention focused elsewhere. Her footsteps were silent, masked by the storm overhead. She hastened her pace. A bolt of lightning crashed a hundred feet from her, illuminating the area. The booming sound exploded through her chest as she fell to her knees and scurried back to her feet. *Shit. Gotta keep moving. Shit.* Ahead, a dark shadow marked the entrance of a large hole carved into the hillside. Eva scanned the tops of the compound walls on either side. No one was watching.

She sprinted for the entrance.

Puddles splashed beneath her with each step. Droplets of rain pelted her face like icy bullets as her lungs filled to capacity. What was only a few hundred feet felt like it took forever. The chasm in the hill was not getting any closer. Her chest burned. She glanced up and immediately noticed the guards starting to turn towards her direction. *Shit.* Digging into the muddy ground with her boots, she pushed into a full sprint. Suddenly, her boot hit an uneven patch of concrete. She dropped to her knees and rolled her ankle, raced back to her feet and managed to stagger the final few yards.

Finally, Eva made it inside the vault, gasping for breath. Her legs burned and her ankle was sore. Luckily, her boot was tied tight enough to keep it from being seriously injured. She was drenched, but a strange cold air came from the darkness ahead. The familiar, faint scent of human decay filled her nostrils. Squinting into the thick darkness, she could not make out the back of the room. Deafening thunder and the waterfall of rain at the vault's opening were the only sounds she could hear. A flash of lightning brightened the room enough for her to see clearly for a split second. Nothing could have prepared her for such an unusual place.

Chapter 2

Strange machines lined either side of the entrance. Their unfamiliarity caused Eva's stomach to twist in knots. She had never seen anything like them before. Cylindrical in shape and stacked in pairs, most were shattered, their glass faces broken and scattered across the floor. At the far end of the room, a few still hummed softly, faint bulbs blinking in green, blue, and red like distant stars. Eva approached one of them warily and studied it cautiously. *Old Time Technology*, she reasoned. She tried to fight the urge to leave it alone, but pressed a button anyway. Nothing happened. Waiting another moment, her gaze fixated on any change in the light pattern, noticed nothing, and moved on. *Well that was uneventful.* At this point, the machines were far too destroyed to perform the task they had once been created to do.

Everything in this vault reminded her of the technology she had seen in old photos and newspapers, but those references never explained what most of the items were actually used for. She guessed the Serpents might have believed the machines were weapons and destroyed them. It was also possible they had been damaged during the blast that opened the door. Without a doubt, this place had been constructed before the War. And somehow, they were able to keep their technology working all this time.

A lamp flickered on the floor in the corner of an adjacent room. Eva saw some papers littered on a desk. They were stained, but she could make out the doodling of a small child. The undeniable smell of rotting flesh passed through her nose. She turned to find the body of the young artist in the shadow of her bed, lying in a heap behind tiny footsteps of blood. Gently clenched in one hand were her coloring utensils. Misery and disgust overpowered Eva. She lurched out of the room, clutching the door frame for support as her knees buckled. With her back pressed against a wall, she put her head in her hands and rubbed her burning, wet eyes.

A shuffling sound down the passageway startled her. She quickly wiped the tears from her cheek and pulled out one of her blades. Out of the corner of her eye, she saw a faint light bobbing up and down. Whoever it was whispered quietly and she couldn't make out what they were saying. Footsteps closed in on her. With her blade at the ready and her fingertips fluttering over the holster of her pistol, she spun to face the sound.

Silhouettes appeared at the edge of the hall. Two of them. Eva pulled out her pistol and pointed it at them. Both of the figures were shaking as they came into view. One was a young man in his mid-twenties, and the other was a child about ten years old. The lantern cast ominous shadows down the empty metal hallway. By the cleanliness of their clothes alone, Eva knew they were not part of the outside world. They were inhabitants of the Vault, clad in matching dark brown pants and white shirts. And though their hair hung around their ears, it was not matted or dirty. Both of them looked terrified. The older of the two fought the desire to run while the younger one stood frozen in fright.

"A-are you going to kill us… or take us with the others?" The older one demanded, voice shaking.

Suddenly, Eva felt something in her stomach shift and burn. Like something had been split open. It spread up to her mind and tingled with a hot numbness. *What the shit?* She had never felt anything like that before, but it could have been anything. Her ears rang for a moment, and then the sensation disappeared all at once. She just shook it off and answered the question.

"Neither," she sheathed her weapons and relaxed her stance. "I came to search for survivors."

"Why? So you can *kill* us like the rest of those people did?"

An unexpected crash of thunder caused the group to jump.

Eva attempted to keep the kindness in her tone through gritted teeth. "No. I'm taking you away from these Gangs to a colony of Rovers."

"Wait. What? Who? We aren't going *anywhere* with someone we don't know. Think we would just trust you? We don't even know your name."

Eva sighed loudly. "I promise I will explain *everything* later. But if you don't come with me, then you'll die here when they come back...or worse."

The image of the little artist in the nearby room flickered through her mind, suddenly, and she swallowed the lump rising in her throat.

"How do we know *you* aren't just going to hand us over to those other people? How do we know you aren't one of them?"

Eva's fists clenched, but in the darkness, neither boy noticed. There was an awkward silence. It took a moment for her to realize that he was waiting for a response.

"I wasn't sure if you were joking or not," she said shortly. "If I was going to *kill* you, I wouldn't be wasting my time speaking to you. So... I haven't killed you yet. I came here to help you and anyone else left here."

"Why are you wearing a jacket like the ones who came before? The symbol is different, but it looks similar..."

Eva was growing impatient and cut the older brother off. "Disguise. There is a road between two Gangs right outside your front door. They would shoot me otherwise. We can't sit here and answer every single one of your stupid questions… We *need* to get out of Gang territory before the sun comes up or we're all dead. Are you coming or not?"

Eva swung her backpack over her shoulder and let it drop to the floor. The older brother stepped back, but the younger one held his ground, eyes fixed on her every move. She knelt down, pulled out two bloodstained leather jackets, and tossed them at their feet. Without hesitation, the younger boy snatched one and slipped it on.

"What are you doing Tommy?" the elder brother asked frantically. Tommy still did not utter a single word. He just gestured at Eva.

She was getting tired of the older one already. She strode over to the kid, crouched to his level, and held out a hand, "My name is Eva Calloway. Nice to meet you Tommy."

The older brother huffed, "I'm Jake. Jake McAvoy. We're brothers… and the only two left..."

His voice trailed off.

Eva pointed to the jacket and stopped. "Wait. It's just you two here?"

"Yes," his voice trailed off for a moment. "We searched the entire Vault after they left. Everyone was killed or taken. They… They shot most of the kids and elderly. Kidnapped the rest."

"You're *sure* there is no one hiding?"

Jake's voice cracked. "Positive. Please. I don't wanna think about what happened."

Tommy nodded in agreement.

"Fine then."

Jake reluctantly put the jacket over his shirt, taking in a sharp exhale as the cold leather touched the back of his neck. Tommy grabbed his brother's hand and they followed Eva to the front entrance. She stood at the threshold for a moment. The unsettling feeling of leaving the Vault without any search whatsoever became too overpowering. *I can't just take their words for it.* She turned on her heels and pushed them aside, her footsteps echoing down the hallway the brothers had come from. As she passed the lantern, she swiped it off the ground.

"Where are you going?" the elder brother called.

Eva ignored him and stared down the first hallway. She couldn't live with herself if she just left without further exploration. The lantern was bright enough for her to see about halfway down the corridor. There were doors on either side, all open wide. The floors and walls were all made from sturdy, sparkling metal. Entering each room, she saw a small living space. Above the door hung a sign with the last name of the family that resided in each one. Inside, there were beds, a small kitchen, a table and chairs, and a doorway to the bathroom. There was nowhere for anyone to hide.

The first few residences were empty, but the stench of death clung to the next handful of rooms. Inside, bodies of countless Vault inhabitants lay slumped in unnatural poses. Each one was riddled with bullet wounds. Eva's stomach turned, but she pressed on, still searching for survivors.

At the end of the long hallway were large double doors. She opened them to a larger set of rooms on either side of the passageway. The closest to her were labeled *Mess Hall* and *Infirmary*. Further down, a sign that read *Schoolhouse* housed a number of young victims. Another massive room was for farming crops and raising livestock. The crops had been burned and the animals had been stolen or slaughtered. Door after door, Eva searched for any sign of life. Still. Nothing.

I cannot dwell on the dead, she thought. *I cannot.*

If anyone *was* alive, they may have been too afraid to answer. "Anyone? I'm here to help. Jake and Tommy are at the entrance waiting for you. Please come out. I swear I won't hurt you."

It was the same story for the rest of the Vault. Eva wondered how and where the McAvoy brothers had managed to hide while the Gang massacred their people. But at the end of the opposite hallway near the entrance was a locked door without a window. A thick metal sign read *Authorized Personnel Only - DO NOT ENTER*. She used her weight to push against the door, but it refused to budge. As she lifted the lantern, she noticed an oddly shaped keyhole. Using the butt of her gun, she banged loudly and called out. No response. In the chance that anyone was still alive in there, she could not get to them anyway.

Lucky for her, the storm was still raging overhead when she returned to the entrance. Jake and Tommy were waiting for her, hesitant to leave the place they had been all their lives. Eva said nothing to them as she passed. Her mind was still lingering on the last door.

"Should we pack anything before we leave?" Jake yelled over the rain and thunder. He was trying to stall.

"No time," Eva called over her shoulder and lifted her hood. "We have to leave now if we want to get out of this territory by morning."

Eva disappeared into the downpour. Tommy pulled his brother into the rain at her heels. Lightning struck one of the watchtowers nearby with a brilliant explosion of sparks. That was when the brothers laid their eyes on the compounds for the first time. Between the slits in the walls, through the fencing, were hundreds of silhouettes working in the rain and mud. Above them were armored guards with large guns, pacing and yelling over the storm. An occasional gunshot rang out and someone would scream between crashes of thunder, but not one guard turned to the three leaving the cliffs. Tommy, Jake, and Eva were able to make it through The Blooded Row without incident.

The rain continued for the next several hours, drenching the three travelers. Jake kept a firm grip on his brother's hand and a watchful eye on their so-called savior just a few steps ahead. He was waiting for the moment she might turn on them, though he wasn't sure what he would do if she did.

By the time Eva began searching for shelter, they were all freezing, soaked, and exhausted. She wanted to be certain they had put enough distance between themselves and the Gangs before stopping for the night. As they entered the line of old subdivisions in No Man's Land, she finally veered off the road and led them into a house that looked slightly sturdier than the others around it.

"Why are all of the homes around here falling apart?" Jake asked as they stepped into the home.

"It's been over two hundred years since the bombs dropped in the city south of here," Eva said as she threw off her soaked jacket and pants to hang them on the stair banister. "According to what I've read in old newspapers, the shock wave reached out to the hills. Millions of people died. War spread throughout the world and we are what remains in this region. Well, we are the descendants of those who survived."

Eva continued taking off her clothes while Tommy and Jake stood and watched. She had stripped down to undergarments in complete nonchalance. Jake shielded his brother's eyes.

"What are you doing?" he whispered loudly to her.

She threw her arms up. "I'm drying my clothes. What does it look like? *Relax*. It's just a person's body."

"A *woman's* body," he corrected.

"It's all the same," she said shortly. "Alive or dead. Take off your clothes and hang them on the banister. I'm not going to be responsible if you both get sick."

Jake huffed and began to undress. His brother followed suit as Eva carefully made her way to the second floor in search of anything dry. In the dusty bedrooms, she spotted piles of human bones from the Old World inhabitants. A closer look revealed they had been gnawed by animals long ago. But this was not an uncommon discovery. She simply kicked the bones aside and began poking through old wardrobes filled with torn fragments of clothing. Underneath one of the beds was a large plastic bag. None of the contents, including the clothing, had been destroyed by insects or time. She filled her arms with shirts, pants, a towel, and some blankets and returned to the brothers.

Jake was leaning against the windowsill and watching the dark, empty road. He spun around just as an armful of clothing was launched at him. "What about you?"

"I have clothes that are practical for this life," she wrapped herself in one of the blankets and dried her hair with a towel. Without either of them noticing, Tommy had already made himself a small bed and fell asleep.

Jake walked over and covered his brother before collapsing down onto an old armchair next to Eva. Both faced the window in silence. The rain had subsided to a drizzle, its hypnotic sound made their eyelids heavy. Eva had her gun on the armrest of her chair and her blades leaning against a table in between them. The lantern flickered as Jake reached over and lowered the light to a dull glow.

"How long will that light last?" Eva asked.

"Hopefully until the morning," Jake answered. "As long as we keep the flame low."

Eva nodded and gestured at the sleeping boy. "Your brother is so calm. I can't even remember a night when I fell asleep that quickly. Especially at that age."

"Yeah," Jake whispered, fidgeting with the buttons on his pants. "He has always had an open mind. Wish I had that myself, to be honest."

Again, silence.

Jake could not take it any longer. Questions burned in his throat and started to make his head swim. "So what the hell happened here all those years ago? All we were told was the world had ended and there was nothing left."

Eva watched a particularly large raindrop run down the cracked window before she slid to the edge of her seat and interlaced her fingers together. Jake leaned in. Tommy was fast asleep on the floor while the rain pattered on the ancient roof.

"You aren't too far off," she began slowly. "No one knows exactly what happened because it was so long ago, and there aren't many surviving records from the Old Times. Most of what we know was passed down by word of mouth. You know, it could be true or partially true. The only part of the story that is the same from everyone is the bombs dropping. Anyway, this is what *I* believe happened…"

Jake was now touching knees with her. She lowered her voice even more.

"All those years ago, leaders of the world became greedy and power hungry. Tensions were building up all over the world. People were fighting with each other and it got more violent with each passing day. Countries threatened each other and the people here were just left to the mercy of their governments. Threats of war were spoken of every day. I think that, finally, someone released a deadly bomb somewhere, and that was it. An entire global war broke out. The people then called it the War of Rebirth. All we really know is that most of the population was wiped out. There are other settlements just outside of this region, but I don't know what they are like. I've never left the region, so I have no idea what lies further out than that. But… there *has* to be other colonies out there… way out there. There must be."

Jake's eyes did not break from Eva's. "What about the city nearby that you mentioned?"

"It's mostly overgrown," she pointed towards the direction of the city. "It was a destructive explosion, but a lot of the city still stands. Parts are just rubble. But when it dropped, a lot of people were killed. Even all the way out here."

"And those who survived are your ancestors?" Jake leaned back in his chair.

"Yeah."

"It sounds like the Old Times was just as bad as it is now."

"From the journals and newspapers I've read, it sounded like they were fighting over a lot of different issues. The weather was changing drastically. People getting massacred in public places. Inequality and hatred was an everyday thing. Unfortunately, that much hasn't changed."

"Is that how it is now? With the people in the compounds?"

"The Gangs? Yeah. I won't even begin to describe the horrors I've seen in my lifetime. But one of the Gangs near here, The Serpents, use slaves as their main source of trade. They kidnap Rovers and Nomads, torture them into submission, and sell the ones that are still fit for work and aren't murdered in the process. Women work as pleasure slaves and men do hard labor. At least, that's most of the time. Even children are forced to work. And that isn't even half of what goes on inside those walls."

Jake's stomach dropped as he glanced at his brother. Eva's gaze shot to the floor as her final comment lingered over them like an echo. At first, she thought that it would be easy to tell the brothers everything. They had been sealed off from the world their entire lives, unaware that anyone survived just outside their doors. And now, their whole life had come crashing down when the Gangs slaughtered and abducted their people. Jake's friends and family were either dead or being sold around the region and there was nothing either of them could do.

After what felt like an endless silence, Eva spoke again. "I can't save them all. And neither can you. So, don't dwell on it. You just have to worry about you and your brother out here."

"Sure…" Jake trailed off.

"What about your life in the Vault?" She tried changing the subject. Her back relaxed against the chair. "What was it like?"

"It was great compared to this life," he chuckled nervously, staring blankly out the window. "My community was about two thousand or so people. We were taught many things like math, history, and science. But to be honest, it was probably outdated. We had electricity… clean water. Food. It was easy living. When you became 'of age', you were supposed to learn a trade to help the community. I was going to be an electrician. Stupid, right?"

"What are you talking about *electricity*?"

"The generators. Y'know, the machines you saw in the front entrance. They ran all the lights and technology in the community. The Gangs destroyed most of them. But they're useless out here anyway… and I guess my studies will be just as useless."

"What about your family? Parents? Other siblings?"

Eva knew immediately that she brought up a sour subject. Although twilight shrouded the room, Jake's silence spoke for itself. The feeling of uneasiness permeated the space between them.

"I'm sorry if I-" Eva started.

"No," Jake interrupted. "It's fine. I figured this would probably come up at some point…"

Eva tilted her head.

"Our mother died a long time ago. Someone in the community killed her, and we never found out who or why. Everyone was in an uproar since it was the only murder in our town, *ever*. But… um… We do have a father. He actually left the vault about eight years ago. Right after our mom was killed. We were just told he was distraught after our mother's death and knew secrets about the vault that no one else did. And since Tommy and I weren't captured, we were hoping to find him. A- and you seem to um..."

Eva's tone was unsympathetic, but not intentionally. "He was probably taken by the Gangs like the rest of them."

Jake cleared his throat and clenched his fists. "Maybe… Or he could have escaped like we did. If you could just help-"

Eva stopped for a moment. She was not going to risk her life for a man who may or may not even be alive. There was a good chance that he was now working as a slave for one of the Gangs. An even better chance that he was dead. Still, she did not want to break the harsh news to Jake or Tommy. Not yet, anyways. They had already witnessed enough for one day.

"I'll tell you what," her voice sliced through the dark air. "I'll teach you both how to survive out here. Then *you* can go find him."

"What about you?" Jake asked. Eva sighed loudly. "You help people."

Eva ignored his question, "Goodnight Jake." With that, she dozed off in the chair.

***

Everyone jolted awake in a daze, their hearts pounding in their ears as a gunshot rang down the street. They must not have been sleeping long as it was still dark. Eva threw on her damp clothing and holstered her weapons as fast as she could. Jake could hear her voice shake, though the tone was surprisingly calm.

"What's going on?" Jake ran over to Tommy.

"Gang," she pointed to the door and shoved the lantern in his hands. "Get down to the basement *quietly*. Turn that thing on low. I will come for you once I know it's safe."

Jake grabbed his brother. They were already by the door when he called back. "Will you be okay on your own?"

"I will be much safer alone than with you two standing here," she whispered harshly.

Jake and Tommy raced downstairs. Little did they know, the smell of rotting flesh would be waiting at the landing. They wanted to turn on their heels and run, but hurried across the basement, trying to use their clothing as a barrier for the smell. But it was too strong. Choking down vomit, both brothers moved as far away from the stench as possible towards a broken window.

Eva caught a whiff when she closed the door. It was undeniably human. And it was recent. The Gangs had designated certain structures in neutral territory called Posts, used for trading goods and slaves, and it seemed she had unknowingly stumbled into one of them. Perhaps a trade went bad. But Eva had no time to dwell on her thoughts. The sound of footsteps had moved up the driveway to the front porch. Light from a lantern bobbed across the dusty window. On the other side of the home, near the back door, three people entered the building.

Eva found herself in a bathroom on the main floor with the door cracked just enough to squeeze through without drawing attention. As everyone filed into the foyer and exchanged greetings, she started counting shadows. *Five*. She waited, hoping that they would just do their business and leave.

One group slammed a heavy box of metal objects onto the floor. The crash tore through the air and shook the home.

"Scrap metal we found in the city," the first said. "No charge as long as we get some decent armor out of this."

"Why? You doubting our contacts?" a woman's voice mocked.

"Not saying that," one of them spat. "Our *King* was not happy about the shit you gave us last time."

The first woman responded quickly. "Fine. Whatever."

Another voice chimed in. "We heard what happened in the East Rover colony. Sorry about your comrades. As long as that *monster* is left alive, we are all in danger."

"There is no way just *one person* did that," said another. "You're trying to tell me that one person killed five armed and trained Gang members with no help?"

"I've heard stories that he's butchered more than that at one time," said another woman's voice. "Us Rats have sent at least six to that colony before. Same result. Can't get any more slaves from there anymore. Not as long as he's there. Our King won't risk it."

"It must be the Rovers then," another argued. "Starting to fight back for once like the ones out West. If you back anyone up in a corner, even *that* scum for long enough, they're bound to bite at some point."

"None of them are trained like he is," the woman contradicted. "*He's* a calculated killer."

"I've heard it's a woman, not a man… Either way, the *Serpents* are clearly better trained than you

Rats," another woman laughed. "We wouldn't fall to *one* person. There's no way. But there is a price on her head. We just got the news."

"Him, her, who cares?" a man's voice added. "The Wanderer is bad news."

"Does anyone know what the story on them is-?"

The conversation was cut short. Everyone stopped when they heard a loud bang come from the basement.

Eva felt dizzy as adrenaline shot through her body like lightning. *Dammit Jake!* She screamed in her head. Her heart rate rose and her vision tunneled. The lantern illuminated The Gang Members' shadows against the far wall. She could see that they were arming themselves. The clicking of guns filled her ears. Now was her chance to slink out of the bathroom and into the hallway that separated her from the guards.

If they split up I can cut down one or two at a time.

Lucky for her, they seemed to follow her intended plan. No one gave orders, so the assailants began walking around aimlessly. Their footsteps and whispers blended together, making it hard to discern which direction they were coming from. The darkness concealed her figure, aside from the glint of her blades. As one of the armored figures rounded the corner, she moved in silently behind him. Just as he entered the next room, she grabbed him from behind. Quickly lifting his head with one arm, she made a deep cut across his throat with the other.

The man dropped to his knees grabbing at the wound. He tried to scream but only a gurgle seeped out from his blood-filled mouth. She could feel his eyes turn to her before he dropped to the ground in a pool of his own blood. His comrade raced in. But Eva was already gone, slipping back around the corner just as the second Gang member rushed past without seeing her. He met the same end.

The other Gang Members were closing in. The sound of bodies dropping to the floor was drawing them in.

I need to keep them away from the basement door. Without a second thought, Eva rushed upstairs, making a point to stomp loudly on each step, luring them away from Jake and Tommy below.

"They're upstairs!" one of them called. "Two of us are down already."

Eva couldn't help but laugh to herself. This was not the first time that her attackers overestimated the number of opponents they faced. She was a killer whose skill was simply unmatched. And that realization both delighted and terrified her.

Jake and Tommy heard the pounding of boots on the stairway to the second floor of the home. They held onto each other tightly. While Tommy feared for his own life, Jake was focused on Eva. He prayed she was still alive and the attackers were pursuing her. Because he worried that if they killed her, he and his brother were next.

Adrenaline fueled Eva's heart. She attempted to calm the explosive pounding in her head by taking a few deep breaths as she sheathed her blade and pulled out her pistol. Although she always felt more comfortable grasping the hilt of her swords, she was a decent shot.

The glow of a lantern brightened the landing as the head of the first person appeared over a partially-collapsed wall. Eva stowed away in a bedroom with only a thin door between her and the hallway. As soon as she fired off her first round, the rest would come bolting up the stairs. So, each shot had to be fatal.

She took aim and squeezed. The pistol kicked back a little and warmed in her hand, followed by the sound of a heavy object tumbling down the stairs. *One down.* More gunshots rang throughout the house. The Gang Member must have had his finger on the trigger when he toppled backward, spouting bullets in all directions. The commotion was so loud, it made Eva scamper away from the door. A piercing scream burst from the bottom of the stairs.

"Robert! Delilah! " screamed one of the women. One of the stray bullets must have hit another Serpent by accident. "These Rovers are going to pay!"

Eva heard another set of footsteps race up the stairs. Bullets whizzed over her head as the woman entered the hallway with her gun hot. Eva ducked behind a dresser as small explosions pelted the walls. She covered the back of her neck and tried to move further and further from the doorway.

All of a sudden, silence. The smoke cleared and the dust settled. The Gang member was out of ammunition and resorted to creeping down the hallway, dagger in hand. Down below, Jake and Tommy believed the battle was over.

On the contrary. Eva had snuck through an adjacent bathroom and circled around the house during the chaos. Now, she was standing behind the last of her attackers. She quietly cocked her pistol and pulled the trigger just as the woman turned towards the sound. The shot hit, entering through the chest, causing her to fall back onto the floor and drop her weapon. As Eva stood up and stepped towards her final victim, kicking her gun aside. The woman scrambled backwards until she hit the wall.

During the scuffle, the lantern had fallen on the floor nearby, but did not break. Eva could see the fear on the woman's face as a trickle of blood dripped from the side of her mouth. As Eva passed the stairwell and holstered her gun, she glanced down to the main floor. The bodies of two Gang members were motionless in the twilight. Turning her eyes back to the Serpent lying in a growing pool of crimson, she pulled out one of her blades to finish the job. That was when the woman spoke.

"Who the hell are you? Where are the others?" she shivered and spit blood at Eva who did not flinch.

She laughed coldly. "The *others*? It's only me here."

"You must be The Wanderer," she choked. "No one else I've *ever* heard of could have taken on all of us… with such…precision."

"And *you* are vermin. You worthless Gangs do nothing but destroy the lives of the innocent for your own gain," Eva spat. "And now, all of your decisions have finally caught up to you. Count yourself lucky that I'm ending your miserable life quickly. Especially since you don't provide that same mercy to your victims."

The woman swallowed hard. Eva felt like a wolf closing in on a wounded rabbit. Anger seethed through her veins. Images of what this woman may have done to others flashed in her mind. Without another word, she eviscerated the Serpent, snatched up the lantern, and made her way downstairs.

Two levels below, Jake and Tommy were still afraid that Eva had been killed during the gun battle. Tommy cried silently as the dragging footsteps stopped at the doorway to the basement and slowly unlatched the lock. Jake's chest felt like it was going to explode. With each step, he wanted to scream for help, but bit his tongue. A dark figure slowly walked towards them from the landing, the lantern light obscuring their face. As soon as the beam of light shined on the brothers, they both threw their hands up in the air in surrender. That was when they heard Eva's laughter.

"Relax guys," she said, wiping the blood from her face. "It's only me."

Jake was both relieved and irked. His head was swimming so violently, he thought he was going to faint. "How can you be *laughing* at a time like this? You just murdered people." He pointed to the gray shirt underneath her jacket.

Eva noticed that she was covered in a little blood, but her face hardened immediately as she jabbed her finger into Jake's chest. "Me? You had one job. *Keep quiet*. Would you rather I had stayed quiet while they came down here and dragged you and your brother back to their compounds?"

"Well there are bodies over there." Jake changed the subject. "When we backed up against the wall. I knocked over a metal chair."

Her nose had grown numb to the smell of decay over time, so Eva had forgotten about it at first. She turned to the other side of the basement to investigate. When Jake and Tommy began to follow her, she lifted her hand in protest, telling them she would call them if it was safe. In reality, she wasn't sure how gruesome the scene would be. The moment she cast her light on the other side of the room, her worst fears were confirmed.

She shook her head and her mouth became dry. "You do not want to come over here."

"Why not?" Jake called back. "There are dead bodies upstairs, too."

"This is different," she said.

"Don't you think this is part of training us to *survive*," he mocked.

"Fine then," she spat. "If you think your stomach can take it."

Jake instantly heaved up whatever food was left in his stomach. As he wiped the vomit from his mouth, he took in the scene before them. Tommy was clutching tightly to his brother's arm, shielding his nose with his shirt. For a moment, the three stood motionless in the blood soaked room. Eva could not even muster the words to describe how she felt.

A row of Rovers, half-decomposed, were collapsed in the corner. It appeared as though they were all forced to face the basement wall and executed. Near the foot of the stairs, several women of varying ages lay motionless, their clothing torn and ragged. Each one had a single bullet hole in their skull. Browned blood stained the floor and spattered across the walls. The part that stood out the most was an older child who looked as though he did not succumb to his wounds right away. He used his blood to write on the wall. Just one word was painted on the concrete - *Serpents*.

"This is just a *taste* of what they can do." Eva choked back the lump in her throat. Her eyes remained locked on the Gang's name for a moment as she paused. "What they *have* done. What they *will* do."

Jake did not dare make eye contact with her. "*This* is what you're protecting the Rovers from?"

"Yes," she said, hiding her face. "And your friends may have met the same fate. Trust me when I say that *this* is the end you would beg for. This is a merciful killing. If you can call it that. Servitude is *much* worse… The Serpent's compound was where your friends were most likely taken before being traded for goods."

"How can you be sure it was the Serpents?"

"A few reasons. They are the largest Gang in the area, first of all. Their largest trade goods are people. They sell women to be forced as Doxies and men as Bondsmen. Basically, whatever Gang trades for these slaves can do whatever they want with them. Also, I found a map and a note that led me to you."

"Bondsmen and Doxies?"

"Doxies are pleasure servants. Bondsmen are laborers. They slowly become soulless shells that are forced to work at least twelve hours a day or risk indescribable torture. No matter what, the death toll is high."

Silence again. Jake did not even want to glance up from the bodies. Tommy teared up. Eva put a hand on the boy's shoulder. She wished she could keep both of them from witnessing such a horrific display of the Gang's cruelty, but understood that they would see it eventually. After lingering in the basement for a few more moments, Eva turned on her heels and went upstairs.

"You have to learn to be hard in this world," she cleared her throat as they began to follow. "You have to make a choice each time you wake up - *survive* or *die*. No hesitating."

"Then why did you risk your life to come for us?" Jake asked.

Eva stopped. She didn't really know how to answer the question because she did not know the answer herself. "Because I'm different," was the only thing she could say.

That was the last time they spoke for a while. The sun was rising over the horizon, but they were able to sleep for a few more hours while the bodies of the Serpents and Rats lay just a few dozen feet from them. Jake and Tommy struggled with the scene below their feet still fresh in their minds. Once they had finally rested, Eva woke them and resumed the trek to the Rover colony.

Throughout the rest of the day's walk, Jake tried to ask questions, but Eva's mind was fixated elsewhere. She pondered the reasons why she remained alone and why she had bothered risking her life to save these brothers. For years she chose who to save, but only if she believed she would make it out alive. Survival came first. Everything else was a matter of kindness and courage. Over time, she tried to become numb to the middle-of-the-night raids. The countless screams that still haunted her every step. She reminded herself that self-preservation was every survivor's primary goal. Even still, she refused to talk about her life before the colony. She could never relive that.

"Eva." Jake waved his hand in front of her face. She jumped backwards and nearly punched him.

"*What*?" she yelled. "We aren't in danger."

"No," Jake said slowly. "But is that the colony?"

"Obviously," she responded.

Truthfully, she did not realize how long she had been ensnared by her thoughts. The sun already started to set in the distance. The Rovers would be eating soon. Eva led the brothers to her home and told them to wait outside. She walked through the door and removed her jacket, disguise, and pack. Before she left, she grabbed the journal near her bed.

She motioned for the brothers to follow her to the food hall, where a large crowd had already gathered.

"Welcome back Eva," one of the cooks called. Rovers filled the hall, talking and laughing. "Who are these kids?"

"Survivors from the Vault," she responded. "The *only* survivors."

All eyes were on Jake and Tomm, who rolled their shoulders and kept their eyes glued to their feet. Other Rovers who were queuing had overheard the conversation. They stared at the two newest members of their colony, studying them. Even though their welcome was warming, the brothers were still wary.

Jake cleared his throat and looked up at them. "We are the only two left. The rest were taken or killed. We hid in an air vent."

"Sorry to hear that," the cook shook his head. Others around him expressed faces of pity. "Luck was on your side though. Not so much for the others. But, that's life."

Jake was offended at the lack of empathy. The screams of his friends, forever ingrained in his brain. They had lost *everything*. He and Tommy had hidden for hours while the footsteps, gunshots, and cries for help rang through the halls of the Vault. And then, they were saved by an equally bloodthirsty woman and thrust into a world where torture and death awaited them at every moment.

Sure. Eva killed with ease and no second thought. She was so cold in her view of death. But it seemed like the Rovers also shared the same outlook.

Eva pulled Jake back into reality when she shoved him a plate of food. All she said was "Eat. I'm sure you're starving," then threw her hood over her head and marched over to her table in the far corner of the room. When Jake and Tommy started to follow her, the cook stopped them.

"She prefers to eat alone," he said and nodded his head towards another table.

Jake was annoyed. "Really?"

"Yeah kid," the cook pointed his ladle at him. "Know your place here. We are *lucky* to have someone as skilled as that woman. She has saved *all* of us at one time or another. Respect is something hard to earn these days, but she has all of ours here. So, you need to respect her too. She lived a much harder life than either of you could ever understand. I don't care how many people you saw die where you are from, her count is at least ten times that."

Those within earshot of the conversation turned their attention to the boys. Younger Rovers smiled sympathetically, but the Elders shook their heads in disdain. Tommy elbowed his brother in the side and walked over to a table by himself, silent as usual. Jake followed, slightly embarrassed. As he glanced over at Eva, her back was turned to the rest of the room and she was scribbling in her journal.

I HAVE NO CLUE WHAT THE HELL I GOT MYSELF INTO. I'M REGRETTING GOING INTO THAT VAULT. I SHOULD HAVE NEVER RISKED MY LIFE IN THE FIRST PLACE. BUT I FOUND SURVIVORS — TWO BROTHERS. I DOUBT THEY HAVE EVER EVEN TOUCHED A WEAPON BEFORE. I SEARCHED THE REST OF THAT PLACE. NOTHING.

WE FOUND WHAT LOOKED LIKE AN EXECUTION OF ROVERS IN A POST NEAR THE BLOODED ROW. BAD SCENE THERE. I DON'T EVEN WANT TO THINK ABOUT IT RIGHT NOW, BUT IT'S SO CLEAR IN MY MIND. JUST LIKE EVERYTHING THAT HAPPENED BEFORE. SEEING SCENES IS LIKE A TRIGGER TO OLDER MEMORIES...

Eva closed her journal and shoved it back into her pocket with her pencil. As she started to eat, she reached in her pocket and pulled it back out. She had forgotten to read the next entry from the Old Times.

coasts had been completely leveled and the Midwest was next. Then they listed off the cities that were attacked with a special type of nuclear warhead - New York City, Washington DC, and a few cities in California are now craters filled with radiation. Other countries across the world have already been wiped off the map before we were hit.

Four days before the attacks on US soil, there was a message for everyone to take shelter if they were lucky enough to have a place to go. As for everyone else, the government and news outlets told them to do what they could. Absolutely ridiculous. I wish I could house more people here. I don't know how many survivors are going to be left after this. Most people are not going to be lucky.

My kids haven't stopped crying. My wife and I can't sleep. Her parents haven't said a word since we got down here. They are all scared. And truthfully, I'm scared too... terrified.

The last sentence caused the hair on Eva's arm to stand on end. She stared blankly at the page a while, connecting the experiences of this past author to her present. After a few lingering moments, her attention shifted to the noises at her back. She glanced over her shoulder. The bustle of people filing in and talking with their friends and family. The smell of cooked food and fire burning. This colony was safe for the night. Hopefully. Just as she went to turn around back to her seclusion, she saw one of the Elders hobbling her way.

"Eva," he bowed his head. "You will be training those two brothers, yes? They need to contribute."

She made a fist and put it over her chest in respect. "Yes. I plan on taking them to the city to give them a couple survival tests. Then, we will see how they want to contribute."

"Scavenging I hope," he offered.

"Yes."

"Perhaps they can become productive members here. We do not want them to become a burden for the colony."

Her tone shifted to annoyance. "Agreed. But we both know that I won't allow that to happen. We need more warriors besides me. I would *love* to train some of the other Rovers if they ever stop relying on me to protect them… and if the rest of the community didn't enable it."

The Elder shrugged at Eva who clenched her fists and continued.

"...Anyway, I'll have our weapons woman create something for them. I haven't trained anyone in a while, so we shall see how it goes."

The Elder nodded and limped back to his table. Rovers began leaving the food hall in groups after cleaning their dishes. Jake and Tommy had been joined at their table by a young couple and their two children. The woman was the colony's weapons maker and the man was a farmer. Eva handed her plate to the Rovers who were cleaning and thanked them for another meal. As the brothers caught her eye, they joined her near the front door. Eva waited until the weapons-maker finished the meal with her family and stopped her as she was leaving.

"Wanderer?" She bowed with a fist on her chest. "What is it that my family can do for you?"

"I need two weapons for them," she pointed to Jake and Tommy. "If you have the time to complete them by midday tomorrow."

"Of course I can! I haven't had a chance to make weapons recently. We haven't had a warrior trained here in some time."

Eva agreed. "With the exception of the other night, we haven't had a need for a battle lately, either."

"A good thing," the farmer added. "We haven't lost many Rovers since the summer. Winter will be upon us soon, though. Crops will be scarce, but at least that means the Gangs will not venture out as far or as frequently."

Eva nodded and thanked them, whisking the brothers back to the street. It was now well past dark, the sun replaced by twinkling stars. The earlier storms had cleared and the night was crisp and cool. A slight breeze brushed against them and rustled the trees nearby. Behind a few shacks, Eva could see an owl perched on a tree, hooting softly.

"It's beautiful," Jake was tearing up. His face was aglow against the luminous sky. Eva opened her mouth to respond sarcastically, but remembered that neither brother had ever seen the sky before.

"It's [probably the only beautiful thing left in this world," she commented, admiring the moon. Tommy walked ahead of them, out of earshot.

"Not the *only* thing." Jake didn't know exactly why he had said that, but his face immediately felt hot. He glanced over at Eva.

Her face was obscured by the darkness and her hood, but she felt herself blush. She had not been complimented in years, and admittedly, she was flattered. They walked back to her home. The brothers made two beds near the back of the shack while Eva stayed in her room. With a belly full of food, Jake and Tommy fell asleep almost instantly. Eva spent a long time thinking about her life before the colony. The torture she endured as a child.

Thoughts of her past transformed into visions of terror as she slept.

Chapter 3

Waking up in a cold sweat was a regular occurrence for Eva. By day, her memories lay hidden, but as night fell, the gates of her mind were thrown open. The nightmares had only worsened with age, haunting the darkness behind her eyes. These visions always felt so real. Every slash of a whip, every fist in her face… But her torturers never bore a face - only black pits or hazy distortions where their heads would be. And each time she tried to fight back, the scene would become more painful. It was only when she awoke in a puddle of her own sweat that she was granted some relief. This time, though, Jake was standing over her.

Eva was so startled that she tore a small knife out from under her pillow and pointed it at him. It happened so fast, Jake barely had enough time to stumble back with his hands in the air.

"It's me! It's me," he said frantically. "I wanted to make sure you were okay. You spent a lot of the night crying and looking like you were in pain."

"Fine," she could barely hear him over a high pitched whining in her ears. "I'm fine."

Her chest was glistening with droplets of sweat, rising and falling with each labored breath. She shooed Jake from the room and took a moment to calm herself. The entire ground felt like it was spinning and her hands were shaking uncontrollably. Once again, she forced the lingering, horrific images out of her head. Jake popped his head back in the room while she mopped up her sweat with a rag.

"Are you *sure* you're alright?" he asked.

That was the first time he caught a glimpse of the caged monster within her.

She shot out of her bed and threw her arms out. A few veins in her neck pulsed. "I already told you, Jake. I.. am… *Fine!*" she yelled. "Do you ever stop asking stupid questions? Why can't you just keep your mouth shut like your brother?"

The pure rage that flickered in her eyes for a moment petrified Jake. He wondered whether the last thing her victims ever saw was that look on her face. It made him recall the night at The Post. Eva's voice, completely calm, before she pulled the trigger. He shivered. It seemed that every waking moment for her was filled with the intention of ending someone's life.

Momentarily, she thought Jake was part of her night terror. It took a long time for her to wake up completely. Through the haze, one of the enemies from her dream had dissolved right into the silhouette of the McAvoy brother. If Tommy hadn't poked his head out from behind his brother, she might have attacked him. Jake dropped his shoulders and backed out of the doorway. But Tommy remained. He did not stray from her threatening stance. Rather than speaking, he walked over and grabbed her by the hand. She jumped a little, but did not pull away. He looked up and smiled.

Eva was speechless. An unfamiliar emotion tried to blossom within her, but confusion snuffed it. Her heart softened for this peaceful boy. It may have been his forced smile that melted her. Or perhaps it was his soft, innocent eyes. She could not help but smile back.

"I'm fine," she repeated calmly.

Jake peeked from around the door.

"Let's go," she said quickly and started packing.

"Go where?" Jake asked.

"To the city."

"Why?"

"It's time to start training." Eva sat up next to Tommy who nodded excitedly. "See Jake? Why can't you be as enthusiastic as your brother?"

Tommy shrugged. Jake sighed loudly.

After the three shared a small meal, they finished packing a few more supplies. The trembling had stopped, but Eva's palms were still clammy. A few more flashes of the nightmare followed by something she did not see before. *Odd.* She thought she saw a dark, hooded figure noiselessly float out of the corner of her view. When she whipped her head around, there was nothing. *Was that part of the dream?* Maybe her mind was playing tricks, but the undeniable feeling of dread felt all too real. Before either Jake or Tommy noticed her staring through an empty doorway, Eva secured her blades around her back and pushed them out the door. She turned one last time towards her room, just to be sure something wasn't standing there.

"My imagination is getting too damn strong," she whispered to herself.

The three of them stepped out into the morning, greeted by the warm sun and large, fluffy clouds drifting noiselessly in front of it. Dew-dipped grass glittered beneath the three pairs of feet. As they neared the last few homes of Rovers, Eva spotted two weapons leaning against one of the buildings. They had been fashioned from old street signs nearby. The smaller of the two, which read "Smith Street", was sharpened into a blade, pointed at the end and a handle wrapped in thick leather. The other was an entire "STOP" sign with jagged edges cut on both sides. The pole was used as the handle and covered in the same hide.

Neither of the brothers went to grab their weapon at first.

"Go ahead." Eva crossed her arms and tapped her foot. *"Let's go."*

Tommy walked up to the smaller knife and held it in his hand. It was the perfect size to use it with ease and sharp enough to slice through bone. Jake picked up his axe and slashed the air in a downward motion. He was surprised by the weight, but using it did not feel natural. It was plain to see that neither he nor his brother had ever used, let alone *touched* a weapon before. Jake expressed his discomfort.

"So um, when do we get guns?" He kept his eyes focused on the hilt of his new weapon. Tommy elbowed him in the side.

Eva took a deep breath, clenched her fists, and shook her head. *What the hell is with him and the constant whining? Why can't he just shut up and do what I say?*

In the nicest voice she could muster, Eva explained.

"The Gangs have almost every single firearm in the region. Long ago, when they ransacked the Rover and Nomad colonies, they robbed us of every last gun and every bit of ammunition they could find. If you refused to give it up... well... you can guess what happened. And the only reason we have a few here is because *I* took them from their corpses."

"Oh," Jake tightened the grip on his weapon and strode towards the crumbling skyline. Eva followed after him, Tommy catching up soon after. When the Rover colony had disappeared behind them, Eva decided to prepare the boys for the tests she had planned.

"...You will be split up." That comment struck Jake like a brick. "I want to test your individual skills. You will be scavenging for necessities. So, I'm leaving it up to you to decide what that means. Then, you will bring me the most useful items you can find. Just a few, so don't fill your pockets with junk to try and win..."

Jake mocked her, trying to mask his anxiety. "What do we get if we win this 'game' of yours?"

"Dinner," she half-ignored him. "And the knowledge that you have a surviving chance to be out here by yourself."

She cleared her throat and continued.

"Second, I will test your stealth. You will hide in a block of buildings and try to keep away from me. The second you find yourself staring down the edge of my blade, you lose."

Jake grimaced.

"I don't expect either of you to keep away from me forever, though. I have been doing this all my life… In one way or another. When I was a kid, I saw this life… this existence… as a game - If you want to win, learn the rules. After you learn the rules, become the best by bending them to your advantage."

"Okay," Jake said, not sure how to respond.

A couple hours passed before they reached the outskirts of the city. Eva slowed her pace to let the brothers absorb the landscape. Their mouths dropped open at the sight. Remnants of the War that their ancestors had been protected from. The haze of the early-afternoon sun created sheets of glimmering radiance against the crumbling buildings consumed by vines and other greenery, glowing with a golden hue. At their foundations, trees had burst through the deserted roads. Shells of abandoned vehicles remained clustered together, forever a reminder of their inhabitants' final moments of chaos and terror. A flock of birds chittered from an open window and baby rabbits hopped around the field of green separating Jake, Eva, and Tommy from the roads ahead. Eva seized a moment to close her eyes and take in the serenity of the late-summer air.

"This place holds so many memories," Eva said gently. She couldn't help being swept away by the moment. "We are those who were born from the survivors of this."

"My people hid like cowards," Jake added. "While everyone else was dying right outside their walls. Your ancestors weren't afraid or selfish."

"Selfish, perhaps. But fear of death is natural." Eva's eyebrows furrowed. "I lost that fear a long time ago. But when that fear is gone… you lose a part of yourself along with it. You lose your *humanity*. To have nothing to live for… It's what makes me a strong warrior. But if you linger at Death's door long enough, you are forced to make a choice. Let him drag you into the dark, or fight back."

Jake could hear the pain through her words. He could not even begin to imagine the events that Eva had witnessed in her lifetime. By the way she spoke, he knew it was horrific. Part of him did not want to know. Tommy looked from his brother to Eva with solemn eyes as they all stood in silence for another moment before Jake suggested that they get started.

Eva adjusted her jacket and cleared her throat. "Right. Okay. Um… Stay around this side of the city. We don't want to run into any Nomads."

"Nomads?" Jake repeated.

"They roam the city. Never in one place for too long. They stay within its borders and know the streets better than the Gangs. They worship nature and animals and all that nonsense. Silly, I know. But they are *very* intelligent, and *very* quiet. The Nomads are not part of the Gangs or the Rovers. Just crazy fanatics for the most part. I'll admit, I'm not sure whether they would distinguish you as a friend or a foe. They may attack without warning."

"And what happens if we *do* come across them?" Jake stopped in front of Eva, facing her.

"You won't," Eva said shortly. "As long as you stay where I tell you. They don't usually come to the outer limits of the city."

Although Jake was not comfortable with the tone of 'usually', he shook his head and stepped aside. While she did not give the exact impression that the Nomads were hostile, it was implied, at the very least, that they kept to themselves. Before he could dwell on it, Eva gave the signal for him and Tommy to split up and start scavenging. She would be watching them from the top of one of the tallest buildings in the area, which was still stable enough for her to perch herself on the roof and overlook a large portion of the city. It was one of her favorite places to relax when she was able.

Eva made her way up the old marble steps to the ground floor. The front lobby was a large room with high arched ceilings carved of white stone, riddled with piles of bones from various animals and a few Gang members. Eva could tell from their clothing that it was a Western Gang, not the Tigers or Serpents. A dozen tables and long counters were scattered around the room. Every surface was covered in thick dust. Footprints of predatory animals were all around but Eva found no sight of them. It was just silent. While most would have found this place unsettling, she had always found serenity in the shadows of the past.

She passed through the entrance and began the ascent up to the fifth floor. Surprisingly, the stairs were in great condition, untainted by time. This was probably because they were made from a much stronger stone than much of the city. Broken cracks of sunlight zigzagged on the walls. This particular skyscraper had been twice its current height before the War. The top had been torn in half and pushed into the building behind it at an angle. As Eva climbed the last handful of stairs, she was met with a flock of black and yellow birds which quickly took flight around her.

Finding a comfortable spot to sit, Eva hung her legs over the edge of the half-wall and observed the scenery below. In the blocks nearest to her, she occasionally noticed Jake and Tommy weaving in and out of the streets. They would pop into a building with an item or two in their hands. Between the two of them, Tommy seemed to be less meticulous in searching every miniscule nook and cranny, while his elder brother would stop, lay down his weapon, and search through old dumpsters, rotted boxes, and the shells of vehicles.

Tommy is an impressive kid. Speed is key. Jake is going to get himself killed. Every time he puts down his weapon, he lets his guard down. And diving in dumpsters... She could only shake her head.

The two brothers were blocks away from each other for hours. Shortly after the sky had gone dark, they returned to the building where Eva was watching them. They found her waiting for them as they approached the front doors. Both of them looked drained, but were in good spirits.

Jake volunteered Tommy to go first, clearly uncertain about his own findings and eager to measure them against his brother's. Much to Eva's surprise, Tommy had discovered a few useful items. He presented her with a small knife, a well-fitting jacket, and a potted plant growing from what looked like an old paint bucket. Tucked into his back pocket was a semi-intact book titled *Farming for Beginners*.

"Wow, Tommy," she nodded in praise. "Not bad for your first time out here."

As usual, Tommy did not utter a word, but gratitude was plastered all over his face. A smile grew from ear-to-ear. Jake looked at his brother, dark brown eyes glittering with pride, then dimmed from his own lack of self-confidence. Just as he was about to reveal what he had found, Tommy placed the plant on the floor and pulled out the book, pointing frantically to a picture of a bean crop and then to the plant. Eva looked closely at the picture and admitted that she did not know much about farming.

"The Rovers would know more about this than I would. I would ask them. I was never a farmer. I'm better at *killing* things, not growing them, unfortunately."

"Yeah." Jake shook his head and rolled his eyes. "We know."

She scoffed. "Okay… What did *you* find then?"

Jake cleared his throat uncomfortably and revealed his cache. The first item was a multi-tool in decent condition. He paused, waiting for any indication of approval from Eva. When she did not respond, he presented a pair of boots that he had already changed into. They were in much better shape than the shoes Eva had found at the Post.

"They fit really comfortably," he said, puffing out his chest. "And they're like new."

"Did you get them off of a body?" Eva laughed, half serious.

"Actually… I found them in an old store."

"Next time, make sure you aren't dropping your guard when you are scavenging. Like dumpster diving without being cautious of your surroundings. You dropped your weapon no less than *six* times that I was able to see. Keep doing that and you'll end up dead or captured real quick. But… good job to you too."

Eva was impressed. They seemed to be catching on rather quickly. Until Jake removed the third item from his pocket. At first, Eva did not recognize the spherical item that had a pull pin on top. Her eyes widened. She snatched it from his grasp and ran down to the end of the block, placing it carefully in an alley.

"What are you doing?" Jake panicked. "What is it?"

"That was a *grenade*," she breathed. "A small bomb. The pin hasn't been pulled so it could still be dangerous. Useful, sure… but unpredictable, being as old as it is."

Jake apologized. "Well… this is the last thing I found. It isn't really… um… a survival tool though."

Jake showed her an old newspaper that was in remarkably good shape. The headline read: *The End Times - Bombings Reach America*. Eva had not read this article before and was immediately fascinated. At this point, her association with Jake was built on sarcasm and annoyance. So, when her feedback was genuine, he became concerned.

"This is actually a good find," she said with her eyes locked on his. "It isn't useful for survival, but I am very interested in reading it."

"You don't have to be an ass about it," Jake said as he shoved the paper in her hands and frowned.

"I wasn't." She looked away and held the newspaper in her hands, letting the pages run between her fingers.

Tommy yawned. Even through the street, dimly lit by the moon, the brothers saw Eva's face change.

"And now," she smirked, "It is time for you to hide from *me*."

"But it's after dark," Jake whined. "And we're tired."

She shot a dirty look at him. "*That's the point.* Out here, there will come a time where you will be forced to hide from the Gangs when you are drained of every last drop of energy. Like at the Post. Perfect example. You *will* have to hide. You *will* have to fight. And you *will* have to kill. Stay within these two blocks. The longer it takes me to find you, the better off you do. Buildings around here are mostly intact and much safer than other parts of the city so there are plenty of places to hide. But know that I *will* find you eventually."

Jake and Tommy hesitantly agreed as Eva turned around to let them split up. She plugged her ears so she couldn't hear their footsteps. After a few moments of soft humming, she turned on her heels and stuffed the newspaper in her bag. The street was dark and devoid of movement. Clouds were drifting in front of the moon casting ominous shadows on the ancient asphalt. Jake and Tommy probably thought they had the advantage in this challenge. Little did they realize, Eva spent most of her life learning to rely on senses other than vision.

She waited for a while, taking in a few deep breaths to center herself. While adjusting each sense, she craned her neck in an attempt to hear any sign of the boys. The only noises that met her ears belonged to the nocturnal animals scurrying around on the pavement or floating through the sky. Other than that, stillness. Nothing.

Good for them, she snickered. *They managed to make it through the first minute.*

As a young woman, Eva watched predators roaming the cities and suburbs. Their careful steps. Their calculated movements. Their composure. Because she had neither parent nor guardian, her survival relied on observance. And learning from the very animals that had hunted since the Old Times was her only option.

Before sundown, while she was watching Jake and Tommy scavenge, she had studied the buildings nearby. The structure and condition of each one, even considering which to choose if she were hiding from the Gangs. Although neither of the brothers had experience out here, Tommy appeared much more methodical. Jake, on the other hand, was very unpredictable and reactive.

Their unique personalities was what Eva used to hunt them down. *Know your prey, know them well. And* because I didn't mention how long I would wait for them to hide, Jake probably jumped into the first building he saw. Tommy, on the other hand, will stay hidden in the shadows, searching for the perfect spot while staying away from me.

Admittedly, Eva loved a challenge, so she decided to go after Tommy first. And although he had not spoken a word since they met, he was obviously clever. She believed the reason behind Tommy's silence was to absorb the world around him and speak only when it was necessary.

After nearly missing it the first time, a small building drew her in on her second pass. Hidden behind rows of shops and boutiques, this ancient storefront looked intentionally placed at the back of a larger alleyway. She took care in placing her feet if anything on the ground would give away her position. It would have been pitch black if not for six small windows at the wall to her left, allowing the faded moonlight to penetrate into the room. With each step, she listened for any unusual sound. A couple of mice scampered across the wooden floors under her boots. They had not even sensed her closing in on them.

The building itself looked to be in poor shape long before the War. Shattered dishes strewn across the creaking wood floors and tall tables with stools placed haphazardly around the room. A shattered neon sign hung over shelves of broken bottles read: Pub & Grill. The name of the bar was now illegible. Against the far wall, there were stairs on the right and a door to the back rooms on the left. Directly in front of the back door was a large piece of metal that had fallen from the second story, pinning it shut. The stairs were built from the same wood as the floor, warped and rotted. She swiftly scoured the rest of the main floor but did not find Tommy. He may have gone up the stairs and found refuge on the floor above.

Eva first placed her foot on the stair and drew it across the length of the plank, searching for any rot or loose boards. Only after she was positive that it was safe, she put her weight onto it. Same motion for the second. She slid her foot to one side and noticed that the wood had warped upwards and would snap or creak. She carefully moved her foot back towards the other side. It was stable.

This strategy was arduous, but she eventually made her way up to the second floor. Again, she closed her eyes to focus on her hearing. Nothing. But when she reached the top landing, she felt something. The presence did not feel like an animal, but human. Eva's heart rate quickened. There was a doorway to a smaller room near the front windows, caked with dust. The wall opposite her was completely destroyed and the light from outside draped loosely on an ancient desk and a few lounge chairs. She remained in the shadow of the stairway, waiting for movement. Suddenly, the silhouette of a child peeked from around the corner. When the sound of soft giggling filled the air, an intense chill ran up Eva's spine.

"I see you Tommy," she whispered and the shape disappeared.

Eva rubbed her eyes. *What the shit?* She walked over to the doorway, which only opened to a small room used for washing clothes and linens. It looked like it had been used recently, as if someone was living there. But there was no one to be found. She began to doubt herself. Doubt her senses. Did she see someone that *is* or someone that *was*? A few years ago, she became obsessed with stories of the afterlife and individuals who remained on earth after they passed. This topic seemed to be a favorite among the Old Time peoples as numerous books filled stores all over the city. She had never seen a spirit before, but there was nowhere for that shadow to have gone. And there was no exit out of this floor aside from the stairwell behind her.

Before she could dwell on it any further, the sound of movement caught her attention from the bottom of the stairs. As quickly and silently as she could, Eva made her way back down to the bar. She finally made it to the bottom and glanced around. But again, she saw nothing. This time, it was what she *heard*. Scrambling down the street, the light pitter patter of footsteps.

Eva raced outside to try and spot the culprit, but they had already vanished from sight. They had to be close as she could still hear pacing—either down the alley or up in the next couple buildings. She jogged down the sidewalk, wary of the cracks and rubble below her. The first alley was empty, as was the first building. Most of it was destroyed. Tommy would have a difficult time navigating through the rubble quietly. Whirling around, she followed the sound of the same set of footsteps. They moved into a building further down the street.

If this is Tommy, she smirked, *He is good. But not good enough.*

The moment she rounded the next corner, Eva knew which building that Tommy was hiding in. It was the old food mart where she had been just a few days before. Upon entering, she explored the front area. However, the only realistic hiding space in this building was a small room in the back, used for storage. Still, she checked behind the front desk, the aisles that had not toppled over, and in the bathrooms.

Finally, Eva closed in on the storage room. Her back was against the wall and she peered into the cracked doorway. This time, she knew someone was in there. The faint sound of shallow breathing entered her ears. Bursting through the door, she spotted him immediately. Tommy's face was plastered with fear as he tripped backwards. When he realized it was Eva, his face relaxed into an embarrassed smile.

"You did a great job Tommy," she laughed and helped him back to his feet. "Didn't mean to scare you so bad. But you had me on a chase. By the way, how did you get out of the room in that other building?"

Tommy shook his head and pointed to where he was hiding.

Her heart skipped a beat. "Wait… You weren't the one I saw before?"

He shook his head and pointed again to his hiding spot. Eva's palms started to sweat. Was it a Nomad, a Gang Member, or something else entirely? Or maybe it was Jake and she had mistook the shadow to be smaller. She shuddered to think about it.

"Let's go find your brother," she motioned for the boy and walked out of the building. "I went looking for you first because I knew you would be harder to track down."

Eva noticed, even in the near-complete darkness, Tommy's grin. She turned back to the alley where the Pub was hidden. *My mind must have been playing tricks on me.* The moon peered out from behind a cloud and illuminated the street again. Where the alley met the sidewalk, a dark figure stepped out into the street and faded away. Eva blinked hard. In the pit of her chest, a heavy weight made it difficult to breathe for a moment.

As the sky cleared, a serene glow blanketed the desolate streets. Eva's tightening chest relaxed. She had seen pictures of the Old Times, and imagined herself basking in the streetlamps of a bustling city at twilight. Streets lined with people. Cars dropping people off for their late dinner dates. Laughing and the countless conversations in each building. Friends and family enjoying each other's company. Then suddenly, bombs raining from the sky. Laughter turned to screams.

And Eva opened her eyes once again to the pale, broken metropolis. Nothing left but the remnants of a world that had forgotten itself.

"This city before," she whispered to Tommy, still keeping her wits about her. "It must have been so amazing to live here… Until..."

She trailed off.

The young boy responded with a pat on her arm, still as silent as ever. Even though she did not know a single person from those days, she still mourned their loss. It was almost an obsession. She smiled down at him again, a simple act she had not allowed herself in what felt like ages. And once again, she responded to this softness by clearing her throat.

Now, it was time to find Jake.

Eva and Tommy stayed close to the buildings and looked through each one as they passed. At one point, they decided to double back and comb each structure more carefully, including those that were clearly too unstable to hide. They had traveled well past the first block when they began to worry.

"I told you both to stay in this block," she whispered loudly.

Tommy felt a cold tingling over his body when they stepped into the crosswalk to the next set of roadways. At this point, Eva regretted letting them split up. After spending a significant amount of time in the next part of the city, she began to feel sick to her stomach. The whole block was completely devoid of humans, friend or foe.

She tried to remain calm in front of the young boy. "We are venturing into more dangerous territory. The Gangs like to pillage around here. But these are the Gangs from across the forest in the West. I don't have many dealings with them, so we have to be extra careful."

Tommy swallowed the lump in his throat and stopped in his tracks for a moment, then raced back up to Eva. The further that they ventured down the street, deeper into the city's center, the more her concern grew. However, she refused to admit that she was wrong for teaching these brothers skills to survive.

It's not my fault that Jake can't follow simple directions, she reasoned. *His brother is ten years old and he does exactly as I tell him. Why is it so hard for the idiot older brother? I can't help it if he got himself captured or killed. That's his fault for not listening to me.*

Jake had indeed run off, but Eva and Tommy were close behind. While he was attempting to hide at the end of the block, something caught his eye. A person wearing layers of thick animal hides ran through the streets in front of him, bare feet slapping against the asphalt. At first, Jake believed it was Eva disguising herself as a distraction. He imagined how satisfying it would be to find her first - the hunter becoming the hunted. When the figure rounded a corner a few blocks down, he was immediately surrounded by rugged people with torches, weapons, and unusual markings on their faces.

Eva had also noticed the bobbing lights along the buildings a few blocks down. The jerking feeling in her stomach became more violent. Somehow, she knew Jake was there. With one deep breath, she raced off towards the light leaving Tommy far behind her. He was safe, Jake may not be. And when she heard the sound of Jake's scream, she dug her boots into the cracked pavement and burst into a full sprint.

Why am I risking my life again for this idiot again? she asked herself, but her feet continued to carry her forward.

"Please don't kill me," Jake begged. His weapon, brandished in front of him and his back against a brick building. "D-don't take m-me to your compound."

Eva finally made it to the small crowd with a blade in one hand and her gun in the other. Her lungs felt like they would explode when she finally reached the crowd. Suddenly, the group turned to her. She was ready to kill.

The moment she realized who they were, Eva lowered her weapons.

Chapter 4

Eva immediately recognized the rows of unkempt warriors by the unusual markings on their faces. Jake could see her between the group of disheveled people. As she lowered and sheathed her weapons, he called out to her. His heart was racing.

"What are you doing?" he yelled frantically. A few from the mob turned to him and scowled. "They're going to *kill* me."

Are we done for? Are there too many? Why isn't she fighting them?

"They don't even have their weapons drawn," Eva pointed out. Tommy finally caught up to her, gasping for breath.

"Isn't this a Gang?" he called back.

She laughed. "No Jake. You would have already been dead if this was a Gang. These are Nomads."

Jake was still paralyzed with fear. One of the Elder Nomads ordered his tribe to stand down, proclaiming that he recognized Eva's voice. He walked up to her as she removed her hood. As soon as the Nomads saw who was under the cowl, they all bowed and chanted "Wanderer" in unison.

Jake lowered his weapon with his shaking hands. "What. The. *Shit*… is going on?"

Eva put her hand up as the Nomads rose again. The Elder smiled and looked at Tommy, who had hid behind her. Both brothers watched in confusion as she grabbed the forearm of the Nomad and he returned the gesture. With her other hand, she made a fist, placed it over her heart, then opened her palm and placed it over his chest. Again, he did the same.

"You and your friends are welcome for a meal Wanderer," he said and began walking around the next block. "It has been too long. Come. We have made our camp nearby. Please, we insist."

Eva's stomach yawned with hunger. "Thank you. We would love to join you."

She followed the Elder with Tommy at her heels. Jake rushed up to them after realizing that they were going to leave him whether or not he decided to follow. He grumbled something inaudible under his breath about these people. The Nomads followed behind their leader, silent as they strolled through the grass.

They were led to a part of the city that had been flooded for decades. The sidewalk had been replaced with greenery and a flowing creek filled the street. Nocturnal animals and insects filled the air with their calls. Life flourished in this part of the metropolis. It was no wonder the Nomads set their camp up here. The sound of trickling water soothed Eva and the McAvoy brothers. It was breathtakingly serene. As they walked down the path, a herd of deer passed by them, undeterred by the sight of the group. One of the fawns passed in front of Tommy long enough for him to reach out and touch its fur. Neither he nor his older brother had ever seen one up close. The whole experience was surreal. It was almost as if the Nomads had a divine connection to the earth and all living creatures.

By the time the group reached the camp, fires had already been lit and soup pots were boiling with herbs and vegetables. A few Nomads had been carrying the carcasses of various animals, holstered by rope and twine over their shoulders or around their necks. They presented their catch by bowing to their kin who had stayed behind rinsing vegetables in the stream nearby. Eva's stomach began to rumble.

"Nomad cooking," Eva whispered to the brothers. "Best food in the region."

She and the rest of the Nomads began taking their seats around the large bonfire. On the outer ring were more of the mismatched hides and fabrics used for their lean-to tents. Smaller children who were playing there had stopped to join their families near the fire. These people were much more joyful than the Rovers.

The Elder grabbed Tommy and Jake by the arm and pulled them to the center of camp. The congregation began howling like animals. The brother's hearts were pounding in their ears and their legs grew soft and jelly-like. Eva found a small nook to watch from the perimeter of the congregation so that she could be alone. She pulled her hood over her head and covered her face, watching from the shadow of two brick walls. Even from afar, she could see the fear flickering in the McAvoy brother's eyes. She snickered to herself.

Here we go. Time for Nomad theatrics.

"Tonight!" The Elder settled down the crowd of Nomads. "We gather in the name of our Great Mother."

Eva rolled her eyes.

"Our Mother is who blesses us with these beautiful flowers, this delicious food, and these wonderful people. Our very connection with nature was bestowed upon us by *her* and her alone. Let us never forget that we have a duty to preserve the beauty of her gifts during this time of rebuilding and rebirth."

It started as a low hum and rose to a high pitched screech. The Nomads all howled in unison. Such a haunting sound chilled Jake and Tommy to the core. Only the Elder and the brothers were near the fire, the rest of the Nomads remained at the edge of the camp.

"As our tradition dictates," the Elder continued, motioning at Jake and Tommy. "We must bathe these boys in the love of our clan… and our custom of initiation. They are good friends of The Wanderer."

I wouldn't call them 'friends,' Eva thought. *Let alone 'good' ones.*

Whispers of "The Wanderer" started to arise in the congregation. Many in the crowd looked around, but did not see Eva. The few who were nearby placed their fist over their heart and opened their palm to her in greeting. She returned their gestures. Two children from the crowd walked towards Jake and Tommy carrying tunics made of animal hides. Both bowed and draped them over the brothers. The rest of the crowd began chanting in unison.

"What is going on?" Jake whispered out of the side of his mouth.

Tommy just shrugged and watched on in silence as the Elder continued.

"Be it that they are safe from harm, Blessed Mother. Be it that they are given your favor. So mote it be. So mote it be. So mote it be."

For a moment, the Elder disappeared into the crowd towards the tents, returning with a bowl of a thick red liquid. He lifted his wrinkled hand in front of Tommy and shut his eyes. It hovered a few inches from the boy's forehead before being placed softly upon it.

"Your energy is strong little one," he began. "It flows with such ease through your body. Our Mother has given me insight into your heart, but your openness allowed me to enter into the energy and swim through it like a river. May you always remain this way under her guidance. You and Nature will become one. There is much change in you yet to come. You will be at the end of a cycle of which you do not yet comprehend. Rich is your fate. I will bestow the mark of the Owl upon you. May you cut through your enemies with the same ease that they cut through the night sky. Silent and stoic."

The Elder placed a dot between Tommy's eyes and a line down the bridge of his nose. On each cheek, he drew a crescent moon shape, and three small dots down his chin. Eva leaned forward and watched Tommy bow to the Elder in thanks. She recalled the mark she had been given by Mother Nature five years before.

He does have a very strong yet passive air about him, she thought. *These Nomads and their spirituality is a silly thing, but it seems to work for them. They have been around for a long time.*

Next, it was Jake's turn. Truthfully, his fear had been replaced with anticipation of what animal he would be marked with. *It has to be something stronger than an owl.* As the Elder walked over to him, he puffed out his chest and lifted his chin. The Elder's brow furrowed as his hand hovered over Jake's face. He moved his hand down to his heart area and he lifted his head.

"Interesting energy you have," he chuckled. "I have not felt a heart so hardened in a time. You try to shut out your feelings by projecting your insecurities onto others… but someone with the same blocked energy will break down that barrier. Stubborn… but you bear the weight of the past on your shoulders. Your courage will come with time. My advice is to know yourself and trust those who care for you or it may be your own undoing. Do not dwell on those who you cannot save.

The Mother chooses for *you* the mark of the Coyote. They are headstrong, but care deeply for their small pack. May you always remember who your pack truly is."

Jake was taken aback by the Elder's words. Stubborn? Him? Definitely not. However, he once read that coyotes were great hunters, so he did not argue. The markings he was given was one circle on the tip of his nose, two horizontal zig zags under each eye and a complete handprint on his chest. Another Nomad grabbed some soft dirt and sprinkled it on the brothers and then poured water in their hair.

"The five elements are now gifted to these two new family members," the Elder turned back to the crowd with his hands raised. "We are each marked with an animal - the element of life. Sprinkled with earth, dipped in water, breathed in the air, and burned with fire in our hearts. For our Great Mother! *So mote it be*! Now, let us feast!"

All of a sudden, some of the Nomads began dancing and playing instruments. Others formed lines around the cooking pots for the meal. Eva had pondered the symbol that Jake had been given. She wasn't too sure that he would have been a coyote. *More like a donkey or a fly.* Laughing to herself, she stood up and leaned against the toppled brick wall. A small Nomad girl brought her a platter of roasted meat and vegetables. Jake and Tommy grabbed a plate for themselves after the Nomads took turns welcoming them.

Tommy was quickly swept up by a girl around his age and sat next to her. She was very talkative, so he just listened to her while he ate. His older brother spotted Eva from across the crowd, sitting in the nook, almost completely hidden. As he went to sit near her, Yidi, the Elder, pulled him aside and offered him a seat next to him and his wife, who introduced herself as Masha.

"Do not take my husband's words too personally," said Masha as Jake sat down. Her voice was slow and melodic, almost hallucinatory. "I read energies better than him anyway. But he likes the attention from our clan. However, stubbornness can sometimes be a *good* thing. Especially when you know what to fight for. Coyotes are known to be followers of what they believe is a righteous path."

Jake nodded and smiled. The old woman's words comforted him.

"From where do you hail?" she inquired. "Your energy intrigues me. You do not look as hardened as any slave, Nomad, or Rover."

"We came from a vault in the hills," Jake responded. "Eva came looking for any survivors, and we were the only two left. My brother and I are searching for our father who left our home a few years ago. Do you happen to know anyone that came from there?"

Masha turned to her husband. Yidi thought for a moment, "Not here… But now that I think on it… I did hear rumors about a Gang through the forest enslaving an older man that came from the hills. He would be about the right age from what I heard."

"Thank you so much." Jake smiled. "It's better than nothing."

"I'm surprised The Wanderer allows you to walk with her." Yidi said. "Ever since her parents were taken from her as a child, she prefers to be alone."

"What happened?"

"That girl became a great warrior through a hard life," Masha shook her head. "She's experienced much pain. And through that, she has gained much resilience. More than any of us. The Wanderer bears stronger energy than I have ever seen, but also the hardest soul to break."

"Do you know what her life was like before?" Jake moved closer to them as they nodded.

"It was years ago," Yidi started. "She was born to a Rover family near the Serpent's compound, from what I was told. Those people no longer exist today. I heard she was a sweet child until the Serpents came and ravaged her colony. They were much smaller back then, but they slaughtered *everyone*. No one, not even The Wanderer herself knows how she made it out of there."

Jake glanced over to Eva who kept herself in the shadows. Yidi continued.

"Back then, they would rather massacre the settlements they raided rather than enslave the people… Her kin were burned, along with the town. Our only guess is that one of the Serpents must have felt her strong energy and dragged her back to their compound where she was enslaved for a decade or so."

"But she told me that no one *ever* escapes the compounds-." Jake finished his food but stayed at the edge of his seat.

"And that is true to this day." Masha lifted her hand in protest when Jake started to speak. "No *slave* ever has. But The Wanderer is different. You see, she did something that no slave had ever done before. She challenged the leader."

Jake's eyes widened.

"Granted," Yidi stepped in quickly. "She endured *years* of unspeakable torture before that day. Passed around by the men. Beaten and tortured by the slave-drivers. Scars… mental, physical, and spiritual. Watching her whole colony murdered along with countless others in the Nest. I'm *sure* those scars never really healed."

A large lump formed in Jake's throat that he could not swallow. He wanted to vomit thinking about Eva in the compounds as a young girl. Everything she had gone through. No wonder she was so cold and distant. Her trust for other humans had completely vanished, and understandably so. But what was most unsettling to him was the knowledge that there were other countless children who were still slaves to the Gangs.

"We don't know for sure, but she must've watched the Gang members train," Masha nodded. "She has always been a silent observer, hidden in the shadows. That is how she learned to fight. Through the days of torture, she practiced battle. She learned the hierarchy of the Gangs. And finally, one day, she openly challenged the leader. She called him out for a battle to the death. Only victory could grant her freedom. Defeat would offer it as well, but at the cost of her life."

"Did she win?" Jake instantly realized the stupidity of his question.

"Why do you think she stands before you today?" Yidi laughed. "And she bested him with only a piece of metal pipe. The Chief at the time fought with the same short blades she now carries. After she ended him, she took them… And she has been alone ever since."

Jake stared blankly into the crowd of dancing Nomads. "How do you know all of this?"

"Six or seven years ago, she came to us before she moved to the Rover colony," Masha answered. "We tried getting her to talk, but we were only able to get some of her story from whispers as she battled with the demons of her dreams. I'm sure there are many more secrets that she will take to her grave."

Jake's heart dropped. He had treated Eva poorly since they had met. Questioning her every move. Fighting about every direction she gave. But now, he felt pity for her. After a few moments of pondering what he had just heard, he excused himself from Elder Yidi and Elder Masha. Slowly, he weaved his way around the celebrating Nomads. His gaze was fixed on Eva.

"Saving this seat for anyone?" he joked.

Eva reluctantly offered him a space near her. As he glanced back at the Elders, his mind went blank. "So what animal did the Elder give you when you joined them?"

"I never *joined* them." Eva lifted her head and locked eyes with him. "I *saved* them."

Jake forced his focus on her story though his mind was elsewhere. "How?"

"They were a small group," she readjusted her legs to be more comfortable. "They ran the risk of being exterminated by the Gangs. I taught them to fight because they wanted to protect themself, unlike the Rovers. They taught me to scavenge. And now their numbers have grown ten times over. Some stay to themselves, others are led by Yidi and Masha. Even some of the old colonies of Rovers came here to join them."

"That's amazing." Jake tried to hide his pity, but Eva caught onto it quickly.

Her half smile dropped and her eyes became narrow as her voice became stern. "They told you, didn't they?"

"What are you talking about?" He tried to lie, but realized it was pointless. She saw right through him. He felt the color drain from his face and changed his tone. "Yeah... they did. I am *so sorry* for everything you had to go through."

"Don't be," Eva said shortly. "I don't need your pity. But I guess you would've found out sooner or later."

"I didn't mean it that way. I haven't seen the amount of death or torture that you've faced. I doubt anyone has from what they told me. But I have had personal loss too. My mother died before our dad left."

"Everyone has experienced loss out here, Jake." Eva's tone softened slightly. "It's hard to move on, especially when it is someone close. But that is why I *live*. I live for the ones that I have seen suffer and die. I *fight* for the children whose lives were cut short. The women who have been ravished by men. The men who tried to shield themselves with their hands against the barrel of a gun. It's just… never enough."

Jake slid closer to Eva. She lifted her head and let the light from the bonfire fill her hood. He thought he saw a tear sliding down her cheek. Their gaze remained locked. He was at a loss as he thought back to the gruesome scene at The Post. Eva did not want to hear his words. The calm and warm feeling between them was oddly comforting. She felt drawn to him for a moment.

"I was given the symbol of the lioness," she said, breaking the link between them. "Though we don't have any around this part of the world. They are the ultimate predator, Masha says. And yet, they will protect those who give them respect until their dying breath. Unpredictable and deadly. So… I would say fitting."

"Amazing way to describe you," Jake smiled. "You've already protected Tommy and me *and* risked your life ten times over for the Rovers and the Nomads. I know that he hasn't said anything since our mother died, but my brother and I are grateful. And even though I've given you a hard time, it is not intentional. I guess what I'm trying to say is… thank you."

Jake took a leap of faith and leaned towards Eva, and she followed suit. Their lips only brushed against each other before they heard the screams. Without a second to think, Eva grabbed Jake by the shoulder, ripped him to his feet, and shoved him behind a brick wall as the sound of an explosion rang through the city streets. Fragments of metal clashed against the walls around the camp. The sound was soon followed by gunshots.

Jake screamed over the ringing in his ears, his voice overflowing with panic. "Tommy! We have to find Tommy!"

As he began to run for the crowd, Eva threw him against the wall again. Her fists grabbed bunches of his clothing. She forced him to look at her.

"You *need* to get back to the colony," she pleaded. "Do. Not. Let. Them. Follow. You."

"But Tommy," Jake tried to peer around the corner but Eva shoved him back against the wall a third time. His eyes were welling with tears. "I can't leave him."

"I *will* find him," she promised. "But you have to get out of here. *Now.* There is *nothing* you can do for these people. Most of them will escape. They always do. Take these roads north and get out of the city. You will see the colony on the outskirts to your right. Get back to my home and bar the door until I return."

Jake desperately wanted to run into the hail of bullets, but took one last look at Eva's pleading face and grabbed his weapon. Soon, the gunfire and screams had been absorbed by brick walls and trees. Only the sound of Jake's footsteps passed his ears. His mind was numb. All he could think about was Eva and his brother. If anything happened to them, he wouldn't know what to do.

Lucky for him, the sun's rays flooded the horizon as he exited the city. A burning in his chest tried to force him back to the camp, but he pushed himself forward as tears streamed down his face. He looked over his shoulder. No one had followed him. This was the life he lived now, running from death.

***

Eva had to be extremely careful in how she handled the Gang that was massacring the Nomads. There were too many to fight or pick off one-by-one. Plus, she was low on bullets. Her lone goal was to save Tommy. While most Nomads slipped into the safety of the city, some stayed behind to fight. Countless others fell, their bodies scattered around the still-burning fires.

Eva fought her emotions as she desperately scoured the crowd for Tommy. Smoke and gunshots coming from all directions became disorienting. She was just about to give up but then, she saw him. He was hiding under one of the cloth tents on the far side of the camp. Cradled in his arms was the girl he had been eating with. From the distance between them, Eva couldn't tell whether the girl was dead or dying. She only saw the blood. Worst of all, there was no easy way for Eva to get to them. She would have to brave the hail of bullets.

Dammit, she took one quick, shaky breath and sprinted across the battlefield. The Gang members must have been near the stream because she could not see them, but they were still shooting. Eva ran into a few Nomads who were trying to escape, almost knocking them over. Unfortunate souls lay hunched over their loved ones in a final attempt to shield them. Gang Members and Nomads alike. All dead or dying. The Wanderer's ears were drowning in sounds of moaning, screaming, and gurgling. Her eyes locked onto nearly every victim who was still clinging to life, watching them cry out for their families. Off in the distance, she saw a hooded figure with long bony hands. Its presence felt eerily familiar. She blinked and it disappeared. All of this was almost too much to bear, but she kept her focus on Tommy.

Although it felt like eons, she finally reached him. The young girl he was cradling had a piece of metal shrapnel jutting from her right side. The color was draining from her terror-stricken eyes. She shook uncontrollably, trying to take in a full breath. Rage boiled in Eva's body as the girl struggled to breathe for just a few more moments and relaxed for the final time. Tommy had tears streaming down his face. His hands and shirt were covered in blood, but he said nothing.

"Let's get out of here." Eva's voice was cracking with emotion.

Tommy laid down the little girl and threw his arms around Eva. At first, they did not notice that the rain of shots had gone silent. Pulling away from the hug, she grabbed Tommy's shoulders and squeezed them.

"Do you know where the safe house is?" she asked. "*My* house?"

Tommy nodded.

"We need to get out of here," she nodded with him. "But I need you to get out first. I'm going to find out which Gang did this."

He started to get up, but something caught his gaze. A trickle of blood dripped down Eva's leg. She had been shot. Fear flushed his face as he pointed to her wounds. Pain tinged from her thigh up to her back. Ripping a thin strand of cloth off the side of the tent and wrapping her leg tightly, she pushed Tommy out of the tent. He ran out of sight just as the sound of footsteps closed in.

"Damn near got all of them," a male voice said. Eva pushed herself as far back in the tent as she could, careful not to shake the sides.

"They got a good few of us as well," said another male voice. "Damn Nomads."

"Nah," a female voice said. "This ain't shit for killings. They have numbers. We were lucky to catch them by surprise. There are *many* more."

"Check the bodies," a deep male voice called out. "I want that bounty. The Wanderer wouldn't be dressed like the rest of 'em. If we happened to bag her head, the Eastern Gangs would pay a hefty price."

Eva's wound stung and her legs started to shake from fatigue. She carefully wiped the sweat from her brow. With each breath, the smell of burning corpses and blood permeated her lungs. The body of the little girl was lying at the entrance to the tent, her eyes wide open. She pulled her tourniquet tighter and tried to silently adjust her legs. The pain almost caused her to pass out.

From outside the tent, she could hear them sweeping the campsite. Occasionally, a shot would ring out. She closed her eyes and winced. A bead of sweat ran down her nose, across her lips, to her chin. A couple of the Gang members closed in around her. They had been checking all of the tents by knocking down the supports. A large boot and the bottom of a gun came into view. Before she could blink, the barrel was pointed right at her face, but its owner did not bend down to look inside. All Eva could do was stay perfectly still and silent. She bit her lip when his boot kicked the support. It didn't budge. He tried again. Still nothing.

"Damn tent," the voice outside cursed.

"Don't worry about it. Just finish off the ones who are still dying," a female voice laughed. "They'd've run off by now anyway if they weren't hit."

"Too bad the Serpents didn't get to these guys first," the man near the tent joked. "They would have sold these guys for great trade."

"Hey, The Wolves may not be as large as them," a younger man's voice called from much further away. "But we are just as deadly. If we can sabotage the Serpents getting any bigger… then why not?"

They laughed in unison.

Wolves, Eva repeated in her head. *From the other side of the forest. Why are they all the way out here?*

"Our servants are better than any of these Nomads," an older woman said. "Especially that man from the hills. He takes half the beatings the rest do, but works twice as hard. Smart man."

"What?" Eva mouthed. *Man from the hills? The vault? That must be Jake and Tommy's father. It has to be.*

That was more information than Eva needed. Good information nonetheless. All she had to do was wait until there was an opening where she could slip past them, unnoticed. Her legs were screaming. She pulled her wrappings tighter over the oozing bullet hole. It was only a matter of time before she would either bleed out or pass out. After what felt like an eternity, she saw the Wolves gather near the far side of the campsite. That was her chance. She took it.

When she went to stretch her legs with her back against a wall, she nearly collapsed. The pain from her injury shot up her spine so quickly it made her head swim. She had to hold onto a crate inside the tent for support. A dark spot forming on her pants told her that she had to get medical attention soon. Quickly grabbing a sturdy wooden beam, she limped back towards the city outskirts as fast as her legs would carry her. The distancing sound of Wolf voices had finally silenced. That was when she let out a loud sob and fell to her knees.

The image of the little Nomad girl clung to the front of her mind. Bodies of countless others flashed into her view. No one was around to hear her cries. Same as before, her cries of sadness twisted into screams of pure rage. She was seething, shaking, and bleeding. All she could think about was revenge. But that would have to wait until she healed. Her hands tightened around her crutch and she struggled to her feet.

Wolves.

Each step became significantly more painful as Eva made her way towards her colony. What was normally a two hour journey would now take double the time. Luckily, her wrapped leg was cutting off most of the blood flow. The cool wind soothed her body, yet she was becoming weaker by the moment. Splinters dug into her hands, but the tinges of pain seemed to be keeping her alert.

The rest of her journey was a daze. The only thing she could remember was seeing the colony over the horizon as sunlight beamed down over the metal shacks. After that, she could only recall standing in the middle of the town. And then, her vision went dark.

****

With Eva's directions, Jake was able to make it to her home with ease. He had been pacing in the home, peering through the holes in the metal for an hour before he saw Tommy. The rush of relief was almost unbearable. He hugged his brother tightly. Tommy pushed him out of the way to shut and lock the door. Both of them looked into the street, but did not see Eva.

"Where is she?" Jake asked his brother, still covered in the Nomad girl's blood.

Tommy wiped the tears from his eyes and shrugged, pointing towards the city.

All they could do was wait.

Time dragged on, and soon Jake's stomach began to churn. *She should be back by now.*

When he attempted to question his brother a second time, the boy's look sent him into a panic. Jake could not wait any longer. He rushed to the door, unlatched the lock, and ran outside, looking towards the city. Right past the furthest row of Rover shacks, he saw a limping figure drop to the ground. It was Eva. His heart jumped out of his chest as he raced to her side, hoisting her into his arms.

He immediately felt the warmth of blood running through his fingers and began banging on the Rover's doors.

"Please!" he cried out. "Someone help Eva. She is injured. She's been shot."

Not one door budged. Daylight meant lockdown in the Rover colony. Jake didn't care. He needed Eva to survive, and he would do whatever it took to make it happen. Finally, at the last shack, someone opened the door to let him in. And luckily, it was the home of the Colony's healer.

"Thank you for helping us," Jake breathed. Tommy snuck into the shack before the door closed and latched shut. "She is badly wounded. And I think she's lost a lot of blood."

The woman could hear the panic in his voice. "It will be okay. I'll do everything I can to patch her up… But I may need your help."

Jake laid Eva on a wooden table and the woman got to work immediately, cutting her pant leg off at the tourniquet and grabbing long, rusted forceps. She also took off Eva's thick jacket and tossed it at Jake, checking for any other injuries. Tommy's eyes widened in horror. His brother shooed him back to Eva's home reassuring him that he would look after her until she was well enough to come back.

"You are going to have to hold her down for this," the woman instructed. "If she isn't completely unconscious, this is going to… *sting a little*."

Jake's palms started sweating. The way she had said '*sting a little*' sat in his stomach like a boulder. He caught a whiff of the open wounds and gagged. His breathing quickened as he grabbed her arms and pinned them to the table. When the woman poured alcohol over the forceps and started reaching towards the bullet hole, he whispered loudly.

"What are you doing?" His eyes darted between the instrument and the woman.

"I have to get the bullet out," she flicked the forceps in the air, irked. "Otherwise she could die from infection or metal poisoning."

Jake nodded hesitantly and braced himself over Eva's body. This is not what they would have done in the Vault's Infirmary. Still, he could not break his gaze from the instrument going into Eva's flesh. The woman yanked out the first bullet with some force. That was when Eva screamed and struggled to break free, nearly knocking Jake off of her. She was incredibly strong.

"Do you have anything to help the pain?" Jake pleaded.

"You think I find it *fun* torturing people?" the woman asked sternly while snatching out some shrapnel. "If I had something, I would give it to her. Trust me. This isn't my first time doing this. Or hers."

Eva strained again. She must have woken slightly because her cry was much louder. Veins started to pop out of her arms as she attempted to free herself.

"You can't give her something to help?"

The woman stopped for just a second. Eva was fighting for air as sweat dripped down her neck. The room was quiet, but only for a moment. Pure annoyance was the emotion plastered on the healer's face.

"Do you want her to die?" she asked.

"No - but," Jake responded.

She took a piece of balled cloth and shoved it in Eva's mouth. "Look. Let me do my job, alright? I don't *enjoy* hurting people, but we don't exactly have the luxury of pain medication. I don't know how you did it where you came from, but we aren't so lucky here."

Jake bit his lip and let the woman continue. This time, Eva's scream was stifled from the gag. He closed his eyes tightly and winced with every one of her screams. He blamed himself.

If I had only listened to her, he berated himself. *She wouldn't be dying right in front of me. Stupid piece of shit. If I had just stayed in the block she told me to... instead of following those Nomads...*

"Done." The Healer's voice made him snap out of it. She had already dumped some alcohol on the bullet wound and sewed it up. Eva had relaxed, her entire body drenched in sweat. Carefully, Jake removed her gag and wiped her forehead softly with a dry rag.

"I'll take her back to her home and take care of her," he declared as the woman wrapped the wounds. "Is there anything else I can do?"

"Just don't underestimate her again," the woman smiled softly. "Or yourself."

Jake nodded, lifted Eva into his arms and carried her back to the eagerly waiting Tommy. For once, Jake said nothing to his brother. He just laid The Wanderer's limp body on her bed and sat by her side, promising himself that he would never let her get hurt again.

But deep down, he knew it was an impossible vow.

Chapter 5

Eva's recovery was going to be long and arduous. Her condition in the first week caused Jake to worry. She winced with every movement. Each day was spent in a semi-conscious nightmare filled with whispered pleas of mercy. Neither Jake nor Tommy slept much. And when he was not by her bedside, Jake criticized himself under his breath for putting her in danger. He had vowed to care for her, so he remained in the shack. The Rovers brought food each night and took turns checking on him throughout the day. At first, he refused, but Tommy finally convinced him to eat.

The Healer confirmed what the brothers feared. Eva had lost a dangerous amount of blood on her way back to the colony. Each day she reminded them that Eva might not wake for days, if she survived at all. Still, she urged them to give her water whenever she stirred. Despite everything, the Healer remained hopeful, and in time, Eva began to show signs of progress.

"You cannot blame yourself for what happens out here," a middle-aged Rover explained to Jake. "The Gangs have always been ruthless. And she has been their target ever since she started protecting this place. But she's always been… different."

With each passing day, Tommy would wake up early and fetch water from a nearby well. His brother would lay the cool washcloths on Eva's face to lower her fever. She would squirm and her breathing would be sharp, then relax. Occasionally, when Tommy was in another room reading through old newspapers and magazines, Jake would just watch her as she slept. The guilt was crippling. Deep into the night, he would whisper apologies in her ear, hoping she would hear them through her dreams.

By the second week, Eva finally opened her eyes. Jake hadn't left her side for longer than a few moments and was there when she awoke. His sigh of relief was so loud, that Tommy ran into the room and jumped onto the foot of her bed.

She whispered and cleared her throat. Arms shaking, she slowly raised herself to lie against the cold metal wall behind her. "Thanks for whatever you did."

"Are you doing okay?" Jake twiddled his thumbs. "You should be lying down. I… *We've* been worried."

"I'm fine," Eva gave him a heavy pat on the back. "Just in a lot of pain. Nothing I can't handle, though."

She spotted a bowl of food near her bed and slurped it down without tasting a single bite. Jake turned towards her and shot a look at Tommy who left promptly. Sunlight creeping through the cracks fell on Eva's chest. Faint, yet prominent in the light, scars hashed across her collarbone and below. They were slightly lighter than the rest of her skin and made X shapes in various places from shoulder to shoulder. He had not noticed before, but from what Yidi and Masha had told him about the years she spent within the Serpent's compound, he was not surprised at the sight.

Eva had noticed him looking and quickly grabbed her shirt and covered her chest and shoulders. She cleared her throat, trying to convince Jake that she was just cold, but he wasn't buying it.

"It's okay," Jake touched her hand in reassurance. "The Nomads told me about your past. That *you* were the only one that ever escaped a compound. There is nothing to be ashamed about."

Eva bit her lip and snatched her hand away from Jake. *But these scars are reminders of the darkness... when I wasn't strong enough to fight back.* She tried to bend her legs, but the pain from the wound felt like lightning. Part of her wanted to ignore Jake for the remainder of the day, but she could not leave her bed. There was no way to get away from him if he chose to stay. Instead, she crossed her arms and kept her eyes glued to the shelf near her feet.

"You know about my time before becoming The Wanderer?" she asked.

Jake almost missed the inflection on her voice. "Yes."

"Then you can understand why I will *never* set foot in another compound again," she started. "Because it would be suicide."

"The Nomads told me about a man from the Vault," Jake quickly spouted his thoughts. "They believe it could be my father. In a Gang across the forest."

"Yeah," Eva sighed. "I know. And I know which Gang too."

"Wait… You *knew*?" Tommy entered the room when he heard his brother raise his voice. "You knew all this time and you didn't tell us?"

Eva raised her voice over Jake's. "You think I would have risked my life if I could have just pointed you in the direction of your father when you told me about him? You *really* think I would have allowed myself to be shot in the leg if I could have just told you?"

She pointed her finger in the direction of the forest. Tommy walked over and punched his brother.

"So how did you find out then?"

"After I rescued Tommy. I stayed behind and heard the Gang speaking about a man from 'the hills'. It was the Wolves. They have him, most likely."

"What are we waiting for then?" Jake stood up but stopped dead in his tracks when he saw the look on Eva's face.

"Did you even hear what I *just* said?" She completely ignored the fact that Jake had forgotten about her leg. "Or do you even *remember* what you said to me at the Nomad campsite? That you would *not* argue with my choices. Did you actually mean that or are you just a liar?"

The room went completely silent. Whistling from the late-summer wind coming into Eva's home was the only thing that broke through the tension. Jake looked at the floor. Tommy just stared at his brother, shaking his head. Eva remained steadfast in her words.

"Please Eva." Jake fought back tears. Tommy's eyes were glittering as well. "He is the only family that Tommy and I have left. We won't stand a chance without you."

Eva closed her eyes and tilted her head to the ceiling, sighing loudly. She decided not to argue in her current state. "Can I at least heal before I make any more stupid decisions to get myself killed again?"

Jake was not unhappy with the response and did not dare press for more. He simply nodded and shuffled into the other room, returning with another plate of food from the night before. Eva's mouth immediately started salivating. She was still hungry. Tommy saved some of the water from the well each day in a large jug for Eva to drink. Watching Tommy slop water onto the floor, struggling to bring it into the room made Eva laugh.

"Thank you," she chuckled. "Y'know, I'd almost prefer if your brother was as quiet as you."

Jake scowled at them and helped his brother pour some water into a cup for her. She nodded in thanks and scarfed down the food. Once she was done, she grabbed her stomach and dropped her plate on the floor.

"Much better," she said. "Alright… I need to clean this wound and the rest of my body. So both of you need to get out."

"Do you need any help with your leg?" Jake offered.

Eva just pointed to the other room. Jake threw his arms up in the air and stomped out of the room behind Tommy, mumbling something about 'trying to help'. As soon as they were out of sight, she poured the rest of the jug into a basin that she pulled out from under her bed. Dipping and wringing out a cloth she wetted, she started wiping the sweat and dried blood off of her body. She carefully removed her clothing, glancing at the doorway to make sure no one was looking in. When she reached her pants, she took a few deep and quivery breaths before removing her bandaging. The Healer had not changed the dressing as often as she should have. The dried blood stuck to the wrappings and tore at her sensitive skin.

Idiot, she mouthed as she slowly tried separating the scabbing from the cloth. With each inch, she tore a bit of dead skin off with the dressing, gritting her teeth in agony. A few minutes went by and she was finally able to remove everything, including her pants. Everything was torn or stained with blood, so she tossed it in a heap near the door. Luckily, she had a spare outfit on her shelf near the door. It took quite a bit of effort and suppressed screams for her to get to her feet. Dizziness swept over her for a moment, but she was able to stand and wash her lower half. As she turned to face the wall Jake decided to check on her. He wanted to make sure she was all right.

What started out as just a passing glance became a fixation of horror. The room was bright enough for him to see Eva's past carved into her back and upper legs. Deep indentations stretched the length of her back, though few in number, were much more visible than those on her chest. They resembled claw marks, but did not look like they came from any animal that Jake ever read about. And just as she was about to turn around, he flattened himself against the wall.

Wow. That was the only word he could find to describe what he had witnessed. He slowly sunk to the floor and ran his fingers through his hair. He wasn't sure if he could ever look at Eva the same way again. Even after seeing half-decomposed corpses at the Post, bodies of The Wanderer's victims, and Nomads massacred in front of him, nothing compared to those scars. It was real to him now. The realization that no one, not even a warrior like Eva, was left completely unscathed by the Gangs. From the other side of the room Tommy was reading something and paid him no attention.

Eva did not notice Jake in the doorway. But as she limped over to the other side of the room, she saw him sitting against the wall. He stared at nothing. She knew he had seen something—his face was sheet white. Fighting the urge to say something snarky to him, she chose to bite her tongue. Truthfully, she already had a good idea of what he had seen. And Jake, who could feel her eyes over his shoulder, hoped that she would never ask.

After she had finished getting dressed, Eva allowed them back into the room. She had redressed her injury. The smell of stale blood lingered ripe in the air. She sat on the bed with the newspaper that Tommy had discovered in the city in her hands. When the brothers noticed this, their eyes lit up. Both made a seat nearby as she read.

BOMBINGS REACH THE UNITED STATES

Midwest News Will Continue Reporting

as Long as Possible

In an unprecedented global conflict, the United States has launched its full nuclear arsenal, joining countless other nations in a catastrophic series of retaliatory strikes. Major cities across the country have been annihilated. Washington, D.C. is reportedly reduced to rubble. The West Coast has been leveled. Mid-sized cities like St. Louis have sustained smaller-scale attacks, but casualties remain high. Exact death tolls are still unknown.

Survivors are flocking to emergency vaults, though many across the nation are nearing capacity. Authorities have confirmed that only individuals with proper Tags will be granted entry. Military efforts are underway to establish Ration Stations wherever possible, but resources are stretched thin.

The assault on U.S. soil follows President Smith's controversial July 4th address in which he initiated military action on "inferior countries." The reasons for this declaration remain unclear, though many speculate it stems from escalating tensions among the world's major powers.

Retaliatory strikes began on July 8th, before Congress could vote on a declaration of war. Coordinated nuclear attacks from multiple nations targeted key U.S. infrastructure. Overseas reports now indicate that American allies have also been neutralized or severely impacted.

President Smith's current location is unknown. Communication with the White House and the First Family has been lost since the initial strikes. The last verifiable global

death toll stands at just under 6
billion.

Midwest News has confirmed that
additional missiles were spotted over
the Chicago area. Survivors fear that
cities including St. Louis, Cleveland,
and Denver may soon be targeted.

We at Midwest News remain
committed to providing the public with
critical updates for as long as we are
able. We apologize for the lack of
editing or formatting during this
time, as our priority is delivering
accurate, timely information to those
who need it most.

God help us all.

Eva dropped the newspaper into her lap and stared blankly at the wall, arms crossed. Jake and Tommy were silent. The whole room was still. The last four words of the article lingered in their minds. None of them knew who "God" was, but Eva had an idea. When Jake went to open his mouth, Eva was already struggling to stand up. Her eyes locked onto a box in the other room.

"So who is this *God*?" he asked.

"I'm not sure," she replied. "But I'll show you who I think it may be."

With some effort, she limped back to her bed and stifled another cry as she fell onto the thick blankets. She did not lift her leg up high enough to avoid her boots on the floor and tripped over them. Jake jerked his arms out to help her, but he was too slow. Tommy had to nearly jump out of his seat to avoid being sat on.

Eva apologized after a few angrily spat curse words. "Sorry Tommy."

Carried softly in her hands was a small wooden box, about the size of her palms. The wood itself was extremely aged. Splintered sides curved up to a top that had been warped by moisture. As she opened it, the rusted latch creaked and strained. Tommy and Jake lifted their heads and hovered over her to get a better look at the box's contents.

"I found these in a few buildings across the city," she explained. "A long time ago."

Inside, there were about a dozen figurines of varying sizes. No two looked the same, but all of them bore similar features. Halos made from rays of light carved into the back of most of the figure's heads and the positioning of their hand gestures were all similar. Some were men, others were women. Some fat, some thin. But all of them shared one thing in common, the feeling of 'otherworldliness'.

"Did they worship these people?" Jake took one in his hands and inspected it closely.

"Yeah, I think so. During the Old Times," Eva caressed one with her fingertips. "Not anymore, though. But I think at least one of these things is *God*... Maybe all of them... Ancestors of survivors wouldn't have asked an ordinary person to 'save' them. Right? The Elders told stories about Old Time religions and worshiping deities like the Nomads do. But instead of animals or nature, it was these things. Religion is all but lost now, I guess."

Jake finally knew something that Eva did not and paused with a smirk. He wanted to relish it. "We studied religions while in the Vault."

After a moment of silence, she raised her eyebrows and made a circular motion with her hand to quicken his speech. "Go on."

"As you mentioned, it is similar to the worship of the Nomads with their animal guardians. But instead of animals, many people in the Old Times believed in human-like deities. The one that oversees them has no form, but he is called God or goes by some other name. People talk to him or her before going to bed at night. They would ask their god for things or safety. That's about all I know. I just didn't know if the Rovers or Gangs worshiped the same gods that we read about. Do any religious stories get passed down here?"

"No." Eva tossed the figure in her hand back in the box. "From what I've read, just about everyone believed their *god* left them to die… And I've found religious tablets and plaques, but they don't make sense to me."

Tommy chose the figure that looked different than all the others. Wooden in nature, this statuette did not have a halo like the rest. Instead, on the crown of his head was a circular flame over short and curly hair. His eyes were horizontal slits. Most of the other figures were standing tall, clad in extravagant gold and purple robes, with remnants of the paint still flecked on them. But his figure only had one shoulder covered with a simple, yellow garment and he was seated with his hands placed calmly in his lap.

"That one is my favorite too," Eva glanced over at him. "He doesn't look like a god, or whatever. He looks like a calm and simple person. Like you. Maybe he can be your deity."

Tommy smiled and shook his head. He pointed at the other figures and continued shaking his head as his finger pointed back at his statue.

"He doesn't think that one is a god," Jake chuckled. "He probably isn't. He doesn't look much different than any of us."

"He looks calm," Eva corrected, laughing and wincing. "Which is *very* different from any of us."

"We should be more like him then." Jake looked over his brother's shoulder. "I say we name him."

"Name him whatever you want." She rolled her eyes and handed the box to Jake. Her leg was starting to make her extremely uncomfortable. They both knew that she would not be leaving the house anytime soon. Even if she did decide to go after Jake and Tommy's father, they would have to wait a while.

***

Dusk fell quickly, and the scent of food drifting from down the street made Eva's stomach rumble. Tommy and Jake had gone to the food hall, but only Jake returned to her home with a plate. He explained that Tommy had chosen to sit with the Weapon-Maker's family. For the first time in a while, Eva didn't eat alone. Jake insisted on staying.

"Look," he swallowed hard. "I didn't know what was going to happen in the Nomad camp between us. You know…"

"Okay?" Eva raised an eyebrow. "What of it?"

"Well I wanted to know how you felt about me. I mean obviously you had to feel something in order to… want to… you know… *kiss me…*"

She paused. Her face felt white hot. Desperate to change the subject, her eyes darted around the room for something else to talk about. *Literally, anything else.* She cleared her throat and avoided Jake's gaze. When she realized that she wasn't getting out of a response, she slammed her plate right on her lap. Big mistake. Pain shot up her back from her injured thigh. She cursed loudly and threw the plate across the room. Jake dodged it. He stood up, pushing his dish to the side.

"Will you open up to me for *one second?*" He threw his hands in the air. "Shit Eva. Give me the courtesy. You are so cold all of the time. And then you try to kiss me? How the shit am I supposed to interpret that?"

"I don't know, okay," Eva whispered loudly. Admittedly, she was stunned at the anger in Jake's voice. "I don't know how I feel about you. Some days, I just want to *kill* you. On other days, you are… tolerable. I care about you enough to save you, anyway."

"Well I care about you too, Eva," Jake spat. "A lot. Even though we just met, I want to protect you. I mean, I know you can protect yourself and all but… Shit… I can't even protect *myself*. But I want to be there for you… Or at least *with* you."

"It's just that… I don't exactly know how it feels to be cared for, Jake. By anyone. My parents were murdered, along with just about everyone else around me. I can't even remember their faces. All I know is how to be alone. But I also don't want to fall for anyone. Shit. I *barely* know you. If I acted on my feelings and something happened to you, I would never forgive myself. I would -."

Jake's lips were already on hers. Acting out of instinct. She closed her eyes and returned the motion. His soft hand grabbed hers as their lips continued to dance for a moment. When they both realized what was happening, they pulled away.

"Eva… I'm so sorry," he bit his lip and stood up.

"Don't be," Eva looked away, clearing her throat. Emotions swam through her head and stomach, making her sick. "Understand. People die all the time out here. There is no place for affection or love out here. Especially when you risk your life every day. If I start caring too much, it could be the death of both of us."

She tried to be lighthearted. And yet, the space between them was still awkward. Jake would cough and glance over at Eva who faced the foot of her bed. She would look up at him, only to see him jerk his head towards the door. It was only when she went to clean up their dishes and splattered food scraps that he spoke up.

"You rest," he said, holding his hand out. "And I'm sorry by the way. I don't really know what it's like out here. I may not be able to understand why you do the things you do, I can't really change that. *I can't change you.*"

She wasn't sure how to take his tone in the last sentence. He had spoken so rushed, it sounded wooden. The pit of her stomach twisted into a knot. Faking a half-smile, she nodded in agreement and watched him leave her home, closing the door behind him. As his footsteps faded from hearing, she let out a loud sigh.

"What is wrong with you Eva?" she scolded herself. "You show weakness like that. Love is a death sentence. If one of the Gangs had seen that display…"

But I do care about him. Her mind was torn. *I care about Tommy too, but… I dunno… differently.*

"You can't let that happen again," she whispered to herself and shut her eyes tight. "*Not again.*"

You owe them enough to help find their dad. Eva fought the thought.. Honestly, the McAvoy brothers were not ready to be on their own, let alone, infiltrate a compound and come out alive. No one had done it before. But she was unsure whether she could relive any part of her past. The nightmares that plagued her mind had never completely disappeared in the last few years. It was her constant reminder of mortality.

Without warning, Eva's mind suddenly ruptured, wrenching her back to childhood. The first days inside the Serpent's Nest, years before. Her chest began to tighten. She grabbed her shirt and breathed heavily, trying to calm herself. The longer she could not regain control, the more distressed she became. Flashbacks erupted through her head like lightning. Her vision narrowed. The room felt smaller by the second. She tried standing up. Searing pain from her leg only intensified the images. Whips made of rope tipped with metal claws ripping into her flesh. Laying naked on the frozen stone floor of a small cell, staring at the shadow of a man at the door. Dead eyes of children at the feet of men and women with guns. The little Nomad girl who fought to stay alive while Tommy held her in his arms. Through every flashback, a looming and hooded creature stood in the background. *What is that thing?*

She had forgotten the intensity of the trauma but would never forget the attempts to end her own life. The scars may have blended with her skin, but they were still freshly opened in her brain.

Jake's quick action may have saved Eva's life at that moment. Suffocating on her own terror, she almost didn't notice him pry the knife from her hand. She did not even remember grabbing it in the first place. An imprint of the handle embedded deep in her palm. The pure shock of another person's touch had been enough to force her back into reality. A few moments passed, and her breathing became steady. Her vision cleared and she was able to speak.

"Jake?" Genuine gratitude displayed on her face by a few tears. "Shit. *Thank you.*"

"What happened?" He was still holding the arm he had to pry the knife from. "What in the hell just happened to you?"

"I-I-." She paused and debated telling him the truth. That it had always been that way. That this had happened before. And that she had stopped it in the past. "I don't want to talk about it. It's probably from the blood loss."

He waited for a moment, then let her be. She did not intend to elaborate any further. The rest of the evening was spent in complete silence. Jake and Eva retired for the evening, much earlier than Tommy, who returned from the food hall hours later. He felt the cold heavy latch to the door lock tightly and made his way to the back room. With a singular candle, he studied the book he had found in the city.

***

A mundane routine was established for the rest of Eva's recovery. Morning hours were spent strengthening her leg by increasing the weight on it each day. What began as a short limp across her shack soon expanded to the end of the street, and then the edge of the colony. When she returned in the afternoon, she would hastily scrawl in her journal. Most of the entries were battles of her own mind, fighting between saving the McAvoys' father and continuing to survive in a 'mundane but safe existence' as she described. On the very last page was a running list of pros and cons alongside possible escape plans. It was only when she realized the sheer number of pages she had filled with ramblings that she stopped. Every fiber of her being screamed for her to avoid the horrors behind the barbed wire and towering walls. And yet, the itch to feel her blades sink through warm flesh was buried deep within her soul. Somewhere.

Jake and Eva had spoken very little since he stopped her from ending her life. He knew that something had come over her at that moment. The fear he saw on her face told him that it had happened before. Other than occasional small-talk during the day, the home was silent. He had even chosen to take his evening meal in the food hall. His preferred seat—Eva's table.

Tommy was the only one who seemed to be enjoying the change of pace. He spent his free time studying the art of growing crops, and when he returned home, he settled at the foot of Eva's bed, reading literature from the Old Times. Within days, he had become a farmer's apprentice. In his pocket, the statue of the peaceful mystery man. He believed it brought him good luck.

In the weeks Eva spent regaining her strength, not a single Gang attacked the colony. During the day, they would hear the sound of footsteps and muffled voices from time to time, but no raids. Zero casualties.

Eva had nearly forgotten about kissing Jake. As autumn swept through the region like a soft whisper, she was finally strong enough to take long walks near the forest to clear her head. It was one of the few times that Eva felt truly at peace.

At the end of the fourth week, she decided to reward herself with a longer walk around the edge of the forest. This was the gateway to the rest of the region. A path she would have to take if she decided to rescue Jake and Tommy's father. With her bare feet against the soft grass, she began her stroll along the border of trees. Deep and lingering breaths filled her lungs. Eva drifted into a meditative state. She imagined roots springing from her feet deep below the earth. A soft wind brushed against her face, tousling her hair, carrying the scent of colorfully decaying leaves and rain-softened earth. Her only passing thought was that the Nomads may have had this 'connection with nature-thing' figured out. Time seemed to slow down as she whispered to the sky for a sign of what to do.

"I need some guidance," she said.

Out of nowhere, a decision shot through her like a bullet. It was like an explosion of energy coursing through the ground, up through her body. Epiphany in bliss.

With one swift motion, she turned on her heels and jogged back to her home. The tingling of her injured leg had not completely alleviated yet, so she still ran with a slight limp. Jake and Tommy were tidying her home.

As she burst through the door, it nearly knocked them both off their feet. Tommy had reached for his weapon, brandishing it at the door until he realized who was standing there.

"I have made my decision."

Jake's face contorted to confusion and then fear, "What?"

"About your father. About the Wolves. About a lot of things."

The brothers looked at each other. Tommy's heart was racing but he kept a straight face. Jake shifted his weight from one foot to the other impatiently. The silence was maddening. Waiting for the answer was pure torture. She opened her mouth to speak.

They were shocked.

Chapter 6

"We're going." Those were the words Jake and Tommy had been hoping for since they first met Eva. However, the comment that followed was completely unexpected. "*Tonight.*"

The brothers said nothing. They had been certain she'd refuse to rescue their father, especially once they learned he was in a Gang compound. But something had shifted in her and neither of them dared to ask why. Eva was unsure how to read the room. This feeling of optimism was foreign to her. She stood in the doorway waiting for one of them to say something or thank her. Jake and Tommy just stared at one another. Her toes curled in the dirt as she shifted her weight to her uninjured leg. She dropped her hands to her sides and groaned, trudging over to her bed. Climbing to the other side, she pulled out her journal and opened it to a specific page she had marked.

"I'm not sure what's gotten into you," Jake finally said. He chose his words carefully to not change her mind. "We are grateful… but we… didn't think you would want to go back inside one of those places. Especially right *now*."

"You're right." She scanned her writing and flipped to another page. Jake frowned and looked around in confusion.

"Wait, what?"

"I said, you are correct. I really don't want to step foot in there. In *any* compound. Honestly, I don't know exactly why I'm doing this, but I am… For some reason, I feel like I need to. Maybe it's to prove something to myself."

Maybe I'm hoping these nightmares finally stop if I face my fear, she thought.

Jake put a hand on Eva's shoulder. "Like I said before, you help people. You have a good heart. And if anyone can get us into a compound, it's you."

"I just figured that if I'm going to die, I might as well die helping someone. You're half right, I *do* help people. Usually I'm not waltzing into a trap, though. But… maybe I can make amends for some of the shit that happened years ago."

Tommy's smile had not wavered. Hope was plastered all over his face as he tugged excitedly on his brother's clothing. If they were able to pull it off—infiltrating a Gang compound to save a slave—they would get to see their father again. This was all happening so fast. Both brothers were excited and terrified simultaneously. Eva glanced up, smiled, and then returned to her journal, frantically turning back and forth between pages, nearly ripping them from their fragile binding. The tips of her fingers followed her eyes through the notes, drawings, and lists she had written in the previous weeks. Jake waited eagerly for her to find whatever she was searching for.

"I have never been into the Wolf's compound," she admitted, pointing to something she had written and shut the journal. "I know the forest decently enough. Certain traders knew the paths and taught The Rovers years ago, but it's dark. And I mean *dark*. If we get caught, that's where we run to. If we get separated, that's where we meet. But I need you both to answer truthfully on this… if I'm going to help you."

"What?" Jake stiffened up.

"Are you prepared to take another person's life?"

Any joy in the room was instantly sucked out. Eva's smile had faded long before, replacing it with a slight frown. The look in her eyes was unnervingly serious. No one moved a muscle. For her, it was a simple question. She was not about to waste her time on a plan if neither of them were willing to protect themselves. But they did not feel as though an answer was so easy.

"Are-are you sure you are feeling up to it?" Jake's shoulders sank. He was hesitant now that Eva had decided to help them. Tommy had pulled his weapon from against the wall and stared at it with glazed eyes.

"Oh, so *now* you're having second thoughts?" She tossed her notebook on the bed and walked over to them. "When it's *me* out there. Risking *my* life. Saving *your* stupid asses. Getting shot. Then it's okay? But then I kill someone, and you judge me for it. You call me 'cold' and 'heartless'. And when I risk my ass for nothing in return - *nothing* - and ask you whether you can do what needs to be done to see your father again… you refuse?"

"I'm not refusing," Jake yelled and corrected himself. "*We* are not refusing. I just don't know if I can kill anyone yet."

"Then when Jake?" Eva's tone became mocking as she walked over to the door and slammed it shut. "When is the day that I need to mark down? Huh? That way we can all prepare. Perhaps you should practice on animals? Would that make it easier?"

"No need to be an ass about it." He shoved her. "You don't understand."

Eva clenched her fists. It took everything in her body to ignore his actions. She knew if she lingered on it, even for a second, she would have dropped him to the floor with a black eye.

"No Jake, I completely understand," she barked. "You're *weak*. And let me tell you something, the weak don't last long around here. Not in this world. That is why people like *me* exist…. cold-blooded-killers. But the difference between the relationship I have with these Rovers and the one I have with you two is that they aren't *completely useless*. Shit guys - You want to be a farmer? Or maybe a blacksmith? A cook? Sure. That may be better suited for you. Then get to it, because you have done nothing for this colony or for me. It takes guts and overcoming fear to play the game I play. And if you lack nerve, then there is no point in me going any further with this decision."

Tommy plugged his ears with his fingers. His knees were pulled deep into his chest. Jake clenched his fists tighter. Eva gritted her teeth. She dared Jake to say more. At that point, she would have knocked him back and come out with a handful of his teeth. *One more word* was all it would have taken.

Neither of the McAvoy brothers wanted to lie to her because she always knew the truth. And the truth was that they were petrified.

Tommy was deep in thought while the other two argued. He did not want his brother to speak for him any longer. All he wanted to do was save his dad. If that meant killing someone in self-defense, so be it. Nevertheless, he was not sure whether he could actually do it. But he would try. He stood up, grabbed his blade, and slammed it against the metal wall. The clang was deafening.

Eva spun around with a hand on one of her blades. She relaxed when she saw Tommy proudly brandishing his weapon. Still, she could see the uncertainty in his eyes, but kept her lips sealed. It was better than nothing. He made his decision. Walking over to her, the young boy turned his head up and nodded, using his weapon to point to the door. She tousled his hair and gave him a one-armed hug. With her hand on his back, they both turned to the outlier. Jake, the older brother, remained hesitant.

"Well?" she taunted, "Now you have a decision to make. I need a hundred percent commitment from *both* of you. Kill or be killed, Jake McAvoy. We will be entering into the mouth of a beast. If we survive this, you will have your father back. If not…."

She shrugged.

Perhaps Jake just wanted Eva to stop badgering him. That, or the profound feeling of seeing his father made him speak up. "You're right," he breathed. "I can't keep letting others fight my battles for me. Plus, if I continue to do nothing, my father will think I'm weak. I will *try*."

"Not good enough." Eva stood firm, shaking her head. "I need you to swear that you will ignore the urge to freeze. Even if it feels impossible. Because in a compound, you must protect yourself with a split second decision. You *have* to kill them before they kill you. No hesitation. You've seen only an inkling of what these Gangs are capable of. It will be *much* worse if we get caught."

Jake strengthened his stance and took a labored breath, "I promise that I will take a life if needed. But I cannot promise that it will be easy."

"Nor do I expect you to," she relaxed her shoulders. "It's not easy and it never gets any easier."

"Seems to be easy for you," Jake whispered under his breath. She heard him, but said nothing. She just sneered. He was right, anyway.

Immediately, Eva got to work. She pulled out pieces of blank parchment and started drawing an outline of a compound. They were losing sunlight and needed to be across the forest before dusk. One could easily become lost if they ventured through it at night. It was risky, going to the West on a whim, but she knew a colony of skilled Rover Warriors that may be able to aid her. That is, *if* they still existed. With each intruding seed of doubt, she forced it out of her mind and moved on. Eventually, she had completed a decent blueprint.

"Compounds are all built in a similar way," she explained, pointing to each area on her map. "For the most part, they have one surrounding wall made from fencing reinforced with thick, metal plates. Most have one or two gates into the yard. Usually, they are heavily guarded and, obviously, a dumb idea for us to enter through there. And I am sure you recall that the top of the fence is covered in barbed wire. Basically, these places are impenetrable."

"Then how do we get in?" Jake's hope was dwindling.

"I'm getting to that," she pointed to a tunnel outside. "We have two options: disguise ourselves as Servants to learn where your father is being kept by getting captured. But that would mean that we are without weapons. *Or* we could enter through any sewage system. Gangs use these to travel mostly unseen. These were built in the Old Times and they run all around the region, but not under the forest. Drawback on the sewage system is that it's a maze of tunnels and some have collapsed. Most Gangs use some sort of marking to tell which way to go like a symbol on the walls. So, it may take a while to navigate that. Oh, and I don't really know where in the compound the sewer entrance opens up on the grounds."

"And if we disguise ourselves," Jake started, "Then we are sitting ducks in the middle of all of these armed guards."

"Pretty much," she agreed. "We are going to be vulnerable either way. However, I know of a Rover colony who, as I recall, are very strong warriors. I hope they have been able to keep the Gangs from wreaking havoc in their town. They may have more information. But this isn't going to be easy. My opinion - sewers, after we speak with the Western Rovers. With that choice, at least we can funnel any enemies down one of the tunnels and kill them carefully if we're discovered. If we stand in the middle of the compound dressed in rags with no weapons, we may as well welcome the hail of bullets."

"What if the tunnel opens to the middle of the compound?" Jake pointed to the big open space on her map. "Then we are exposed anyway."

Eva wasn't going to lie. "True. On one hand, it isn't exactly a *stealthy* entrance, but we also aren't barging through the front door. To be clear - I'm not even positive as to what the Wolf's form of trade is. I believe they delve in leathers. If that is the case, their servants do not work all night, and we have a greater chance of making a discreet entrance. That is why I am taking the risk to go at night. If most of them are asleep, we may have a decent chance."

Jake was not about to argue with her. His heartbeat was deafening but he reluctantly agreed. "Fair enough. I'm ready to find our father as long as you are sure those warrior-people can help."

They wasted no time. Eva nodded, rolled up her plans, and stuffed them underneath a bookshelf. Jake and Tommy dressed in the leather jackets that they had been given a month prior. Each of them grabbed their weapons, Eva with the only gun. She double checked her ammo, filled the magazine with some extra bullets in her pocket. Wiping down her blades, she sheathed them behind her back. A backpack just underneath her weapons was filled with various gear and supplies. It was only a matter of minutes before they were ready. Before they left the colony behind them once again, they scarfed down a meager meal and set off.

The three started their journey towards the forest, only carried by the sound of their footsteps and accompanied by their imprints in the grass and dirt. The sky was painted in colors of orange, pink, and purple swatches as dusk briskly approached. At the next hill, they could see the dense line of evergreen and oak trees ahead of them. The tops of the tallest trees unveiled the vastness of the forest as it crested over the horizon. The foliage was packed so densely, it was nearly pitch black after the first few yards. It was no wonder that few dared to travel into this darkness.

As they reached the border, they stopped for a moment. Eva turned to look at the sun which had fallen behind the hill. Time was against them if they were to arrive on the other side of the forest in an hour. They would have to hurry.

Jake nodded when Eva told him to pick up the pace. "Got it." His attempts to clear his mind of any feelings, doubt, or fear was becoming increasingly difficult, almost impossible. And yet, with each step, he pressed on.

The brothers and The Wanderer did not get far before they were encompassed by complete darkness. Behind them, they could still make out the faint light of dusk, but nothing but a black abyss lay ahead. Claustrophobia began to set in. Eva grabbed a rope she had in her pack and wrapped it around her belt. Then she tossed either end to the boys who knotted themselves to her.

"Do not pull me," she whispered. "Just follow close and try to keep up."

Jake and Tommy were blindly dragged through the infinite darkness with Eva leading the way. Neither brothers were sure how their guide was able to navigate, but each turn was precise. Through the soles of their boots, they could tell that they were on a rocky path, occasionally bumping into a tree or nearly tripping over a fallen log. Once or twice, the sound of nearby predators nudged them into each other. Yet, Eva said nothing. Sometimes, they weren't even sure she was paying them any attention.

She wasn't. When she first moved into the Rover colony, the traders in the region trained her in navigating this forest. Sunlight never reached the pathways, so they were forced to find a way through using their other senses. Those who were able to navigate successfully utilized a combination counting their steps and feeling for carved markings on the trees. Traders were afraid of being followed by the Gangs, so they marked the trees with three different symbols: an X, +, or O. One of the symbols marked the true path through the forest. The other two would lead to an endless labyrinth of roads that never truly brings you back to the main road. It had been quite some time since she had traversed here. Eva was unsure which symbol was the correct one. She went with her instinct - O.

She winced when Jake read her mind, "Are you sure you know where you are going?"

"Yes," she lied. Luckily, he could not see her face contorted in uncertainty. She masked her wavering voice.

"Okay. I trust you," he whispered back.

You shouldn't, she thought. "Thanks," she said.

It felt like they had spent hours weaving through the endless mass of branches and bramble. Rustling leaves, crunching grass, and the snapping sound of tree limbs combined with the nauseating smell of greenery was becoming too much for them. A thick cloud of moisture made it difficult to breathe. They were desperate for fresh air.

Eva needed to prove to herself that she was still able to get through this place. Halfway down the path, Eva was finding it difficult to feel the markings on the trees. It was almost as if something or someone had deliberately worn down the carvings in this part of the forest. Normally, the traders would carve deeper into the trees as they passed so they would not get lost, but it was almost like someone tried to carve them out of the trees completely. She stopped and carefully drew the outline with her fingertip. One tree felt completely smooth. Were they still on the correct path?

Of course Jake had to open his mouth.

"Something wrong?"

She paused. "The carvings are, how do I put this, worn away. I can barely make them out."

"Please don't tell me we're lost."

"I thought you said you trusted me?"

"I do. Just not this place. I just feel like we are being watched."

Just then, a growl from a few feet away sent a chill down their spines. Panting of a coyote, wolf, or mountain lion was now within an arm's-length. Something was closing in on them. Eva pulled out one of her blades and yanked the rope, pulling the brothers towards what she thought was the safest route.

Eva's whisper was barely audible. "Get ready to run."

The animal bolted, chasing them as they ran through the trail. No one was sure whether they were on the right path anymore, but it no longer mattered. Soon, the trail stopped and Eva, Jake, and Tommy squeezed between trees and an endless thicket of sharp bramble. Their legs were caught and torn by thorns and sharp tree roots. Just as they braced for the predator to pounce on them, it became distracted by the sound of distant gunshots. The rustle of leaves disappeared into the void and the three let out a collective sigh.

Thanks to whatever led me through this. Eva's mind was elated the instant she could smell the crisp air. Finally, they had fought their way out of the forest. Her mind was suddenly flooded with the saying that the merchants had taught her about the markings on the trees. *X brings death without delay, + won't help you find your way, but O will save you—come what may.* Her instinct had not led them astray. They made it through the forest unscathed.

The West side of the region was completely different from what Jake and Tommy were growing accustomed to. Standing at the edge of a bluff, the city was almost obscured by the edge of the forest and the horizon. A large colony was nestled in a valley to their left, and the unmistakable sight of five Gang compounds dotted their right. They were noticeably smaller than either the Serpents or the Tigers domain, but their fires burned brighter. Uninhabited Old Time ruins filled the remaining space. Eva had not been to this part of the region in years. It was nothing like she remembered. *Great.*

Jake took notice. "You look confused."

She threw her hood over her face while Jake and Tommy untied their tether, "Yeah. I haven't been here in a while. The Rover colony has doubled in size. And the Gangs… There were only two before and neither were the size of any of these. I knew there were more, but I didn't realize they were getting this big."

"Do you know which one belongs to the Wolves?"

"No… And I'm not about to guess. The Western Rovers know this part of the region, for sure. Most likely they won't be aggressive to us."

"What the hell do you mean by *most likely*?"

"Like I just said, Jake. It's been a while. They may not remember me."

"Do they even know who you are?"

"They know of The Wanderer. But they may not remember that it's me."

Jake threw his hands in the air. He felt that Eva was being annoyingly nonchalant about entering a Rover colony that could be hostile. She took off down the bluff before the boys could react. The three of them might be walking into a trap, but she did not seem the least bit concerned. Tommy had already rushed to the edge of the cliff, leaning over the side, looking down at her. Jake ran after him.

Eva was over halfway through her descent when she noticed the brothers were not following. "Are you coming? We're losing daylight."

"We could have used the rope," Jake proposed. "This is really dangerous."

Eva was just waiting for him to stop whining. "So is infiltrating a Gang. Get used to it."

"Seriously," Jake looked at his brother and pointed at Eva. Tommy shrugged and took the first cautious step over the side, hanging onto a boulder overhead. His brother huffed and groaned, then followed after him. Rocks crumbled off to his side and some of the natural hand grips were not solid. Once or twice, he reached for what he believed was a sturdy piece of earth and nearly plummeted forty feet to the rock-strewn ground below.

Eva and Tommy reached the bottom long before Jake had even made it halfway. He hugged the wall and inched down to the next step, cursing and complaining. As he looked down at the ground, he realized how much further he had to go. Sweat was causing his hands to become slippery and droplets slid into his eyes, burning them. Carefully, he rubbed his forehead with his sleeve.

And as he closed in on the ground, he could hear the sound of Eva's boot tapping in impatience.

"You know Tommy," she jeered, "Sometimes I think you are more mature than your brother. Even though he has, like, ten years on you."

I'm starting to question whether Jake has the gall to protect himself if we get into trouble, she thought. *He can't even climb down a cliff.*

Tommy held up ten fingers and then another four. Fourteen years older than him. Eva smirked. Jake grunted and shook his head, trying to focus on the final few steps. When he only had about ten feet left to go, Eva coaxed him to jump. He refused. Shaking violently, he finally felt his foot touch soft ground and nearly collapsed to his knees in relief.

"Jake," Eva hoisted him to his feet. "You *have* to start overcoming fear. If scaling a wall is too difficult for you, well, yeah." She decided to bite her tongue and not finish her thought.

"Isn't there an easier way down here?" Jake argued.

Eva responded. "Not if we want to save time."

Jake shot a hateful look at her and she pulled her hand away. As he passed them, he shoved his shoulder into hers.

"I grew up under a hill Eva," Jake called back without turning his head. He was already heading toward the lights coming from the colony. "I have never had the *pleasure* of climbing down a mountain or any of that shit."

"*Cliff,*" she corrected.

Eva was poking and prodding at him for a reason. To her, anger was a necessary seed for ruthlessness. In an attempt to ready him for what was to come, she tried to keep him aggravated at something. Also, it was rather convenient for him to attack her and effortless for her to return the favor by taunting him. She almost laughed. Almost.

The moon was now high in the air, brushed by thinly veiled clouds. By now, Jake was far ahead of Tommy and Eva. They nearly lost him over the cresting hills a few times. He was mumbling something to himself as they neared the town. The wind would carry his voice back to the other two, but they weren't able to make out the words.

Another hour had passed before they entered the outskirts of the colony. The mismatched metal buildings felt welcoming and familiar, but the atmosphere was different. Unlike the colony that was protected by The Wanderer, these Rovers did not seem nearly as fearful. Gardens lined the front of every home, brimming with different fruit trees and vegetable plants. All of the homes had windows and smaller herb pots hanging underneath them. A small livestock farm lay just outside the rows of homes. Assorted clothing hung on lines between the rooftops and a few of the inhabitants were out tending to their crops.

The Rovers who had spotted the travelers instantly stopped what they were doing and watched them pass. Jake swallowed hard and looked over his shoulder, noticing a crowd forming behind them. Brandished weapons glinting in the moonlight distracted him enough to nearly trip over Eva who had slowed her pace. She spun around and pulled out one of her blades, pressing it against Jake's throat.

"Woah." He threw up his hands and pointed to the angry mob that was closing in around them.

One of the dark silhouettes spoke. "From which Gang do you hail? We would like to know where to send your corpses."

"None." Eva sheathed her blade but kept her face hidden. "We are no enemy of yours, Rover."

"We are just travelers," Jake squeaked as he felt a cold gun barrel press against his temple.

"Ha!" the shadow stepped closer. "Laughable at best. We have not seen travelers around these parts in some time, and we know the trade routes and the traders who travel them. You come bearing weapons and no goods. What *ally* does this?"

"The Wanderer," said Eva. "We come with questions if you would help us. We wish to infiltrate one of the compounds."

The energy of the crowd shifted. Twinkling shards of metal relaxed and lowered towards the ground. The pistol at Jake's head was removed and holstered. A murmur through the mob rose and fell. And then, the same voice spoke again.

"We know of The Wanderer," he stated and took a step closer to Jake. "Bold of you to claim to be such a being. He has not shown his face here in some time."

"*She*," Jake corrected as he felt the man's powerful arm around his shoulders. "It isn't me. It's her."

"A woman," he paused. "That *is* correct, isn't it? I admit, I had not spent much time in this colony until they elected me their leader. Indeed ma'am, you do have a deadly air about you."

The leader's choice of words was very unusual. They seemed meticulously put together and much more eloquent than other Rovers, let alone, any Nomad or Gang member. Either way, it did not sit well with Eva. She had not changed her stance since hiding her weapon. Tommy had backed up to where his brother stood and all eyes were on her, The Wanderer.

"Is it true that you are *she*?" a woman's voice called from the crowd. "One who walks in shadow behind footprints of blood?"

Why do these people speak so weird? Eva scrunched her nose under the darkness of her hood. *And what the shit did she just call me?*

"If by 'footprints of blood' you mean killed many in my lifetime," Eva replied but still did not move. "Then yes. I protect those who cannot protect themselves. And I guess you could say that I also 'walk in shadow' as many know of me, but no one truly knows me."

"Shadow encompasses your past," the man corrected. "Does it not?"

"Yeah," Eva stretched out her response as she lowered her hand to her gun. "But I would prefer to keep that to myself."

"There is no need for bloodshed." *Damn. How did he see me?* The leader had spotted her fingers wrapping around her holster. "You are welcome here. The blades you carry are more than enough proof for me and my family. Our feast hall is open to you and your friends. The bartender knows much about this region. She can answer your questions. Her poor mother was taken into a compound in the East. The wound on her heart is still fresh. However… She is both strong and knowledgeable. We have but one simple request of you, though."

Eva was not going to risk being attacked before making it into the compound. "All right. What is it?"

"I believe my family would all agree. We wish to see the face of the famous Wanderer," his outstretched arm motioned to the largest building in the town. "In the feast hall. Because here in my colony, we have no secrets."

The Wanderer hesitated for a moment.

"I think it would be *wise* of you to oblige."

"Fair enough."

Tommy, Jake, and Eva followed behind the Rovers into the feast hall. Large lanterns burning with bright fires lit the room to near daylight. Parts of the ceiling had been cut away to make for better ventilation, so the air was not thick with smells of old alcohol and rotting food scraps. Rather than rags, most of these Rovers were clad in leather armor. Belts wrapped around their legs and torsos supported weapons of varying lengths, sizes, and designs. People drank together, loudly announcing their previous hunt. The smaller children practiced fighting with wooden weapons near the corner of the hall, awaiting their dinner. What Eva found highly unusual was the smile on everyone's faces. They were not burdened by pain and suffering. These people were warriors. Genuine survivors. The thought crossed her mind to just live here and let the Eastern Rovers meet their inevitable fate with the Gangs.

She was about to instruct Jake and Tommy to sit while she spoke to the barkeep, but the leader of the colony climbed onto a table and called out to his kin.

"My beautiful family," he boomed. The room went silent. "I would like to introduce you to some friends. One of which, you may know as the protagonist of legends that surface around the region."

That was the moment Eva finally got a good look at their leader. Dark skin hardened by the sun, wrinkled but tight against his muscular arms. Around his mouth, a curly beard of silver that connected to his crown in tufts. His arms were outstretched, both burned with snakelike tracks undoubtedly from battle. Calluses caked over his palms. His armor, crafted by hand, outlined his bulky physique as he proudly displayed a string of silver daggers crisscrossed in front of his chest. And although his face bore one pinkish scar from his nose to his left cheek, the peace behind his sapphire eyes was admirable.

He reached down to Eva, beckoning for her to follow. "This woman. You have heard of her in stories… perhaps from whispers from the Gangs and Traders. She comes to us with questions. Her famous blades may be stained with the blood of many enemies, but her heart is pure and untouched by hate."

I don't know about that, she joked to herself and stepped onto the wooden table.

Their leader instructed her to remove her hood. Everyone was watching intently. Gripping the thick cloth, she let it slide softly back behind her head. And then came the longest suspense that she had ever witnessed. Her leg stung faintly. All she could feel were the eyes of hundreds of people and the only thing she could think was the number of ways this could end badly for her and the McAvoy brothers.

She did not reach for her weapon, but Jake and Tommy were half-expecting some type of conflict. Unexpectedly, the whole room erupted with cheers. The volume was deafening. Eva was confused. She had not done anything for these people in ages. So, why were they cheering for her? Their leader could sense the confusion.

"You are a hero in this town," he said as he helped her back to the floor. "Every man, woman, and child aspires to be like you. To show these Gangs that we are a force to be reckoned with. We will never bow to those who would enslave us. The Wanderer is why we fight."

"They shouldn't want to be like me," Eva said shortly.

"And why is that?" The man led her over to the bartender while Jake and Tommy entered the line for food. "You strike with honor. Protect the weak and afraid. Why would any good warrior not strive to be like this?"

The words fell out of her mouth before she could think. "Because I was not always this way."

But the man paid no attention to her comment. He was busy introducing Eva to a woman named Elaine. Then he turned to her, bid her farewell, and mentioned his name.

"William," he said and disappeared into the crowd.

Eva cleared her throat and studied the barkeep for a moment as she swung her legs around a stool. Like the other Rovers here, Elaine also wore leather armor and carried a dozen different weapons. She was in the middle of cleaning tin mugs when William had instructed her to help The Wanderer. Her forehead wrinkled as she slammed a cup onto the bar.

"Yeah?" she said with a shockingly high pitched voice. "You have questions? Oh and don't expect me to be fawning over you or anything. I don't give a shit who you are. I am only doing this because Will asked me to help.”

Much to the barkeep’s surprise, Eva laughed. “You know what? I actually *like* your attitude. Straightforward and no beating around the bush. It’s nice to talk to someone like me for once.”

The woman was speechless. She rubbed her partially-shaved head. Neither of them were sure how to continue, so Eva just started asking questions.

“My friends and I are trying to find the Wolves compound,” she began but was interrupted.

“Truthfully,” Elaine leaned in towards her. “Those two don’t look like your *friends*.”

Eva leaned in too. “No, they’re not. More like… burdens.”

“Interesting,” she snickered. “I always believed The Wanderer only traveled alone.”

“I did. But I found those two in a vault near the hills, through the forest. Y’know, in the East.”

“Vault?”

“Yeah. Apparently they were built back in the Old Times as safe havens for some of the important people back then. Haven’t been opened since those days. Well, until recently.”

Elaine paused. “The Beforetimes. There’s probably more then.”

“Not around here,” Eva was handed a plate of food. “At least, not that I’ve heard of. The Gangs would have probably wiped them out if there were. The only reason this one was unchecked was because it had been covered when some of the hills collapsed during the War. Anyway, we are trying to get in-.”

“The Wolves Den, yeah got it. Suicide mission in my opinion.”

“Trust me. Your opinion is not far from mine. Jake and Tommy’s father is being held prisoner there. I promised to get him out.”

“Then I won’t waste my breath with opinions… So, it’s the closest compound to here. You can see it once you’re out of the colony. And don’t worry about time. Those servants are forced to work late into the night, but they hardly *ever* start working until midday.”

“Well that’s a relief. Any ideas on how to get in there without being spotted?” Eva took a few bites of food.

“There’s an old tunnel that runs from the colony border to their camp. Last I checked, it hasn’t collapsed.”

“And that was when?”

“Few weeks ago. That’s your best bet. It isn’t exactly a direct route and there is no map, but my best guess is that it opens up to the center of their common yard. Most of the Gangs around here use the tunnels for trade. Forces everyone into a funnel so that if there’s trouble or they want to sneak past one of their ‘competitors’, they can do that more successfully. So, if you spend too long in the underground, you may be in for a fight.”

"Great. Thanks." Eva said as she finished her food. "Unrelated question. Why does William talk the way he does? It is extremely odd."

"He reads *a lot*." The edge of Elaine's mouth curled upward. "And he writes fantasy stories about the castles and dragons. He reads them to me sometimes."

Eva tilted her head. Elaine flushed.

"Don't get me wrong," she responded quickly. "He is our best Warrior, which is why he leads us now. But being the best means you sacrifice some sanity. Even *you* should know that. You're supposed to be one of the best, too."

"I'm not sure what you are hinting at. I'm not insane." Eva crossed her arms and leaned back in her chair. Elaine had already left the conversation and tended to patrons on the other side of the bar.

She returned from serving drinks and propped her elbows on the chest-high wood. "You know. You aren't at all like I pictured. The stories always make you seem older and stronger… more menacing."

Eva was rather offended. "Well stories are just that, right? Stories."

The barkeep opened her mouth to say something else when her eyes jumped over Eva's shoulder. Jake and Tommy were standing there, waiting impatiently. She sighed loudly and turned around with an exaggerated effort.

"Yeah?"

"Did you get any information from them?"

"Just as I thought - sewers."

"Well then. We need to go if we are going to do this tonight," Jake motioned to the door.

Eva shoveled in a few more bites of food, thanked Elaine with a fist closed against her chest. The barkeep with the dark skin touched her palm to her forehead, then a fist to her chest, opening it as she pulled it away. "Fight well. Don't get yourself killed." Eva mimicked the gesture. William had been watching the entire time, calling out to them as they stepped into the doorway.

"Remember Wanderer," he said. "Never ignore who you are. Your past defines what you are today. Do not mask it with pride or fear. Become what you were meant to become. And may your blade always strike true."

"Yeah," Eva whispered softly where only Jake and Tommy could hear as she shut the door behind her. "And hopefully no blade or bullet finds its mark on me."

Chapter 7

As they left the Rover colony, fear began to sink in, not only for the brothers, but also The Wanderer. The first thing Eva had promised herself when she escaped the Serpent's Nest was to never return. In fact, she made a personal rule never to step foot inside the barbed wire fences of any Gang compound. Not for a friend. Not even for a lover. And yet here she was, doing the exact thing she vowed never to do again. But she refused to go back on her word despite how much she regretted it. For the first time in ages, she felt like death was holding her by the throat, ready to dig its claws into her flesh.

The haze from the Warrior's food hall disappeared from view and the smell along with it. Three pairs of pounding boots and the thumping of their hearts boomed over the sounds of the evening. Their eyes were fixed on the dark outline of towering metal outposts, held together by strings of jagged wire, awaiting their arrival in an eerie silence. Not a single flicker of a lantern or fire came from that place. The compound seemed to be asleep. But it would take time to reach their destination. A maze of tunnels awaited them first. If they lost themselves underground, they could be exposed to a horde of enemies by dawn. For the moment, time was still on their side.

Eva spotted a cover to the sewers near the shell of a home that burned down long ago. What remained of the brittle exterior creaked in the wind. Bizarre sounds from unknown animals startled them when they tried prying open the manhole cover. Jake and Eva used a piece of hinged metal hidden in the nearby bramble to lift the iron hatch. They lifted it away from the hole. Straining to move it to a soft patch of grass nearby, their rusted metal tools broke, causing it to slam against the pavement. The ear-shattering crash rattled their very bones. Hundreds of yards from them, the sound echoed back from the Wolf's Den. They flinched, pulled out their weapons, and waited for a moment in the darkness, craning for any sound past the edge of hearing.

"I think we're okay." Eva's mouth became dry. She pulled a canteen of water from her bag and took a swig.

Tommy had already climbed inside. Ancient rungs of a ladder descended into the chasm beneath them. Neither of the older two trusted that it would hold their weight on the way down. Eva spotted a nearby tree and fastened one end of her rope around the trunk and the other around Jake.

"Use the ladder cautiously," she instructed. "Go slowly."

Jake nodded and Eva slowly began lowering him to the sewers below. Her arms burned instantly. She knew they could give at any moment. *How is he so heavy? Focus dammit. I hope I have enough strength to lift my weapon. My arms are going to fall off before I even get that far. Why am I doing this again? Why in the heck is it taking so long? If he's taking his time, I'm going to kill him. I. Am. Going. To. Kill. Jake.* Eventually, her arm was freed of the weight.

Eva exhaled and stretched her arms out. A wave of panic flooded her when she thought they had locked at an angle. Biting her lip to muffle a scream, she took one more look at the surface and warily slid down to the brothers. She alternated between her left and right arm, stretching out the unused one. Each time, her bones creaked and her muscles twitched. She began to get worried.

If I can't fight. I'm dead. Dread prickled through her body then subsided. *Shit. I may die anyway.*

She had not realized that she had completely frozen. One foot was still on the ladder, and the other, hanging freely. Jake's voice echoed up to her, snapping her out of the daze.

"Come on Eva," he called. "We are losing time."

"Sorry," she replied and leapt the final few feet to the ground, crouching to cushion her fall.

"You didn't bring a light did you?"

"Damnit. No. You rushed me out, remember? And Elaine, the barkeeper, didn't really give me directions either."

"We just have to keep going as straight as possible, right? The compound is in this direction."

"I can't see you pointing at anything, Jake. It's dark."

"Tommy? Did you get ahead of us again?"

Tommy tugged on both of their pants.

"I know you don't talk," Eva said. "But you need to make some sort of noise or I am tying you to me." He tapped his weapon softly on the damp ground. Eva sighed. "I guess that'll work."

There was really no turning back. Now, they stood on the edge of something they could no longer escape—the darkness of these ancient underground tunnels and the uncertainty of the surface above. They pressed on. Eva had to be certain that they weren't being followed. Every few minutes, she counted the pairs of footsteps. *Three.* Tommy was so quiet that she had to pay an exhausting amount of attention to him while also attempting to navigate a place she had never been in a darkness she seldom experienced.

"Do you think the Gangs even use this tunnel?" Jake whispered softly.

"I don't know," Eva replied softly. "Elaine said that the tunnels were built in the *Beforetimes* and certain areas have collapsed. But the Gangs still use some of them for trade. I would assume they still travel around here. Shit, there may be a group of them just ahead."

"Wow. Thank you for making me feel so at ease. And wait. Collapse? Oh great, another way to die down here."

"Well, on the bright side, being crushed by thousands of pounds of rock and rubble would kill you instantly. Probably. Maybe. Torture from a Gang. Not such a merciful death."

"*Bright side*? You're joking."

Eva shushed him. She flung her hand backwards towards a sound, hitting Jake in the chest. Maybe a whole tunnel collapse would kill them. That *was* the bright side of current circumstances. One, two, three, four, five, six footsteps. Still there. Then they ran into a wall. A dead end.

Smooth, circular walls around them. She could rule out a collapsed wall. A cold metal ladder upwards, but it was made of a newer steel. No rust. *Perhaps this is the way out*. Even though it did not feel like they had gone far, Eva had navigated as straight of a route as possible. There was only one way to find out.

"I'm going up there," she declared. "Just to listen. I won't open the latch for a few moments. But I will call down to you when I know it is safe."

She jumped when she felt a hand on her shoulder. Jake's hand. "Be careful."

"Yeah."

Eva took a deep breath, gripped the cold sides of the ladder tightly, and began the ascent. Suddenly, her chest began to tighten again. The air in the cramped room became dense and difficult to inhale. She was sweating. Flashbacks started materializing in front of her eyes, taking over reality. *Oh no. Not again. Please. Not now.* She repeated the words in Jake's voice over and over in her mind until it was maddening. *Be careful.* It kept the demons at bay. With each rung, she repeated it. *Be careful. Be careful.* Her head was swimming in a struggle for control and she almost collapsed. Then she reached up and touched the cold latch and everything stopped.

"A handle," she whispered back to them loudly. "There is a handle here. I'm going to open it."

She pressed her ear against the cold metal latch and heard nothing. A burst of adrenaline shot through her body as she allowed the latch to unlock. With one slow, meticulous motion, the metal door creaked open. She opened her eyes to a view that she had not seen in a long time. It was bittersweet at best.

A few sparse lights from torches were enough for Jake and Tommy to see Eva's silhouette motion to them from above, beckoning for them to climb. Tommy scurried up the ladder while his brother tarried out of reluctance. In the tunnels, they were somewhat safe. On the surface, they were vulnerable. Elaine was correct. The tunnels had opened up right into the center of the compound—a large common area with various stations for making leather armor. Corpses of animals were strung the length of one side. Tanning racks dotted between the long workstations for cutting and sewing the hides. Everything was desolate. That was, until they looked above them at the outpost towers.

Jake and Tommy felt their clothing being grabbed and yanked to the wall. Eva pulled them into the shadows. She scoured the perimeter, trying to calm herself. From a distance, she was able to make out a couple dark figures marching back and forth above them. Two heavily armed guards at each of the four towers. The building that the Gang members stayed in seemed to be alive with dancing lights at the far end of their territory.

Spanning the length of the compound were the slave tents. Wet leathers as roofing and warped, soaking wooden boards as walls. The Doxies and Bondsmen were separated, but all slept on cold, hard floors. Jake and Tommy split from Eva and started searching for their father, making a point to stay close to the walls and with weapons at the ready.

"He looks like me," is all that Jake whispered before they parted.

Not one of the slaves stirred in their sleep as Eva passed them. Her footsteps were nearly inaudible, just the occasional crunching of gravel shifting under her boots. Children were huddled together closely in one tent, men spread out in the next. Each servant, clad in rags stained with blood and sweat. Their skin was covered in scars. When she finally reached the other side of the compound, someone caught her attention.

This man, unlike his roommates, was not asleep. He was sitting straight up, wide awake. At first, it caught Eva off guard. She brandished her weapon at him, but the fear on his face subsided when he recognized that she was not a Wolf. Through the starlight and torches, she could make out a beard, faint strands of silver weaving through clumps of deep brown or black. He slowly stood up and tiptoed over his sleeping kin, allowing a better look at his face.

Although his skin was wrinkled with age, it was not worn from a life of servitude. Compared to the others, he was better kept. His tunic was not quite as torn and no blood stained its fabric. Some scars were visible over his shoulders, but they were fresh. It was the color of his eyes that grabbed Eva's attention, a honey brown, the same shade as the McAvoy brothers.

"Do you know Jake and Tommy McAvoy?" she whispered as softly as she could.

"Yes," he replied anxiously. "Are they okay? They survived? How do you know them? Who are you? Are they here? How did you get in here? Can I see them?"

Eva shushed him and looked around cautiously. "We don't have much time. You have to come with me."

Jake and Tommy had seen the exchange from the opposite end of the compound. Jake squinted and saw the silhouette step out of the tent towards The Wanderer. As soon as the man came into view, they heard yelling from the nearest outpost.

We're dead.

Someone had seen them from a tower near the gate. A bright beam shone upon them - a bonfire against a large mirror. Eva's heart dropped like a boulder, Jake and Tommy gasped, and their father disappeared back into his tent. She looked around, but it was too late. Bound arms, shoved to their knees, and cocked guns in their ears. The cold, thin barrel of a rifle jabbed her head, but she kept her hood masking her face. A pair of boots and the warmth of torches appeared in her limited field of view. Eva choked on the nauseating smell of body odor. She coughed softly.

"Well, well, well," a scratchy voice heckled. "What have we here?"

"Looks like intruders Chief," a woman's voice replied. "They have some nice weapons. And that one has a gun."

Eva felt her handgun being ripped off its holster. She stayed motionless. Jake and Tommy were whimpering at either side of her, but she remained surprisingly calm. Various scenarios played out in her mind as she considered attacking. A familiar craving for bloodshed bubbled up in her stomach. Her thoughts were yanked back into reality the moment she received a kick in her side that knocked her to the ground.

"One keeps their eyes downcast for two reasons," the Chief used his mud-caked boot to lift her head to meet his gaze. He towered over her prone body. "To show fear or to hide something. And I see no Gang symbol on your person. Yet, you have a firearm. A *nice* one. Very well kept. So tell me, *bitch*, what are you hiding?"

He dropped to a squat. Jake, who was on his knees right behind him, was watching in complete horror. Eva looked up at the Chief with a cold glare. Insulted by the lack of fear, he reached down and grabbed her face, squeezing hard and forcing it closer to his. Pulling out a knife and pressing it against her cheek, he smiled fiendishly, exposing rotted teeth and an indescribable smell.

Trickles of blood ran from her cheek down to her neck as the blade pierced into her flesh. The unwelcoming feeling of dread was starting to swell, and with significant effort, Eva forced it back to the depths. The Wolf Chief must have caught a glimpse of her blades at that moment because his eyes sparkled over her shoulder. He sheathed his knife, then tore the short swords from their scabbards. White-hot rage tore through Eva like lightning. It felt like her very identity had been ripped away. He noticed the look on her face because a glint of fear dropped his grin for a split second. Then, his lips twisted into something far more sinister.

"Well my brothers and sisters," he boomed. "Anyone fancy a guess as to who this bitch is? I've only heard of her from across the region. She's a *nobody* here."

"Looks to me like a future Doxie," one man licked his lips, looking her up and down. "I'd like to get my hands on her first."

"She's your next victim," a woman offered. Other guesses bellowed from the crowd. The Chief then raised his hand to silence them.

"No," he laughed to himself. "Morons. This woman is the *infamous Wanderer*. I can tell by her blades. It *has* to be her."

The Wolves chanted, "Kill her!" Eva stayed on the ground.

"Not this one," he shouted over them. "A Gang in the East is paying a heavy price for her… *alive*. Her friends, though…"

"At least torture her," a voice called out from the center of the crowd. "She has Wolf blood on her hands. *Our* kin."

The Chief shrugged, grabbed Eva by the jacket, and dragged her across the dirt and jagged rocks to the center of the courtyard. Her legs were tearing up underneath her pants but her eyes did not waver from the swords in this man's hand. *Her* blades. He would be her first victim. All she had to do was free herself from these bonds.

"My brothers and sisters." The crowd quieted. "What does this woman have to say for herself? Killing our family? Infiltrating a compound to steal our weapons or kill us all in our sleep?"

Eva scoured the crowd. She could make out the figures of Tommy and Jake, shaking with fear. In the back of the mob stood the boys' father, watching silently with his arms crossed.

I cannot die here, she vowed. *I. Will. Not. Die. Here.*

Eva's words shattered through the murmurs of the Wolves. "I *challenge* the Chief to battle." The Chief dropped his arms and turned to her in shock.

"You challenge *me*," he repeated. "You are unarmed."

"That didn't stop me before." Eva now wore a menacing grin. An old and familiar feeling started to seep into her.

The Chief laughed.

"Well?" Eva repeated. "Do you accept my challenge or will you be a coward like the rest of your Gang?"

The man's face hardened as he inched closer to her face. "I would never pass up a challenge from someone like you."

"Eva, no!" Jake called from the crowd. She spotted him just as a Wolf struck him with the butt of his gun, knocking Jake over. Tommy sobbed silently.

"I want that boy to watch his *girlfriend* take her final breath," he jabbed his finger at Jake.

Eva's bonds were cut and the crowd created a large space around the two combatants. Although she was exhausted by the journey into the Wolf's Den, she prepared to wring out every ounce of endurance she had left for this fight. If Eva was victorious, she could plan their escape. Her eyes darted towards the front gate. It was now completely unguarded. Even the Doxies and Bondsmen were permitted to watch the battle from the outer ring.

The Gang jeered as Eva and The Chief circled each other. He toyed with her swords, one in each hand. Two pistols stuck out of pockets near his belt. One of them was hers. Instead of charging, he decided to provoke her.

"I won't kill you right away," he toyed. "I mean - I could shoot you. It would be over in an instant. But I want to have some fun before you bleed out."

She sneered. "You will just be another corpse. No one will remember your name. They've already remembered mine, you *insignificant piece of shit*."

With a twitch of anger, the Chief charged with her blades flying in all directions. She almost fell trying to dodge the first flurry of blows. But in the second wave of attacks, she was not so fortunate. While one blade had missed her torso and arm, the Chief's elbow bore down on her back. She dropped to the ground on all fours, gasping for air. Glancing up to see the Chief barreling towards her again, she was able to roll away to avoid another strike. She was quickly losing the upper hand in an already unfair fight.

Eva jumped to her feet and sprinted to the other side of the makeshift arena. Turning on her heels, she had a split second to access his stance. *Perfect, high bearing.* His arms were above his head, leaving his guns free for her to swipe. Right behind the raging man knelt Jake cringing in pain from the blow to his back. There was no time to tarry on the emotions that continued to boil inside her. She leaned forward, pushing the ground with all her might.

Bam, contact. It felt like she collided with a brick wall. Her boots dug into the soft earth and reached around, locking her arms behind him at the waist, throwing him off balance. Frantically grabbing at anything she could get from his pockets, the hilt of a knife found Eva's palm. The Chief's back hit the ground hard, knocking the wind out of him. He pointed Eva's blades toward her face, coughing and wheezing for air.

"What are you smiling at bitch?" he panted. "You're losing and you still don't have a weapon."

Eva pointed at his thigh. During the scuffle, he did not notice that she had stabbed him. She yanked out the knife and blood spurted from the wound like a fountain. A piercing scream and the clang of her blades on the ground at her feet rang through the compound. The Chief clutched his leg. In an instant, the howl was cut to silence. Eva's blade sang as it entered through the bottom of the Chief's chin, now dripping with crimson beads. She clutched the other blade above her head as her sweat covered chest rose and fell. But it was a short victory. All she heard was Jake screaming her name then felt her arms nearly being dislocated from her shoulder.

She was kneeling again. Someone grabbed her hair and yanked backwards revealing her neck.

Jake was hysterical. He was screaming through the barrage of punches coming from the Wolves around him. Spit, blood, and mucus sprayed out of his face as he frantically tried to crawl to Eva before being held down and beaten. She closed her eyes as the cold blade, *her* blade, pressed against her throat. This was the end. Breaking her first rule turned out exactly how she feared. *What was I thinking?* Staring up at the peach-colored sky as the sun rose to greet her for the final time, she smiled as a single tear rolled down her cheek. The man above her noticed.

"Why'r'yew smilin'?" he spat. "Y'er about to die."

"It's just... funny." She held back tears of unexpected euphoria. "To have my life ended by the very weapons that I have used to end countless others. But - I suppose I've always been ready for death… when the time truly came."

Suddenly, an explosion detonated at the gate. It shook the ground so violently that the shockwave knocked them backwards. Everyone went deaf, but through the mist and dust, they could see the spark of guns firing in all directions. Eva wavered for a moment then jumped to her feet and sprinted straight for Jake and Tommy.

They were dazed, but she managed to drag them behind a metal lean-to. The ringing in her ears was deafening. Tommy and Jake's faces were covered in dirt and sweat as they scrambled to unbind each other. Jake's face was swollen and oozing blood as he tried to scream directions to Eva, but she couldn't hear him. Their father found them at the lean-to and watched as a shower of bullets pelted both slaves and Wolves alike.

Without warning, there was a whooshing sound and the four cowering behind the sheet of metal regained their hearing. Screams of horror and pain, the explosion of gunfire, more screaming. Only one word was audible through the firestorm.

"Rats!"

A horde of enemies flooded into the compound grounds. Servants were being used as human shields for both sides. Eva peered around the corner. One of the assailants spotted her. Two shots whizzed past her head, but he was out of bullets. He beckoned to a couple of his comrades to follow him, ducking through the cloud of war. At their feet were Eva's blades.

Jake and Tommy's father looked at The Wanderer for their next steps. "What do we do? There are too many."

"I have to get my blades back," she yelled over the crowd. "Stay here."

Jake nodded.

A cloud of smoke formed between Eva and the two Gang members, making it nearly impossible to see. A second bomb exploded near the far corner, but it was much smaller than the first. The sound of spraying shrapnel echoed through the compound. She dropped down on all fours and reached around blindly for her weapons. Both hands met familiar metal. *Finally*. One blade was still on the ground when someone stepped on her hand with their thick boots but did not seem to notice. With a firm grasp around the hilt of both blades, Eva grimaced and scrambled back to the safety of the lean-to. As the dust began to clear, the attackers were upon them.

As the two Rats rounded the corner, Eva drove her blade deep into one's chest. Blood sprayed across her face as she ripped the sword free and plunged it into the next. Both dropped at her feet. Something ignited in her soul—she let out a rage-filled scream and charged into the fray, cutting down anyone in her path. For a moment, Jake and Tommy stood frozen. Their father gave a quick nod, urging them forward. In the distance, they spotted The Wanderer—indistinguishable from the bloodthirsty Gangs around her. But her fury had carved a way through the chaos, and it was the only reason they could escape.

They took their chance. Jake grabbed Tommy by the arm and ordered him to hold on tight. He took two guns from the bodies beneath them, handing one to his father and kept the other for himself. With his face still stinging in pain, he trudged through the chaos and slaughter. The gun he found was cocked. He pointed it at each passing Gang member but did not pull the trigger. He would only kill if they attacked them first.

In the mayhem, they lost sight of Eva. Jake changed his course to weave in and out of the battle to hunt her down. Tommy pulled him back to the outside of the horde and they continued towards the direction of the exit. The three of them coughed and gagged through the smoke, using their hands to navigate as it thickened. Distant moaning and sputtering faded when they finally felt the edge of the gaping hole where the gate once stood.

Jake sighed in relief as soon as he thought they were safe. They made it to the old subdivision where the sewer entrance was. "Thank whatever the hell is watching over us." He collapsed to his knees and rubbed his swollen and burning eyes. That was when he realized that they were still missing someone. *Eva.*

Completely exhausted, he struggled back to his feet and scanned the horizon. A dense cloud hung over the Wolf's Den as sounds of battle continued. It was still barely dawn, so he could not make out much aside from the glowing torchlight from the compound. Tommy, Jake, and their Father waited eagerly for any sort of movement. No survivors. No one walked out of the gates.

"Eva," Jake pleaded. "Eva, please. Please hurry. Please be alive."

"Jake… I don't think she…"

Tommy looked up at his father who was watching Jake with a sympathetic stare. Just as the old man was about to finish his comment, Jake bolted. His younger brother hurriedly examined the horizon and saw a heap near the edge of the Wolves' territory. He squinted as the dust and smoke cleared. The dark silhouette, whatever it was, was moving.

Jake rushed over to Eva's prone body. He caught the glint of her blades as she slumped over. As his last bit of strength left him, he inspected her body for wounds. Her bright aqua eyes slowly turned up to him.

"I am fine, Jake," she whispered with a smile on her face. "Didn't get shot this time."

After a few moments of catching her breath, she rose to her feet. Her body and weapons were caked in blood and mud. Sweat marks drew tracks down her cheekbones. Her hair was matted. Sheathing her swords, she reached down and helped Jake up. He could barely take a step without stumbling and she was forced to use various trees for support. Both were breathing heavily by the time they made it back to Tommy and the McAvoys' father. Eva smiled and nodded, but said nothing. From the look on their father's face, she knew that her actions had terrified him. In fact, she probably reminded him of his captors. Ruthless like the Wolves or any other Gang, despite the fact she used her skills to save others.

"Well that was fun," Eva said sarcastically between breaths. "Let's never do that again."

The rest of the group laughed uncomfortably.

The group finally reached the Western Rover colony after a long and arduous journey. Every street and front porch was completely desolate. William and his warriors had disappeared into the Feast Hall for their midday meal. Eva was not usually one to beg for hospitality, but she knew that they needed it, particularly Jake. They were enticed by the smell of freshly cooked food and nearly bumped into William as they limped through the doorway.

"Legends ring true about you Wanderer," he said, taking her shoulders in his hands. "A *true* warrior."

She couldn't help but to smile. Flushing underneath the layers of blood, she thanked him. William looked over Eva's shoulder at Jake, Tommy, and their father. Eva turned to Jake, who was using a nearby table as a crutch, and asked for medical attention.

"I know it's pretty obvious," she mentioned. "But Jake is badly -."

William interjected and quieted the other warriors. "Say no more. Healers! Please tend to the young man. Get these fatigued warriors some hot food and comfy beds tonight. Let us show them what the Warriors of The West can boast in hospitality."

Eva, Jake, Tommy, and the boys' father were all lifted off the ground by large men and brought to the back room. Eva was placed softly in an area with a pump for water. Elaine walked in and handed her a new set of clothing.

Eva began rinsing her blood-stained body. "I'll admit," Elaine started. "You surpass any of the stories I've heard about you Wanderer. We heard the explosion from here."

"That wasn't us," she admitted. "Rats attacked the Wolves after I killed the Chief."

Elaine spun her back to Eva and laughed. "So you *did* get caught. Predictable. But, hey, you made it out alive. A better outcome than if any of us would've done it."

"We got lucky."

"Sometimes that's how the game is played, right? Luck is what we live by day-to-day. As warriors. It is the only reason we wake up every day after the hunt. Skill only takes us so far."

Eva nodded and Elaine left the room with her soiled clothing. Soon, the water ran clear and she dried herself in a large piece of cloth. She drifted over to the fresh pile of clothing and noticed that William had gifted her brand new armor. Her thick cargo pants had been replaced with leather pads woven through tightened and durable fabric, stained black as night. Underneath the pants was a gray tank top and new wraps for undergarments. Her favorite jacket had been replaced with layered leather pieces, dyed dark brown and pressed with metal rivets and a thickened hood. They had even given her a new set of boots. Each piece of armor fit perfectly.

Feeling like a completely new person, Eva made her way out to the Feast Hall. Jake was being patched up near the door. The Healer had cleaned his face, but it still looked rather grotesque. Tommy and their father were sitting right behind him, eating. She strolled over to them and displayed her new gear.

Jake gave a thumbs up. "Very nice."

"How is your face?" she winced.

"Better now," he smiled then grimaced in pain.

"You look like shit… You know that right?"

"Yeah, I figured."

Eva laughed and pointed to the silver and black haired man. "Have you at least said 'hello' to your father yet?"

"Wait." The man overheard them and turned around. "*Father*? I am not the father of these boys."

"What?" Her smile vanished. She felt like she had been punched in the gut.

Chapter 8

The entire feast hall fell completely silent. The Rovers held their breath, bracing for what might come next. Jake broke eye contact with Eva, suddenly fixated on his feet. His hands turned cold and clammy. He felt like he was going to vomit. Tommy stared at his brother with a look of bewilderment. The man she believed to be their father stood slowly, inching backward until his back pressed against the wall.

"What… did you just say?" Her lip twitched and her fists clenched.

"I-I," the large man completely flattened against the wall. Eva shortened the space between them, closing in on her prey. "I thought you knew that. I thought they would have told you. I am not their *father*, but I left with him. A family friend. Tommy probably doesn't have a clue what his father looks like, but Jake should have remembered *something*. He should have told you *something*."

"Don't blame this all on me, Michael," Jake squeaked. "I *barely* remember what dad looked like."

Eva spun around and grabbed a knife from a nearby table, gritting her teeth as she took a few steps towards Jake. With a red face and white knuckles clenched around the handle, she grabbed a fistful of his shirt and held the blade up to his jugular. Warriors of the Rover colony waited silently for The Wanderer's next move.

"You-you *knew*?" She kept her eyes glued to Jake's petrified gaze. "And you said *nothing*?"

"I couldn't just *leave* him there, Eva," Jake pleaded. "He was a friend. And-and we were already there. We were already in the Wolves Den."

Jake managed to slip away from Eva and backed up behind another table, hands raised. As he pathetically stumbled backwards, she grabbed dishes, cutlery, and anything else she could reach and hurled them in his direction. Food and dishes went flying in all directions, ringing through the food hall. Eva's voice grew louder and louder. A few of the Warriors backed away from the quarrel.

"You," *smash*. "Knew," *crash*. "Jake! We were going after your *father*. I could have died! You knew and you said nothing while I stood there. I was almost beheaded right in front of you. You saw what happened after I was shot in the Nomad campsite. You've *seen* how much I struggle with my past. The *torture* I endured. I-."

"I had no idea that it wasn't my father until I saw him," Jake pleaded as she gained ground on him. "I *swear*. How could I have known? I would never have put your life in danger if-."

"No Jake," Eva interrupted. She stopped dead in her tracks.

The feeling in the room immediately shifted.

The Wanderer took a deep breath and her voice became chillingly calm. "You know what? I have fought too many demons for you. For Tommy. I pushed all of my past away for you two. All against my better judgment. To save your father. And this guy I risked my life to save… is a *nobody*."

She tore her pistol out of its holster and pointed it at Michael. Turning off the safety and cocking it, she paused with her finger on the trigger. Her vision tunneled. To her, he was a victim. A lie. He blubbered and pleaded for his life, falling to his knees as she took two steps forward, with the barrel pointing down at the top of his head. Tears streaming down his face and snot bubbling out of his nostrils.

Pathetic, she thought. *He won't last out here. He's too weak*. She wanted to squeeze the trigger. To end his life in front of all these people.

But she couldn't. That was not her. Not anymore. She could never kill someone who had escaped the compounds. If his fate was to die, it would catch up to him, eventually. Noticing her hand was trembling violently, she lowered her handgun and flicked the safety back on. As Jake was about to get up from behind her, she let out a scream that toppled him back to his rear.

"Do *not* follow me," she ordered. "If any of you follow me, I *will not* hesitate to kill you."

"Eva, wait." Jake reached towards her.

She walked over to the doorway and stopped. "Shut up Jake. You don't care about me. That much is clear. If you even *think* about following me, I *will* tear you apart. *Slowly*."

That was the last she saw of the McAvoy brothers. She slammed the large metal door behind her, and the rumble of voices started up again inside the food hall. The pleading look on his face was the last she saw of Jake. He seemed lost without her. For some reason, tears started welling up in her eyes, but she immediately shrugged it off.

She set off towards the forest as the sun began its journey back to the horizon, stewing in her thoughts. *I have no pity or feelings for that man. He betrayed me. Used me. His father probably isn't even alive. I was right all along. Pathetic.*

Eva made her way to the bluff, still seething from the confrontation. The cliff felt steeper than she remembered. On the way up, there would be no support. One missed foothold or a patch of loose earth mistaken for a root, and nothing would stop the fall. No second chances. Only the desperate urge to get home carried her forward. She climbed slowly, testing each step and every handhold. The rock wall dragged the minutes out, but she pressed on, grit in her teeth and fire in her limbs. At the top, breathless, she turned and looked west one final time. Smoke was still billowing from the Wolf's Den and an orange glow lingered like coals. Off to her left, the Rover colony. The warriors spilled out of the hall and into their respective homes. A mix of rage and depression washed over her as she turned towards the darkness of the forest.

Back to my life, alone, she thought. *I am free of them. That burden is now gone. For good.*

Nightfall had long since passed by the time Eva reached the other side of the region. She had chosen to go around the forest rather than through it. Going in alone was far too dangerous with the animals lurking around. As she neared her colony, she heard the rumbling of voices coming from the large building for the evening meal. Because of her clash with Jake, she had not eaten in an entire day. Her stomach twisted and groaned as she strolled towards the smell of food. The Rovers welcomed her with a hot plate of vegetables and venison, acting as though she never left. Each one greeted her with a fist on their chest. She nodded to each one of them, smiling softly, but a void in her chest still remained.

"Where are the boys that were with you Eva?" they inquired.

She grabbed her tray. "Dead." She lied. "Died trying to infiltrate a Gang in the West. I didn't find their father, either. I risked my life for an imposter. They were gunned down while I escaped."

They questioned her no more and left her in peace. She sat down at the table in the corner and threw her hood over her head. For the first time in months, she was able to eat in solitude, without a care in the world. But slowly devouring her soul, deep down, was not peace. A gloom washed over her. A nameless sadness. Doubt. It spread from her heart, blackening and rotting her insides, twisting them into uncomfortable shapes. Tears welled up again so she finished her food quickly. Once the door to her shack was closed, she could no longer hold it in.

Eva crossed her arms over her knees and she slid to the floor, sobbing. The cold metal against her back gave her goosebumps. Why was she crying? The betrayal was still so raw, but the tears refused to end. She felt so pitiful and weak. The only thing in her mind was the look on Jake's face. That, and the kiss they shared.

She wiped her red, puffy eyes. "What is wrong with me?"

After a few moments on the dirt floor, she tore off her weaponry and sank into her bed, staring blankly at the ceiling. A numbing sensation blanketed her entire body. She felt dead inside. Empty. Tears continued to trickle down the sides of her face as she let that emptiness consume her.

"You have a choice Eva." A Rover Elder was standing in her doorway. She hadn't seen him enter her shack and apparently forgot to lock the door. Gradually, she sat up, shoulders slumped, head in her hands.

She had only half-heard him. "What are you talking about?"

"You have two choices," he repeated. "You can let this darkness envelope your soul. Or, you can show your strength and get past this. Just like you always have. He was just *one* man, Eva. Tragedy to lose him and his brother, but that's life. You know loss well, so why is this any different? Remember, you *chose* to help those boys. You chose to help us. Now, you have to choose to help yourself."

He disappeared through the doorway, shutting it behind him, leaving Eva to ponder his words of wisdom. Images of her past began to arise. *It's about time I faced them. Perhaps facing these demons would make me stronger. Maybe they won't return.* They were becoming more intense by the minute, but she had suppressed them for too long. She stumbled into the next room. Claustrophobia clamped around her ribs and flashbacks tore through her skull like claws, one after the other, without mercy. Every sound warped. Too sharp. Too loud. Her chest tightened further. Her vision blurred. Hands trembled. She clutched the doorway, nails digging into the frame, trying to anchor herself—trying to remember what was real.

But the past didn't care. It came anyway.

Gruesome scenes split open her head. Screams. Being whipped mercilessly, *feeling* the metal claws across her back where her scars now lay. The pain was just as intense as before. She dropped to the floor on all fours, watching drops of sweat splash against the dirt. Suddenly, the hallucination of a hooded figure stepped from the shadows. A hooded figure, silent at first.

Its voice came sharp and metallic, like metal grinding on bone.

It said her name.

And something inside her snapped.

"Just end it Eva," he taunted. Its voice was a metallic whisper. "End your life. Your pain. You are worth *nothing* anyway. You are weak. The Wanderer is not a protector."

He cackled. She squirmed in pain as the mental torture continued. A scene of dead and decaying bodies enveloped the other images. The effigy still stood at the edge of her room, taunting and laughing as she writhed. She was losing control as more horrific scenes started to creep into view. The demon's laughter became louder and louder until it sounded like he was screaming in her ear. Deep down in the depths of her soul, she found the strength to stand. Using a bookcase as support, she became level with the shadow's face. The only feature she could make out was its crooked, pointed teeth.

The figure continued to taunt her. "You are weak. Death is all you deserve."

"*No!*" Eva did not remember whether she had ever screamed so loud in her life. Lunging towards the figure, she swiped the air with her fist, rattling the walls and splitting open her knuckles. In an instant, everything disappeared. The man. The images. The pain. It was just her, a pool of sweat, and a hand dripping with blood. Her trembling breath was the only sound that remained. A wave of relief washed over her.

She breathed through a wavering voice, "I did it. It's *gone*."

The voice cackled like the wind past her ear.

She spun around, eyes wide, goosebumps rising across her skin. Something flickered in her peripheral vision, a shape too familiar, too dark, vanishing before she could focus. Deep down, she knew the images would return, and maybe the evil figure along with them. But for now, she had forced them back into the shadows, along with whatever feelings she still carried for Jake McAvoy. She could finally return to her life as The Wanderer.

***

Eva was able to finish the day in peace. She cleaned her blades and wrapped her injured hand. Fortunately, the Healer told her that she did not shatter any bones from the incident. The remainder of her evening was spent with a hot meal and reading the last few pages of her journal. Knowing she was nearing the end of this author's story was bittersweet.

I've lost count of the days we've been down here. It's just me and my son now. We have been out of food for days... I think... Maybe weeks... We were so hungry. And they were going to rot down here if we did nothing. I'm not proud of it. Neither of us are. I just couldn't let it go to waste. We're starving after all. I just don't know what's worse, braving for the surface or dying down here. Do we risk what's on the other side of that latch? Either way, this could be the end.

***

The next morning, she opened the journal and turned a couple more crackling pages and stopped. At the next page were the notes she had scribbled weeks before. Hastily drawn maps with notes stemming off of the doors and gates on every square inch. The images made her stomach bubble with rage. With one quick swipe, she ripped it from the spine. She tore the spine wide open and ripped every page, including her own writings, from its tethers. She cursed. As she passed the fires in the food hall that evening, she tossed the crumpled papers and the rest of the journal into it, watching it smolder. A small part of her wanted to save the wilting leather. The last five years of her life were recorded in those pages. But now, it was ash.

She just wanted to start over.

But in the back of her mind, was Jake McAvoy.

***

In the coming days, Eva occupied herself with replenishing food and supplies for herself and the Rovers. As soon as the sun's first rays crept into her shack, she awoke, got ready, and left for the city. Winter was fast approaching. Each year, she would search for seeds and small plants for the Rover farmers to plant for the next harvest. When the snows came, trade would come to a screeching halt as the land became treacherous with storms blanketing the land. Hunting was difficult and the Colony would rely on any food they could, sometimes barely making it through. But she was determined. And they relied on her skills so that they could survive.

Each morning, a brisk wind greeted her as Eva moved toward the distant, hazy skyline. Vivid purples, oranges, and reds danced across the glass and metal of the broken skyscrapers. Lately, she spent more of her days wandering deeper into the city, letting the remnants of the Old Times consume her senses. The sound of crumbling brick, the scent of aged furniture. Each detail sparked her imagination. Sometimes, she saw herself standing in a crowded city street or seated in a bustling restaurant, surrounded by voices that no longer existed.

One morning, she stumbled upon a building that had caught her eye many times before but had never explored. Curious, she stepped inside. Ivy and other creeper vines had overgrown the towering pillars and statuary. Greenery wound around the faces of sculptures she did not recognize. The sound of a babbling brook calmly flowed through her ears. She followed it. Much to her surprise, an entire stream had formed through the aisle down the middle of the building. Trees sprung through the wooden floorboards, warmed by the autumn sun that shone through broken stained glass. Small mammals and birds hopped and fluttered through the morning light reflecting in the ripples of the pool near her feet. She tarried at each bench, brushing her fingertips across the ancient, hand-carved wood. A shelf of books hung at the center of each bench, swollen by years of moisture. At the head of the building, between two large trees, stood a marble table. Behind it was a statue of a man, arms outstretched and nailed to a cross.

This must have been a place of worship and he was their god. Eva climbed onto the table to get a better view of the idol. *Silly though. Looks like he let himself get killed. Why would anyone worship someone who was killed? Only a survivor is worth worshiping. History is only written by those who live. Either way, I guess, stories get twisted by their followers.*

After having her fill of this city's secret gem, she continued on her way. Exploring that ancient building gave her some peace. Even in a crumbling world of death and hate, there were places like this, untouched by evil. Just as she exited through the large archway, she noticed a basket of rotten vegetables. She carefully plucked out the seeds from the mush and put them in her pack.

It wasn't long before Eva found herself carrying a backpack overflowing with leathers, seeds, and tools. As she ventured back to the colony, she took a different path. She happened upon another building that was just as unfamiliar. This one was definitely built in the Old Times, but the sturdy wood had not rotted or collapsed. It stood strong despite its age. She pulled out her handgun and carefully stepped up the front stairs. The door was unlocked but nothing stirred inside. With one hand on her gun and the other wrapped around the brass door handle, she crept into the single-room structure.

This temple was much different than the one before. There were no chairs or benches, rather, torn cushions and worn rugs. Dusty windowsills devoid of glass allowed in much more daylight. As her eyes scanned the front of the room, her heart jumped. Sitting in the front of the room was a near mirror image of the tranquil deity that Tommy had taken from her collection. One hand was touching the ground and the other was near his chest, palm softly facing her. Even in this pose, the man with partially closed eyes was peaceful and relaxed. An invisible energy seemed to draw her to the statue, beckoning her to sit with him.

Ensuring the door was locked, she laid out her weapons and backpack and sat on the floor, mimicking this man. She leaned forward and read the word "Buddha" on it. She didn't understand the meaning. *Perhaps that is his name? Or title?* Then, as Eva closed her eyes, took a deep breath, and was instantly whisked away into a state of relaxation by the soft breeze. She sat there, motionless for a while, taking in the scenery. The time she spent here was incredibly healing. She wondered whether this place could completely draw out her demons if they returned.

* * *

The McAvoy brothers chose to remain in the Western Rover colony for a while. In the weeks following their encounter with the Wanderer, fear kept them from venturing beyond the Rovers' protection. Traveling alone was out of the question. William took pity on their situation and allowed Jake, Tommy, and Michael to stay. But he gave them one condition.

"You must provide for your new kin," he told them. "Contribute to your family. There are those who would not dare raise arms to strike down any foe. Yet, they cook, they farm, they tan leathers. I care not which craft you choose, my brothers, but I do not tolerate idle hands."

Obviously, Tommy took up farming. He had already read the book he found in the city countless times over. Jake, who decided to become the armorer's apprentice, became very impressed with his younger brother's skill. And much to his own surprise, he found leather tanning rather enjoyable. Michael, on the other hand, spent most of his days cooking, scarcely speaking to anyone and only working when he was in a decent mood. As time went on, Jake began to lose respect for the man his father had once called a *friend*.

The McAvoy brothers remained in the Rover colony for a couple months before Tommy remembered the Nomads. He would draw the markings of the Owl on his face with mud, and after a while, he managed to convince his brother to leave the comfort of the Warriors and venture into the city. William was sad to see them go, but offered them some advice.

As he led them to the border of the forest, he put a reassuring hand on Jake's shoulder. "Follow the path through the trees and venture to the city. My people roped off a faster path. Take heart boys. Nomad numbers are many. Greater than you may have witnessed before. Seek them out. I feel they may have a story to tell, but I am wary of the context."

Michael did not even come to see Jake and Tommy leave that day. Elaine was the only one who accompanied William. She had grown fond of Jake and attempted to make advances, but he simply pushed her away. His heart never left the East. Painful as it was to accept, it belonged to Eva. Still, it frustrated Elaine, but she let him go, hoping their paths would cross again.

"When you find whatever you are looking for," she took his hand. "Please, come back to me."

"I… I cannot make that promise," Jake replied as he pulled away and disappeared into the darkness. "I'm sorry." His brother trailed behind him.

Truthfully, Jake had fought to keep his memories of Eva. As her image began to fade, he would recite her features. Her intense aqua eyes, soft nose, pronounced cheekbones, and graceful lips. Although her expression was almost always somber, he preferred to remember her that way. Her strength wasn't just admirable—it was what captivated him. The last melody of her voice lingered in his ear. It was music to him, even though it had been a threat of death. But it was all he had, at least, all he could recall.

Finding the Nomads would be both risky and challenging. The city was large and Jake had discovered them purely by accident before. He was not thrilled about the journey, but there was a chance that William's words were correct. Perhaps they had more to tell him about this region. Tommy's intent was to protect those he could not save before. He never forgot about the girl who ate with him that night. She also bore the mark of the Owl.

They made their way through the forest with little delay. William mapped out the trail for them, using the tree-markings and rope as a guide. Jake made only one wrong turn, and he realized immediately they had drifted deeper into the tree line. Growls from predators rumbled around them. Hours lingered on, but they eventually found themselves staring at a beam of light on the path ahead.

They stepped out of the forest beneath a peaceful sky, stars twinkling in the distance. A bright moon hung above them like a gentle guide, illuminating the path into the city. Familiar sounds and smells greeted them at the border. Both brothers felt a strange comfort beneath the towering ruins, safer among crumbling stone than beneath the open skies of the Western Rover colony. The thought of staying with the Nomads and learning to fight with grace and meaning stirred a quiet thrill deep within them.

"You know Tommy," Jake rounded the next block and called back to his brother. The silence was starting to bother him. "You'll have to talk one day. It's been *years* since mom was killed and dad left. You have seen some of the worst shit out here we could ever imagine. And still, you have not made a sound."

Tommy ignored him.

"What happens if you get lost?" he continued. "I mean, there are so many things that require at least some sort of noise. Express yourself through words. Y'know? It gets kind of lonely when I talk to you. It feels like I'm talking to myself. She isn't around anymore… All I have left is you."

Jake's memories of Eva bubbled up and he cleared his throat. His brother could sense his sadness and patted him on the back but still said nothing. As they stepped out of another dark alleyway, the distant beat of drums reached their ears. *Nomads*. They rushed toward the sound, hearts pounding with anticipation and excitement. The flicker of bonfires came into view, and in the dancing glow, they saw them. Yidi and Masha had survived the massacre. Tears welled as the two rushed forward and pulled them into a tight embrace. They were alive. They were safe.

"You seem to have washed your markings my Coyote and Owl," Masha joked. Her smile was warm and welcoming. "We will get those back on you."

A woman brought the paint over to the Nomad Elder and she retraced the symbols on their face. Jake and Tommy felt like they were finally home. The Nomads gave them food and drink as they sat by the fire next to Yidi. He explained that he had taken a few bullets to the hip and now walked with a limp, but was grateful for his life.

"Our numbers are many," he explained. "We're still at least four or five hundred strong. After you escaped, my healers took good care of me. I may be old, but I can still fight. Ahh… But time has been kind to us these past few months. Not long ago, we had the privilege of meeting another Nomad tribe deeper in the city. They outnumber our tribe by the thousands."

Jake tried to imagine a group that large. "How do they manage to stay away from the Gangs with so many people?"

"The city houses many secrets," Yidi replied. "Many that we cannot comprehend. Perhaps they are the masters of those secrets. Nevertheless, their food is good and they praise our Mother with the same passion and love. And that is all that matters, yes?"

His lighthearted laugh made the brothers smile. Some of the Nomads they recognized from before. Others were new faces. After the ceremonial dance and thanks to the spirits for another safe night, they had full stomachs and warm beds. Jake, who had received a large axe similar to the one the Eastern Rovers had once gifted him, stayed awake to speak with Yidi and Masha.

"We have so many questions for you youngling." Masha settled in her seat. "It has been too long."

Yidi chimed in. "Indeed. And you seem to be missing someone."

Jake swallowed hard. He knew that they were going to mention Eva, but hoped that they would avoid asking outright. For a few moments, he pondered how to best answer, but ultimately decided to be honest with them.

He hesitated, choosing his words with care. "We had…a falling out. She promised to save our father. We, no, *I* failed to mention that we do not really remember what he looked like. And we didn't really know where he went off to. When we ventured into the West, we got word that a man from my Vault was being held captive in a nearby compound. We were *sure* it was him. It had to be. Eva risked her life to save him. But it wasn't our father…just a pathetic excuse for a human being. I was too scared to say anything…"

"So after you found out that it was not your father." Yidi closed his eyes with a pained expression. "You said nothing."

"I felt as though he deserved to be saved as well," Jake said.

The old Nomad stared into the young man's eyes. "At the expense of her life… I know Eva's story too well.

Her *whole* story. Perhaps… It is time you know it too. Lies and betrayal mark her like deep scars. Parts of it, I did not intend to speak to another soul. But it may bring some perspective into your heart… The Wanderer's path is filled with courage, but also stained in the blood of the innocent."

Jake was confused. *Innocent* blood? Yidi beckoned him closer. The Elder leaned in with his wife at his side, looking at Jake with wide, intense eyes.

"You know of her time spent as a slave - Doxie I think they call them - in the compounds?" Yidi put his hands on Jake's shoulder, who nodded. "Well… after she was victorious against the Chief, but *before* she left the compound, she spent a number of years inside."

"Doing what?" Jake shuffled closer.

"*Leading it,*" Yidi's voice dropped. Jake's heart skipped a few beats. "The Gang that calls themselves the Serpents. They are the largest in the region, by far. But they weren't always that way. Only under the leadership of a merciless killer could they become so great. That 'merciless killer' was, and still is, The Wanderer."

Jake could barely believe what he was hearing. "Wait… You're telling me that Eva was *the leader of a Gang?*"

"Not just any Gang," Masha corrected. "She built the largest, strongest, and most ruthless Gang in the region. By her blades, thousands of Rovers and Nomads alike were sent to their deaths or lives of servitude. Perhaps it was revenge for the torture she endured?

Maybe she allowed the power to get to her head? Whatever the reason, she was a slaughterer of many."

Jake's stomach rose to his throat. Color drained from his face. He did not want to hear any more. Any trust, love, or affection he shared with Eva before was now completely consumed by fear and hatred. He did not want to believe it. This was not the Eva that he knew.

"How do you know all this?" he asked. "You have to be lying."

Masha looked at her husband and dropped her head. They both took a deep breath and Yidi spoke for both of them. "We were there as part of her council when the Nomads and Gangs were under a peace treaty."

"Peace treaty?"

"For a time, whatever The Wanderer said was law. We could only obey. If we did not, our people would end up the same as the rest of the slaves. She was too tactful, too ruthless for us to resist. Her numbers were too many."

"So you sat there and let her take the lives of innocent people and did nothing?"

"For our own survival, we had no other choice."

"Then why the *shit* do you treat her with any shred of respect?" Jake became angry. "You bow to her like she is some sort of deity. Why do you allow her to be here with your people when you know she has *Nomad blood on her hands*?"

Yidi tried to keep his composure. He knew that Jake was only hearing his words, not listening to them.

"Because she *changed*. I have seen both sides of that woman. Her eyes that were once filled with hate, pain, and a thirst for power. Now… Now they are filled with only pain and regret. She realized the error of her ways. We cannot judge her past deeds because she has done so much to *save* us."

Jake stood up. "No. This doesn't make any sense. If you're telling me the truth, then Eva *brutally killed* thousands of people. Shit, she created the Gang that now slaughters your people for sport. In case you forgot, this Gang that sells *human beings* to a life of horrible torture and inevitable death."

"None of us are without offense, Coyote," Masha said with her hand raised. "We've all had to protect ourselves. Sometimes, from our own ilk."

"But you did not send thousands of people to their deaths."

Masha and Yidi looked at each other with pained expressions. Jake's eyes widened.

His voice squeaked, grappling with whether or not he wanted to hear their answer now. "Right?"

"There was a time when Nomads and Rovers sacrificed their own for food or medical aid. We sent family and friends to their deaths because it was the only way to survive. We have never claimed to be honorable people. Elders before us once sent my husband and me to our deaths as part of The Wanderer's council, but we hold no grudge now. Today, we consider ourselves lucky. At least it is the Gangs picking us off, not our own.

It draws a clear line between who we can and cannot trust."

Jake stood frozen, mouth slightly open, silent. His eyes flicked between Masha and Yidi, his feet rooted in place. They spoke so calmly about the horrors of Eva's past—and their own. The Elders noticed the judgment in his expression, and their faces hardened in return.

Yidi's tone sharpened and his face dropped to a frown. "Bearer of the Coyote Spirit, you have *no right* to judge anyone out here. Both you and your brother came from a place of safety and peace for the last two centuries. And you come here to condemn *our* past? *Her* past? You have no right. You know nothing of this world and what it was before. Nor what it is at this very moment. Our hands were forced to battle long before your time. Everything we know, we had to learn. The Gangs have taken *everything* from us, but we had to survive. Do not make assumptions about us. Survival is *everything* out here."

At first, the three caught in a quarrel thought the loud pitter-patter was either rain from the sky or a trick of their imagination. But then came the screams. Bloodied Nomads running from the next street seized them into battle. Too late. The Gang was already upon them, snatching people off their feet, binding their hands and legs, and slinging them into a cart. Women were ripped from the arms of their children. Some were executed. Others fought back with everything they had.

Many fled into the darkness, their footsteps lost in the chaos.

Jake found himself wrestling with a large man. The Gang Member was trying to rip the axe from his grasp and grabbed the blade by mistake. Jake pulled hard and severed the man's fingers from his palm. His opponent yelped in pain and grabbed his wrist.

When Jake was able to free himself, his eyes locked onto the patch on the man's jacket, a Tiger baring its teeth. A moment later, he was on top of Jake again, trying to hold him down with bleeding hands, calling out for someone to help him.

"Not today," Jake yelled, wrenching one arm free. He raised his weapon and drove the blade deep into the man's stomach. When he pulled it out, the Tiger's steaming entrails spilled into his lap, pulsing and twitching. He watched in horror as the man tried to pull his intestines back into his body in desperation. A scream tore from Jake's throat as he looked down at his blood-soaked torso and hands. He sat there in a stupor for a moment, until his mind jolted back to reality.

He scrambled to his feet and sprinted toward the tents. *Tommy*.

When he finally found the yurt his brother had been sleeping, he ripped back the leathers blocking the door. Nothing. An audible thump and a sudden pain seared in his head as he fell to the ground. Someone or something had struck him, hard. His vision narrowed into darkness. Just before he fell into complete unconsciousness, he heard the sound of struggling behind him. Right in front of his eyes, his brother was being shoved into the cart.

Chapter 9

The Tigers must have forgotten about him or left him to die. He would never know which. But Jake certainly felt like he was dying, at least until he was able to move his arms and legs. He reached up to check the back of his head. There was no open wound where the butt of the gun had struck him. He felt only a knot, accompanied by a splitting headache and dizziness. He had no idea how long he'd been unconscious. It was daytime, not yet noon. *Focus.* What was the last thing he remembered? The image was still fuzzy. Jake shut his eyes hard. Gradually, then all at once, his memory began to clear.

Tommy.

Jake crawled over to the tent where his brother had been sleeping a few hours before. He was not sure what he expected to find, but pulled back the curtain anyway. It was empty. The Nomads were gone. Bodies scattered the camp, both Tiger and Nomad alike. Each one, their lifeless gaze staring blankly ahead of them.

The grass was saturated from the blood of battle, damp and springy to the touch. The elder brother did not know what to do or where to go. For the first time in his life, he was completely alone.

Quickly, his mind went to Eva.

No. Why would she help him? After everything that happened with the Wolves. She vowed to kill him if they crossed paths again. Still, she was the only one he knew who could infiltrate a compound. Eva knew the region and its people better than anyone. But now that Jake knew the truth about her past, he feared her more than ever.

She's the only one who can help, he reasoned. *Last time she nearly got killed. Shit... And she'll definitely refuse to do anything for me. But maybe Tommy is a different story. Yidi and Masha said that she changed. Maybe.*

The voice of reason spoke up. *She threatened to kill you. If she sees you, you're dead.*

"Dammit," he whispered, snatching his weapon off the ground. He turned toward the road leading out of the city, heading for the Eastern Rover colony. Tears blurred his vision as he wiped them away. "I have to try. For my brother."

Jake decided that his best option was to wait for Eva to return from scavenging. Before she could speak, he would plead for his life and explain everything. Tommy was never at fault for not knowing who their father was or what he looked like. He was too young to remember him. Besides, The Wanderer always had a soft spot for his little brother. If she killed Jake, so be it. But perhaps she would still save Tommy.

In the hours it took to reach the Rover colony, Jake argued with himself over the choice to find Eva. *I should just turn and run. She is going to kill me slowly. Remember? But Tommy. If I leave him, he's worse off than dead.*

Leaves rustled at his feet, crunching under his boots. The smell of autumn air soothed him slightly. When he lived in the Vault, he spent some of his free time researching weather in different parts of the world. Books from the Old Times became his obsession as a child, especially those about the weather. The greenery all around had changed from reds and oranges to yellows and browns. Being able to comprehend the feeling, the sights, and the smells of the seasons changing first-hand was euphoria. Survival made him afraid, but being outside the Vault was indescribably freeing.

He was so distracted by his own thoughts that he nearly knocked over a Rover woman farming in her garden. She had to slam her shovel into his shin to pull him from his reverie. "Hey! Watch where you're going!" He apologized profusely and jumped back out of her crops. The moment he asked where Eva was, she recognized him.

"You must've really angered her," the woman said sternly. "She told us you were dead. And you have the nerve to crawl back here begging for her mercy after endangering her life for your own selfish reasons?"

She told everyone that we died?

The farmer jabbed a finger hard into his chest and ignored any further questions. Jake turned to some of the other disheveled men and women around the town. But the second they recognized him, they turned away. No one would help. Not even the children.

"Fine," Jake spat at one of the Elders. "I'll just wait for her to return."

The old Rover-woman mocked. "And we will be waiting to watch your head roll down the street."

He swallowed the lump in his throat and walked over to The Wanderer's shack. While she was out scavenging, Eva would leave the latch unlocked to her home. Closing one eye, he squinted through an opening and saw no movement. He could feel the eyes of the Rovers on his back as he slipped through the door. After finding a seat, he began his long wait for Eva's return. Each passing hour increased his anxiety.

If she kills me, I hope it's a quick death, he pondered. *Maybe I'll have a heart attack and die before she has a chance to kill me.*

***

Eva was, indeed, hunting and foraging. Rovers in the colony had run out of fresh meat as they turned their focus on harvesting crops before the first frost of winter. She happily took the responsibility to bring back as much game as she could carry. Early that morning, a small wooden cart was waiting for her outside. The city, she believed, would be a good place to start. Many of the animals would begin preparations for hibernation and they typically utilized the ruins as their dens.

On the pavement, the cart rattled loudly. It looked like one of the wheels was smaller than the other and had been worn in places, making it unstable. The misshapen wheel made it exhausting to drag the cart down the road. It was also very loud. She skidded to the right and hauled it to the grass. Wiping the sweat from her forehead and chest, loud voices echoed in her ears from down the street. Quickly pulling the cart from sight, Eva crouched behind a rusted dumpster at the mouth of a nearby alleyway and waited.

Throwing her hood over her head to mask herself in the darkness, she spotted two men and a woman carrying large guns, clad in thick leathers and short cowled robes. They were all hiding the mark of their Gang, but Eva knew from the condition of their firearms that they belonged to one. Joking loudly and making no attempt to be stealthy, they marched down the road. They unknowingly passed The Wanderer and a name caught Eva's attention.

"McAvoy, at least, works hard," said the woman. "I've never seen a man work so hard. Crazy."

"Yeah," the man agreed. "I heard he's been here for ages. You would never know lookin' at him. Did you know he came from that Vault the Serpents raided a while back? Not a callus on his hands. Zeke told me he did something with science or some shit like that. I don't know what that means. What I do know is work. And that bastard outworks all of us."

"Wonder how we got 'em?" the woman wondered.

Eva's heart was racing. Memories and events flooded back into her mind along with the demons. *Shit, no*. She tried to repress them again, to no avail. With ease, the feeling of dread and claustrophobia infected her. Luckily, she was able to stay silent long enough for the Gang members to turn out of earshot. Choking on the rapidly thickening air, she opened her eyes to the shadow that had taunted her before. It provoked her.

"I told you I would be back," he chanted. "You cannot escape me, Eva Calloway. I will be here until you take your final dying breath."

She could not relax enough to open her airway. With fists clenched, she gathered as much focus as she could muster and took a deep breath. A voice yelled loudly in her mind. That voice she recognized instantly as Jake McAvoy.

You have a choice Eva, he said. *Me or an eternity fighting with this anxiety. The guilt of leaving me is eating away at the darkness of your past. If we find my father, then maybe this will go away. It's just guilt. That's all.*

She fought back. *I can't. You lied to me. You betrayed me. I will not help you.*

Then you cannot help yourself. Jake's voice chimed in again. *If you do not help me and Tommy, then the good in you will fade.*

All of a sudden, Eva heard a small voice in the depths of her mind. It was quiet. A whisper. *I choose Jake*, it said sternly. Then it came again, louder. And again. By the fifth time, the shadow vanished. She gasped, drawing in a full breath. After steadying herself and making sure no one had seen her, she walked over to the cart and pulled it to the city.

It wasn't long before her cart was almost too full to carry. When she was satisfied with her hunt, she headed back to the colony. One deer and a dozen rabbits lined the length of the carriage. Still, her thoughts drifted and her head was light with exhaustion. The name *McAvoy* clung to her mind, tangled with the memory of the mysterious Gang she encountered.

Eva unloaded her cart at the back of the food hall, but her thoughts stayed submerged, drifting through the depths of her mind. She returned home before the evening meal, still dazed. It wasn't until a few moments later that she even noticed her door was closed and that Jake was inside. He stood tense, gripping a raised axe, ready in case she attacked. When she finally saw him, she screamed and stumbled back. After what she had experienced only hours earlier, she was not entirely sure he was real.

A mix of anger, relief, happiness, and betrayal bubbled up to the surface. "Jake? Is that you?" She wanted to throw her arms around him, but also considered removing his head from his shoulders. And by the look on his face, he noticed her reach for the hilt of her blade.

"Yes, it's me. And I know you are still upset with us," he pleaded. "With *me*. And I should have said something. I'm so sorry. I would never intentionally put your life in danger. I had no clue it was Michael and not my dad until I saw him for the first time."

"You have some gall showing up here." She lowered her hand and pointed at him. "How do you expect me to respond to you showing up here? Especially after I told you I would kill you if I ever saw you again? How *do* I respond, Jake? I don't. Want. Apologies."

His eyes were burning with tears. "They took Tommy. Eva. The Tigers took Tommy. I wouldn't have come here if I wasn't desperate. *Please.*"

Eva's heart sank. Her arms felt cold. She turned her back to Jake, trudged over to her bed and sat down. She ran her fingers through her hair and rubbed the back of her neck with a loud exhale. Keeping her eyes locked on the door rather than Jake, she changed her tone.

"Shit." she whispered. "How did this happen? You were with the Western Rovers when I left."

Jake sat down next to her and rubbed his eyes in exhaustion. "Yeah. But we came back East. To the Nomads. Tommy wanted to protect them, or something. He felt guilty about the last attack, I think. It was a stupid idea. I should have never let him come. This is all my fault. *Why is everything always my fault?*"

"Oh shut up Jake," she shoved him and stood up. "Stop blaming yourself for everything. Stop whining and acting like you are a victim of this world. Guess what? We all are. And let me tell you, you won't get an *ounce* of pity from me… Or anyone for that matter. The sooner you realize that, the better."

"I just came here to ask for your help to get my brother back," he said. "I know where he's being held. He was taken last night. Or the night before. I can't really remember... *But he can't die, Eva.* I'm supposed to protect him and ever since we got out of that vault, he's been doing everything right… and I keep screwing everything up. I'm just a huge disappointment."

"I am not responding to that, Jake. Grow up. For *shit's sake.*"

"Can you help me? Just this last time? For Tommy. Then I will leave you alone for good. I swear."

Eva paused. Jake did not like the silence at all. It made him nervous. She would be infiltrating a Gang for a second time, risking her life for the lives of these brothers. Again. *But you help people.* A comment that Jake had made months ago fluttered past her thoughts, as did Tommy's innocent face. She could not allow him to suffer like she had all those years ago.

"To be perfectly clear. If I do help, I'm *not* doing this for you, Jake. I am doing this for him. Also, I am breaking my number one rule *again*. So I need you to focus. I need someone at my back. No hesitating to kill anyone. Got it?"

Jake nodded as they caught each other's gaze. Eva crouched in front of him and looked him dead in the eye. The look on her face sent an ice cold shiver up Jake's spine.

"I'll have your back. I *swear*."

"If you lie to me again. I'm leaving you the moment you choose to hide like a coward. The Wanderer won't come after you. I'm not going to protect you. They'll tear you apart. You won't stand a chance. And I won't feel a single ounce of guilt about it."

Jake nodded again. He had disemboweled a Tiger at the Nomad camp, but did not feel comfortable telling her yet. Admittedly, Eva was relieved to be back with Jake, though she would never admit it. She stood up, shoved some supplies into her pack, and walked over to the door, adjusting the blade sheath on her shoulders. As she reached for the front door, she put her hand up and turned to him.

"Wait." she said. Jake's heart was pounding. "If we're going to do this. I have to be completely sure where Tommy is and what we're getting into. We're going to do this *my way*."

Jake lingered at the look on her face, not completely sure what she meant. "Um… Alright…"

"That means," she said in a condescending tone. "No arguing with me. No questioning my methods. No whining. Keep your mouth shut and do as I say. Be ready for anything. If you screw up, you'd better hope the Gang kills you before I do."

Jake agreed. Eva mimicked his nod then spun around and made her way through the doorway towards the Tiger's compound. She knew exactly how she was going to get through those walls. Darkness descended upon them swiftly as they reached No Man's Land. Houses in varying stages of wreckage lined the cracked pavement with Old Time vehicles in front of nearly every building, relics of another time, with all but the ghosts of their former owners behind the wheel. It was silent between the two adventurers until that point.

"The Nomads told me *everything* about you Eva. The *whole* story." He was not sure how she would react, but he couldn't hold it in any longer. Knowing about her past made him cautious to be traveling with her, alone.

He was nearly a block away when he noticed she had stopped. She didn't need an explanation; his meaning was clear. She met his gaze, daring him to say more. Feeling cornered, she went on the defensive.

"This place," she said, gesturing around her. "This life. It changes everyone. You don't get that. That story. *My story*. No one understands. How could they?"

Her tone shifted.

"In the compound, as a Chief, the Serpent's Mistress, I wanted for nothing. *Bloodlust was easily satiated*, as they say. Food - more than someone could ever eat. Supplies - My men had to expand the walls multiple times to fit everything for myself and them. I was given the nicest bed, the best weapons, the most filling foods. I was worshiped for what I did for that Gang."

Jake crossed his arms and shifted his weight to one leg. He had enough. "Then why *did* you leave?" They were yelling at each other from the edges of the block. "I mean, you really don't give a shit about other people in the end. You just said you had *everything*. Why leave?"

Her voice did not waver. No emotion of guilt passed through her lips. "You're right. I didn't want to leave. I had no choice."

"What are you talking about?" Jake rolled his shoulders. "The Nomads -."

"They don't know the whole story Jake," she interrupted. "No one does. I was betrayed by one of my followers. He staged a mutiny."

"Really?"

"This man… I know nothing other than his face. He was a whelp. A *New Blood,* as we called them. One day, I got word from one of my men that he was murdering my servants under the cover of the night. So I decided to poke around his living space.

"I found a notebook filled with obsessive things about overthrowing me. Things like, "How could a woman rule with such cruelty?" and "Imagine what a man like me could do." He wanted to be me. But his skills were… lacking. He was nowhere near my ability."

Jake closed the gap in between them a few steps. Eva continued.

"Knowing this, he got my men to distrust me. Staged a coup. Said something about me being soft with the servants and sympathizing with the Rovers and Nomads, and I'm pretty sure he killed a few of my men in No Man's Land and told the others that it was a direct order from me. He got his hook in about half of them. Promised a better life under his rule or some shit. I'm not even sure how it all happened, but there was no way I could fight every single one of them. So, I escaped."

"So you never really changed. You just chose to kill the Gangs instead of *lead* one."

"Well.. at first, yeah. And the Rovers and the Nomads welcomed me with open arms. They held no grudge against me. I grew to care for them. For people like you. I figured, if I can't rule with an iron fist, then no one should be able to."

"Sounds selfish."

"So what, Jake? Like you care anyway. But, guess what? I *do* care now. I still care about *you*, if that means anything. A lot. And Tommy."

It felt like she ripped her heart open for Jake. She was not entirely sure why, but she decided to follow that little voice in the back of her mind. Everything was on the table now and the vulnerability was terrifying. This time, it was her own heartbeat that rose uncomfortably. Jake said nothing, just walked towards her. Part of him was still processing what she had said. Truly, he cared for her. *Loved* her even. But the sheer darkness of her past changed things. Trust seemed impossible for her. But then, Eva realized how Jake had felt when she rejected him. And it hurt.

"Well," she stiffened up. "Now you know."

He had stopped halfway down the block and turned his back to her. "Yeah. I do."

Eva walked a few steps past Jake and pointed to a familiar sight. It was the Post where they had taken shelter their first night together. The same place where Gangs would trade goods without fear of being ambushed. This time, The Wanderer had a plan.

"What are we doing here?" The two stepped into the darkness. Rats and Wolves must have come back for their fallen comrades because the people Eva had slaughtered were nowhere to be found. Only dark brown stains remained behind as a warning of The Wanderer's presence.

"We are going to wait." She plopped down on a nearby chair. A plume of dust formed over her and settled on the floors around them. "The Tigers and Serpents trade here more often than the Eastern dens. Serpents will always need weapons. Tigers will always need Bondsmen and Doxies. It is only a matter of time before they come here to do business. That is when we pounce."

"Pounce?" Jake repeated, sitting beside her, still mulling over their exchange on the street.

Eva found some flint and lit a candle on the table between them. "Well, I need information. And one way or another, I am going to get it."

"I already told you the *Tigers* have Tommy." He watched her illuminated face.

"Yes." She pulled out her gun and set it on the armrest. "And I believe you. But I need to know the best way to get Tommy out and whether or not he is still with them. Do they have a secret entrance? Is it going to be guarded? Any additional information that will avoid us having a repeat of our last 'adventure'."

"Fine," Jake crossed his leg at the ankle and laid his axe beside him. Truth was, he was eager to rescue Tommy. Sitting around got under his skin. Crossing Eva was worse. His only hope was that a Gang showed up soon so they could be on their way.

"The Tiger and Serpent compounds are built around structures from the Old Times," she yawned. "A network of tunnels and basement levels span around each one of them. Same as the East. Usually, that is where they keep their prisoners. The cold, dark, and damp basements."

"Do you think it was a prison in the Old Times?" Jake asked.

"I don't think so," she shook her head. "Maybe for the Tigers. But the building in the Serpent's Nest was just a building that we made into living quarters. The lower levels were gutted and rebuilt as prison cells and torture rooms. I spent a lot of time both looking in and out of those cold, damp cells."

Jake stayed silent.

Neither the Tigers nor the Serpents came to the Post that night. Eva and Jake had fallen asleep after a few hours, their hands hanging from the armrests almost touching. Honking from migrating geese startled them both awake the next morning. When they realized that no one had come, they decided to stay another night.

"Let's try one more," Eva suggested as they sat on the back porch. "If no one shows up, then we will just have to go off of my memory."

Jake reluctantly agreed. She left him for an hour that morning and brought back a few rabbits she had caught. To her surprise, Jake had picked up the skill to clean animals during his time at the Western Rover colony. It was something she never took the time to learn properly, so she watched him carefully.

"I'm impressed Jake," she mentioned while cooking their meal.

"Yeah," he laughed. "I know. I *actually* learned something useful."

"I mean *I* wasn't going to say anything," she chuckled. "Other than, 'See what happens when I leave you alone to figure shit out yourself'?"

For the next few hours before nightfall, their tone was lighthearted. Jake was warming back up to Eva, despite what the Nomads had told him. Soon, tension replaced the jovial tones from before. They were, once again, sitting in their chairs, waiting. Everything that Jake had heard of Eva the past few days started eating away at him again. Despite everything, he could not help to care for her. So he told her everything.

"I just can't get over the fact that *you* created the Serpents," he started. "You were part of the people trying to kill us."

She shuffled uncomfortably in her seat. "Yeah. I know Jake. *Trust me.* You have every right to feel the way you do about me. It's just… really difficult to explain to you how survival works in this world. As a child… Especially when you grow up alone in all of this. I witnessed so much death growing up. Perhaps, instead of hating them, I *envied* the Gangs. Their power, their prowess."

Jake was hoping Eva did not notice him frowning in the candlelight. "I guess… but on the other hand, I care about you more than anyone else out here. Besides Tommy, obviously. I know it sounds so stupid, but I really do. I feel stupid when I think about these feelings. I just… I can't imagine a life without you."

She paused, smiled, and sighed.

"Despite everything, I think I feel the same way. We both know how we feel. But, right now, there is too much out there that could end everything. The Gangs *can* and *will* use our feelings against us. You saw how they acted in the Wolf's Den."

"I get that," Jake replied. "And I understand the risks involved. Could we not try to be together?"

She shook her head. Jake bit his tongue. "Not until this is all over. And I'm not just talking about saving Tommy. As soon as I feel that we are safe for a while. Then… maybe we can try."

Footsteps on wood boomed through the house. *Back porch*, Eva mouthed and extinguished her candle. With Jake's arm in one hand and her gun in the other, she pulled him over to the stairwell, opposite the back door. They watched as two armored Gang members stomped into the kitchen. One was carrying a lantern, illuminating guns and ammunition under winter robes. The two in hiding searched for any symbol that could indicate whether they were part of the Tigers.

"Bingo." Eva's voice was barely audible when she pointed to the back of the robe. *Tigers*.

"Thought I saw a light in here," one of the men grunted. "Not sure if we gon' get that shipment tonight. Serpents said somethin' 'bout the 'quality'f servants today'."

"Good that we found those Nomads," the larger of the two said. "If our Chief would just let us raid more towns, we wouldn't need to trade with the Serpents. Last haul had some kids in there though. Tiny fingers for cleaning the guns."

The first one cackled. "'Till you chop 'em off," he added.

"One looks like he ain't never worked a day in his life."

"Tommy," Jake whispered. Eva put a hand on his shoulder.

"On my signal." She turned to him. "You grab the larger one by the arm and use as much weight as you can to get that gun out of his hand. I will take down the little one. Sounds like the big guy knows about Tommy."

"What was that?" The voices in the kitchen grew louder.

"Shit!" Eva said and shoved Jake. "*Go.*"

In an instant, Eva had pinned herself on top of the smaller of the two Tigers. Ripping off a piece of his shirt, she shoved it in his mouth to muffle his screams. She looked over at Jake who somehow managed to knock the larger one to the ground. He was now standing over his victim with a Tiger gun in his hands.

"Who are you people?" the bigger one demanded.

Eva ignored him and adjusted her legs to hold down the smaller man. "We need some information. Now… I'm going to end your friend's miserable life. Then I'm going to make you *wish* you were him. Unless you tell me what I need to know."

"What the shit?" The man went to sit up on his forearms, but Jake kicked him down. He kept glancing over at Eva with a look of uncertainty and fear.

"Tell me everything you know about those Nomads you kidnapped." She pressed a blade to her victim's neck. A small stream of blood dripped down the blade from the tip. The man stiffened and inhaled sharply. "Tell me *everything*, or your friend is dead. *Now*!"

"W-w-what Nomads?" the smaller Tiger stuttered. His partner stared at him in shock.

"I'm not playing around. *One. More. Chance.*"

"You don't have the guts to kill someone else." He hoped she was bluffing.

She wasn't. Eva snarled and raked her blade through the Tiger's jugular. Blood spurted from the wound as she stood up, covered in the red liquid, and took a step back. She wiped her eyes and watched the man scramble to his knees, holding his neck. He gagged and coughed, sputtering everywhere. His fellow Tiger watched in horror as his comrade fell back against a wall. With a few more labored breaths, his body was limp.

Eva squatted next to the man Jake was holding at gunpoint. She grabbed onto his armor and jerked his face to her. "You test me Tiger. I am a very impatient woman. His death was swift, but yours will not be."

With one swift motion, her blade was sheathed and her gun pressed against the man's temple. She ordered him to stand and strip down to his undergarments. Jake tucked the handgun into his pocket and leaned his axe against the wall. Eva tossed him a coil of rope the Tiger had carried, and Jake bound the man's arms and legs tightly to a nearby chair. Eva rifled through the man's pockets, pulling out several knives and loose bullets. She tossed the bullets aside and laid the knives on the table, slow and deliberate. Then, finally, she strolled over to him.

"Shall we begin?" she asked with a maniacal smirk.

"Wh-whutareyougonnadotome?" the Tiger rattled off. "There's another Gang on the way. J-Just you wait."

Her tone sent shivers down Jake's spine. It was completely emotionless. "Oh you'll be *long* dead before then. And we will be well on our way. Now, let's get started. I guess the first question you should ask yourself is 'Who is this woman who stands before me?'."

"I know exactly who you are, demon." He looked Eva up and down.

"Your description is truer than you realize," her melodic tone rang with the chime of the blade she tapped against the table. "So your second mistake is not knowing who you are dealing with. The first was kidnapping one of my friends."

"What are you talking about?" The man's face bled instantly as Eva cut a thick chunk out of his cheek. He howled in pain and she shoved a piece of cloth in his mouth. When he quieted to a pant, she pulled out the gag and repeated her demands.

"Tell me *everything* you know about the Nomads that you and your people kidnapped."

The Tiger paused for too long so Eva sliced at the meat on his chest. This time, he did not scream. He just bit his lip hard enough to draw blood and spit it at Eva's face. She lifted her head just in time for it to splatter across her neck. But she said nothing. Jake watched as she responded by smiling and wagging her finger at the man.

"You are making a huge mistake," she warned. "You have two choices: tell me what I want to know, or face a long and *painful* night."

"Why does it matter? You're just gonna kill me anyway."

"Maybe. But do you want to risk the possibility of leaving here a free man? This is a transaction, not a mercy killing. I am a woman of proposition and reason despite what you've heard."

The man paused again, considering his choices. Eva grew impatient. She knew that every second wasted torturing this Tiger could mean the end for Tommy. Flipping the blade downwards in her palm she buried the blade deep into his thigh, missing his artery. Her victim screamed as she twisted it deeper. Jake leapt to his feet and gagged the man, looking down at Eva.

"Someone is going to hear us," he said frantically. "He isn't telling us anything."

Eva shot a glance at him. "Where is your patience? He looks ready to tell us something right now."

Jake removed the gag, now soaked in saliva, blood, and sweat. The man was breathing heavily, but kept his eyes glued to Eva. Her hand was still firmly grasping the handle of the knife. From the open door, a frigid breeze chilled the tension in the room.

"Ready to talk?" Eva's voice was firm, almost to a yell.

"We took them back to the compound," he blubbered in between gasps. "They were processed and sent to work. P-please don't kill me."

"Tell me about the younger children you took," she ignored him. "The one you said looked like he never had a hard day's work."

"He is working as a food runner, I think." The man was growing more pathetic by the moment. "H-He's still with us. We didn't sell him or anything. I *swear*."

"Easiest way to get to him," she sped him up. "Easiest and safest way for us to get in there."

"Part of the basement was dug out into the tunnels further down. Please. *Please don't kill me*."

The Tiger began to cry. His voice became hoarse from the screaming. Still, Eva pressed for more answers. The look in her eye became more animalistic than Jake had ever witnessed.

"How do we get into the tunnels?"

The man continued to sob. The Wanderer had to twist the knife a little more and repeat her question. Her victim screeched in pain.

"Any-any of the sewer entrances out here will lead there. We marked the way a long time ago. Red "Ts". Follow them. *Please, let me live*. I don't want to die. I don't wanna die. I don't wanna die like this."

"What?" Eva taunted. "You mean die like the low life piece of shit that you are? Oh dear, you are *way* past that point."

Eva turned to Jake and handed him a knife. At first, he had no clue what she wanted him to do. Then, she used her thumb and drew it across her neck. His face felt hot as he took two steps toward the man pleading for his life. Even though a life had already been taken by his hands, it was more of an accident. This guy was not even able to fight back. His hands were bound. He was defenseless.

"Don't think about this scum," Eva ordered. "His people have your *brother*. They murdered Nomads and who knows what else."

"You have more blood on your hands," reminded Jake frantically.

"Doesn't matter," she said shortly. "If you don't do this, he'll go back and tell the others. And then they will *torture and kill* Tommy."

The mere thought of his brother suffering at the hands of the Tigers was infuriating. Something in the back of Jake's mind finally clicked. Everything made sense. Survival was about him and the people he cared about, first and foremost. People who did not possess the strength to protect themselves would be enslaved or killed. The Gangs take what is not theirs, like his brother. He recalled the gruesome scene right below his feet, picturing each victim with Tommy's face.

"Jake," Eva softened her voice. "You have to do this. *These people never change.*"

"I understand." Jake slowly raised the knife above his head and took one last look at the Tiger. Fear twisted the man's face, tears mixing with the blood running down his cheeks. The blade plunged through his eye with a wet crunch, then scraped against the back of his skull. Jake yanked it free, leaving a gaping hole where the eye had been. He stood up, breath catching, stomach twisting as vomit rose in his throat. He stumbled back from the chair, the metallic scent of blood thick in the air. He had to get out.

Silence spread through the home as another winter breeze moved through the room. Then, a soft hand. It was covered in blood, but it slid its fingers to interlock with Jake's, gripping tightly. Eva took a step closer and stood over Jake's shoulder while he stood in the kitchen, completely numb.

"I understand how hard that was." She turned her eyes up to him and then behind her to the other room. "As much as you're struggling right now, I can promise that it never gets easier. But that feeling of emptiness? As cruel as it feels, is part of survival. It makes the act more simple. Embrace that feeling."

"I." Jake paused. "I think I'm finally starting to get how survival works. Your story, though completely terrible, it - well - it makes sense. *Why* you did the things you did."

"Most of what goes on here is a reflex. When you pause, you are cut down. So you cannot hesitate. *That* is what keeps you alive. It doesn't seem like much, but now there are two less men that can hurt your brother."

"And we have some information," he offered.

Eva smiled and released his hand. He did not want to let go.

She was already at the door when he grabbed his axe. Like always, she was right. Tommy was still suffering at the hands of the Tigers and that was their first priority. For once in his life, Jake felt confident that he could protect himself *and* Eva. And it was time to show his true character.

Chapter 10

Eva and Jake, still soaked in blood and haunted by the memory of the Post, stood at the edge of the Old Time sewer tunnels, staring into the darkness below. Similar to those in the West, these tunnels were cramped, humid, and in disrepair. Eva murmured something about them being "completely unsafe." However, her hesitancy came not from the sewers themselves, but what lay on the other side. Even so, she was the first to splash down into the ankle-deep, putrid water. Although no one had used the tunnels as a sewage system in over two hundred years, that did not stop animals from dying and rotting down there.

Jake had snatched the Tiger's lantern before they left, using it to illuminate the T's they were instructed to follow. "How far are the compounds?"

"Not sure." Eva kept one hand on the wall at all times. "Could be a few hours, a few minutes… or a day."

"A *day*?" Jake repeated.

"I don't *exactly* know how complicated this tunnel system is," she snapped. "I never used these when I was in the Gang. If the easiest route collapsed, we have to take a detour. But what if that is impossible to get through? Then we find another way. What if we have to stop and fight? It could take some time. I never make guesses with places I have never been."

"Sorry."

"Stop stepping on my feet. You're going to get water, and whatever nasty shit is in the water, in my boots."

"Sorry."

"And stop apologizing. Talk about something else or shut up."

"Sorry."

Eva's sigh came out like more of a growl. The darkness and uncertainty of the tunnel kept them on edge, wary of a potential trap at every corner. A thick haze hung like a curtain through the darkness. Rotting animal carcasses floated in the ankle-deep sludge, and the smell left the taste of death on their tongues. Lucky for them, the winter air muted some of that pungency. Occasionally, a rat would skitter past their feet, nearly sending them stumbling into the muck. They would laugh nervously and continue on their way. And with each step closer to the compound, their fear grew.

"I hope Tommy is okay," Jake said.

"Me too," Eva admitted. "He's a strong kid. Give him some credit."

He sloshed through the deepening waters. "Oh I do. I just… have seen how ruthless the Gangs are. I can't imagine what I'd do if they hurt him."

"It's so different when you're a servant," she breathed and slid her fingertips across another T on the concrete wall. "I think I was thirteen when I realized how many times I begged for death. Once for every time they beat me unconscious. For every time they would take me into their rooms to whip me or cut me or… some other form of torture. I didn't scream. I never cried. Only begged for them to end my life."

Jake opened his mouth to say something when Eva continued.

"One day, I made the decision that I wasn't going to die. I couldn't let them have the satisfaction. Living and enduring was a sign of my strength. Plus, I needed revenge. Maybe that was most important to me. But that was when I started training. When I took over the Serpents, I rose to a level I couldn't control. Too much too fast. Shit, even when I left the compound in the middle of the night so I wouldn't be killed by my own men. Each time… I knew I was going to survive after it was all said and done."

"Why the change of heart? Why change from a ruthless killer with so much power?"

"Something clicked. I didn't exactly have a choice, but… I wanted to live. Somehow, one day, I knew I was put on this earth for… well… a purpose."

"And that was?"

"I think… it was… to help people. Like you said a while ago. To find and rescue you and your brother. That, for some reason or another - by deity or fate - is my purpose right now. And honestly, I didn't realize it until recently."

Jake grinned sheepishly and then pointed to another T on the wall. This marking had an arrow pointing upwards. Next to the arrow was a ladder and, at the top, a latch to the surface. They looked at each other as Jake extinguished the lantern. Neither of them knew how long they had been down there, or where the door would open. They were shaky. Ghosts of the previous infiltration still lingered and tainted their mind.

"I really don't want to do this again," Eva breathed as she reached up to the latch with her handgun over her head. "But it's for Tommy."

Jake was right on her heels as she pushed the door upwards and off to the side. Their eyes adjusted to the flickering light of torches lining a stone hallway. Cell doors, haphazardly built with barbed wire wrapped around iron bars, stood between each torch. Moans and pained grunts echoed from the narrow, damp rooms. Some called out for food or water. Others pleaded for an end to their suffering.

But it all stopped when the prisoners heard the latch screech open. A few of them popped their heads through their cell door towards Eva. Jake was still climbing the ladder.

"What do you see?" he whispered up to her.

"Prisoners," she called. "We must be in the Tiger's prison. No sign of Tommy."

The tortured souls must have thought Eva was one of their captors. As she got to her feet and traded her gun for her blades, the sobbing from within lowered to whimpers and the prisoners' faces disappeared. Jake poked his head out from the sewer and took in a deep breath of fresh air. It still smelled of death, but there was a cold breeze coming through the corridor. The ominous glow of the lanterns greeted him.

The two infiltrators started down the hallway, peering into each cell as they passed. The inhabitants scattered to the corners, shaking and cowering like animals. One after another, they shrank from Jake and Eva's gaze. Smells of human waste, infected wounds, and rotting food caused their stomach to lurch. Jake pulled up his shirt to cover his face, gagging against the smell.

But there was one who did not shy away from them. The last prisoner, an old woman. She sat in complete tranquility, mousey hair in wired strands pointing in all directions. It covered most of her leathery face, but one pale eye shimmered through. She grinned, revealing five large teeth between gaping emptiness.

She stared blankly at the space between them. "I can tell by your footsteps that you are not a Tiger." Eva looked back down the hall and noticed the outlines of faces now looking at her and Jake. Whispers amongst themselves about being saved as they tried to grab The Wanderer's attention.

"Don't mind them," the woman said loudly. "They do not realize that you cannot save us all. Such is the way of survival. But I am sure you did not come here seeking your own deaths."

"No." Eva crouched in front of her. "We are looking for the boy that brings you food. He was taken here fairly recently. Within the last few days. Do you know him?"

"Ah," she nodded her head slowly. "He has been sweet to us. Quiet, though. I have not heard him speak a word since he arrived."

"Do you know when he'll be back?" Jake dropped to his knees. "We are going to take him home."

Voices started calling from the other cells. "What about us?"

"Save us too."

"I've been here for *years*. He has only been here for days."

A hard lump formed in Jake's throat that he could not swallow. The pain and the desperation that shook their voices made him sick. Guilt draped over him like a heavy shroud. Eva looked over at him and shook her head. Countless times before, she had told him how difficult it was to survive in this world. *You cannot save everyone*. A simple fact that tore his heart wide open. His mother, before she was murdered, had always taught him to care for others, especially those who needed it most. The strong exist to protect the weak.

But Eva had always preached that the strong exist because they overcame their weaknesses. There was no place for those who cannot fend for themselves. Still, he couldn't take his eyes off of the gaunt figures in the cells, starving to death in cramped rooms that reeked of waste, left alone in their misery. That was not a way to die. But his mind circled back to Eva's words. Over and over, the word 'survival' ate at his most primal instincts.

"Do not mind them." The old woman lifted her willowy hand. She could sense his urge to help these people. "It is a natural thing to want to live. We all seek it. Life and freedom. However, we were bound to be caught all those years ago. We are lucky they still remember to feed us. And for that much, I am grateful. Please, young man, do not burden yourself with thoughts of us. This is the way of the world. Go and save your brother. Deep in my bones, I feel like that child is destined to do great things."

Eva's tone was soothing. "Can you tell me when he will return?"

"Soon," she replied. "Yes. It will be midday soon. But be wary, my child. Tigers always accompany him. Prepare for a fight."

"Thank you deeply," said Eva. "I'm sorry that we cannot save you all."

Jake clenched his fists and shut his eyes. "No. You *both* are right. We don't have any keys. So, the only way to save everyone here is to destroy every Tiger in the compound. It would be impossible."

"This man speaks the truth," the elderly woman nodded. "True, it is a difficult decision. I can feel that your spirit is fresh to this world. But you are beginning to realize."

Eva thanked the woman once again and rose to her feet. She said nothing, but guilt sat heavy in her chest. If she only had the keys, she could open the cells and let them escape through the sewers. She would leave these people a fate she did not have the strength to stop… and it haunted her.

She and Jake silently slipped into a small cutaway in the wall near the stairs. Tommy would arrive at the cellar with both food at any moment. They had to remain in the darkness until he returned.

"I understand how hard it is." Eva's whisper cracked under the heaviness of her emotions. "I've been on both sides."

Jake never considered how The Wanderer grappled with the weight of her past. Hard to imagine that she was once slaughtering these defenseless servants for sport. And years later, she defended them with her life. Maybe, in her eyes, her life meant so little that spending it to save others was the only thing that gave it worth.

His silence made her stir. "You know, when I was the Mistress of the Serpents, I was colder than I am now, believe it or not. I guess I have always been heartless to some extent." She let out a nervous laugh.

"No Eva." Jake touched her hand. She pulled away. "It takes a lot of courage to do what you do. And yeah, your past was pretty shitty. But you changed."

Jake nearly stopped in mid-sentence. His voice sounded like Yidi's for a moment. Back in the Nomad camp, when the Elder was trying to explain The Wanderer's past, he had spoken the same words. The Nomad's wisdom had been correct. Eva *had* changed.

"Thanks Jake," she said. "Just, please, don't beat yourself up about this. We're here for Tommy. We can't free an entire compound with two people."

"Hey. I get it. It's hard to leave anyone behind, especially when you know what will happen to them."

"I know I've said this before. This doesn't ever get easy. You just learn to ignore those emotions. Sad? Yeah. But that's the only advice I have." One of her blades was resting on her thigh, loosely grasped by her fingertips.

Jake nodded and leaned back against the cold stone wall, causing his whole body to shiver. Eva jabbed her blade into the soft moss between the cracks at her feet with her hooded silhouette hunched over it, like she was ready to pounce. A leak in the roof dripped down onto her hood, rolled off the edge, and saturated the ground. She did not move a muscle. All of a sudden, the moaning from the corridor had fallen silent once again.

Someone was coming.

Footsteps descended the concrete steps. Two men and a small boy passed Eva and Jake's field of view. The boy was dirty and clothed in rags. In his arms was a large pot of sloshing liquid and a stack of bowls that were nearly toppling over. One of his escorts carried a loaf of dry bread. The other had both hands on his rifle—one on the barrel, the other on the handle. He took the gun and slammed it across the bars of the cells, laughing at the screams of agony coming from inside. Eva pulled her blade from the soft earth noiselessly. Remaining crouched, she slid one foot back, ready to sprint towards them.

"Time'a wake up if ye ain't dead yet," said the man with the gun. He was burly, with a beard of red and gray. Again he banged on the cells and howls of pain filled the air. "Time'a eat."

"Feed 'em." Jake saw his brother being shoved to his knees by the other Tiger, almost dropping the food. The bowls scattered on the ground. *"Pick them up, or there will be a good lashing for you later."*

He almost burst out of the shadows as his chest burned with rage. Gritting his teeth hard, Jake watched his brother being tripped, then smacked over the head for dropping the bowls. He stood up and wiped the tears from his face with his sleeve. Although he was hurt, Tommy nodded to the Tiger and smiled warmly to each of the prisoners as he passed them a bowl of food. The two Gang members went back to sit on the landing to watch the boy, taunting him every few minutes. For the most part, Tommy was able to ignore them. Until they became impatient.

"Hurry up!" the man with the bread commanded as he flung a chunk of bread onto the moist floor of each stall.

Tommy must not have served the food fast enough for the Tigers. The moment he handed the last bowl of soup to the old woman, a guard stormed over, kicked the pot from his hands, and seized a fistful of his wavy hair. An ear shattering crash rang through the corridor as the man forced the boy's face towards him and cracked him hard in the ribs.

By the time Jake had said *"That's enough,"* Eva was already upon them. She had been watching over his shoulder the entire time, clenching the hilt of her blade until her knuckles went white. When the Tiger had kicked the pan out of Tommy's hands, she pounced. She knew what the Tiger was going to do next and scolded herself for not attacking sooner.

Tommy was doubled over in a heap, gasping for air between cries of pain. The Wanderer was standing over a corpse. A jolt of alarm hit her and Jake simultaneously. They made one miscalculation. The other Tiger had a gun. The second mistake came from his reaction to Eva's swiftness and deadly accuracy.

He ran.

An alarm had been tripped.

The floor seemed to sway underneath Jake as the sound of guns being loaded grew louder and closer. Eva began to panic. She tossed her sword back in its sheath and rushed over to Tommy, skidding to her knees. His dirty face, stained with rivers of tears, turned to her.

"Everything is going to be okay," she said. "Jake and I are here. You're safe now."

Jake ran to his brother's side, dropped his weapon, and lifted the boy into his arms. Tommy buried his head in Jake's shoulder, still breathing heavily but starting to fall into unconscious exhaustion. The Wanderer spun on her heels to face the onslaught of enemies heading for them. Her gun was loaded and pointed at the stairway. Vision was narrowing and the only sound was the rush of blood in her ears.

"Go! Jake," she demanded.

"But Eva," he called. "You can't take them all. There are -"

"Too many." She tilted her head back to him. "I know. But I can hold them off until you make your way down the ladder. I will be right behind you."

"Promise?" Jake called to her just as he pulled the latch to the sewer below. She said nothing more to him. He bit his lip and glanced up at her one more time.

"Prisoners of the Tigers," she boomed. "Back against the far wall of your cell. No innocent blood will be spilled by my hands."

Truthfully, Eva was more terrified than she could ever remember. Her legs felt like they were losing stability, but her voice remained strong. She gripped her gun with both hands to keep it from shaking as Tigers began pouring into the room. *Bang.* One down. *Bang Bang.* Two dead. *Must be lethal shots. I cannot miss. Please do not let me miss.*

Shit! I missed.

A bullet whizzed past the face of one enemy and hit the wall at his back. There was a deafening echo in the passageway. Eva knew that Jake had at least gone two thirds of the way down the ladder if he was hurrying. She needed more time, but they were gaining on her fast. The man she missed shot back and missed. Others stepped over the bodies of their comrades, fumbling to get to her.

One of them got close enough to recognize her. "It's The Wanderer," he shouted. "Get her!"

She took two steps back. A few more rounds. They did not all have firearms, thankfully. One was bolting right at Eva. Five more steps backwards. Her heel hit something. Turn to the exit for one second. Even if Jake was yelling up to her to say it was safe, she could not hear him. The Tigers were too close. They were starting to surround her. Ten feet, maybe, between them and their prey. Screw it.

Eva threw her handgun back into its holster and grabbed the lever on the trapdoor, swinging it closed while jumping into the darkness below. Gunshots still rang out through the prison as reinforcements entered the corridor above.

"They're coming," she yelped out to Jake and Tommy as she crumpled to the ground. An excruciating pain shot up her leg from the ankle. She had almost cleared the ladder, but her foot had caught the final rung, twisting it at an uncomfortable angle before she landed on the ground. She screamed. The latch above them exploded open and Eva crawled away just before a hail of bullets showered them. Jake almost dropped his brother to grab her. But she managed to scramble to her feet and limp away as fast as she could.

"I'll be okay," she breathed as they sprinted through the tunnels. "Shit. Shit. Shit. They're right behind us."

"Where do we go?" Jake heaved his brother back up to his arms.

"Back to the Rover colony," she winced. "We will gain some ground if we hurry. They'll turn around when they lose our trail. Let's make sure they do."

"It's a two day journey."

"I know. But we can't stop. We have to keep moving. We have to survive this."

"We will follow you anywhere Eva. No matter what happens."

"Keep going. I'm right behind you."

With every other foot drop, Eva flinched in pain. Her ankle was starting to swell, but the laces on her boots were tied tight enough to ease the pain somewhat. Jake wanted to act as a crutch, but with Tommy bundled in his arms, he was useless to her. Light from the Tigers' torches became distant, but bright enough for the three to make out the "Ts" on the concrete walls. If they made it out of the sewers, they could slow their pace.

Jake tried reassuring Eva and Tommy. "We can do this. Almost there."

She tripped. Yelling in anger and agony as Jake turned to go back for her. The sound of footsteps was getting louder. With the remaining strength he had in one arm, he lifted her back to her feet, carrying his brother over his other shoulder. He was sweating profusely. Turning to run the last few hundred yards, he called back to her again.

She reassured and pointed ahead of them. "Look! The way out."

They reached the bottom of the ladder and the cool breeze drifted downwards from the opening. It was a welcoming sight. Eva looked at Jake who was struggling to carry the limp body of his brother. She could tell Tommy was still breathing. His chest rose and fell softly. Jake turned back and saw how much pain she was in. All of the color had drained from her face and she was covered in a layer of sweat. Breathing was becoming more difficult by the moment. Neither of them were able to determine the extent and severity of her injuries.

"Go Eva," he motioned his head upwards.

"*No*." She used the ladder for support on her good side and winced in pain. "No. You have no weapon. You have Tommy. Get up there."

"*You* are wounded," he called over the rising volume of voices. "Hurry. Go first."

"I am not *asking* you Jake," she spat. "Get your ass up there."

He let out a roar of frustration and started up towards the surface. She looked up at him for a moment and wrapped her other arm around a rung. She clung to it with most of her weight. Her swollen ankle was shaking, the rest of her body ached, and left arm began to sting. Dreams of torture from long ago bubbled to the surface and the Hooded Figure appeared on the other side of the ladder. But this time, he was more transparent than before.

Jake finally surfaced carrying his brother who he laid against a tree before diving back for Eva. He leaned down and grabbed her shoulder, forcing her to climb. The dreams and images faded. At first, she thought Jake was part of her nightmare. Light beams shone from behind his head like a crown. He looked similar to the deities that she had seen in the city.

His voice echoed through her daze. "Come on. They're gaining on us."

Once again, she snapped back into her own body. It was a battle, but Eva forced herself up that ladder with one good leg and one good arm. Jake, who was pouring sweat, pushed the door to the sewers shut. The sound of distant voices silenced and the bright and silent sunlight greeted them.

"We cannot stay here," Eva gasped.

Jake agreed and lifted Tommy back into his arms. When Eva had made it to the surface, his eyes were instantly drawn to a hole in her jacket. For the time being, he chose not to mention the bullet wound in her arm. He was focused on getting her and Tommy back to the Rover colony.

But The Wanderer followed Jake's gaze and noticed the wound herself. The stinging pain was nothing compared to the swelling of her ankle. She tore a piece of fabric from Tommy's tunic and wrapped it around her wound.

Luckily, the Tigers lost their trail as they escaped the tunnels. Only a few hours, however, separated them from a brigade of Gang members. The Tigers would be hunting. For now, at least, Eva's home would keep them safe.

But she was losing more energy with each labored step. Her panting had progressed to gasping. By the time they had made it to the Post a couple hours later, her vision was hazy and her muscles were beginning to shut down. Fortunately, she had only been grazed by the bullet that struck her arm. But her ankle was another story. Jake choked back tears, as he could only watch her struggle back to the town. He was physically useless as long as Tommy remained unconscious.

Come on Tommy, he pleaded to himself. *You were just punched in the chest. There is no way you are still knocked out of breath. Eva is dying right in front of me and I can't do anything because you are too busy sleeping.*

He hated himself for the way he was thinking, but couldn't keep the thoughts from pervading his mind. The only thing he was able to do was offer a shoulder to Eva. When she fell to her knees, he was stern, almost rude to her. A few times, she begged him to leave her. He refused.

He forced her hands on his arm and pulled her up again. "We have to survive. *All* of us. Get up. You aren't weak."

"I just do not know how much more I have -" she started, "how much more I have in me. I can rest and catch up."

"No. You have more in you than anyone." He jerked her back to the road as the homes from the Old Times faded from the horizon. "We can do this together. Eva, you make me strong. Let me make you strong this time."

Eva licked her dry, cracked lips and nodded. Jake would never let her lie down and wait for death. Normally, she would not have given up so easily, but she was in a debilitating stupor and losing stamina. The pain was causing her to become increasingly disoriented.

Following Tommy and Jake was what kept her going into the night. *They are my purpose,* she repeated. And suddenly, every step seemed further from death. The very pain itself seemed to leave her body. Hope filled the void. Jake's words floated down like a harness that lifted her further. *Let me make you strong this time.*

They had reached the outskirts of the colony when Jake stopped hearing Eva's gasping. Rovers had seen them coming a mile away and flocked to him when he called out for aid. Handing Tommy to a couple of men, he sprinted over to a group surrounding something. *Eva.*

Her face was relaxed, almost expressionless. Her eyes were closed. His heart stopped until he saw the faint movement of her stomach rising and falling. A small trickle of blood was pooling underneath her arm and her ankle was facing out awkwardly. Expressions of disgust were whispered under hushed tones. Some of the Rovers were accusing Jake for Eva's current state.

"I don't give a *shit* if you think this was my fault or not." He jabbed his finger towards the shacks. The muffled gossip ceased. "Help. Her. *Now*. She needs to live. I promised she would. I - I - I swore to her."

The healer pushed through the crowd. She knelt down and looked at Eva's injuries. "Calm down. She isn't going to die. She just overextended herself… again… for *you*."

Elation finally overtook him. Exhaustion followed. Blackness encompassed his view of the Rovers as they carried Eva's limp and weary body. He expected to feel the hard, uninviting ground meeting his back, but it never came. The Rovers had caught him.

They were carrying him to the Healer's home. They were giving him a second chance.

Chapter 11

Jake was the first to awaken in the care of the Healer. He had suffered a few minor injuries like scratches, bruises, and general fatigue. It was a struggle for him to even lift his head to look around the room. He spotted Tommy laying in a bed at one corner, near the fireplace. They had removed his shirt and wrapped his chest with white linen. No one was tending to him, so Jake figured that his brother was just resting. Eva, however, was nowhere to be found. Jake swiveled his head back and forth, searching for any sign of her. His body went numb when his eyes locked onto her gun and blades near the door.

As he attempted to rise to his elbows, the Healer pushed him back onto the bed. She had just entered the room when she noticed him trying to sit up. Dropping a pile of blankets, she hurried over to him and forced him to lie down. Jake hesitantly agreed, huffing to himself.

"Where is Eva?" he demanded. "Please tell me she is alright."

The Healer was silent. She picked up a jug of water and handed it to him, then picked the blankets up off the floor. Because she was usually blunt, no matter what, her silence made him sick. After clearing her throat a few times, she answered him, but not with the answer he was hoping for.

"I'm not sure. Ankle's messed up pretty bad. And her arm must have got infected when you all were trudging through sewage. She broke her fever yesterday but hasn't opened her eyes in days. None of you have. It could be worse, though. She's going to make it. Just has -"

Jake took a drink of water and nearly spit it out. "Hold on. I have been sleeping for *days*?"

"You all have." The Healer pointed to Tommy. "And the Tigers have been here looking for you. We've all been forced to stay inside. They were tearing people from their homes and interrogating them at one point. Luckily, they haven't reached this home yet. Only in the middle of the night are we able to pass around food."

His eyes widened. "They followed us? They're still here?" he repeated.

"Yes. Which is another reason Eva is not faring well either. I have to wait until after dark to get anything I need. Lucky for the children, and for you, they haven't started killing anyone… yet."

Jake glanced at the front door. He could make out the faint sound of voices on the other side. Tommy stirred in the corner. The room itself was warmed from hearth fire, but Jake pulled a blanket towards his chin. As the Healer stepped into the next room, he posed one more question.

"When can I see Eva?" Again, her answer was not what he was expecting.

"I don't think that will be a good idea for a while," she murmured. "Just rest. My Apprentice and I will do everything we can keep her comfortable. But you need to rest and tend to the little one when he wakes."

Jake nodded and turned his back to her before she disappeared into the other room. Straining to listen to the hushed voices of the Healer and her apprentice, he tilted his head back towards the doorway. Eva was definitely in that room. Part of him wanted to jump out of bed to be by her side, but any motion below his neck was almost impossible. He was still extremely tired. And right outside the front door was a group of Tigers bearing more weapons than all the Rovers had combined. And the only one who would even stand a chance at slashing their numbers had been in a coma for days. Exhaustion hit like a wave and suddenly, his worry melted into the soft bed as he drifted back into sleep.

***

A full day passed before Jake opened his eyes again. This time, most of his strength had returned. The Healer's Apprentice allowed him to sit up and walk around. The fire near Tommy had been out for some time. Now, the frigid air and rustling of dead leaves drifted under the space between the front door and the ground. Jake shivered and pulled another blanket over his legs. He asked again how Eva was. The Apprentice smiled softly but avoided his gaze.

"She's in a lot of pain," she replied. "Good news, though. The infection has almost cleared up… but… I can't even comprehend how she managed to limp so far with an injury *that* bad. The Healer was confident that we were able to set it right and mend properly."

"Well, she is an *amazing* woman," Jake said with a smile. "To me… well… When I first met her, I really believed that she was invincible, possibly immortal. Stupid, right?"

The Apprentice was gathering a few medicine bottles from a box near where Tommy lay. She gave Jake a glass of water and he chugged it down. "No. We *all* believe those types of things from time to time. When you're exceptionally good at something, people start to see you as something unreal—almost mythic. If I wasn't a healer, I would believe the same."

"When can I see her again?"

"Speak to the Healer. Eva is improving, but it is not for me to say. If she can pull through and wake up, maybe then you can see her."

"And if she doesn't wake up? Please. I *need* to see her. Not as a corpse."

The Apprentice looked at him with pity. She paused, nodded, and left the room. The Healer returned in her place. First, the middle-aged woman tended to Tommy who looked up at her and nodded in thanks. She laid a bowl of soup near him and patted him on the head. He had heard his brother talking and slowly turned with his food in hand and waved at him.

"How are you doing buddy?"

Tommy nodded in contentment with a mouthful of food.

The Healer moved in between the table and pulled a chair next to Jake's bed. She plopped down, crossed her legs, and sat her chin on her interwoven fingers.

"If I let you see her," she started, "Just this *once*. Then you must swear not to touch her. I don't want to hear about needing to see her until she gets better. You may have a virus or bacteria that she could contract."

Jake was speechless. Originally, he believed that the Healer was refusing to let him see Eva because he was still recovering. The thought of him carrying something that could *kill* her had not crossed his mind. He felt selfish - battling between the permission to see her, but not wanting to risk her life further.

"I will just tend to my brother for the time being," he sighed. "To me, Eva's health is more important than my need to see her."

"Assume that nothing has changed with her unless I say otherwise," she agreed. "Like my Apprentice mentioned, Eva's temperature has dropped to normal. But she is still in a significant amount of pain due to the infection, mostly. Her leg will heal in time."

"And the Tigers?" Jake hung his legs off the side of the bed. "Are they gone?"

She glanced at the door. "Most have returned to their compound," she said. "A few remain here and I fear they are the most vicious."

"How much longer do you think they will be here?"

"Difficult to say. I'm not sure. Just stay inside and away from the door. Hope that they do not start breaking it down. But they still haven't interrogated us yet."

Jake thanked the Healer as she vanished into the other room. He gingerly let his bare feet drop to the icy, stone floor. A chill crawled up his legs and made him shudder. He looked at the doorway into Eva's room, just once, and pondered going in to see her. Instead, he pulled one of the blankets around his shoulders and brought another over to his brother. Tommy had been focused on his meal until Jake sat with him.

"You doing okay?" he asked.

Tommy nodded but tapped his chest and winced.

"Yeah," Jake wrapped the blanket around him tightly and stared at the glowing coals in the fireplace. "I am *so sorry* I let this happen to you."

Tommy sat up and shook his head aggressively. He wore his usual innocent smile and patted his brother on the arm. Jake half-smiled. The Healer's Apprentice brought him a bowl of soup and some soft bread. His stomach growled loudly as he slurped it up. Piping hot liquid burned his mouth and throat, but he was so hungry that he hardly noticed. His brother giggled as a spoonful of soup dripped onto Jake's chest.

"What?" he laughed. "I'm starving." It was nice to see his brother smile.

All of a sudden, someone pounded on the front door. It was a heavy bang, a sound no fist could make. The Healer rushed in and motioned for the McAvoy boys to hide in a small closet behind a curtain. Tommy was the first to jump to his feet, grabbed the dishes they had been eating from, and ducked behind the drapes. Jake lumbered to his feet, nearly tripping over his blanket, and sprinted into the closet just as the door burst open. The Healer narrowly had enough time to unlatch it and dodge out of the way to avoid being hit by the swinging sheet of steel.

"We're checking houses now," said a brawny woman. Her voice was low and grating. "And it's your turn. You should feel lucky that we aren't taking any of *you* back with us... just the three we're looking for."

"Who are you looking for?" The Healer stepped out from behind the door. Her face was expressionless. "Perhaps I could help you."

Jake could see them through the crack between the curtains. A cold fog covered the view to the street along with a light snow, but the dark shadows of Tigers moved about. They were all carrying guns. From a distance, he could hear other doors in the colony being busted open. The screams of terrified children seemed to be cloaked by the thick haze. His stomach churned when he caught sight of Eva's blades out in the open. The Healer, too, had spotted them and leaned against the wall in an attempt to hide them. Thankfully, the Tiger paid no attention. Jake wondered if they had hidden Eva as well.

"Two people came this way," she stated, "Carrying a third. A man and a woman. The one they were carrying was a servant of ours. Seen 'em? Young-ish. One was limping. Looked pretty bad. Kinda hope she's dead by now."

Rage burned white hot inside Jake. His vision turned red and his breathing stiffened as the woman let out an evil cackle. It took every ounce of energy not to explode into the room and beat her senseless. Tommy noticed his brother's chest puff out and wrapped his arms around his torso.

"My men and I are *not* leaving until we find them," she announced. "We're checking *every* house."

The Healer bowed helplessly. The Tiger scoffed and flipped a table onto its side with a crash as she walked through the room. She was carrying an assault rifle strapped over her shoulder. Her pants boasted pockets overflowing with various blades and ammunition. Jake and Tommy backed against the wall as she walked over to the closet and stopped. Both brothers covered their faces to still their breathing as her gun poked toward them. The thin barrel was nearly touching Tommy's nose when she yanked it out impatiently. She started knocking over things in the room in anger. Various bottles of homemade medicines shattered on the floor and pooled at her feet. The Healer winced with each crash. It had taken years to gather the ingredients to make those tinctures. The Tiger spun around at the Rover, smiled with her hand on another bottle, and pushed it onto the floor.

"Too bad your shelf here is so unstable." She made a fake frown then laughed. The Healer bit her lip and stared at the floor. "And you're *sure* you don't know where they are?"

"No ma'am," the Healer repeated, now red in the face.

"Haven't checked this other room."

The Tiger hurried over to the adjacent room. Jake and Tommy let out a sigh in unison, but now they could not see the Healer, the Gang member, or the Apprentice. Jake went into a panic. While he knew that the Healer would have hid Eva, he still did not know whether the woman with the gun would give up on her prey so easily. When the Tiger entered the adjoining room, it was empty, but she spoke so loudly, the brothers immediately thought that Eva had been discovered.

"What is this in here?" she yelled.

The Healer's response was inaudible.

"Repeat that. I can't hear you, *scum*!"

Again, only a murmured response.

"Don't lie to me. I *know* this place is watched by The Wanderer. That's how you got these guns. You and your people are dirt. You are shit. You are *nothing*. And you had your chance. Now, I am going to have my men search *every single home* for what is rightfully ours."

With four heavy footsteps, the Tiger was out the door. She barked a command to her troop, and they began kicking in the doors of every home they had missed. Screams of fright echoed through the fog as the woman disappeared into it—carrying two more guns than she'd arrived with. The Healer quickly shut the door behind her, locking it tightly.

"It is safe to come out," she breathed and wiped a few beads of sweat from her brow. "All of you. She won't be back."

"How can you be so sure?" Jake stepped out from behind the curtain.

"When she saw those guns," she shifted her weight. "She knew they belonged to the Gangs. I thought she was going to kill me. But she just took them and left… and I hope she will do the same with the other Rovers. I grow tired of the needless bloodshed."

Everyone in the room jumped as a gunshot rang through the colony. A woman wailed as a second shot went off. Then a long, eerie silence. The Healer shoved Jake aside and rushed over to a small slit in her wall, scouring for the source of the noise. She whispered "oh no" and stepped back from the peephole. She shook her head, eyes filling with tears.

Her voice was shaky. "Fate save us… They just murdered a young couple and are hanging their bodies in a tree. Somehow, I just knew we weren't getting out of this unscathed."

She stepped aside so Jake could peer through the crack. Through the dense fog, he saw most of the Tigers leaving for their compound in the north. A handful of them were surrounding a large tree near the center of town by the well. His heart dropped when they stepped away to join their comrades. Two bodies swayed in the tree near the colony well. Though difficult to make out, it appeared the Gang had hung a sign from each of the Rovers' necks. What they wrote, he couldn't read from afar. Before he turned to speak, he noticed that Tommy had also seen the gruesome display. In the past, he would have scolded him for looking, but censoring this life was hopeless. Innocence had become a figment of his imagination.

The Apprentice rushed into the room. "Eva is awake."

Jake nearly knocked the Healer to the ground in his haste. *The gunshots must have woken her up.* Eva had opened her eyes. As he entered the room, he found her lying on a table with a thin mattress on top of it. Her body was drenched in sweat and her wounds were wrapped and treated with various salves and herbs. The Apprentice had already helped her drink some water for the first time in days. Her first word was so faint.

"Jake," she whimpered.

Neither Jake nor Eva could hold back the tears any longer. He took three long strides toward her and scooped her up in his arms. She cried in pain as he bumped her arm, but when he went to apologize, she put her hand on his cheek and kissed him. Tommy giggled. The Healer and her Apprentice exchanged a look and shook their heads. After a moment, the lovers pulled away.

"I thought I had lost you," Jake admitted as he brushed her hair between his fingers. A wave of relief spread through his body. "There were moments I thought you would just stop and let them take you. I was so scared."

"You're not going to get rid of me that easily Jake McAvoy," she teased. "I didn't want to die without saying anything. So… Jake… I can't imagine myself without you. It sounds stupid but, while I was asleep, I fought with many of my past crimes. But each time it felt hopeless, I saw a beacon of light. It spoke in your voice, pulling me back from the darkness. I may have chosen death if not for that voice, begging me to keep breathing."

"So my annoying voice kept you alive," he laughed and wiped a tear from her cheek.

"Pretty much," she smiled and hugged him tightly. "I can't get you to leave me alone and let me die."

"Is this how they always act?" The Healer asked Tommy. He nodded and rolled his eyes.

The two women left Jake, Eva, and Tommy alone in the room to clean up the mess the Tigers had left behind. The younger McAvoy joined his brother at Eva's bedside. From outside the shack, they could hear the Rovers filing out of their homes, sobbing loudly near the center of town. Eva tried to sit straight up but her fatigued body slumped her back against the cushions. She sighed in frustration and turned to Jake.

"What happened out there?" she demanded. "I heard gunshots."

He told her everything the Healer had told him - the Tigers following them back to the Rover colony but most leaving after a few days. The first time he woke up and heard the interrogations outside. And the Tigress leader busting through the door, taking the guns, and instructing her men to pillage the town. Finally, he told Eva about the 'examples' they had left hanging in the tree.

Anger and disgust caused Eva's stomach to churn. She blamed herself. After all, she was responsible for killing the Gang members that trespassed into town. Taking their guns, that was her fault too. She should have just escaped to the city with Jake and Tommy rather than risking the lives of the Rovers further. It was only a matter of time before an enemy had discovered them. If they decided not to kill everyone in the town, setting an example was what the Gangs did best. The fear they instilled in the Rovers would be enough to make them wary of ever touching a firearm again. Or fighting back.

This is all my fault.

"Are they gone?" The Wanderer asked loudly enough for the Healer to return. "I need to see what they did to those people,"

"Yes," the Healer said.

Eva laboriously sat up in her bed. The Healer tried to refuse, but knew that there was no use arguing with The Wanderer. Even Jake tried to persuade her to rest. She ignored him and grabbed a Y-shaped crutch at the edge of the table. The Apprentice was on her way back in the room with the Healer by the time Eva had limped right past them to the front door. Jake and Tommy followed her.

"That girl is unbelievably stubborn," Jake heard the Healer say as she was sweeping broken glass. "Not worth my energy to fight with her."

Eva stepped out into the fog and light drizzle. The crutch sunk into the muddy ground, but she persisted. Her body was so fatigued that each motion made her breathless. Still, the Rovers awaited her, forming a semicircle around the tree. The children had been escorted inside their homes as the teens, adults, and elders looked up at the horrific sight. Eva and the McAvoy brothers made it around to read the signs that the Tigers had strung from their victims' necks. Each message was written in blood.

Jake and Tommy's jaws dropped. Eva bore a pained look on her face.

We will find you Wanderer, read one. *Remember your place*, the other.

"We cannot continue to let The Wanderer and her friends stay here," a Rover called out from the crowd. Eva's heart began to race. "They will be the death of us all. We can't take it anymore. Ever since she came here, there has been nothing but death and fear. This is the last straw."

"But she's protected this town for years," another argued. "She scavenged for supplies and food when we had nothing. She saved us."

"She expects us to give her an unfair share of our crops," a woman's voice mentioned. "We give her whatever she asks for, but she spends more time out there than with the town. She doesn't contribute *anything* but death."

"Yeah! There is no protection from the Gangs, like she says. They keep coming back! She protects us only from herself. All of the trouble we have is *because* of her."

Eva tried to make herself seem smaller, but the barrage of insults continued to be hurled her way.

"She does nothing for *us*. It is all for her own greed."

"But she gave us weapons."

"Only to be taken from our dead hands. She knew that the Gangs would be back for them one day. She *built* the Serpents. Don't you think she knows how ruthless they are? They're just like *her*. They always come back. Look what the Tigers did to Tim and Lyla! This is not what we deserve. It is what *she* deserves."

"We're safer without her. The Gangs will stop massacring us if we stop killing them and tell them that The Wanderer no longer protects us…"

"Yeah! Before she showed up begging for mercy, they only took what we sacrificed. We could offer more crops in exchange for our lives. When *she* started killing 'em, they started killing more of us."

"*Stop*!"

The crowd turned at the voice who silenced the crowd.

It was Tommy.

Jake could hardly remember what his brother's voice sounded like, if he had ever even heard it at all. Eva was so shocked she tripped backwards against the tree. No one had heard Tommy speak before. But now, he finally had something worth saying.

"I don't know what happened before my brother and I got here," he yelled and clenched his fists tightly. "But Eva is a *good* person. You are all selfish. Y-you don't even help her fight against the Gangs. But at least Eva tries to keep you safe. She saved me from the Tigers when she didn't have to. And I am sure she's saved you before, too. No one can save everyone."

The entire town fell silent. No sounds came from chirping birds or the rustling of leaves. There was only the pitter patter of raindrops falling on the grass and cobblestone at their feet. Some of the Rovers looked around. Others glared at Eva. Tommy stuck out his chest until Eva put a hand on his shoulder. He turned to her to find tears in her eyes.

"No Tommy," she choked. "They're right. I am nothing but a danger to these people. I have brought them into my sick game of survival by slaughter. These people have paid dearly for my sins for all these years…"

"You're *wrong* Eva." Tommy hugged her waist. "You're not a bad person. You're good."

Her voice cracked. "Maybe it's both. My title suits me better than I realized. *The Wanderer*. That is my place. To wander."

"Then go already." An Elder broke away from the crowd. "It seems my trust has been misplaced for all of these years. Perhaps my fear blinded me to the truth. Blinded us all. My duty is to protect these Rovers and I believed that you had shared that same loyalty. Now I can see how little you care for my people. Returning here after saving the boy was pure idiocy. You *knew* they would follow and slaughter us."

Jake threw his arms out and stomped towards the crowd. "But you can't just banish her while she is still so injured. She can barely walk."

A few in the crowd huffed and shook their heads.

"She made it here didn't she?" The Elder turned his back. "If she stays any longer, the Tigers will return and finish us all."

Jake and Tommy could scarcely believe what they were hearing. Both of them were glued to the ground, mouths agape. Eva had already turned her back to the crowd and started walking towards her home, stopping by the Healer to grab her armor, handgun, and blades. Eva thanked her one final time and labored down the road. The feeling of dread returned and materialized. When she passed the shadowy creature in the space between two homes, she finally caught a glimpse of its face. It was her own.

"You will all die without her." Jake's voice rang through the street. Eva looked over her shoulder at him. "It is nothing more than you pathetic people deserve."

"This is how you thank us *boy*?" The Elder spat. "After we gave you food, medicine, and shelter when you have done nothing for us."

The Shadow disappeared by the time Eva turned back around. Jake and Tommy were by her side, helping her to her shack for the last time. As the door opened, they found that it had been ransacked by the Tigers during their pillage. Every single one of Eva's trinkets had been stolen, even her box of deities. Her bookshelves were bare and her food supply had been emptied.

"Eva I-." Jake was at a loss for words.

"Everything I have ever found in the city was here," she said with tears streaming down her face. "All of the memories and stories of the Old Times. My collection of gods and worshiped idols. Every. Last. Thing."

"I still got this." Tommy held out his hands to Eva. They were clutching something. "Sorry if I wasn't supposed to take it."

In his child-sized palms was her favorite idol, the man wearing a common robe, sitting in a peaceful bliss. Eva stepped over to him, dropped to her knees from exhaustion and relief, and wrapped her arms tightly around the boy, sobbing into his shoulder. They all knelt on the floor of the shack, holding onto the only thing that remained of Eva's collection. Even in defeat, there was a ray of hope.

Jake knelt down and helped Eva stand. Exhaling hard to stop the flow of tears, she staggered over to her bed and grabbed the bag that she had hidden underneath. Luckily, the Tigers did not find it when they flipped over her mattress. Solace washed over her as she opened it and checked inside. It was still filled to the brim with small knives and one other handgun. She held it to her chest and looked up at the ceiling. Then, handing the gun to Jake, she threw on her armor.

Jake fumbled with it. It was fully loaded. "What do we do now?"

"We *survive* Jake," she sniffled. "I have done it before. I can do it again."

"*We* can do it," Jake corrected. "You are not alone this time."

"Thank you both." She tossed her bag over her shoulder and pushed herself up with the crutch. "I never knew what it felt like to have a family. Or, shit, someone who didn't just use me for my skill. It's nice to have someone who cares."

Jake and Tommy smiled and followed her out of the shack. The Rovers were removing the bodies from the tree, watching her with deep scorn and hatred as she labored down the street. Her sorrow quickly switched to anger. She shot them a threatening gaze, causing them to avert their eyes. Before they left the Rover colony, she looked over her shoulder at the village. One man insulted her as she turned to journey to the city.

"What?" he said. "No last words?"

Eva's lips curled to a fiendish smile. She thought for a moment. There was a lot she wanted to say, but she chose a single word instead.

"Hope," she said under her breath. The man saw her lips move, but did not hear her.

"Say that again," he demanded.

She stopped. Jake and Tommy turned with her simultaneously. The Rovers formed a crowd to hear what she had to say.

"I said *hope*," she repeated louder. "You… All of you… had better *hope* that you can survive without me. Your days are numbered and your thankless attitudes are what led you to this fate. The Gangs will never stop hunting down every Rover and Nomad they can. Banishing me will do nothing to appease them. All I did was slow the inevitable. So, just *hope* that your deaths are quick and merciful."

The man's face drained of color. Eva's tone sent a shiver down his spine. Although she swore that she would never return to this place, there was always a chance that destiny would lead her back. Those who had gathered left as quickly as they came. As she turned her back for the last time, she sighed. It was not a sigh of defeat, though. No, this was a breath of elation. The burden of protecting these people was gone.

Eva and the McAvoy brothers looked to the city as the fog began to clear. A large ray of sunshine burst through an opening in the overcast sky. Suddenly, the horizon changed to a sparkling skyline. Greenery that remained with the winter chill lined the old buildings with a welcoming blanket of warmth. For the first time in a while, Eva was content with being uncertain of her future.

Perhaps I can rest a while, she thought. *Gather my bearings and start over.*

She hid her face and laughed knowing, deep down, that The Wanderer could never truly rest.

Chapter 12

Because of Eva's injury, the half-day journey to the city stretched into three. She shoved her boots into her pack before she left the Rover colony and was forced to stumble barefoot down the asphalt highway. Her feet were just too swollen. Jake had offered to take breaks when he noticed her pain worsening, but she refused. The Tigers may have sent a small group to search for them in the city. Now that they had evidence of The Wanderer arming the Rovers with guns, they sought her blood even more. Crossing paths with them would result in instant death. And although Eva did have one good arm to shoot, she could not run. This time, she had to hide.

"Let's set up camp near the middle of the city," she told Jake and Tommy. "I need to wait until my leg heals before we decide to do anything crazy."

"Do you think the Gangs travel that deep?" asked Jake.

"Most of them stay around the outer edge," she breathed and winced as her foot touched the pavement. "The wildlife they hunt stay on the border, so the Gangs don't need to go any further. Except if they're scavenging for supplies. Also, the buildings closest to the center are in much worse condition than the rest. I'm almost positive that was where the bomb dropped during the war."

"Is it safe to live there?" Tommy squeaked.

"Not sure. I haven't been there in a *long* time. Heavy winds pulled down what was left of the larger buildings there. There's no telling where or when the beams will fall. But…Quite a few of the smaller buildings are safe. We just have to go a few blocks out from the center. Plus, it's a better option than coming across the Tigers or any other Gang."

After a few more hours had passed, they finally reached the outskirts of the metropolis. Clouds now obscured the sun and the drizzle had returned, but the view was welcoming nonetheless. Eva was surprised by the freedom she experienced abandoning the Rover colony. Four months had passed since she saved Jake and Tommy. They had grown so much. In their time spent with the Warriors in the West, they had acquired some necessary skills for survival like hunting and cooking. All she had to do was say what she needed.

Being forced to limp miles from the Rover colony began to take a toll on Eva's body. She battled with her pain just to get to the outer part of the city. Now, they had at least another mile to venture. And after that, they would still have to find a place to stay for the next few weeks.

Tommy noticed the bloody footprints Eva was leaving behind, but he decided not to tell her. He could tell from the grimace on her face that she already felt it. She did. But stopping now would be dangerous so he just swept dirt over the prints so they would not be followed.

After it had gotten dark, Jake realized that he had been leading the group for a while. Both of Eva's hands were clutching onto the crutch. She was dripping with sweat and breathing heavily. Tommy took it upon himself to watch her closely. If she tripped, he vowed to do his best to help her back to her feet. Jake had walked for a long time before turning back to see her in excruciating pain.

"We are stopping for the night," he commanded. "Pushing yourself so hard is only going to kill you and you are no good to us then."

Eva reluctantly nodded and collapsed to her knees. Jake lifted her into his arms and carried her into the closest building. An old neon sign read "HOTEL". *Room 5* had two beds, both destroyed by moths and other small animals hundreds of years earlier. Tommy checked the front closet and found a large pile of blankets that had been wrapped in plastic to keep the bugs out. Jake laid Eva in an old chair and threw a pile of blankets on the floor for her to rest. Looking closely at her cut foot, she noticed a sharp rock right underneath the skin.

Jake rushed to her side. His words were frantic. "What do you need? Anything. Something."

"I'm not going to die." She bit her lip and dislodged the rock from her foot. "Ow! Anyway, it isn't that deep. Just some water and any clean linen to wrap it."

"Water." Tommy had already disappeared through the door.

Jake and Eva looked at the empty doorway, then back at each other and smiled. She crawled to the floor and propped some rolled blankets against a wall for her to lean on. Jake threw another blanket nearby for him and Tommy to sleep on for the night. Before he left, he asked whether she would be okay while he searched for food. She pulled her gun from the holster and set it near her uninjured hand.

"I also have a special tool that they used in the Old Times that may help you," she mentioned as Jake was turning to leave. "It's two pieces of metal that start a fire when struck. We can cook a meal in between the vehicles outside."

"You don't think it will draw unwanted attention?" he questioned.

"Predicting the future would be a *great* ability," she laughed. "My confidence is based more in my ability to deal with problems as they arise. And luck. The occasional luck that I have in surviving every bad turn of events is beneficial too. But, no, I don't think anyone will find us."

Jake leaned against the door frame and shook his head. He noticed her smile was genuine, admiring how it brightened her face. The twinkling in her eyes and a dimple on her right cheek… but not the left. He had come to know her face well. It seemed like Eva had become much more open to laughter and honesty lately. Part of him even considered an infection to be the culprit of her attitude change. But either way, he appreciated her change of heart. He could not put his finger on it, but the energy she now exuded was much warmer.

He waved and left Eva in the room. For some reason, she could not stop smiling. It felt like a heavy chain had been cut from her neck. The burden of protecting the Rovers had been more significant than she realized. She was able to fully appreciate the sight around her—an ancient hotel. Shards of glass were strewn across the floor near the window, and walls of painted brick held together this ageless room. A family of mice skittered across the floor, not even noticing a colossal human in their midst. Her eyes were abruptly drawn to them. Sure, this place was old, damp, and smelled of mold, but the mice seemed to enjoy it. It was their home.

For what may have been the first time in her life, Eva could not recall a time when she was happier. Her ankle was in bad shape and her arm was at risk of another infection. On top of that, her other foot was cut from the pavement outside. But despite her injuries, banishment from the Rover colony after defending them for so many years, nearly witnessing Tommy being beaten to death, and being forced to start over with nothing - she turned her face to the ceiling and furrowed her brow with a smile on her face.

"Fate has never been kind to me, but now I have Jake and Tommy," she whispered to herself. "They care for me. I'm no longer being thanked out of fear. Jake and Tommy looked right through me. What they saw was not the exterior of a demon -"

"But the heart of a hero." Jake had returned with his brother. He winked at her. Eva was startled at first and cleared her throat while the mice scattered back into the safety of the walls.

"I was… um," she tried to explain.

"Talking to mice," Tommy giggled and brought her a basin of water. "At least you said nice things about us."

She messed with his hair. "Well I couldn't have said anything mean about you. But are we just going to ignore the fact that you started talking for the first time in…"

She paused. Jake finished. "Years. Since mom died."

"Was that when you stopped talking?" Eva leaned closer to the young boy.

Tommy nodded as his brother went outside to set up the fire. Eva could tell he wanted to talk about his mother. He was standing uncomfortably close and gazing at her. His body had become rigid, but his face was soft and pleading.

"You can tell me anything Tommy," she said while washing her foot and redressing her arm. "You know that right? I promise not to tell Jake if you don't want me to."

He knelt down and sat beside her. "He remembers everything that happened," he said. "We are different. *Really* different. When I tell him things… he hears me… but he doesn't *listen*."

Eva paused, unsure how to respond. For the first time, she was getting a glimpse into the mind of Tommy McAvoy. From the moment they met, it was clear he was always thinking, always watching. During their training in the city a few months ago, he had proven himself remarkably resourceful. She had never seen a child adapt to this harsh life so quickly. Now, as he spoke, his words were just as thought out as his actions. *The Owl Markings from the Nomads.*

Jake returned to a silent room and understood that they were having a private conversation. He quickly asked for the fire-starter and jogged out into the parking lot.

"I love Jake," Tommy continued rubbing the back of his neck and wrapping his finger around his locks of hair. "He just can't understand me. You're more like me, I think."

Eva smiled. She put a hand on the boy's bony shoulder. "Well Tommy, not all siblings can be the same.

Or even similar, for that matter. Everyone is different. And your mother's death affected Jake differently than you."

"Mhmm," he agreed. "When my mom died, I just went quiet. I don't exactly know why. I just did. Jake always talked for me. He never asked why I stopped, just helped be my voice."

"Why did you stop? I mean, other than not having anything to say."

"I guess I was scared. My dad left before I could remember. I sort of remember my mom, but I really *really* remember what she looked like when she was dead. It was me who found her first. At home. In our kitchen. I have bad dreams about it. They still happen. Jake tries to make me feel better, but he can't make her go away."

"Are you scared of dying too?"

"I dunno… maybe. But, but, but when I saw *you* that night. In the storm? You looked scared and lonely too. Jake always shows when he is scared. But you are *strong* all the time. Even when you are scared. And really brave! That's why I wanted to go with you. I wanted to be strong just like you. Maybe to save someone else one day."

Eva was at a loss for words. *Be strong just like you.* Never in her life had anyone told her something so honest and loving. The innocence of his face and the sincerity of his voice was enough to make her cry.

"Tommy," she choked. "Thank you. But you *are* strong. And Jake and I both see how strong of a man you will become. One thing I learned, being alone for most of my life, is that strength will never be found outside yourself. It has been in you all this time."

He smiled and hugged her around the neck. Jake returned from the fire glowing in the parking lot and his chest puffed out in pride. Eva laughed as he deflated.

"What?" he said smiling. "I started a fire."

"Proud of you Jake," she said sarcastically. "We are both so happy for you."

"I mean it helps that this fire-starter-thing works every time," he mentioned. "It's really easy to use."

She pointed to her bag. "I have a few of them. Got them in an old store. No one had even touched them and I can't figure out why."

Jake shrugged and held up three rabbits. "So I have one for each of us. And before you say anything snarky or mean, Elaine taught me some hunting tricks."

"And I learned how to get them ready to eat!" Tommy snatched them from his brother's hands and ran outside, laying them on the hood of an old car, and starting to prepare them for cooking.

"That kid is something else." Jake laughed and rested next to Eva. "His voice is so different than I would've guessed."

"He hasn't said a word in five years," Eva said. "Now the floodgates have opened… And yeah, he is a special kid."

"How is your foot?" Jake backtracked. "*Feet.*"

"Fine. Now that I'm not walking on them. But I have a feeling that I am going to be laid up through winter."

"Are the winters bad out here?"

"Depends. We get snow. And sometimes it's a lot and lasts for weeks. But the ice is worse. Much, *much* worse."

"Then we will have to prepare."

"We will. And I will do my part."

Jake turned to look at Eva and rolled his eyes in front of her face. "You are going to stay here until you heal. Why don't you ever listen to anyone but your own stubborn-ass self?"

"I am *not* arguing with you about this again. And I won't *quit being stubborn.* I'm not just going to sit around and do nothing all day."

He sighed loudly and made her swear that she would rest for a week at minimum. At least the newest cuts would be healed by that time. She reluctantly agreed.

"You know something Jake McAvoy?" Eva snorted. "I love you and I hate you at the same time and it is so damn frustrating."

"*Me?*" As he exited the room, he threw his arms up and chuckled. "How do you think I feel dealing with *you*? Gotta get used to me because you are stuck."

Eva shooed him out of the room to help his brother cook. She watched them from the comfort of her makeshift bed while they worked. It was well past midnight before they ate and retired for the evening. Tommy, as usual, fell asleep first. Finally, Eva understood why Jake waited up for a while every night. He was protecting his brother from the nightmares of their dead mother.

"You and your brother dealt with a lot growing up," Eva murmured through the darkness. She could feel Jake's eyes on her. "Even though your basic needs were met in the Vault."

"True," he replied. "But nothing compares to what you went through in the compounds. The torture. It's a surprise that you decided to trust anyone at this point."

She heard him sliding closer to her so they would not wake Tommy. "Let's not make comparisons here. All I am trying to do is give you a damn compliment."

"Well thanks," he said. His voice was much closer now.

"Yeah, Tommy told me about your mother's death a little. About discovering her body… and well… about his nightmares."

"They don't happen as often as they used to. But I still want to make sure he is okay."

"You're a good brother, but sometimes your jealousy of him obscures that."

"How can I not be jealous? He picks up this survival shit like it is no big deal. I would kill to have that ability."

"That's just it Jake. You shouldn't worry so much about him. Shit, you killed someone. He hasn't done that yet."

"Still pure in that respect."

"That will change at some point. And you will change too."

"*All* of us have done a lot of changing lately."

Jake paused for a moment. So long, that Eva had thought he had fallen asleep, until she heard rustling near where Tommy lay. In her hands, all of a sudden, was the leathery cover of a book and a pencil. Her brow furrowed as she studied it with her hands like she was blind.

"I found it for you when I was gathering wood," Jake whispered. She could hear the grin on his face. "And it's completely empty. When the Tigers destroyed your home, I suppose they took your old one with them."

Her silent laugh was more like a breath. "Actually, I burned the other one. When I left you both with the Warriors… I was just… *so mad*. I wanted to start over."

Another pause.

"I understand. Regardless, I knew you needed a new one. Maybe start over in this one? Write a new beginning?"

"Sounds nice. I'd like that."

Eva felt Jake's fingers interlace with hers. She yawned and drifted into sleep before either of them uttered another word. A cool draft from the windows caressed their hands, but did not erase the warmth hidden between them.

***

Dawn broke through the Old Time Hotel and awakened Eva before the others. Her and Jake's hand had come undone sometime during their slumber. They both knew that this was neither the time nor place to let their affections run wild. However, that didn't mean they could not express their fondness at all. She carefully sat up and studied her wounds for a few moments. Pressing against the bottom of both feet as hard as she could, she wanted to see whether her body would allow her a walk. When the pain was noticeably lessened, she grabbed her crutch, dressed herself, holstered her weapons, and rose to her feet.

The stiffness of her limbs prevented Eva from bending her knees for the first few steps. As she dressed in her gear, she turned to see both McAvoy brothers deep in their dreams. It was peaceful to watch, but she needed to heal as fast as possible. Knowing Jake, he would never allow her to venture out in her current condition. Winter had nearly arrived and the Gangs could attack at any moment. Every minute wasted was dangerous. She had to be ready.

Her eyes caught the notebook Jake had given her. It was still near her pillow. The pencil was waiting to be used and the pages beckoned for Eva to write her tale. There were so many things rushing through her mind. Should she start with when she left Jake and Tommy? Or perhaps when the Rovers banished her? No. She had to start with last night, and the freedom and peace that leaving had given her. And at the very least, she had to leave the boys a note.

Noiselessly, she stepped over to her bedside and picked up the journal. It was undoubtedly from the Old Times, yet it looked brand new. The pages were untouched, free of stains, and did not crackle when opened. She picked up the pencil and leaned into the morning sunbeams to begin her letter.

THE ONLY WAY I CAN HEAL THESE WOUNDS BEFORE WINTER IS IF I PUSH MYSELF. YOU PROBABLY WON'T AGREE, BUT I'M GOING ANYWAY. WILL BE BACK IN A COUPLE HOURS. -EVA

Ripping the page from its bindings seemed like the single loudest thing she had ever heard. Her eyes darted from the book to Jake over and over. In her old journal, the papers would fall out if you shut it too hard. But this parchment was crisp and firmly attached to the spine. Her tongue stuck out the corner of her mouth in concentration while tearing the page as slowly as she could.

Come on you stupid thing. The final bit finally separated from the binding and she was out the door. When she reached the parking lot, the pain in her legs had dissipated. Trees that had broken through the pavement wore shades of red, orange, and brown. Many stood bare, their delicate branches stripped of leaves. Smaller shrubs were either bare as well or still clinging to the last hints of summer. The only green came from the firs and evergreens clustered around the city's edge. Cold winds from the street seemed to go right through her body, and carrying with it, a scent of what was to come. Autumn had always been Eva's favorite season. As a young girl, it had taught her that the end to some things were beautiful. Death was not to be feared. For without death, life would be meaningless.

There was no particular reason for her walk around the block other than to build strength. Jake and Tommy would worry about her when they woke, but she would go crazy staying in the stuffiness of a hotel room for weeks. This was the time where she could be alone with her thoughts. And some of these reveries would never be written in the pages of her journal.

A short breath before the next plunge. We can make it deeper into the city. Find a place to stay, gather the basics, and perhaps last until winter. If we don't make it, well, the Nomads will find us. Hopefully.

Eva stopped. She thought of the Rovers and her banishment.

Maybe the Nomads will say the same of me, calling me a demon, forcing me into exile. They have not been hostile and hateful to me before, but I'm not sure if I can trust anyone except Tommy and Jake now.

The word *trust* embedded itself deep in her mind. Had it been misplaced all the time? Was the innocence of these two strangers from the Vault enough to earn her trust? What if they broke it? Thoughts like these were the reason that Eva had been alone for so long. Betrayal was in her veins. It had always been.

Paranoia does horrible things to you Eva, she argued. *It will be what gets you killed. Keeps you off your game. Keeps you from being the best. Once you heal, you will be better than you have ever been before.*

Suddenly, an unwelcome sight appeared in the window of a nearby building. The Hooded Figure.

"As soon as they learn to be like you, they will betray you too. Leave you for dead. You will be used as a human shield. When you find their father, they will not think twice about you. End them before they end you."

Eva limped quickly past the effigy with a shaky exhale.

As she rounded the corner to the next block, she noticed an abandoned garden. Its only inhabitants were rabbits, squirrels, and birds. Upon closer inspection, she saw fresh vegetables were growing right underneath the soil. Plucking the first bunch of leaves, carrots. Second bunch, potatoes. Third, an onion. She harvested as much food as her pockets could handle. They were bursting at the seams when she made her way back to the hotel.

Luck.

Jake had woken up not long after Eva left. He spotted the note where she'd been sleeping and waited a few minutes, hoping she might return. When a half hour passed with no sign of her, he decided to venture out. But the moment he started tying his boots, she appeared in the doorway, arms full and pockets overflowing with vegetables.

"See?" she commented while Jake opened his mouth to argue. "I can be useful even in my current state."

His eyes darted to her pockets as she emptied them on the floor at his feet. Again, his worry was misplaced. Tommy sat up and rubbed his face, yawning. When he noticed the pile of vegetables at the end of his bed, his face lit up. He adored cooking.

"You need to realize that I have done this before I met you," Eva said to Jake. "I just wish you would see that. I am *begging* you to stop worrying about me going out alone. It's not like I won't come back. And that look on your face tells me you want to argue. But you don't get it. I don't want to change my independence. That is a feature that I actually like about myself."

Jake crossed his arms and tapped his foot. "Then you don't need us?"

"No, I don't *need* you," Eva mirrored him. "I *want* you both here. Why don't you get that?"

"I'm not sure Eva. Maybe it's the fact that you're injured and don't want our help. That's what family is supposed to do. *Help* each other when they're hurt."

"I do not need someone freaking out when I disappear for a while, though."

"You need to rely on us Eva. A little bit, at least."

"But I'm not completely useless. I have walked these streets countless times. Shit, I scavenged here as a *child*. And that was all before the Serpents kidnapped me. Just because I'm hurt does not mean I am helpless."

"Shut up!" Tommy said with armfuls of the vegetables. "Both of you. Jake - If Eva wants alone time, leave her alone. She's better than us."

Jake huffed, murmured something under his breath, and walked out the door and down the street. Tommy dropped the vegetables back on the floor, running after his brother. Eva returned to her bed to write and rest for the day.

As the weeks passed and winter broke into the region, the three exiles had gotten into a routine. They had moved deeper into the city after the first couple weeks, lugging bags filled with vegetables and scavenged supplies. It would not be enough for the entire winter, but they could get by. Eva and Jake had softened to each other once again. Tommy was as happy as ever. All of their wounds, physical and mental, had diminished. The Wanderer felt stronger and faster than she had in a long time.

An old clothing store became their residence. The top level had been a home two hundred years before. Almost all of the windows were boarded up to keep out the cold, but there was ample light during the daytime. Most importantly, it was dry. They made their beds with blankets from the hotel which also served as additional insulation when the snows came. In fact, the first snowstorm of the season swooped in just as they had completed preparations for their shelter.

Jake and Tommy were in awe. Neither of them had seen snow before. The moon basked the untouched whiteness with a sparkling brilliance that words could scarcely describe. The brothers stood in the storefront and watched as white flakes cloaked the ground. Eva stood out in the middle of the storm, picturing the street bustling with people, as she always did. People casting shadows on the ground from the streetlamps. Vehicles cautiously making their way through the slushy streets. But now it was simply a colossal graveyard. A reminder of once was or what it could have been.

"Every time it snows," she told Jake who had come out to stand with her. "I am dumbfounded at the sheer brilliance of it all."

He reached to her side and warmed her hand with his. Their breath formed a cloud in front of them. She smiled and kissed him on the cheek. His face was warm against her frozen nose.

"When I read about snow in schoolbooks." He nodded toward the end of the road. "I always had this feeling that the author could never capture its true beauty. Frustrated me to no end. I would look at pictures and then read poems. Something was missing. But only now do I truly recognize that there *is* no way to describe it. Well, describe it well enough to do it justice."

Eva rested her head on his shoulder. The fire where they were cooking flickered out of the corner of her vision. She closed her eyes, taking in the smell of fresh snow. The sound of the crackling fire nearby, muffled by the blanket of the white flakes. She felt the soft touch of Jake's hand and his hair on her forehead. Clinging to the moment, she wanted to hold onto it for an eternity.

***

Eventually, the snow melted but the cold lingered. Eva and the brothers had run out of their food supply, so they resorted to exclusively hunting. Originally, they had all agreed on taking turns, but Eva continued to volunteer. She believed that if she stopped for more than a day, her skills would begin to dull. Ultimately, Jake and Tommy chose to accompany her for the very same reason.

"We need practice too," Tommy declared.

That day marked the first time they had traveled together since the Rover colony. Eva almost forgot the presence of two others with her. It wasn't long before she resorted to her old self, complaining to them of breathing or walking too loud. And just like the old Jake and Tommy, they obeyed without rebuttal.

Until they heard unfamiliar footsteps.

At first, they blamed each other. Jake thought it was Tommy. Eva swore it was Jake. And Tommy thought it was the elder two. But after a moment of listening, it was the unrecognizable voices that signaled them to hide. They had almost forgotten about the Gangs until this one showed up at dusk. As the strangers came into view, Eva's heart shot straight up into her head. She recognized them from months ago. The three hooded and cloaked figures who had spoken about a man named McAvoy.

"Jake," she said as they passed out of sight. "I had forgotten until now. Please don't be upset. Those Gang members. I've seen them before. They spoke of a man named McAvoy, but I never got a good look at any symbol. So, they could be from anywhere."

"We'll have to follow them then," said Jake. This suggestion was unlike him. Eva took notice and raised a brow. "If they go back to their compound. We will find my father. There's no way it could be anyone else."

"Fine." At this point, she had stopped trying to avoid the compounds. "But this time, we're doing this right."

Chapter 13

Jake turned to Eva as they quietly pursued the three Gang members through the city. "They must be from this region right?"

"I really hope so," Eva whispered back. "No one that I know of has ever ventured past the city borders in the south. Except for traders. I've never been out that far, but rumor is that it's just an endless wasteland. Whatever lies beyond that is a mystery."

Eva and the McAvoy brothers made sure to stay at least two blocks behind the cloaked travelers, being mindful of the placement of each step. The winter winds had broken brittle tree limbs and scattered them across the street. Any pressure placed on a fragile branch, dead leaf, or icy surface would signal their location. Eva felt like her predatory instinct was returning, and she welcomed it. It filled her with prowess. She was stalking her prey. The feeling was so invigorating that she trembled a little.

Based on their route, Eva believed the three shrouded figures entered the city from the East. She, Jake, and Tommy were forced to stop every few blocks as the Gang Members looted for scrap. For a while, the scavengers said nothing to one another. Perhaps they felt the presence of the three hidden in shadows. As they moved on, they loosened their uncertainty and began chatting. Each time the wind blew, it carried back a few words here and there, but they were indiscernible. Jake pondered whether they had been talking about their Gang, so he begged Eva to close the gap between them to find out.

"The closer we get," she said and looked around the next corner. "The more dangerous it gets. If they hear any of us, we're dead. Did you see what they were carrying?"

"Uh guns?" Jake questioned whether Eva was joking. "They won't see us."

She crossed her arms with a gun in one hand. "And if they do?" Her voice was a loud whisper. She was losing her patience. "What happens then, Jake? You both could get captured or they could execute each one of us. Like what happened at the Post. *That's the problem.*"

"Stop arguing," Tommy whispered and pointed down the street. "We're gonna lose them."

Eva shoved her gun in its holster, hard. "I'll scout ahead. You stay here. After a while, we meet up and, if they say anything about your father, I will tell you. Keep following them until they lead us to their compound and we can figure out what to do from there. We *have* to plan this out. No more guesswork. Okay?"

She looked at Jake. He nodded. Then, she looked at Tommy. He also agreed. And in the blink of an eye, she had vanished from sight. Shallow breaths and silent movements made Eva completely invisible. She remained in the shadows. Only one block now stood between her and the Gang Members, but she still could not hear well enough. A hand remained tightly gripped around an unsheathed blade. There could be more of them waiting to spring a trap at any moment.

This is what you were born to do, Eva. She psyched herself up. *You play this game better than anyone else. This is why you continue to survive. This is why you are feared and revered. Because alone, no one can hold you back.*

Confidence washed away any seed of fear or doubt left in her mind. A mere twenty or thirty feet now stood between Eva and the mysterious Gang. Finally, she was close enough to hear them. She found a secure spot behind a brick wall so she could see down the road where Tommy and Jake were hiding. If either group moved, she had a clear path to escape.

"As I was *trying* to say, asshole," a woman laughed. "We never find anything good out here. So, *why* do we keep coming back?"

"For the metal to melt and trade," the man replied. "Gotta keep the Gang profitable. Otherwise we have nothing to trade and the other Gangs will overthrow us."

"Lest we fall into history where no one remembers our name." A second woman sounded like she was reading from a script. Her voice sounded like a yawn.

The first woman made a gagging noise. "That sounds like something the Chief would say. Does he always talk like that?"

"Everyone who works for him says so," the other woman replied. "How would any of us know? We just do the runs."

"And torture the servants," the man reminded. He stepped closer to where Eva sat hiding. She could hear the gravel crunching under his shoes. "Don't forget about that."

"You just take advantage of the women, Dirk," the women said in unison. "Disgusting."

Eva reached up and slowly pulled out her other blade. The laugh from the man materialized images in her brain of young women being abused by his hands. It made her sick.

If I kill him… then I give away my position. Both of the women have guns and will shoot without question.

"A man has needs ladies," he snickered. "And the rest of you are off limits."

"I should drop you where you stand Dirk," one of the women said as a gun clicked. "Even though they're

Doxies, what you do is disgraceful. If the Chief knew… You men are sad excuses for human beings."

"Well they aren't really people are they?" Dirk pulled out his gun as well. "Servants are sub-human. And we all know that *you* enjoy a good torture as much as the rest of us."

"That's different."

"Is it?"

Eva wanted to smash their heads against the brick wall. It took everything in her not to pounce. She took a crouching step closer to the edge of the crumbling half-wall that she was hiding behind.

"Only because you end their miserable lives out of *mercy* or some shit," the first woman chimed in. "Then we have to find *more* metal to trade and replace the Doxies and Bondsmen you kill. It's wasteful. Do you know how much one slave fetches in trade? Of course you don't because you are a moron."

"Shut up, Olivia. Don't forget that you have a weakness for some of the better-looking ones," Dirk smiled fiendishly.

"And the Chief made a good spectacle out of your last love," the second woman spat at the first. "I remember Nora. Too bad she met her end so horribly. I mean, really, how is it even possible to fall in love with a servant? Despicable. He should have killed you as well."

The first woman growled. "Don't. Go. There."

Dirk flicked the safety on his gun and the tension dissipated. "At least that McAvoy works hard. My favorite so far."

"Such a surprise that he came from that Vault." Olivia picked up a heavy chain from the ground. Eva could hear the clanking. "He always talks about it. Did you hear he put out a reward for his sons? If the Serpents got to them, they're dead… or working at least."

"It would be nice to find them out here though," the nameless leader yawned. "We'd get *real* good with the Chief. Two Bondsmen that we paid nothing for."

By the time Eva heard McAvoy's name, she had already returned her blades to their sheaths and was on her way back to Jake and Tommy. Some sort of reward had been placed on them. But how could a servant ask that of a Gang? Maybe he traded his skills for his sons? Or his life. The moment she returned, she told them everything.

"He has to be a prisoner there," Jake declared. "There's no other way. I knew he wasn't dead."

"My question is why would they care about any reward from a servant?" Eva was thinking out loud. Her eyes watched the Gang members digging in a large pile of rubble for metal to fill their bags.

Tommy tugged on her jacket but she shooed him away. Jake cocked his head. "What do you mean?"

"A slave does *not* make demands to a member of any Gang unless he has something to give in return. They already have his life in their hands. What else could he offer?"

Jake thought for a moment. "I remember that he was great with strategy. He always beat me in board games. Maybe he helps the Chief with organizing his slaves and troops."

"That would be something of value," Eva gently touched her chin. "Because it isn't a *thing*, the Gang can't simply take it. Back when I led the Serpents, most of the smaller settlements we absorbed lacked any real strategy. The only reason the Tigers survived was their size. But now, they could rival each other. Interesting."

Once again, the Gang members were on the move. The three cloaked enemies continued to weave through the city streets in search of more scrap. Every so often, they would stop and comb through piles of rubble, saving only certain pieces of metal. The McAvoy brothers and The Wanderer were only a few steps behind, all deep in thought.

Dirk, a rather bulky man with slicked blonde hair and a deep scar running across his eye, had seen a deer. Without thinking, he shot it. Jake and Tommy thought that he was just hunting, but Eva watched with intrigue. This prey was not shot to be consumed. He had a clear shot to kill it, but chose to aim low, striking the creature's leg.

Sickening as it was, Eva stared him down, jaw clenched, while he tortured the poor animal. Tommy and Jake had to look away. Even the women who were with him ignored the sounds of pain. After a few excruciating moments, it was over. Olivia, the one with the dark hair, put the poor beast out of its misery.

"I am going to kill him before the others," Eva promised. Her face felt hot and the grip on her blade tightened a bit more. "And it will be *slow and painful*."

"Not if that girl does it first." Jake pointed to Olivia. She stood behind Dirk as he knelt beside the deer, her gun aimed at the back of his head.

Bang. He dropped with a thud, motionless. All of his darkest thoughts and actions, gone in a flash of light with a single bullet. *Shame*, Eva thought. *Should've been me behind that smoking barrel.* His comrade and killer tore the pistol from his hand and emptied the contents of his pockets. She only took a few things, including his bag of scrap, then stood up and spat on his corpse. The woman with no name had been observing her comrades silently. As Olivia met up with her, they continued on.

Daylight was dwindling and the two mysterious women had not yet left the city. As they distanced themselves from the pale corpse of their kin, Eva jogged over to examine it. Tommy positioned himself as a lookout, and Jake watched the women as they stuffed their bags to capacity.

"Damn." Eva threw a rusted knife to the ground. "*Nothing*. She must have taken his insignia."

"Why would she kill one of her own?" Jake did not glance back once. "Doesn't make any sense."

"They have the right to end anyone's life," Eva said as she searched through his pockets and glanced at the hole at the back of his head. "And this piece of shit deserved it. He was cruel, even by *their* standards. Guess they just had enough."

"Merciless," said Jake. "All of them."

"We all are merciless executioners Jake," she sighed loudly and stood up. "Even *you* have taken a life."

"What?" Tommy jerked around. Eva instantly knew she had made a mistake. She bit her lip. "You *killed* someone?"

Before Jake could respond, his brother shoved him and turned his back. The two remaining Gang members were moving again. Eva grabbed Tommy and Jake and pushed them onwards. There was no time to be upset. They had to keep moving if they were going to find their father.

"I had to find you," Jake reasoned. "If I had let that guy go. He would have gotten both of us. We would both be dead."

Tommy refused to hear any of it. His brother tried to explain, but The Wanderer's fist was already at their backs, pushing them after the Gang-women as the last bit of daylight vanished. Eva was the first to notice that Jake was getting too noisy and hurled them into an alleyway. The women had heard them.

"Shut up," she berated. "Now is *not* the time for this shit. Jake did what he had to do. *I* told him to do it. Because, unlike both of you, *I* know what it is like inside the heads of these people. Tommy, you need to understand that. Jake had to do it. And it won't be his last. Now stay quiet."

"Is anyone there?" one of the women called up the street. Their footsteps quickened. Eva jumped inside of the only thing in the passageway, a dumpster. It reeked of death and decay, but Jake and Tommy did not hesitate to follow. With the lid shut above their heads, they covered their noses and waited.

"Better not be playing tricks on us," the one named Olivia said. "If you know what's good for you. We don't play nice."

I swear, I am going to disembowel Jake if they find us. Eva's thoughts ran wild. *I have had enough of this hiding shit. It smells so bad in here that my puke would be an improvement.*

Two sets of footsteps marched down the street, stopping in front of the dumpster. Rust had eaten a hole through the side of the bin where Eva could see their shadows in the moonlight. The first woman peered down the alleyway but saw nothing. The other woman mentioned "I could have sworn I heard voices," shook her head, and turned in the same direction they came. Eva and the brothers wasted no time jumping out into the fresh air, forcing back any vomit that was starting to make its way up their throats.

Both women were far more alert now. At the beginning and end of every block, they checked behind them as they exited the city. Jake and Tommy were still queasy from before. Everyone moved much slower and it was getting late. Neither of the groups lit a fire nor ate that night. They could feel someone watching them. The air itself was unsafe, but they slept nonetheless.

***

Eva jerked awake to a crow's ear-splitting caw. Her leg had fallen asleep and she completely forgot where she was. Off in the distance, the two women from the unknown Gang awoke when one of their packs had spilled from a second story overhang. The noise from the crashing metal sent a flock of birds bolting into the sky. Jake and Tommy sat straight up with their heart beating in their ears.

"Come on Olivia." The woman's voice echoed through the empty street. "We have to get back sometime this week."

"Let's go," Eva said and they continued tailing their targets. It was not long before they saw the Rover colony on the horizon to their right. A couple months had passed since she last stepped foot there, but her anger still burned with the same intensity. The highway they had taken separated the forest and the town. Even in the late-wintertime, the pine trees held their greenery. The other trees had been stripped of their leaves and loomed over the street like gnarled hands. Above them, the sky had thickened with clouds and the smell of snow filled their nostrils.

"Dirk deserved what he got, right?" The other woman was within earshot. "I mean, I don't think what you did was wrong."

"They're going to ask questions," Olivia responded as she hoisted her bags over both shoulders. They had taken a short break to eat a small meal. "We may get demoted."

"What do you mean *we*?" The woman stood up with a hand caressing her handgun. "Chief would believe me if I told him that I tried to stop you. And after you killed Dirk, I delivered justice."

Olivia now brandished her weapon. "You'd do me in for a stupid promotion?"

"Why not? It'd make me look good. I could work directly under the Chief."

"Or I could shoot first and blame the whole thing on you."

Jake looked at Eva in bewilderment. The Wanderer's eyes remained fixed straight ahead. "Are they really going to kill each other?" he mouthed. At this point, they had hidden themselves between two cars that were mostly intact. But they were dangerously close to the battle.

Eva's only response was holding up one finger and using it to draw a line across her neck. She believed that, by the time they reached the compound, there would only be one returning member. The next second confirmed her answer. None of them were paying attention when the shot was fired. When they peeked over the trunk of the car, both women were still standing. The look of total shock was plastered on their faces, but only one slumped at the other's feet. Olivia was the lone survivor. She threw the third bag of scraps over her shoulder, dug through and removed a few of her victim's belongings, and made her way down the street, whistling.

"What the shit just happened?" Jake, Eva, and Tommy had distanced themselves from the deranged Gang member.

Eva stepped over the woman's dead body after finding no indication of the Gang she once belonged to. "I think that's pretty clear, Jake."

"She killed her friend," Tommy said. He had been silent for the majority of the day. Deep down, he still struggled with the news that his brother was no better than Olivia.

"Unfortunately," Eva squinted at the Old Time homes that were beginning to appear in the distance. Snow started falling lightly on the ground. The pavement was becoming slick. "There are no real friends in those compounds, Tommy. No one really cares about anyone. All they want to do is impress whoever's in charge to rise through the ranks. Those on top reap the best of everything."

"Oh." Tommy dropped his head.

"This world really does suck," she said. "I know it does. But there are those who care. Like your brother. He would do *anything* to save you. Believe me. He risked his life to find me. Risked it again when he helped me kidnap two Tigers… And risked it a third time when he took the life of that Gang Member. It was all to save you.”

The little boy with almond eyes nodded up at her with a half-smile. Her words had lifted most of the weight he had been carrying. Jake hugged him tightly. Tommy quietly thanked his brother for rescuing him from the Tigers.

Olivia had started to fade from view as the blizzard moved in. What once had been a calm covering of snow was now dropping in thick sheets. Eva caught the outline of her target slipping into a building, so they chose the one next door. Just down the street stood a familiar place: The Post, the home they had spent a couple of nights in. They had put a few miles between themselves and that memory since then. The houses on this street were in especially bad shape. She eyed the sagging roof above them, worried the weight of the snow might bring it down, but the other homes weren't much better.

“We have to wait out this storm.” A large white blanket had already formed on the yard separating the Gang member from Eva and the McAvoy brothers.

Tommy decided to keep to himself, adopting his old, silent nature. Even as they ate nearly frozen food, he sat in the foyer of the old home. Eva and Jake made their beds in the living room at the back of the house. Attempts of getting Tommy to talk were unsuccessful. The rest of the evening Jake spent looking over his shoulder at his younger brother.

"He'll get over it." Eva had been trying to get Jake's attention for some time. She was annoyed.

"Tommy doesn't just *get over it*." Jake's first sentence of the entire night. "Why do you think he stopped talking after our mother was killed? I know him better than anyone. Trust me, he lingers on things."

"So do you. Like right now. About this whole stupid thing."

"What do you mean *stupid*?"

"Think about it Jake. Your brother just found out that the one person he looks up to just murdered someone. How do you think that makes him feel?"

"He admires *you* too. Probably more than me."

"But the difference is that *I* have been killing since you first met me. I've already been *tainted*. There was blood on my hands long ago. The blood on yours is new."

"It's not like I enjoyed it. It was horrible!"

"It isn't supposed to be a pleasant experience. Ugh. I really hope you don't see me like that Olivia woman. I have never *had fun* killing anyone before. Even in the Nest, I was more power hungry than anything."

"Well you shouldn't. I mean. I never thought that. I mean… I would never think that about you. Or anyone. That woman is just nuts."

"But that's just it, Jake. Many of the Gangs are like this. People are like this out here. Like *that*. Which is why I made you kill that Tiger back there. To make you realize that mercy isn't always an option. It rarely is."

Jake got up and walked out of the room. Now they were all separated. *Just like I like it...alone.* Eva reached in her bag and grabbed her journal, jotting down the day's events. It was nothing special, just something to keep her mind busy.

***

Another day had passed before the storm had finally subsided. Every moment she was awake, Eva watched the other house to see if Olivia had left. Tommy bought some frostbitten vegetables from a garden near the house that were still edible. It was mostly carrots, but they were filling nonetheless. When they finally noticed that their target was on the move once again, they left in a hurry.

It was much more difficult to stay silent while their boots crunched in the snow. Although it was lightly packed together, treading through the ankle deep trenches was exhausting work. It was likely that they would make it through No Man's Land by midday. Originally, Eva thought the woman belonged to a smaller Gang, but she was beginning to suspect she hailed from either the Serpents or the Tigers. Either way, it was just as dangerous.

Her guesses were confirmed a few hours later. *Tigers.* The brothers' father had been held by the same experts as one of his sons for a few days. But even if

Tommy had seen him, there was no way he could have recognized his own father.

The three of them huddled behind an overturned truck as Olivia called for the gate to open. Her fellow Tigers pulled large ropes attached to the doors and she stepped inside. An unnatural heat permeated from where the gate had been opened. It came from the forging fires of the Tigers trade—*weapons*. Sounds of bustling slaves, whipping, clanging, and yelling rose over the metal walls and barbed wire.

"Second largest," Eva said. "This Gang is the second largest in the region. Serpents only have them beat by a hair. Their walls are equally impenetrable and their inhabitants just as deadly. Of course it's the Tigers. Shit. I have no clue how to even get in there at this point."

"What about the entrance we used before?" Jake offered.

"Come on Jake. They'll have it either heavily guarded or destroyed by now. Infiltrating a Gang is *not* taken lightly. It makes them feel weak. So we'll have a target on our heads. A big one."

"What about that?" Tommy pointed to a building that barely rose over the towering walls. It was difficult to see originally, but they noticed that one side shared a border with the outside world. It was not protected by reinforced metal. Off to their right, the Serpents had a similar layout, but their building was surrounded by both a wall and the outer ring of the compound itself.

"I wonder what that building is for." Jake took a step towards the end of the truck and crouched.

"The basement is where we found Tommy," Eva said. "The upper levels, if they're anything like the Serpents, is where the higher ranked members live. If we can find an open window, that may be a good way in."

"I was only on the first floor and basement," mentioned Tommy. "It was the prisons and the kitchens. Everyone there only had knives. Not guns."

"Okay," Eva smiled nervously. "Well. As usual, I am probably going to regret this, but we have to try a different tactic. Something I've never done before."

She took a deep breath. "We're going to pose as servants."

***

Sentinels were stationed at the towers surrounding the compound, marching across its perimeter. Each one of them was armed with an assault rifle, staring out into the snow-covered landscape. Dense clouds obscured most of the sunlight, so their vision was drastically reduced. Only the faint outline of Eva, Jake, and Tommy could be seen if they stayed far enough away.

Rounding through an old parking lot and weaving between old vehicles, Eva led the way. As they approached, the compound loomed over them. The fence had now stretched into the back of the building. Not a single guard tower stood on that side. Broken windows dotted the entirety of the structure. Within them, occasional shadows moved about. Danger grew with each step. At the bottom, there was a section that had broken away from the rest of the structure, leaving just enough space for them to squeeze through. Only a white, snowy clearing separated them now.

Eva took a deep breath and lumbered into the field first, holding her hand behind her for the boys to wait until she made it across. Her gun stayed pointed up at the windows in case anyone spotted her, but no one looked out. The snow was too deep to run. It dragged at her legs, slowed every step. But she made it. Reaching the brick wall, she turned and waved them forward. Jake crossed next. Then Tommy.

For now, they were safe.

"No one spotted us," Jake said as they all peered into the opening. "I'm surprised."

"Let's not get overconfident," she reminded. "We haven't even made it inside. We have to do this with the utmost care. *The utmost care*."

They first had to dislodge a few bricks to free up enough space for them to crawl through the mud. On the other side of the wall was a small, windowless room. The door was shut tight. Eva dragged herself inside and cracked open the door. It led into a desolate hallway with lanterns hung on either side. There was nobody in sight. Jake and Tommy dropped into the room behind her, nearly knocking over a metal shelf filled with supplies and weapons. She shot them a fierce look as they struggled to their feet.

"Sorry," Tommy whispered.

Eva shook her head, heart pounding, torn between pressing forward or turning back. "I'm going to check out the hallway. Stay here until I get back. Don't move."

Holstering her gun and pulling out her blades, she opened the door and cautiously stepped into the passage with her head on a swivel. The darkness brought back memories of her time as a Serpent. Odd, but she felt a certain level of comfort. Her footsteps echoed through the corridor as she tried each door. Nothing. At the end of the hall where it turned right sharply, she pressed her ear against one of the rooms, just to see if anyone was inside. Silence.

Further down the adjacent hall was a T-shaped corridor. Before she ventured further, she held up her hand at Jake and Tommy, who peeked their heads out of the cracked closet door. *I will come back for you,* she mouthed to them. The next hallway looked much the same, though the doorways were spaced farther apart. Once again, every door was shut and the rooms deathly quiet. But this time, Eva swore she saw movement in the slivers of darkness beneath a few doors. Was everyone asleep? Or were these something else—more cells, maybe?

Just as she reached the end of the hallway, the sound of approaching footsteps froze her in place. They echoed sharp and steady, growing louder. The hairs on her neck stood on end as The Wanderer backed up to the nearest door and tried the handle. It gave.

She slipped inside. Luck was on her side. The room was empty, except for a few overturned, dust-covered desks shoved into a corner. She spun and pressed herself against the door, peering through the narrow gap. A small group of Tigers filed past, their boots thudding loudly across the floor. They moved in formation, following a single man at the front. He was dressed in the finest leather armor she'd ever seen. Polished rivets caught the lantern light, flickering like shards of silver. A black cape draped over his shoulders, flowing down to ornate, gleaming boots.

The moment his face was brightened by the beam of a lantern, Eva's heart stopped beating.

She covered her mouth to mask the sound of her gasp.

It can't be, she repeated over and over in her head. *No. This isn't real. No. No. No.*

"Chief McAvoy." One of the Tigers rattled off his report. "We still haven't found your sons. I've sent word to the Serpents to look for them as well. As you commanded, I mentioned the reward."

"Good." *That voice. That face.* "I hope to find them soon."

His chocolate hair tinged with silver strands combed back neatly on his head. A short but neat tuft of hair around his mouth bore the same color. Face, wrinkled with age, not work. But most all, it was his eyes—those piercing, stony blue eyes burned into her memory like frostbite.

Eva staggered back, her mind reeling.

Jake and Tommy's father… he was not a slave.

He was leading them.

He was the Chief of the Tigers.

But it wasn't just that revelation that nearly stopped The Wanderer's heart. No. This went deeper. She had known him long before Jake and Tommy ever spoke his name. Back then, he went by another. Dan Avery. This man, who stood right outside the door, was the one who betrayed Eva when she was Mistress of the Serpents. The same man who had shattered everything.

He had destroyed her life once before—

And now, he was back.

I must be seeing things.

Peering around the doorframe to be sure her eyes were not fooling her only deepened her fear. Her face felt hot. She could almost feel her blade sinking into his chest. Even if the other Tigers spotted her, it didn't matter. She *had* to kill him. He was much more dangerous now than he was all those years ago.

But that is Jake and Tommy's father, a little voice in her head spoke. *They would never forgive you.*

Before she could decide, the Tigers and their Chief heard a noise and rushed down the hallway. It came from the direction of the closet where the brothers were hiding. Eva was frozen to the floor. She heard Jake screaming her name.

"Help, Eva! Help us!"
Then it was silent.

Chapter 14

The Wanderer was alone. She sat in that empty room with her head in her arms, trying to compose herself. Jake had begged for her to rescue him, but for the first time in her life, she froze. A shadow, the one that materialized time and time again, towered over her. It still bore her face and voice. The malicious laugh still rang in her ears and the suffocating shroud of dread was just as familiar.

"I failed." Eva sobbed into her lap. The Tigers who had kidnapped Jake and Tommy left only moments ago, but she still couldn't move. *That man has taken everything from me. And now, he has taken the only two people in the entire world that I care about.*

"You *are* a failure," the Hooded Figure hissed. "End your life and others will no longer suffer. Give them your head on a silver platter and the Chief will treat the boys like royalty. Until then, you bring them *nothing* but pain and danger."

Eva no longer had the will to fight. The shadow would return along with the nightmares. It did not matter what she did to push it away, she could feel it getting stronger each time. Sweat dripped down her nose and onto the floor as she gasped for air. The shadow's hissing became louder until it was right next to her ear. It wasn't until she felt the cold metal pressed against her neck that she realized she was holding her own blade to her throat.

"Do it." The shadow was inches from her face. "One swipe and it's all over."

Eva banged her head against the wall, shaking uncontrollably. Her heartbeat thudded against the hilt of her blade, every pulse an echo of the shadow's relentless whispers. It pressed in, coiling around her thoughts, its voice the only sound in the barren room. Or rather, her empty mind. Suddenly, cutting through the darkness came another voice. A familiar one. The ground seemed to rock beneath her. What started as a low purr grew in volume to combat any other sound around her. It was warm. Gentle. Melodic.

Jake.

"You can't give up Eva," the voice pleaded. "You can still save us. Don't give up on yourself. Please. Get up or they'll get you. *Hurry! They're coming.*"

Eva felt a surge of self-control and power. She hurled the blade from her grasp, watching it skid across the room and crash against the far wall. Then, silence. The voices were gone. Only the sound of her own weeping remained.

Suddenly, the door to the room creaked open. She shot to her feet, heart hammering against her ribs as her gaze locked on the figure in the doorway.

***

Tommy hung half of his body out into the hallway, waiting for Eva to return from scouting. The dim lighting obscured the end of the passageway, so any movement would be impossible to see anyway. When Eva had turned the corner, the sound of her footsteps faded into silence. Jake was trying to keep his brother inside the closet, but to no avail.

Jake pulled him back into the closet for the tenth time. "Someone's gonna see you!" When he closed the door, his brother pushed it back open.

"There isn't even anyone out here," Tommy whispered. "And maybe I can find Dad if he works here."

"If he is a Bondsman like Eva said," Jake jerked him into the room again. "Then he probably works outside. Plus, you don't even know what he looks like."

His brother ignored him. "I can see the end of the hallway. We can hide if the Tigers come."

Jake just shook his head and crossed his arms. Instead of arguing with his brother, he started pacing around the cramped space. The room would have been much larger if the shelves were not filled to the brim. He studied their contents. One shelf had a few random weapons. Others were packed with ragged clothing for the servants, but none of it had ever been washed. Crusted, brown blood stains saturated some of the garments. On the next shelf were a number of crates that were locked tightly. A large sign hung above them with the word *Slave's Belongings* written in black ink. He tried pulling on a few of the padlocks. Not a single one budged. The last handful of shelves had rows of onions, carrots, and celery. Some of them were beginning to mold. The sign on that shelf read *Slop*.

A cold wind blew in a small pile of snow onto the floor from where they had entered the building. One of the weapons that was precariously placed on a table rolled and fell to the ground with a crash. Jake turned from the opening in the wall back to Tommy. His brother was frozen in fright. Down the hallway was the sound of quickening footsteps. In a flash, he heard one of the Tigers scream "Intruders! Get them!" Black sacks were thrown over their heads and arms bound behind their back. Tommy cried an apology through his hood and Jake called out for Eva. He hoped that she had not been caught as well.

"Help, Eva! Help us!" he screamed at the top of his lungs. Then, he felt the hard metal butt of a gun against the back of his head. The Tigers dragged Tommy and his unconscious brother down the hallway and down into the yard.

Chief McAvoy paid little attention to the two boys as they were taken to be "processed". He stood aside as his men dragged their motionless bodies down the hall and entered into the closet to see how they had gotten in. As he inspected the opening in the wall, a young woman waltzed into the room. She had the tattoo of a Tiger above her left breast and wore a red nightgown that was strung haphazardly on her shoulders. She sighed loud enough for McAvoy to turn around with a knife pointed at her throat.

"Calm down baby," she cooed. "Relax. It's only me."

"For the Old World's sake," he breathed and sheathed the hidden blade under his cloak. He turned and reached up into the opening, gauging how large it was. "You startled me Bethany. I could have hurt you."

"Why have you been so… *on edge* these past few months?" The barefoot woman with thick chestnut locks swirling down her back sauntered over to him. She caressed his bare arm and moved up to his neck, massaging it. "Hmm?"

He slapped her hand away and turned. "You well know the answer to this foolish inquiry. Yet you ask anyway. The Wanderer has been making quite a stir. *She* was the one that infiltrated us months ago. I'd bet my life on it. And she is a very dangerous woman."

"Spare me the patronizing tone Daniel," she said, crossing her arms and frowning. "How could *one woman* be so frightening to you? She stands alone. You have an entire army."

McAvoy gripped her by the neck and threw her against the closest wall. She clawed at his grip, but he tightened as she struggled. A moment passed and she started to lose consciousness. After begging him to release her, he finally let her drop to the floor coughing and gasping. His face remained unchanged, emotionless. Only his eyes flashed with rage.

"I do not care which of my wives you are," he said and crouched down to Bethany. Her hair hung in her face as her breath shallowed. "First or Seventh, I care not. You have been with me since I took this post. Loyal, yes. But know your place, woman. *I own you.* You may be a Tiger, but I am your Chief. I would sooner slice your neck open than relinquish my search for The Wanderer."

Bethany's eyes filled with fear as she clutched her nightgown.

McAvoy calmed his voice slightly. "Poor girl. I do not expect you to understand. But one day, you see the carnage The Wanderer has left in her wake. But by then, it will be too late."

The Tiger Chief smiled an empty smile. He reached down and grabbed her chin, forcing her face to meet his. He was strikingly handsome, but there was something predatory in the calm, commanding tone of his voice. Almost every Tigress fought for high ranks within the Gang in hopes to become a wife to their newest leader. But even still, they would have to wait for him to select them.

"I'm sorry my love," she whispered softly.

He nodded softly. "Know that I am only doing this so that you realize how important it is for me to find her. When she's gone, we will experience true peace."

Bethany left the room with him, their hands touching softly as she led him back up to their room. The hallway was silent once more. If only McAvoy knew that his greatest rival, The Wanderer, had only been a few doors down from where he stood moments ago.

***

Jake had regained consciousness just in time to feel the Tigers hurl him and his brother into a tub of frigid water, their bare skin hitting the surface like stone. They wore nothing but their underwear. Armor and weapons were stripped away, carried back to the building where they'd been caught. The brothers shook violently, every breath a ragged gasp as the winter air bit into their soaked flesh. After long, punishing moments of frozen agony, someone shoved coarse, ragged clothing into their arms.

Then a man stepped forward, holding a white-hot branding iron that hissed in the cold.

"Gotta teach these new Bondsmen how to work," he smirked. "Looks like they never worked a day in their life."

Jake dropped to his knees and pleaded. His eyes were drawn to the glow of the torture device. "We will work. We will work. I swear. Just please don't hurt us."

The man turned to his comrades and roared with laughter. Tommy had backed up into a corner, cowering in fear. His brother pleaded again, but it made no difference. *Where is Eva? Shit. Did they get her too? If they did, we're done for.* Jake's screams ripped through his lungs as the guards slammed him onto the table, forcing his arm down at an angle so sharp he thought the bone might snap. A searing pain exploded through his entire body as the white-hot poker pressed against his flesh. The smell of burning skin filled the air. When they finally pulled the iron away, a bubbling scar remained. His arm remained twisted on the table. Tommy watched in horror, but no words came to his lips. Only the unforgiving realization that he would be next.

"Please," Jake panted as he tried to regain his balance. "Not my brother. He's just a kid."

"Should've thought 'bout that before sneaking in here, *boy*," the man said as he returned with the brand reheated. "And now, you are property of the Tigers."

One of the guards straddled Jake's chest, pinning him down while his brother received the brand. Tommy's scream was so piercingly loud, Jake thought his eardrums would burst. A bright red "T" now blistered both their arms. A mark of ownership mixed with the pain of discipline. They were then hurled into a semi-dry tent with three others and were left there for the evening. Jake stared unresponsively at the vast yard while Tommy wiped the tears from his eyes, sniffled, and started asking questions of their roommates.

"Have you seen a lady with red hair and green eyes?" he asked. They shook their heads. "Her name is Eva."

Still nothing.

"Do you know anyone named McAvoy?"

Silence.

"Eva's probably dead." Jake turned to his brother. His hair was soaked with sweat as he held snow to his arm and cooled his wound. "She just got swept up like we did. Take one look at her blades and *bam*. They found out who she was and killed her."

"Don't say that Jake." Tommy teared up and shoved his brother. His voice cracked. "Don't *ever* say that."

"What do you mean *who she was*?" Jake immediately recognized the blind woman from before. She had been fed by Tommy in the prisons. He swore that the Tigers must have killed her. But there she was, sitting just as quiet and as calm as usual.

"No one." He lied.

She smiled. "Well then… Your *friend* may be dead. But there is a greater chance that she is still alive. Speaking of her so negatively will do nothing but impede her energy."

The old woman with wiry hair threw her head back and cackled. The noise that escaped from her lips sent chills down Jake's spine. A Bondsman and Doxie, who shared the same tent, just shook their heads at the madwoman. For a while, Tommy and Jake sat near the opening in the cloth, looking out into the compound's immense yard. There were large piles of metal waiting to be thrown into massive barrels which drained out into bullet molds. Glowing coals from the work day created an eerie glow over the muddy slush. In the distance stood the building where they had been caught, and where Eva might still be.

"Hey boys." The Doxie they shared their tent with slid over to them. Underneath the layer of dirt was the face of a pretty, young, and extremely thin girl about 16. She had long, orange hair that was almost as messy as the old woman's, and a patch of freckles on each cheek. One of her eyes was black and swollen. "I'm sorry about your friend. Maybe she works out here. Tigers don't kill anyone who can work unless they deserve it."

"No one deserves this." Jake remained fixated on the building. "You all should be free."

A sheepish grin grew across the girl's face and she looked at the "T" branded on her own arm. "That is nice of you to say, but most of us have never been *free*. Out there… you are forced to fend for yourself. At least they give us meals and a safe place to rest our heads here."

"And yet they work you to death and beat you senselessly," Jake replied. "I would rather starve to death out there than live with *this*."

"Not all of us are fit for the outside world." The Bondsman whispered from the dark corner of the tent. "I could never hunt. I don't have any skills. That's why I make ammunition for the Tigers… I came here willingly. Years ago."

Jake snickered to himself and turned towards them. "Let me tell you something. Me and Tommy here… We were raised away from all of this. When we were freed, I had no clue about fighting Gangs or finding my own food. I didn't think I was capable. But the woman who saved us also showed us kindness and patience. She taught us both how to fend for ourselves. We learned how to survive. Yeah, it's tough killing someone, but sometimes it has to be done. "

Jake opened his mouth to continue, but closed it when he replayed what he had just said. Eva's own words were speaking through him. He bit his lip hard to force back tears. *She can't be dead. I will never believe that.* Even Tommy smiled over at his brother.

"Your enthusiasm," the old woman yawned. "It is nice to see. Not many slaves have that here."

"That's because it's beaten out of us," the Bondsmen sighed. "I had that spark when I was your age, but it has long since gone."

The Doxie girl smiled and slid over to her bedroll. "Hey. Let's get some sleep. You both will be working in the Pits tomorrow, I bet. Make sure you get your rest."

Before Jake or Tommy could speak with them further, the slaves had all fallen asleep. The younger McAvoy brother made himself a bed in the corner, away from the cold of the winter snow. Jake decided to stay near the slit in the tent. If Eva was taken down into the yard, he would be the first to know. It was almost impossible to sleep with a mind so full of worries, but he forced himself to rest for a few hours.

***

Clanging of metal pipes rang throughout the compound. It was still dark, but early morning. The sun's rays had not even found their way over the horizon when the slaves poured out of their tents and queued towards the middle of the yard. Jake and Tommy were snatched out of bed by the Bondsman and shoved into a line. Hundreds of dirty, gaunt faces attached to bruised and bloodied bodies caused the McAvoy brothers' stomachs to churn. A few nearby forced a pleasant smile, but most just stared blankly ahead. Waiting for something.

Aside from the wet crunch of footsteps through the snow-packed ruts, the line stood in silence. Now and then, a slave driver would berate a servant in the distance. The cracking of a whip would sound through the brisk air, cutting through the cloud of breath above them. Some of the slaves would flinch, but kept their eyes locked on the shoulders straight ahead.

"What are we filing for?" Jake asked as silently as he could.

"Morning meal," the Bondsman replied through the side of his mouth. "They only make so much food. Sometimes, you don't get to eat if you're at the back of the line."

"Shut up over there or no food!" A Tigress stomped over to them. She lifted her whip over her head and came down hard on both their backs. Tommy whimpered but kept his eyes glued on the person in front of him. He did not dare turn back to his brother. Jake gritted his teeth in pain, but did not cry out. He refused to give his torturer the satisfaction.

After a painstakingly slow pace, they made it up to the table where the food was being served. Somehow, Jake had gotten in front of Tommy. The last bowl of food was sitting on the table in front of a large man. As Jake stepped aside for his brother to grab it, the man bounded over the table. He started screaming at Jake, only inches away from his face.

"You don't get to choose who eats." The Tiger's spittle landed on his face. "That's *my* job."

"He *was* in front of me." Jake looked at his feet. His shoulders tensed for the beating. "I screwed up and got in front of him. Accidently."

The rest of the servants had already started working when Jake received his second beating of the day. When the Tiger was done, he pointed him to a large bonfire surrounded by burly Bondsmen. Tommy gulped down his food and followed his brother to the mountain of logs. The man that shared a tent with them was there as well.

"Just keep the fire going," was his only instruction. "It has to stay bright and hot. Otherwise, the metal doesn't get hot enough to come down into the molds. Too hot, and it will start melting the buckets. You screw up, we will *all* be taken to the torture rooms."

It sounded as if he had rehearsed these lines before. Jake and Tommy began throwing piles of sticks and logs into the fire. They kept very close attention to the color and shape of the fire to keep the same temperature. Soon, the Chief began making his rounds. He was surrounded by five guards, all brandishing large guns. One of the guards was Olivia, the woman from the city. Jake ducked his head when the Bondman called out "Chief".

Chief McAvoy, still adorned with his jet-black cape and meticulously slicked back hair strolled around the grounds. His hands were clasped behind his back and he would stop occasionally to observe the servants' production. With a flick of his finger, a Doxie would be carried out of sight in the direction of the building. With another wisp of his hand, a Bondsman working too slow would be slaughtered. Although his face bore no expression except a slight lip curl, his icy blue eyes glowed with joy. He made his way to the Pits and stepped past both of his sons. Neither of them noticed him, but the Chief's brow furrowed for a second and he stepped back to them. Lingering only for a second or two, he whispered a command into his guard's ear and turned on his heels, continuing his rounds.

Once he was out of earshot, Jake turned to his new friend. "Is this a daily thing?"

"Yeah," he replied.

"Has that man been the Chief long?"

"No. Weird thing is, he just showed up one day claiming to be from another Gang. He challenged the old Chief and massacred him so badly, they did not have much to bury. That's what we were told by the Tigers. And… not that they actually *bury* anyone here."

"So he likes death," Tommy panted as he heaved another log onto the fire. Their faces and bodies were burning, but they were not permitted to move.

"He *loves* death and torture." The Bondsman was careful not to speak too loudly as a couple more guards walked by. "He's less merciful than the one who ruled before him. I thought I was scared before, but this guy is much, *much* worse."

Day faded into night, and still Eva did not appear. Dinner was at least plentiful enough for every servant to eat, and Jake and Tommy, bruised and with splinters embedded in their hands, devoured what they were given. Jake's back still burned from the whippings, but at last they were allowed to rest. *Finally*. The young, red-haired Doxie entered the tent much later than the others. On her arm was a red handprint and her hair was matted even more so than before.

"Those men are ruthless to you poor Doxies." The Bondsman looked at the young girl's arm. He scooped up some mud and caked it on her bruise. "That should make it feel better."

"You know we aren't allowed to talk about our work." She brushed her hair with her fingers. She graciously handed her empty bowl to Tommy who took them back to the food line. "Besides, it isn't hard work. You have it much worse. At least we get breaks."

He rolled his eyes and played with his beard. The Doxie jumped in her seat and turned to Jake. Her voice grew jittery as Tommy stepped back into their tent.

"I almost forgot," she clapped. "We don't even know your names. I'm Natalie. I was from a Rover colony that doesn't exist anymore. That's Brandon the Owl Spirit. He was a Nomad a long time ago."

Tommy gasped in excitement. "That is so cool. I was given the Owl symbol too. By the Nomads. When Eva took us."

"*You* were part of the Nomads?" Brandon leaned in. "How long ago?"

"Not long," Jake interrupted. "I'm Jake and this is Tommy. We… um… actually came from the Vault between here and the Serpent's Nest."

"How did you not end up at the Nest?" Natalie's face hardened. "I heard they took *everyone*."

"Not everyone." Jake cleared his throat. He rubbed his still-throbbing arm. "The Wanderer found us."

The whole tent went silent. Natalie and Brandon looked at each other in disbelief. While the old woman slept in the corner, they whispered further questions.

"Wait," Brandon repeated. "You know *The Wanderer*? I thought he was just a legend. Someone that the Gangs are terrified of, but doesn't really exist. The Nomads revered him as a villain turned hero."

"He is a *she*," said Tommy. "And her name is Eva. We're looking for her."

"She is the friend we spoke about earlier," Jake said and tugged on a strand of his hair.

"I'll be damned," Brandon laughed. "Always thought the Wanderer was a myth. I had no clue it was a woman either. I bet she's deadly."

Jake and Tommy both nodded and answered simultaneously. "She is."

"Is she as cold as they say?"

"No," Tommy replied. "She's nice. She saved both of us… a lot of times."

"But she can be harsh," Jake added. "I watched her torture one the Tigers for information."

"Ruthless."

"We came here searching for our father," Jake added. "We were told he would be somewhere in this compound."

"What is your father's name?" asked Natalie. "Maybe we know him."

Right as Jake was about to respond, two guards marched over to him. They reached in and yanked him and his brother into the yard. *What did we do?* Hearts raced in their chests as they were thrown to the ground and commanded to get up. The two brothers were forced to follow their captors to the building. One guard stood in front of them, the other was on their heels.

"Where are you taking us?" Jake asked frantically. Death was certain, whether he asked or stayed silent. The least they owed him was a reply.

Unfortunately, the answer was a single, ambiguous sentence. "The Chief asked for you two, *specifically*."

Jake and Tommy glanced at each other in horror. What did the Chief want with them? They had done their job without any incident. So how did he know who they were if they'd only just arrived?

It felt like hours before they finally stepped inside the building. The Tigers referred to it as "The Castle." It was where they slept, ate, and tortured their slaves. A number of Doxies queued in and out of the building as personal servants for the floor. Some carried food. Others dragged heavy bags of clothing. But they all were dressed in silk nightgowns of various colors. If they were coming in from outdoors, they were allowed better shoes and coats. The ones who bore the tattoo of the Tiger on their body were part of the Gang itself. Women in that rank were free to bear arms and abuse the servants as they pleased. The ones branded with a "T" were slaves.

Winding staircases were built at the corners of each level. The brothers were taken to the nearest and ordered to climb to the top floor. The Tigers followed them closely, nudging them with their rifles each time they slowed. Jake felt his throat closing in fear. He worried for Eva. Neither of them had seen her since she left to scout ahead. A little voice in his head wondered whether she intentionally led them into a trap in order to join the Tigers.

She would never do that... I hope...

At the very top of the stairwell was the steel door to the highest floor. The Gang member in front opened it and pointed to a door on the left. The right side of the hallway was covered in paned glass except for one closet door and a door directly across from the Chief's chambers. Both of the Tigers were behind them as Jake placed his hand on the cold brass handle and turned it. Tommy was shaking and forcing back a barrage of tears. He took a final look at his brother, opened the door, and stepped inside.

The door clicked shut behind the McAvoy brothers. At the other side of the room was a large desk. A figure, shrouded by shadow, sat behind it. The room itself was neatly filled with extravagant things from the Old Times. Books, furniture, clothing, and art covered the edges of the walls. Everything was organized and spotless. Not a single item was out of place. A long, royal blue rug lined the only pathway between the door and the desk, where the Chief sat.

Jake's arms went numb when he saw it. Propped up on the desk were Eva's blades. He had no doubt she was here. But whether she was alive or dead was still unknown.

"Do you know who I am?" McAvoy leaned back in his chair and propped his feet on the wood table.

"The Chief," Jake and Tommy said simultaneously.

"Not a wrong answer," he tilted his head. "But you are missing something… much more… pertinent."

Something about his voice started tearing at Jake. He could not put his finger on it. *Why does he sound so familiar?* It was soothing, sickeningly soothing. He had watched the back of this man only this morning as he massacred at least five of his own servants, but he had not spoken a word until now. And this was the first time Jake had met him face-to-face. At least, he thought it was.

How do I know his voice? And why hasn't he just killed us already? He didn't waste a second with the other lives he took today.

"Tell me boys," McAvoy's voice hastened. "What do you know of The Wanderer?"

Jake gulped. Tommy stayed as quiet as he could.

"Nothing, sir." Jake lied. He hoped this man was not as good as Eva picking up on the deceit in his voice. "Aside from rumors and legends."

"Pity," the man stood up straight. He pushed his chair behind him and guards appeared from either side of the room. "That woman cost me so much of my life. Still, she gave me all of this - this *power*. I will ask you only once more. Do you know me? Jacob and Thomas McAvoy."

Jake backed up against the door. It couldn't be. This man. He had finally recognized his voice.

"Dad?"

Chapter 15

A loaded gun in Eva's hands pointed toward the woman at the door. Her eyes were still fuzzy with tears, so she wasn't able to focus at first. The silhouette looked similar to Eva's demon, but when it spoke, she did not recognize the voice. With her arms shaking in front of her, the scene gradually became clearer and she lowered her weapon. The woman who had come into the room threw her hands up and pleaded for her life.

"I just work here," she stuttered. But then, she noticed that Eva was not an enemy. "Who are you ma'am? How did you get in here?"

Eva scanned the Doxie from head to toe. She was covered in dirt and bruises, but she was rather clean overall. Her face was thin, not emaciated, and her hair was the same shade of red as Eva's, cut to her shoulders. In fact, this woman looked very much like The Wanderer. The uncanny similarity inspired Eva to hatch a plan.

"I asked who you were," the woman repeated, slightly more stern. "You are not one of them or one of us."

"By *them* I guess you mean the Tigers?" Eva holstered her pistol as elation spread through her body. She closed and locked the door behind them. Although she was still reeling from seeing Chief McAvoy, her thoughts shifted to saving Jake and Tommy. "And by *us* you mean slaves?"

"Yeah?" The woman backed up, thinking she was going to be cornered. "So, whose side are you on?"

"My name is Eva Calloway," she responded as she wiped the sweat from her head and chest. "I came here with two boys. A young boy named Tommy and his older brother, Jake. Do you know them?"

The Doxie shook her head. "Sorry, no. Why did you three come here in the first place? How did you get in?"

"We were searching for the boys' father. But the Tigers took my friends captive. Maybe you can help me find them?"

The woman glided over to the overturned chairs, picked one up, and sat near the window. Moonlight shone in with a silver brilliance. It illuminated the Doxie's black nightgown and created a faint aura around her entire body. Eva stepped into the light and repeated her question.

The servant rubbed one bare foot on the other. "It doesn't involve me sacrificing myself, does it?"

"I can get you out of here." Honestly, Eva made a promise she knew she couldn't keep, but noticed the woman's face light up. "But you must swear to return my weapons to me."

"What do you need me to do?"

Eva sat on the floor in front of the Doxie and explained her plan. With each moment, it unfolded in her mind. She would lend the servant her blades in exchange for a disguise to cover her armor. Short swords would be too bulky to hide underneath the rags, but she would have her gun and numerous other small blades. The Doxie would escape through the same space she and the McAvoy brothers had entered the compound. Then she could finally find a place to live in peace.

"Upon finding our hideout in the storefront," Eva continued. "You will leave my blades there and take whatever else you wish. Find the Rover colony to the south of the city. You will pass it on the way there. They will take you in and you will be free. Or you could always remain in the city and find the Nomads. Whatever you choose."

"Why are you doing this?" The woman looked hopeful yet wary. "And why help only me?"

Eva considered the questions carefully, along with her response. "Because I have to save my friends. Can't go into too much detail, but I'm posing as a servant for a few days. I'll scope out the compound and figure out where they're being kept. And then... I make my move."

"Your move?"

"Are you going to help me or not?"

The Doxie agreed with a tinge of reluctance in her voice. "Okay. But you will have to cut your hair. The Tigers will think you are a Doxie if you do not. There are female workers in the Pits, but not many. If you cut your hair, you can trick them."

After Eva ran her fingers through her hair, she was stunned at how long it had grown. When she lived in the Rover colony, she maintained her hair at the shoulders. But with months of hiding in the city, her dark auburn hair had dropped to the middle of her back. Without another thought, she yanked a knife out of her pocket, reached behind her head, and sliced through her hair. The woman sitting in the corner smiled and left for a few moments. Eva let the handful of hair drop to the floor.

The Wanderer is back. As she watched her hair fall from her fingertips, she realized how much she had changed. At this moment, she felt like her old self, before she ever met Jake or Tommy. Stealth and survival. Merciless and calculated. Before long, the Doxie returned with a ragged outfit. It covered her armor entirely.

I'm ready.

Eva immediately felt vulnerable as the woman disappeared down the hall with her blades. Those two short swords were part of her image… part of *her*. She had carried them for as long as she could remember. Its metal craved for the blood of Chief McAvoy. But it would not be satiated. No. Eva would have to resort to other methods. First, she had to rescue Jake and Tommy. Once she was positive they were safe, she would end McAvoy's life however she could. He would be dead before she left that compound.

She promised herself that much.

With one deep breath, she was out the door and descending the stairs at the end of the hallway. It was late in the night, so she could make it to the yard before anyone would wake. Sure, there would be sentinels posted at the towers, but she could hide in the shadows and take refuge in the closest tent. She was not sure how long she would have to pose as a slave, but she was willing to be there as long as necessary. If discovered, a horrific death awaited her. But if she was successful, more than one life would be spared.

Without incident, Eva made it out of the building and into the brisk winter air. The snow covering the yard had been beaten to a muddy slush. Guards marched above her in the towering posts. They chatted about the day's events, a Doxie they had grown fond of, their latest trip to the city, and other nonsense. The darkness cast by the moon created a pitch black walkway along the entire side of the compound to the first row of tents. After the scouts disappeared and no movement was detected close by, she took her chance. The ground sucked her boots deep into a thick mud. She could run, but they would hear her. But if she was too slow, her feet would sink further.

The first tent's occupants were still awake. Three Bondsmen and a Doxie inhabited all but one bedroll. Whispers of their friend who once slept on the vacant bed were still on their tongues. They jumped to the back of the frozen metal wall when Eva came from around the corner. She had her hands up and frantically explained that she was a new servant, neglecting to use her title as The Wanderer. In the depths of her mind, a voice reminded her that she *cannot save everyone*.

"Eva." They responded as she wiped her shoes with the side of the tent. "You are here to rescue *two* people? Why not rescue all of us?"

"One person rescue hundreds?" She laughed and shook her head. "No. That would be impossible. I mean, how many Tigers guard this damned place?"

"I dunno." The youngest Bondsmen realized what they had asked of her. "Two hundred or more."

"If you don't bother me," she cleared her throat. "I won't bother you."

Before any of them could ask what she meant, she was already lying down and pretended to be fast asleep. Little did she realize that Jake and Tommy were sleeping on the other side of the compound. They had just been processed and were awaiting their first day in the Pits. When Eva finally closed her eyes, she was immediately suffocated by her nightmares. The rest of her tent woke up when she started to thrash around.

"I wonder what's wrong with her?" a Doxie asked.

One of the Bondsmen backed away. "I don't even want to ask."

Eventually, everyone in the tents fell asleep. They had to rest to keep their strength up for the next day. Tigers patrolled the yard and the walls above throughout the night, completely unaware that The Wanderer slipped into their midst. Not even Chief McAvoy, who spent the night with one of his many wives, knew that his greatest enemy and both sons were already within his walls.

***

The sound of clanging metal jolted everyone awake. Darkness still filled the yard as the Tigers began lighting the bonfires with their torches. Eva tucked her ragged shirt into her pants and made sure that her weapons and armor were well-hidden. Her boots, though, stuck out underneath. Luckily, some of the Bondsmen who had been slaves for a while wore battered shoes and boots.

Eva filed to the nearest queue for the morning meal. The servants in her tent were right behind her. They said nothing. She kept her head down as the Tigers passed through the lines, whipping at random. As they approached her line, she turned away from them, peering out of the corner of her eye. One of the larger men stopped right behind her, turned to the Doxie who shared the same tent, and slapped her across the face.

"Watch who you are glaring at," he screamed. "The Chief is doing his daily inspection soon. I'll be sure to let him know that you are… insubordinate. You can be sure of that."

Eva's fists clenched, but she did not dare draw attention to herself. If she challenged the Tiger, her identity would be given away. After taking a deep breath, she noticed that she was at the front of the line. A bowl of mostly mashed potatoes and small chunks of unidentifiable meat awaited her. *You have to keep your strength up. No telling how long you are going to be here*. The taste of rotting, moldy potatoes caused her to gag. Those around her slurped up every last drop. Eva paid little attention. She had to focus on finding Jake and Tommy.

As the Doxies rushed to The Castle for their day, the Bondsmen along with Eva and a few other women crowded to the Fire Pits. One of the older Bondsmen, wrinkled but very strong, pushed her over to the back of one of the molds. The rest of the Pits were obscured, so she was not able to scour the rest of the compound to find the McAvoy brothers.

Maybe I can spot them during the evening meal.

"New blood, eh?" A Bondsman taunted her. "They letta lady 'n this side'f the Pit. Hope you'c'n keep up without a lashin' from 'em guards."

Her job was to pull the bullets out of the cooled molds and put them into crates. What the Bondsman did not count on was the fact that she had assisted in the tray design when she was the Serpent's Mistress. They released all the bullets when cracked right down the middle. She would be able to process twice the material of the other workers who simply picked out each bullet by hand.

"You may want to try keeping up with me," she said, irritated. "If you can."

Other workers looked at each other and laughed. Three cool molds slid down the metal slide to her. She kept her eyes glued to the Bondsmen as she smacked the mold on her knee twice and dumped two dozen bullets into the box. They looked at the tray, which seemed broken. Eva smiled, flipped the tray, and popped it back into place.

"Try and keep up without breaking the molds boys," she said, just soft enough for them to hear her. "Takes a *woman's* touch to do it right."

When the first Bondsman tried following Eva's lead, the mold shattered in his hand. His knee made contact just enough off center to destroy the entire tray. Bullets rolled along the ground. One of the Tigers heard it and sprinted over to him. The slave was whipped and beaten countless times. As he tensed with each lashing, the sharp edges of the tray embedded into his hands. That was when the Chief had passed by.

Eva did not notice him at first. His hair was slicked back, each strand in perfect position. His facial hair was trimmed. Not a single whisker was out of place. She had been watching the Bondsmen work until

McAvoy walked up to them. For a moment, she watched his cold stare, then turned her back. She shut her eyes as he flicked his wrist. The poor soul that was already being beaten within an inch of his life was yanked to his knees in front of the Chief.

"My good sir. Why are they beating you?" He had already spotted the broken tray long before he posed the question. "What have you done to hurt *my* production?"

Eva kept working, though every muscle in her body urged her to strike him down in front of everyone. She would have to challenge him alone, but before that, she needed to find Jake and Tommy. The sound of McAvoy's voice sent a chill up her spine. On the surface, it was calm, almost kind. Yet malice dripped with every word, cold as the winter chill. When the Bondsman didn't respond, he continued.

"Now… why on earth would you intentionally destroy one of *my* molds?" he asked.

The battered man gulped a mouthful of his own blood. "Wasn't me, m'Chief. Please. It was-"

"Then whom shall I hold responsible for the shards buried in *your* palms and the remnants littering *your* workspace?" The Chief was clearly becoming impatient. "And do not place the blame on another when the evidence is clearly in your hands."

"I-I dunno. I'm sorry m'Chief."

Dan McAvoy raised a hand softly. "I could send you to the torture chambers… However… I am feeling rather *forgiving* today."

"Thank'yew sir. It won't happen-"

"You're right, it won't."

The man pleaded for his life as Chief McAvoy turned on his heels to walk the other direction. He glanced back and watched one of his men grab the blubbering man by the hair and wrap his arm around the slave's head. Another Tiger pulled out her knife and carved the man's neck wide open, dropping his twitching body to the ground. The guards and slave-drivers strolled away in silence leaving the remaining Bondsmen to witness their friend die in agony. They just resumed their work with sunken eyes. Eva kept her gaze glued on the compound wall.

All of a sudden, she heard plans for revenge coming from the other Bondsmen.

Let them try, she thought. *I will strike them all down. That man may not have deserved what he got, but I couldn't have stopped the Tigers. I would have been their next victim.*

She paused, only for a second.

Stop drawing attention to yourself, idiot. You just got someone else killed.

The guilt she felt was real. The Bondsman's corpse lay on the ground in a pool of mud, snow, and blood. She noticed the warm liquid seeping into the ground where she stood. *One who walks in shadow behind footprints of blood.* Perhaps the title the Western Rovers gave her wasn't meant as a compliment at all.

Not far from where they stood, in the nearest Pit, someone screamed and was quickly silenced. Eva could see the top of McAvoy's head moving across the compound until he started in the direction of The Castle. His sons, Jake and Tommy, were a mere twenty feet from where Eva was working.

Evening arrived and soon, the immense heat from the bonfires was replaced by freezing air and a light flurry. The Wanderer chose a different line for the evening meal. She tried searching for the brothers before she reached the front to be served. Nothing. Not a single sign of Tommy or Jake. Maybe they had been taken to The Castle. Or perhaps they were being tortured.

McAvoy may try to convince Jake and Tommy to join him. If he knows they're here, they may no longer be out in the yard.

She found a seat in the middle of the compound and ate whatever 'soup' the Tigers had given everyone else. Most of the slaves were tucked away in their tents. A hum of voices carried an echo through the yard. She scoured the living quarters as Doxies filed out of The Castle into their tents. Still, nothing. When she returned to her tent after washing her dish, she started asking around.

"No idea who you are talking about, lady."

"Nope. Never seen 'em."

"Sorry, I don't recall anyone like that."

"What were their names again? Nope. Can't say I've seen them. Sorry."

She had made it halfway across the tents when the Tigers started calling for night watch. Everyone must remain in their tents. "We don't give a shit if you stay up. But if you slack off tomorrow, then we'll just kill ya." That was the message. Eva groaned and punched the metal wall of a tower. She jogged back to her tent as a group of Gang members began kicking and whipping anyone who was not moving fast enough. One additional bedroll was empty. The Bondsman that had been executed earlier that day shared the same tent. As Eva stepped inside, the remaining tent-mates were huddled in the corner, talking in low voices. She turned her eyes to each one of them for a moment, slowed her breath from running, and sat down at the edge of her blankets.

"I hope you're happy with yourself," one of the Bondsmen spat.

"What do you want me to say?" She snarled. "That I got one of your friends killed? What good would that do?"

"Because you *did*." Another Bondsmen jabbed his finger in her direction. "And I see no remorse on your face. So, you're no different than the Tigers themselves. You know that right? Or the Chief."

Rage seethed in her chest. *No better than the Chief?* "What the shit do you want me to say?"

The man's hand relaxed, but his face did not. It just contorted to anger and then sorrow. Truthfully, Eva felt partly responsible for the Bondsman's actions. She would never admit to any wrongdoing, but that was exactly what they were waiting for. An apology. But in an apology they would never receive.

Her Shadow appeared and sat beside her. Their legs touched, and she could hear it humming eerily beneath the hood. Eva tried to ignore it. But the dread seeped in from where their knees touched, crawling up into her chest like poison. She shut her eyes and looked away, refusing to acknowledge it. No one else could see the hooded figure, and they already thought she was losing her mind.

"I will not apologize for his death," she said without moving a muscle. "I have known death closer than any of you realize. And *I* have been on both ends of a gun. The one thing that I learned is that only *you* are responsible for your own death. If your friend did not try and boast, he would not have been killed."

"You are *evil*." The Doxie slid further back against the wall.

"We all have our opinions," she replied calmly. "But it's certainly not a good idea to poke a lion. Eventually, they will bite."

"Then we should just kill you."

"Go for it. Best of luck to you."

Just then, a scream from The Castle caught everyone's attention. Eva whirled around and crouched behind the hanging leathers in front of her tent. Sloshing through the mud were two large figures carrying a small, feeble one. At first, she could not make out anything in particular because the fires had been reduced to coals and the sky above them was shrouded in clouds. But when her eyes adjusted, her heart sank. It was the Doxie she had promised to save. The one who she loaned her blades to. *Shit.* Her short blades were gone, and the woman was being dragged off to be tortured. Both Tigers had beaten her savagely, but she was still alive and still fighting to stay that way.

The Tigers marched by the tent with their victim. The Doxie lifted her head weakly and turned to look right at Eva. Her eyes were filled with tears mixed with blood. *I'm sorry. I tried,* she mouthed as they disappeared from sight. Before they were out of earshot, one of the Tigers mentioned something to another guard.

"The Chief said he would recognize those blades anywhere," he stated. "I doubt this woman is The Wanderer. She would've put up more of a fight. But we need to be rid of her just in case."

Eva rested her head on a wooden pole in defeat. Her eyes closed in a pained grimace. It was her fault that this woman would be executed. Everyone else in the tent immediately knew what happened. The moonlight cast a beam as the clouds broke away. It moved across the compound and lingered on Eva for a moment. When the light passed through the Shadow that had stolen her face, it became invisible but returned just as fast as it disappeared. It could hear Eva's thoughts and began to ridicule her.

"Tsk. Tsk. Tsk. You know I will never go away. Silly girl… That *poor poor* Doxie. All your fault… all your fault…" The hair on Eva's arms stood straight up. Each time it spoke, it was both her voice, and yet, not her voice. This voice was much more demonic than she had ever uttered before. *Do I really sound like that? I hope not.*

The Bondsman jerked her out of her mind. "You did that, too, didn't you? *You* caused that woman to be put to death."

Eva had enough. She crawled over to the cornered slaves and brandished one of her knives, pointing it at them. They gasped when they saw how many blades she had hidden in the armor under her rags. Knives belted up her leg on one side and a handgun holstered on the other.

"You're *her* aren't you?" The Bondsman wheezed. "The Wanderer…"

She directed the blade at the one who spoke. "If you tell *anyone* that I'm here, I will *not* hesitate to kill you. All of you. Understand?"

The group nodded. Fear lingered in their eyes, but they knew killing her might be the key to their freedom.

Eva continued. "I am only here in search of two boys. That's it. And now, I have to find my damn blades."

"Do you plan on taking them from the Chief?" The Doxie started her question but was hushed by Eva. "You'll have to kill him to get it."

"I said shush," Eva repeated and looked through the crack in their tent. She had heard a familiar voice. The Tigers from before were returning with two new victims. One was taller but not gaunt like the other servants. The other looked like a young boy. *Jake and Tommy. It has to be them,* she thought.

"Where are you taking us?" Jake demanded. She could hear him clear as day. The sound of his voice brought tears to her eyes.

The relief was soon smothered by the Tiger's response.

"The Chief asked for you, *specifically.*"

Not a good sign. He knows his sons are here. And if he has my blades, he knows I'm here too.

There was now even less time to waste. Her original plan was to find Jake and Tommy and come up with a way that they could infiltrate The Castle. But now that McAvoy possessed her blades, he knew The Wanderer was in The Den. There was no telling how the Tigers would be directed to search for Eva. It was only a matter of time before they discovered her. Jake and Tommy would be offered an opportunity to join their father and Eva would be executed in front of everyone.

Three days. That was all she allowed herself. McAvoy was an impatient man. She would maintain a low profile. As long as the slaves who shared her tent stayed quiet, she could manage three days. It would give her time to come up with a way to invade The Castle. Once she was in, she would find The Chief and kill him.

Is this what my whole life was leading up to? An odd, jittery feeling sparked in the pit of her stomach when she imagined sinking a knife into his heart. Her demon faded from view.

"I'm going to end him." Eva did not mean to speak her last thought out loud. The rest of the people in her tent squirmed. "In three days."

"You're going to kill the Chief?" They whispered simultaneously.

She looked back at them. The expression on their faces had changed from fear to joy. The reality that the Chief's tyranny could end gave them hope.

"I'm definitely going to try." Eva nodded and smiled. She was half talking to herself. "Not only for my own sake, but for the sake of those two boys that were just dragged up to him. The Chief won't kill his own sons unless he knows I am with them. I just need to come up with a plan to get inside that building."

"You could always pose as a Doxie." The disheveled woman pointed to her silk clothes underneath a heavy blanket. "That would grant you access without killing anyone. But you'll have to find someone to get you a nightgown."

That could work, she pondered. *But I won't let those men use me like others have before. If they try... Well... I'll kill them.*

Eva slid over to the Doxie who recoiled. She looked the woman dead in the eye with both hands on her bony shoulders. "Can *you* get me in there?"

Chapter 16

The Doxie stared blankly at Eva. The Bondsmen watched their friend and waited with bated breath. Would the young girl help The Wanderer? It would be risking her life, just as the other woman had done before. The girl dropped her head in exhaustion. She was unresponsive.

Eva shook her gently, lowering her head to meet the girl's. "Did you hear me? Can you help me or not? I won't need you to do much… just smuggle my armor in The Castle. That way I can get to it when I get inside."

"*No*," interrupted one of the Bondsmen. He tried reasoning with the fatigued Doxie. "It's too dangerous. See what happened to the last person who helped her?"

"But what if she *did* kill the Chief?" another offered. "We could escape in the chaos."

"There wouldn't *be* any chaos," the first one snapped. "One of his guards would take the position. Or, they would fight to the death. But they would maintain order. They would gun us down before letting any of us leave.”

The Doxie was still silent. Everyone was weary from the day, but Eva needed an answer. If this woman refused to help her, she would have to search elsewhere. The woman’s eyes drooped closed again. Eva gave up on trying to convince anyone in the tent to help. The limp body slumped to the bedroll and the young woman was fast asleep. With her hands still in the air as if holding invisible shoulders, Eva tilted her head.

“I guess that’s a no,” she sighed. Lucky for her, someone in the tent next to them had been eavesdropping on their conversation. A woman in her mid-fifties crawled into the tent and sat down. Her curly, dark brown hair was cut very short and her long, thin limbs flowed into an equally slender body. There was no doubt she had been a Doxie for many years. She wore heavy bags underneath her soft, dark eyes and the scars of torture were scattered all over. Before she uttered a word, she shot a look at the Bondsmen who were still huddled in the corner.

“You oughta be ashamed of yourselves,” she scolded. “This woman is trying to save her friends from the jaws of the most heartless Chief we’ve ever had. In the process, maybe your asses will be saved as well. Maybe if *you’d* have fought back before, you wouldn’t’ve been brought here.”

Eva smiled. She really liked this woman. Oddly enough, she bore a similar appearance to Elaine from the Western Rover Colony. "Will *you* help me, then?"

"You're damned right I will." This woman was fiery. "What do you need me to do? I heard you mention something about having three days."

"Well I know he will hunt me down regardless," Eva added. "But if I can pose as a Doxie and have my armor and weapons easily available, I can take the first day to scope out of The Castle, find out how to get to the Chief, and the third day will be it."

"And what do you need me to do?"

"Tomorrow, I will work out in the Pits again." Eva explained her plan with great care. She was making half of it up as she was speaking. "I need you to bring in my armor and weapons and hide them somewhere. *Anywhere* that the Tigers won't be able to find it. When you get back tomorrow night, let me know exactly where it's stored. Oh, and I'll also need an… um… uniform… For day two."

"And that is when you scope out The Castle," the woman repeated. "Got it. I am willing to take the risk."

"Wanda." At this point, only one of the Bondsmen had forced himself to stay awake. "You cannot be serious. Don't trust this woman. Two people have already been executed because of her actions. One was trying to help her."

Wanda jabbed her finger towards the man. "And you should not blame their deaths on her. They got caught and the Tigers are going to kill us anyway… one way or another. I understand the risks. Don't patronize me. I was once a Warrior in the West."

"Thank you for helping me Wanda." Eva shook the woman's hand. Fear, anxiety, and a tinge of relief swirled in her stomach. "Wait…. Warrior in the West? Were you a Rover? Are you related to Elaine? She lives in the Western Ro-"

The woman's weathered face contorted into a huge smile. "*My* Elaine? My baby is still alive?"

"Yes." Eva smiled. She was thinking about Jake again. Her family. "She lives with the Warriors in the West. Across the forest."

"Oh… If I ever get to see the light of freedom again," she hummed and cried silently. "I will go straight into that place and wrap my arms around my baby girl. Long ago, when there were dozens of settlements across the West, my Elaine and I lived near the edge of the forest… One day, the Serpents came and destroyed our village. Burned it to the ground. They were far too strong to fight… I… I was quick enough to hide my little girl in a hollow tree stump. They took those of us who survived the 'cleansing' and brought us to be sold into slavery."

Wanda paused, her face contorted into anger. "I was once a *great* warrior. You'd think that was worth a shit when they sold me? Of course not. The Tigers bought me for three boxes of ammunition… *Three*."

She sighed. Eva offered a sympathetic hand on her arm.

"But I cannot change that past. I just prayed someone would find my daughter and raise her safely."

Eva's smile faded. Even though she had not been the Serpent's Mistress at the time, there was a good chance that she had known Wanda as a slave. Depending how long she had been a servant for the Serpents, there was an equal chance that Eva had tortured this poor woman. At that moment, the Hooded Demon appeared next to them, laughing through each breath.

The Wanderer cleared her throat and glanced at the demon out of the corner of her eye. "Well she *is* safe. And I hope you can see her again. Soon."

"I will help you Wanderer," Wanda stood up, having to hunch over to stay in the tent. "Remove your armor, and I'll be back in a few minutes. I have a safe place for it in my tent. Most of my tent-mates have been lost over the years, so it's only me and two other Doxies now. I swear I'll bring you a nightgown to wear when I return tomorrow."

Eva nodded. The Tigers were passing by as Wanda slipped back into her own tent. Under their murmurs, she could make out a few words like "Wanderer" and "kill". When she was sure they were gone, she began to remove her armor from underneath the ragged clothing. She shoved the knives from her pockets into her boots, keeping a few strapped to her leg. Wanda came back into her tent and took the pile of armor, as promised. One Bondsman was still awake, just shaking his head.

"I gotta hand it to ya," he said before turning his back to Eva. "You do have a way to make people do what you want. Follow you to their dying breath. Yet, you wear no remorse or guilt on your soul. Truly an ability."

"You have no idea," Eva replied back to him, but her gaze remained fixed on the imaginary figure in the corner of the tent. By now, it had revealed its skeletal hand and placed it on her shoulder. A sudden chill spread up her back and across her extremities. She wasn't sure if the shiver came from the demon's presence or the chill against her uncovered skin. The blankets, once belonging to a Bondsman, were now wrapped around Eva. Her body heat soon seeped into the fabric. As her Demon loomed over her, whispering torment, she drifted into a restless dreamscape.

***

DAY 1 - Eva

Same as the day before, the Tigers woke their servants by banging on metal pans. One of them shot their gun in the air for good measure. Eva jumped to her feet, forgetting why she felt so naked. After a few moments, she saw Wanda exiting her tent. In her arms was a satchel and a pair of worn shoes. She tossed the shoes over to Eva. The older Doxie wasted no time moving straight to The Castle while everyone else filed for the Morning Meal. They exchanged passing glances and nods but said nothing. Directed to the nearest line, The Wanderer spotted the young Doxie who shared her tent. The young girl looked just as tired as before, swaying as she waited for food. Her face was significantly more gaunt and sickly than before.

The moment Eva turned back to be served in line, the ground under her nearly bare feet thumped slightly. In an instant, the Tigers crowded around the source. Exhaustion and weakness had become too much for the poor Doxie and she collapsed into the thick mud. Guards dragged her out of the mud and tried a few kicks in the stomach to wake her up. She didn't flinch. A few of the servants were watching the event. Tigers posted at the nearby towers took notice. Two of them climbed down the ladder and started whipping those who halted the lines. From the corner of her eye, Eva watched a guard drag away the ghost-white body.

After the morning meal, she made her way to the Pits to crack open molds. She kept her back to the other men. They had not forgiven her from the day prior. As she waited for a new tray, her eyes turned up to The Castle. Towering over her like a lingering nightmare, it remained silent for the day. Each time a guard would pass her line of vision, she would search them for any sign of Wanda, Jake, or Tommy. There was nothing. Not one indication.

The remainder of the day was uneventful. A few of the Bondsmen received lashings because they were not working as efficiently as Eva. She had been setting the pace but was also given a few swipes from a stick for moving 'too fast'.

"Slow down," said a Tigress between floggings. All at once, Eva was jolted back to her time in the Serpent's Nest as a slave. Relentless torture at the hands of merciless Gang members. Her limp body, bleeding and numb on the floor of a cold, wet, stone cell of their torture chambers. Each crack of the whip pushed her deeper into the Hooded Demon's embrace. Memories that she thought had faded, now right in front of her eyes, as plain as day. The pain was amplified by the heat of the fires and the frozen ground, but she did not scream or let the dread consume her. No one would ever see her struggle.

Although it seemed like an eon, the ten lashes only lasted a few minutes. Eva's legs shook as she returned to her feet, half-covered in mud and fresh blood. The Tigress had left. Bondsmen sniggered as they continued their work. Until the Evening Meal, her back stung and her hooded doppelganger followed like an ominous cloud. She ate alone and returned to her tent at sundown. The Doxie who had shared the tent did not return. The Bondsman also mysteriously disappeared during the day. Now, it was just Eva and two others who ignored her.

They cannot blame this on me. She glared at them while they whispered under their breath. *What are they talking about? Perhaps plots of killing me this evening? Maybe I should just confront them.*

"I'm being paranoid," she said to herself. Wanda had finally returned for the evening and sat down at the mouth of the tent. The rest of the tent shifted their backs further away from the women.

Wanda was panting for a moment. She must have run from The Castle back to the tents. "I did as you asked. One thing I am grateful for is my sharp tongue. Almost got caught sneaking your clothes in. I hid it on the top floor, where the Chief's quarters are. There is a room on the right side, just a small closet. No one ever uses it. But in a wooden box near the door… that's where I put it."

Eva thanked the woman over and over. "You don't know how much this helps. It will give me a fighting chance."

The middle-aged woman handed a silk gown to her. It was black and much less revealing than the other Doxies' uniforms. When she caressed it against her fingers, she was shocked at how these women were able to withstand the cold in such light material. No wonder these Doxies were always covered in layers of blankets outside the building. After thanking Wanda once more, she stood up to leave. Before she disappeared back into her tent, she mentioned one more thing.

"Oh, I almost forgot," she crouched right outside. "The Tigers are going to be looking for you tomorrow. Be very aware of your surroundings. I imagine they'll be interrogating *everyone*."

"Great," Eva said sarcastically. "Thanks for letting me know."

Eva wrapped a blanket around her and laid on a bedroll. Nervousness and anxiety began to seep in as she watched flickering lights and moving shadows inside The Castle. Jake and Tommy were in there. That much she knew. Maybe they had decided to join their father and the Tigers. But if they had, would they betray her? Had they said anything about traveling with The Wanderer? She was McAvoy's worst enemy, though she doubted they knew it. Just before she fell asleep, her suspicions about the Bondsmen in her tent were confirmed. She heard their heavy breathing as they crawled toward where she lay.

Rolling over just as they pounced, she pulled out a knife strapped to her leg. The closest slave was cut down when his legs got tangled in the blankets at his feet.

The other one spat at her. "You destroy every life you touch. That stops now."

When the first body dropped to the ground, the other Bondsmen tried to pin Eva against the ground. His hands closed around her neck, pinning her legs underneath his. She gasped for air, clawing at his grip. Then she saw it. Her knife, just inches from her hand. Her muscles flexed and her veins popped as she tried pushing his body off of her neck, but he was too large.

Her vision began to darken and a numbness spread through her cold limbs. Death started to take her. It sucked at her soul deep underneath the soil. Six feet under in complete darkness, she imagined the squirming of parasites eating away at her flesh. The story of The

Wanderer would simply dissolve into myth. A simple Bondsmen—the one to claim her soul.

These were the final moments of her life.

All of a sudden, the weight lifted off of her. Eva was sure she was dead until she felt a heavy body fall onto her arm. Luckily, the weight of the Bondsman's corpse did not break it. Her soul was ripped from the ground and shoved back into her body as the fresh air filled her lungs. She crawled to all fours, gulping for air. The Wanderer had been saved by the dark-skinned warrior.

Wanda had snatched up Eva's knife and plunged it into the back of the Bondsman's head with all her strength. The blade punched through bone with a sickening crack, and his body went rigid before collapsing in a heap. The hilt still jutted out from his skull.

Eva coughed until she regained her breath. Wanda crouched by her side.

"We need to get these bodies out of here now," she warned. "Get up. We *must* hurry."

The Wanderer nodded and rubbed her neck softly. Although the man was dead, she could still feel his palms collapsing onto her throat. She sat up and wavered to her feet. Wanda took one man by the arms and Eva grabbed the other by the legs and they made their way across the yard. Tigers were still making their rounds, but their lanterns bobbed from the other side of the compound. A large rut formed in the ground behind the corpses as they were drug through the mud. The Bondsman that Eva was dragging still had her knife stuck in his skull. She would have to remove it before they deserted the bodies.

Wanda guided them to a place behind the Pits where the Tigers brought bodies to be tossed. The pungent, indescribable smell punched Eva in the face as the cold breeze wafted towards them. She gagged and wondered why she had never noticed this place before. The smell of the fires and molten metal must have masked this graveyard.

In the front of the pile of rotting flesh were newer remains. Slumped over a pile of other Doxies was the girl from her tent. Her skin was just as pale as the prior evening. Her frail soul left her body hours ago, lifeless eyes forever staring at the night sky. Only dark, handprint-shaped bruises remained on her limbs. It was the cost of a lifetime of servitude. Wanda noticed Eva and walked towards the body, placing her fingers over the girl's eyes to close them, and spoke a quick prayer.

"It's a shame that Doxies expire in masses just because of our *uniform*," she sighed. Eva released the Bondsman's legs and jerked the embedded knife out of his skull. "This poor girl looks like she got sick from the cold."

Sadly, the sight of death never made Eva think twice. True, she would shed a tear every now and then, but the bodies piled against the compound wall no longer affected her. Tonight, the tent she returned to would be empty.

Eva hugged the woman tight around the shoulders. "Thank you for saving my life. I promise I will get you to your daughter."

"Do not make a promise you cannot keep," Wanda smiled as they crept back to their tents. "I will not be upset if I do not see her again. Simply knowing that she is happy and safe gives me peace."

Those were the words that lingered in Eva's mind for the evening. Wanda was content with her life, though it was filled with pain and suffering. She knew that she may never leave these metal walls but the happiness in her life came from knowing that her daughter was safe. It was like they had never been separated.

Day 1 - Jake and Tommy

"Dad?" Jake's mouth dropped to the floor. Dan McAvoy did not smile when his eldest son recognized him. Instead, he nodded and snapped his fingers. Four of his personal guards, loaded to the teeth with weapons, blocked the door behind them. He took a few gliding steps down the carpet, almost dancing with each stride. Tommy hid behind his brother until their father bent over to look at him.

"I understand your hesitation," he said. His voice was cold but oddly soothing. No sense of emotion within the words, but the baritone chord was melodic. "You were just an infant when I left. And your brother was fifteen, I believe. I suppose a warm welcome is just a father's dream at this point."

"S-so you *were* looking for us?" Jake questioned. "All this time?"

The Chief snapped his fingers again and the Tigers lit the lanterns around the room. Father and sons were able to see each other for the first time in years. Jake thought he resembled his father in face and hair. Tommy, on the other hand, looked nothing like him.

"Well," his father exhaled a dramatic sigh. "Not this entire time. You see, I was forced to fight for my life until I was given this position of power. And it did not come without its… complications."

"I was eighteen Dad." Jake's voice cracked, unsure whether it was sadness or fear. "*Eighteen*. And Tommy was *five*. And you left us. By ourselves. Without a mother or anyone to care for us."

"Do you not think that your mother's death affected me too, boy?" His father snapped, but did not change his expression. "I meant to escape that vault for years. None of us had an inkling how this world would treat us."

"The rest of our people. *Our* friends and families. They were kidnapped by the Serpents to be sold into slavery."

His father raised his hand either to strike his son or silence him. Jake flinched and looked over McAvoy's shoulder at The Wanderer's blades. But his father was too observant. He noticed in an instant.

"What do you know of those blades?" he inquired. Grabbing Jake's chin, he pulled it back to face him. "I refuse to believe that my most precious, *innocent* children survived this long on their own. You must have assistance. At the very least, you must have heard of this Wanderer."

"Heard of, yes." Jake could feel his face getting hot. Tommy was tugging on his shirt. "But I never met the myth. Just stories of the blades… and… I guess those are it?"

The Chief straightened his stance and released his son's face. Straightening his clothing, he cleared his throat and took a step back. Not one person in the room knew what he was thinking until he opened his mouth once again.

"I have a proposition for you boys," his face contorted to a painful-looking grin, if one could call it a grin and not a jeer. "My *sons*. But first, a teaching moment. Yes… a chance to bestow some… perspective. You will work in my kitchens for a day. One single day. You will not be treated as poorly as my slaves in the yard. However, there will be punishment for your actions. All I am doing is simply *teaching* you the difference between a King and the common man."

With another wisp of his hand, the boys were escorted out of the room, but just before they turned the corner, the Chief called out once more. "Oh and boys. If there is *anything* else you would like to tell me, do not stay your tongue. You may find that I am a particularly good listener. *Liars* have no place in my kingdom." And with that, the McAvoy brothers were brought to the floor below and into a room with two beds, then locked inside. Neither of them had anything to say. Their exhaustion settled in and they were asleep within moments.

***

As sunlight burst through the window of Jake and Tommy's prison, both of them opened their eyes to an unfamiliar sight. They had almost forgotten where they had been taken the night before. They had found their father after all these years. Was their reunion a dream or reality? Everything felt like a wisp of smoke they could not grasp. That was, until the Tigers came for them in the morning.

"Get down to the kitchens," they commanded. "The other slaves will show you what to do. Don't screw it up."

The two wavy-haired brothers descended the stairs to the main floor. They hurried down the hallway to the kitchens. When the door opened, it revealed the harsh conditions awaiting them for the day. A large cloud of smoke billowed through the room. Some of it ventilated out of The Castle through small windows on one side. The soot stained air choked both their eyes and throats. Still, the slaves worked endless hours peeling and preparing vegetables, stirring massive pots of thick liquid and serving the edible food to the Gang. Not a single one of them looked like they had eaten in days, maybe longer. Each one, distinct red eyes with deep bags underneath and rib bones poking out of their skin. They stood almost naked, careful to not overheat. The women donned the same nightgowns as the Doxies. One of them walked over to the boys and grabbed Tommy to peel potatoes.

Jake was given two tasks, stir the pot of gray sludge and feed the fire. "It has to stay hot or it will turn solid. We'd have more death on our hands because it rots so fast."

"What's in this?" He asked the wrong question. The guard who had been stationed right inside the door walked over to Jake and grabbed his upper arm.

"Whips aren't allowed in the low ceiling but we still like to leave marks here." This Tiger had blackened teeth. As he pulled out a small, dull blade, he bit down on it like a joke. "Don't you worry about what's in it. It keeps you alive. That's all you need to know."

Jake watched helplessly while the knife penetrated his flesh. It was not deep enough to cause serious injury. But the edge had been so worn, that the pain intensified as the man drew it across his arm. It was only Tommy that noticed his brother screaming in agony, but the Doxie held him back. "Do you want to be next?" she whispered. The rest of the room remained fixed on their work.

"Get back to work," the man sneered and threw Jake back to his fire. "And don't get blood in the slop. I wouldn't want to make another mark on your *pretty* skin."

For the rest of the day, Jake and Tommy worked their hands raw. The younger McAvoy brother had cut up his knuckles while peeling hundreds of potatoes for the Gang. He was told to only clean the blood off the good ones. If they were bad or molding, throw them in a pot to the left, where Jake was stationed. Jake spent the entire day stirring a thick liquid sludge and tossing small logs into a fire. Even his hands were splintered from the wooden spoon and the wound on his arm had not stopped oozing blood. But the worst part was the heat. It was hot enough for him to pass out for a few moments now and again. No one stopped to wake him up.

The kitchen staff was served their evening meal first. Jake was forced to wait until someone took over his position while he ate. When the others had finished, the two frailest old men began carrying the pots out to the yard. It was slow, grueling work. The Tigers watched and laughed as the gangling men slowly moved to each pot. Both were shaking from age and fatigue. Over time, the skin on their chest had calloused from the burns of hot soup sloshing over the edges of the pots. In the hallway, they could hear the Gang ordering them to "hurry up" or "move faster."

After a while, they returned for the second batch of pots. Both of them panted for air and now bore three or four whip markings on their backs. Jake had enough. He noticed that the Tigers in the kitchen had left for the yard. He took one of the pots and raced out to the queues.

When he returned, the two older gentlemen had tried to grab the next pots.

"No," Jake pointed to a few chairs in the corner. The rest of the room watched in amazement. "You should *not* be doing this job. There are too many of us young servants who are more than capable. You men, carry a pot. We will go out in pairs so we avoid suspicion."

The old men cried into their beards, thanking Jake for his kindness. The younger men looked at one another and smiled. For so long, they had allowed the Tigers to treat them as they desired. Truthfully, the guards did not care who brought out the food. It was just a sick joke to force two elderly men to struggle day after day. Jake was part of the first pair to make it out into the yard. The first wave of cold air brushed against his body that was saturated with sweat. Another gust made him shiver when his bare feet sunk into the cold mud. Both young men hurried to the table, dropped their pots as the lines continued to move and raced back into the kitchen.

It did not take long before all of the full dishes of food were emptied. But the kitchen staff were instructed only to clean the dishes that the Tigers had eaten from. The slaves' leftovers, pots, and pans were to be used the following day. After every dish was clean enough to pass the Tiger's inspections, the overnight crew replaced Jake and Tommy's shift. Their hands were crusted with blood. While the rest of the servants filed out into their tents, the brothers were locked back in their room within The Castle.

It was only before closing his eyes that Jake was given time to think of Eva. Because his father had asked of her whereabouts, she must still be alive. There was a good chance that she stayed behind to save them. But maybe she didn't know that the Chief of the compound was Dan McAvoy, their father. He was terrified of what would happen if he did meet Eva because his father seemed unusually determined to find her.

I miss you Eva. Jake pictured her one final time before wiping away his tears and turning on his side to sleep.

Chapter 17

The familiar bang of gunshots woke the only remaining person in the tent, Eva. She hurriedly changed out of her rags and slipped into the sheer black gown. Crisp winter air blew right through the dress and chilled her to the bone. Her shoulders hunched in a shiver as she made her way towards the warm fires for the morning meal. Unlike the day before, she was much more vigilant. She remembered Wanda's warning. The Tigers were alerted to the presence of The Wanderer. It was evident by the increased number of guards in the yard, combing the food lines and interrogating as many servants as they could. But they did not know who Eva was. As long as she did not draw attention to herself, they would not question her. She hoped.

Two faint outlines of bodies behind the Pits reminded her of the night before. The lines shifted, giving her a glimpse between the large barrels that held molten metal for ammunition. She caught a glimpse of her attackers' bodies in the mound of nameless faces. Tigers had already started lighting the bonfires and the smoke masked the smell of death. But the odor stuck to Eva's nostrils. Her bowl of food carried the same scent as the rotting bodies a few feet away. Wanda sat next to her while they ate. They were alone in the tent.

"No one gives the Doxie direction," Wanda explained. "You see what needs to be done and you do it. When a Tiger requests your presence, you give it to them. If you don't, they bring you straight to the torture chambers."

"How many men do you think I could kill before someone would notice?" It was a valid question. Eva still had weapons and she refused to let another man take advantage of her. She would rather die fighting.

"There are only so many ways you can hide a body here. You may have a day or two before it starts rotting. Then the smell will give it away."

The Wanderer choked down the rest of her food. "I'll be out of here by then. Or dead."

"Just look busy and most of them will leave you be. They'll think you are going to the next room or something."

Eva nodded and stood up when the other Doxies began emptying the yard towards The Castle. Wanda departed with their dishes and urged her to get started with her day. *Day Two*. It would be spent scoping any way in or out of the compound as well as a place to hide in McAvoy's chambers on the following day. Manual labor was nothing to her. In fact, she enjoyed it. On the other hand, the work of the Doxies was unspeakable. What transpired behind closed doors was something that Eva refused to recall. She had endured it for too long with the Serpents. And never would she allow it to happen again.

Like clockwork, the Hooded Demon appeared again. It followed her into the front doors of the building, whispering under its breath. "Your plan will never be successful. McAvoy will find you *and* kill you. He will murder his own sons for keeping you a secret. You are a *burden* to them." Eva shut her eyes hard and shook her head, trying to ignore the Shadow's taunting.

The other women were hard at work, and the cooking staff was changing shifts.. Eva's heart jumped when she saw them. Jake and Tommy. Jake looked right at her, but did not seem to notice. She did look quite different, but she had to keep moving. It was a welcomed relief either way. They were alive. She swallowed her tears and walked right past the small crowd. What caught her attention next were the guards interrogating every woman who entered The Castle.

"New girl," one called. Eva flinched. "Yeah. Black dress, red hair. Turn around and come here. We have some questions for you."

Instinctively, Eva put on a fake smile. It matched all of the other Doxies around her. She raised her voice to sound more upbeat. Even her walk became a more graceful stride. All of it made her disgusted with herself.

"Sir?" She swayed on her feet. "How may I be of assistance?"

"Never seen your gorgeous face around here before," the taller man caressed Eva's cheek. Her hand slid to the side of her dress where her knives were, but she resisted the temptation to slit his throat. *Too many witnesses.*

"How'd you like to come to my room?" he winked.

"Sorry sir," Eva lowered her head to hide the irritation. Her voice still remained singsong. "I already have appointments on the top floors today. But perhaps I could fit you in tomorrow if there is time?"

"What a busy gal," the other one laughed. He turned to his friends. "Got a lot of Tigers to please. But she's gotta be one of the prettiest here. It's them eyes."

"I should be on my way then?"

"One more question. You don't know anything about The Wanderer do you? And look at me when you speak."

Eva gazed up, right into the man's soulless gray eyes. Her answer had to be careful and calculated, but not too rehearsed. "Just the stories that people tell, sir. Heard of her, yes. But met her? No. I was a little girl in the Nomad troupe. In the city. Ages ago. Gangs killed my parents and took me here. Well, not *here*. I was with the Serpents for a while."

The men paused. She remained as happy as she could fake, but she was terrified at her response. The silence was driving her crazy. *Was it too much?* After a few moments, she was shooed away. It would not be the last time she was questioned. With each growing fear, her Shadow became stronger. If it became too large, she knew the darkness would be too deep to crawl out of. After curtseying to the Tigers, she hurried to the stairwell and began the climb. First was to find McAvoy's quarters. It must be on the top floor. The day before, he made his rounds in the yard in the early morning, right after daybreak. Now was her chance to gain access.

Uneven concrete steps caused her to trip and scrape her bare knees. The palms of her hands were scratched up but that did not slow her pace. Three floors from the top. Two. One. She stopped and opened the metal door to the floor directly below The Chief's. She searched for something. Right outside one of the bedrooms was a neatly folded pile of clean cloth. Whether it was for bathing or linen, Eva didn't care. It could be used as a distraction. She scooped them in her arms and ran her fingers through her hair, pulling forward a few strands to cover her face.

McAvoy was up there. The Wanderer heard his footsteps moving down the hallway to the stairs. She could wait on the floor below until he and his guards left, but if a Tiger caught her standing idly, there would be consequences. Unfortunately, she had to keep moving.

"I want more guards posted at every tower." The Chief's voice echoed through the stairwell. Marching boots followed the voice towards the yard. "She may try and move at night. So absolute vigilance is a must. Also, I want my sons returned to me after their work. Evening meal. Then my quarters. And most importantly…"

Eva almost bumped into him as she closed the door behind her. He had seen her, but it was clear he did not recognize her. Only a quick side glance had been exchanged between the two rivals. The Wanderer apologized and bowed. Chef McAvoy ignored her presence entirely. Lingering at the top of the stairs, Eva heard his last demand echo towards her.

"Most important, my Tigers," he said. "If luck is on our side and you just happen to find The Wanderer in my kingdom, bring her to me *alive*. I will be the only one who will have the honor of ending her miserable existence. Understood?"

His cronies agreed. Eva touched her neck. Just as she remembered him from years ago, his voice was devoid of emotion. But something was different when he spoke of executing her. Something was off. A faint hint of excitement rose from the underbelly of his words. As his voice trailed off, her demon changed. Not in size, but it developed claws and pointed teeth.

Inside the highest floor of The Castle was an empty C-shaped hallway with a few doors on its perimeter. Eva stuck her head into the first door on her right. And just as Wanda had promised, an old wooden chest. She slipped inside to make sure no one had discovered the hidden cache. Tucked inside was her armor, folded and placed safely underneath a pile of old cloth. Underneath the cloth was a note. It was sealed, a single line scrawled on the top. *Please take this to Elaine, my beloved daughter.* Without another moment to waste, she closed the box and continued down the corridor to the Chief's chambers.

A single guard was posted right outside the room. Opposite to him was another door with a sign that read *Wives*. It must have been where Dan McAvoy kept his concubines. Eva cleared her throat and threw on her fake smile again. The Tiger tensed up out of instinct and pointed his weapon in her direction.

"What are you doing up here, Doxie?" He demanded, prodding the gun barrel to her chest. "Speak."

"I was told to bring this to the Chief's room. New linens." Eva swallowed hard and continued to play his game. He was armed with at least three guns that she could see.

"No one told me," he snuffed.

Her heart was beating so loudly in her ears that her own voice was almost inaudible. "Would you like me to relay that message to the commander who gave me the task?"

"Absolutely not," the Tiger straightened up and lowered his weapon. "You may enter."

And like that, Eva was inside, completely alone. Her eyes were instantly drawn to her blades sitting on the desk and they were ripe for the taking. It reminded her of how naked she felt without them. Those two silver swords were her mark. Without them, she was just Eva. But risking her life along with Jake and Tommy's would be reckless. There was no way she could take her weapons now.

She hid the linens underneath an end table so The Chief would not know she was there, and swiftly made her way around the room. Any place that was small enough for her to hide would be sufficient. Then, plans of murder started to make their way into her mind. Poison? Too impersonal. She had no knowledge of any deadly concoctions. Gunshot? Too loud. Bodyguards would barge into the room in an instant. A knife through the chest? He could survive if the aim was off. But if it was dead on…

It seemed like the only option of concealing herself was a small space between two bookshelves. They joined together in a diagonal pattern. The gap was wide enough for her to slide through, and the darkness would conceal her. So as long as her back was against the wall, she would be invisible. In the morning, after the meal, she would return here and wait for McAvoy to return. When his guards left him for the evening, she would strike.

If this works, she looked at her Shadow, *then I can finally start living my life with Jake… and Tommy.* The thought of them brought up a few tears. Suddenly, the guard outside became impatient. He started banging on the door then threw it open to find Eva standing right in front of him. She stifled her breathlessness until he released her and she was out of sight.

"How long does it take to drop off linens wench?" the Tiger growled and smacked her in the back of her head.

"My apologies," she bowed, stifling the rage that bubbled in her stomach from being struck. "I got caught up in all of the beautiful treasures."

Midday arrived too quickly. The Wanderer hoped that no one had noticed her absence. She made herself look busy, as Wanda suggested, and most of the men ignored her. Truthfully, she had no idea what she was doing just moving piles of clothing and linens around. It scared her more that the Tigers would notice that she was walking the same supplies and leathers back and forth on the floor. On the next floor down, she felt her arm being grabbed as she was yanked into a room.

At first, she believed she had been caught. Someone had snitched on her. It wasn't until the Tiger locked the door and forced her against the wall that she realized what was happening. Both of her arms were held above her. They refused to budge against the Tiger's tight grip. The large man towered over her, easily larger than anyone she had met before. She jerked her head in disgust as he sniffed her neck. He licked his lips and reached up her dress. When he shifted his weight, he accidently released one of her wrists. Fatal mistake.

Eva's knife was already lodged in his stomach. She twisted and felt her hand slide through the man's flesh.

Staggering back, the Tiger tried to reach into his wound to pull out the blade, somewhere in his organs. Blood poured onto the floor like a waterfall. He was able to gurgle one last question. "Who are you?"

Eva dropped to the floor and stood over her kneeling victim. "The wrong Doxie." Sparks of power surged in her body. Her demon shrank in size as the man died at her feet. She needed to figure out how to hide the body. Quickly snatching her knife from the Tiger's chest cavity and wiping the blood on his clothing, she rolled his body on the concrete floor next to the bed. Lucky for her, the concrete was almost black, so the blood blended into its darkness. He was far too heavy to push underneath the bed so Eva managed to wedge herself between the wall and the limp carcass and pushed with her feet. Sweat beaded and dripped from her forehead. One more push and he would be concealed for a couple days. So long as no one knew he was gone, only the eventual smell would give him away.

Evening meal was upon her but she had no appetite. The rest of the Doxies had left The Castle long before Eva made it out of that bedroom. She was so focused on the length of the food lines that she did not see Jake running pots from the kitchen and back.

But he noticed her. Those unmistakable aqua eyes gave her away. Inside, Jake wanted to shout her name, but he forced himself to stay silent. The Tigers would be on them in a second. They would be brought to The Chief, and who knows what would happen next. Even though every fiber of his being wanted to wrap his arms around her, he fought the urge.

"How many Tigers did you take down today?" Wanda joked. Eva was still shaken by what had happened in the Tigers' quarters. Neither she nor Wanda had the stomach for food that night.

"Only one," she said and stirred the slop around in her bowl with an old spoon. Her shadow was seated next to her. Quiet. How unusual.

"I can smell the blood on you. And you didn't even think twice about the color uniform I gave you. No credit."

"Credit is due to you," Eva smiled weakly. "That's for sure."

Wanda lowered her voice. "Are you scared?"

"What?" She had drifted off again.

"For the plan? The *third day*. When you strike down our Chief. You know, save your friends?"

"Oh yeah." How could she forget? Danger loomed over her from the instant she stepped foot in the compound. "I'm just trying not to think about it. If I dwell on it, I might hesitate or make a mistake."

"If I never see you again, know that your bravery gives me hope." Wanda took Eva by the shoulders and hugged her tight. "Someday, I *will* see my daughter again…"

Eva was about to retire for the night when the middle-aged woman with curly hair whispered from her tent. "The place where you entered this compound has not yet been rebuilt. Second floor, closet at the end of the second hall. Maybe I will sneak out before you do."

Eva stirred in her blankets. "You should...Because if I'm discovered, there will likely be an entire army after me."

Day 2 - Jake and Tommy

Their father had only promised one day of hard labor, but he must have forgotten about them. The next morning, they were jolted from their dreamworld by the sound of guards banging on their door. Sunlight had only just begun to seep through the window, its faint warmth pushing back the bite of winter. Both brothers knew another long day awaited them. The smoky coffin that the Tigers called 'the kitchen' would singe the skin off of their arms and blacken their lungs. Sweat would be cascading down their backs within the hour. But anything was better than the Pits.

"I haven't heard anything about Eva." Jake had been worrying about her since they had been captured. He had no clue she had spotted him the day before. *What if they got her? What if she's being tortured at this very moment? What if she's...* The thought of witnessing Eva's death terrified him even more. His stomach twisted in knots. The image of her famous blades at his father's desk hung heavily over his mind.

As they entered the first corridor of The Castle, Jake glanced at someone he swore he recognized. She had short, red hair. It was wavy, not curly. Clad in a black silk nightgown just like the others. It was a Doxie about his age, but they had passed each other so quickly that he did not get a chance for a second look. As they turned their backs to each other, he glanced over his shoulder. This poor soul must have endured years of torture by the scars on her back. They were not numerous enough to cause her torso to deform, but there were a few prominent slashes from shoulder to shoulder. Jake convinced himself that he must have met her in the Rover colony or Nomad troupe. He had seen her before but his brain could not pinpoint where.

"Those Doxies ain't for you!" A guard smacked him on the back of the head, hard. "Not for your eyes. Or your hands. So don't get any funny ideas."

"She's probably hiding." Tommy tried to remain level-headed because his brother looked like he would explode at any second. "You know Eva. If we saw her, our dad *would* find out."

"You're right," he said. Admitting that his brother's words were comforting was difficult. But they were. Without another word, they traveled down the last hallway on the main floor to the kitchen. Tommy went back to peeling potatoes while Jake took charge in keeping the contents of the pot from solidifying. The smell of rotting food was particularly pungent that day. Every single servant gagged as they passed the fires.

But that was not the only thing that had changed. Something else was different. Rather, *missing*. Two people were gone. And not just any servants. The elderly gentlemen who were forced to carry heavy dishes to and from the yard were gone. Jake had seen them cutting other vegetables only a day ago. In the corner of the room, there was nothing but a lonely table with food waiting to be prepared. Blunt knives lay motionless next to them. He feared the worst. If they were no longer useful, the Tigers had disposed of them.

"*Don't stop stirring*," one of the servants warned.

Jake nearly fell off the stool where he was sitting. He had dozed off from the heat again. "Where are the older men that were here yesterday?" Jake pushed back a few strands of hair from his face.

The servant's reply did not surprise him. "Dead. Most likely… Good eye, though. We need someone at that station." He called two women near Tommy to replace the elderly men.

Jake felt the urge to be angry at the man's lack of sensitivity, yet he knew this was something they witnessed daily. *Their entire lives are built around death. You have to be numb to survive.* He continued drawing the spoon around the pot, staring deep into the lumpy gray sludge. Whiffs of rancid onions curled his toes and he swallowed the vomit in his throat.

Finally, their break for the evening meal arrived. It felt like days had passed. For the first part of the shift, the Tigers refused to open the windows because they were too cold. It didn't take long before the air became unbreathable. They could feel their lungs blacken as they exhaled the same smoke that went in. After a few beatings of pleading servants, they finally agreed to crack the windows to let the smoke clear. When Jake looked for his brother, the cloud of smog had become too opaque to see past an arm's length. By the time it was clear enough for his eyes to stop burning, the slave-drivers rang the bell to serve the food. And as usual, the kitchen staff was allowed to eat first. They had all spent the day smelling the spoiled food. They cut and prepared the mushy, moldy vegetables that went right in with the rest of the slop.

"I can't eat this." The whole kitchen murmured in disgust.

"I can smell it through the sweat in here."

"You don't have to eat it."

"Yeah, but *they* do. Outside."

"People will die because of this."

"It's not like we have never served this before. Slaves are not allowed to eat the good stuff. And if we try to go on a hunger strike… They'll just let us starve. If we stop working…well, you know."

"Maybe tomorrow will be better."

Children were the first to pour the contents of their bowls back in the pots. Tommy led them. Although he did not want to go hungry, he had a bad feeling that the food would make him ill. Jake, too, followed in his brother's footsteps but could not help thinking of Eva. *If she's out there and eats this food and dies, it would be entirely my fault.* The hope that she would be late for dinner was all he could muster.

The other servants had been taking turns running the food out to the yard. Again, Jake lifted a pot to his chest and started out the door. Most of the Bondsmen stood at the front of the line and the Doxies filled the rear. He was part of the third pair to switch out the food and women were still leaving The Castle. The cold handles of the empty pot froze his sweaty hand to the metal and burned. Instead of crying out in pain, he bit his lip and hurried back into the building. Only a few steps towards his brick sanctuary. Then, he saw her.

Eva. He was positive it was her—the woman he had seen before. He scolded himself for not recognizing her earlier. His heart screamed for him to stop, wrap his arms around her shivering figure, and kiss her, but his brain yanked his feet forward. She had not even noticed him.

I bet she knows we're here, he reasoned. *That's why she hasn't left. And that's probably why she's dressed like a Doxie. She has a plan. I know it. And it will work. It has to.*

When he returned to the kitchen, masking the smile on his face, three of his father's personal guards were waiting. Tommy was with them. His stance seemed solemn, but his face read fear. The leader of the group pointed up and said nothing. Jake made a guess as to where they were going. Their father had requested their presence again. He had spoken of a 'proposition' before.

***

Dan McAvoy waited for his sons. While they might have thought the two days of work were meant to offer perspective, he knew better. His reasons were darker and far more sinister. It was a test. Not a pass or fail test, per se. He thought of it more like a test of character for his proposition. But there was one thing that he did not account for. Normally, when he overlooked a possible outcome, he would take his frustrations out on innocent lives. But it was this very result that had given him an idea. It excited him, but he remained calm and stoic.

Jake and Tommy entered their father's chambers alone. Half of the torches were lit inside. Their father stood at the other end of the room, behind his desk, facing the large window. It overlooked the entire compound. And in the distance, the Serpent's compound glowed dimly, still bustling well after dark. Jake put his hand on his brother's back for comfort. Silence weakened their tired legs and exhausted their minds with worry. When he did finally speak, his gaze remained fixated on the horizon.

"My sons." A dead voice came from his curled lips. "You have completed your test. How do you think you fared?"

"A test?" Jake didn't understand. "I thought-"

"Obviously your thoughts were incorrect," he interrupted. "But if you were to consider the past two days as a test. How do you think you performed? We had schools in the Vault. What marks would you give yourselves?"

"I would say that I was not the best." Jake was unsure how to answer. He could not gauge what his father desired as a response. So, he tried to be as honest as possible. "However, given the circumstances, I rose to the occasion. I worked hard. Took initiative."

"Interesting." The Chief gave no indication of liking or disliking his eldest son's answer. He directed his attention to his younger son. "And Thomas? What about you?"

Tommy took a deep breath. "I think I did my job as I was told. When someone needed help, I helped."

"But did you help only because you feared punishment?" He had not asked any questions of Jake. This raised their anxiety even more. "Or did you choose to help because it was the correct thing to do?"

Tommy was silent. He did not know the answer to his father's question. McAvoy turned around. In one hand, glinting in the moonlight, was one of Eva's blades. With it swinging off to his side, he strode over to them. Holding it playfully in his grasp, he pointed it at each one of his sons. In turn, they each stiffened, waiting for the strike. Another moment of silence, then Dan McAvoy's perfectly groomed beard widened to a smile. A cackle of evil erupted out of him and sent his sons backing against the wall.

"This has all been very fascinating for me, boys," he said as he lowered the weapon. "Truly enthralling. My spark of genius to test you worked better than I could have hoped."

"What are you talking about?" Jake squeaked.

His father's face dropped in a flash. "Well, if you *must* know… When I happened upon you in the Pits, I was going to request that you both join me in the Gang. You would not be a very high rank to start out. No. But you would learn what is required of you. How to serve me. You would be given all of your desires. Good food, warm beds, training, power, *women*."

He paused and shoved The Wanderer's blade into Jake's grasp.

"But then I thought more logically. I considered the fact that I no longer know my boys. How *did* they survive for so long in this unforgiving world? Too suspicious, if you ask me." His back turned to them and he continued. "The Rovers may have taken you in. But then, how did you get past The Blooded Row between my kingdom and the Serpent Nest? Again… too suspicious. But then, it dawned on me. Perhaps, at least one of my boys… was truly like their father. A *survivor* who understood what it takes to live out here. Maybe you slaughtered a few people for food or supplies? Who cares."

"And the test was to prove what?" Jake had a clear shot to his father's chest. He grasped the hilt of Eva's blade so tightly, his knuckles turned white. But if he pounced, the Chief would be ready. He knew that much. *Why do I want to kill him so badly? This isn't like me.* After begging Eva to find him for months, what he found was not what he expected.

"My dear boy," he sighed and shook his head. "To prove which one of you was worthy. If not both of you, one of you must have the heart of a Tiger in him. My proposition that I mentioned... The test that I administered... only *one* of you passed."

Jake looked around in confusion. His hands were trembling violently. Tommy's eyes were glued to his brother. Their father turned on his heels and lifted his arms.

"And now," he bowed to them. "My proposal is this... Jacob McAvoy, my eldest son, you have made me proud as your life giver and thus have a choice. So, choose carefully."

Chief McAvoy paused and smiled menacingly.

"... Strike down your *weaker half* and join me or I will cut both of you down where you stand."

"W-what?" Jake stuttered. He stared in horror at his brother. "P-Please. You can't be serious."

"Power is the *only* thing I am serious about," his voice twitched with anger and impatience. "I only breed leaders. And I will only allow my blood to flow in the veins of a leader. Your brother is a sheep among wolves."

Tommy had tears of anger and terror streaming down his dirty face. "I'm standing right here! You want me dead because I'm not like you?"

The Chief snatched the blade from Jake's hand and returned it to the sheath on his desk. He returned to his position at his desk. "Precisely Thomas. I *cannot* have any child of mine be weak. I *will not* have a child of mine be weak."

Jake and Tommy were at a loss for words. Dan McAvoy circled the desk and slammed his fist down. It had been a signal for the guards to enter and grab the boys to take them back to their room. This time, they would be separated. Just before they were dragged off the floor, their father called out to his eldest.

"You have one day to make the decision Jacob," he said. "Be grateful that I am giving you time to consider your choice. If you do not choose. *I will.*"

And with those parting words, The Chief's chambers were closed behind them.

Chapter 18

Sleep became impossible for Eva that night. Her body and mind were exhausted but rest was fleeting. Most of the twilight hours were spent staring at the leather overhang of her tent, blowing in the wind. After hours of deliberation, she decided that it no longer mattered whether she survived or not. There were only two things she cared about, Dan McAvoy lying in a pool of his own blood and Jake and Tommy's safety. That had to be the outcome, no matter the cost.

Morning was soon upon her. She rubbed her eyes and sat up the moment she heard Tigers marching into the yard to wake the servants. Wanda was sitting at the edge of her tent, as silent as the winter air. Something pained her. She hugged her bony knees to her chest, resting her chin on them. Everyone was filing to the meal lines after the gunshots, but one Doxie stayed behind with The Wanderer.

Eva crouched next to her friend, knowing that this could be the last time she ever saw her. "Is everything okay?"

"I should ask the same of you," she sighed. "But no… I'm afraid of the world out there. This has been my life for so many years. What if I don't make it out there?"

"Freedom is for *everyone*," Eva smiled. She put her hand on Wanda's shoulder. "You fight for it every moment you are in this compound. And you will still fight tooth and nail out there. But you will survive. And you *will* see Elaine."

"And I hope that you are successful in your plan," she added. "Whether or not I gather the courage to crawl out of this place…doesn't matter… You need to fight for what you believe in. Revenge. Love. Whatever. Just never stop fighting."

The two women embraced and Eva picked up a bowl for her final meal. She would go straight to the top floor while The Chief walked the grounds of his "kingdom," waiting for him between the two bookshelves. When his guards retired for the night, she would strike.

Then she would rescue Jake and Tommy.

But that's if everything goes right, she reminded herself.

It could have been the fact that she had not eaten since yesterday morning, but the slop in her bowl tasted better than normal. A chill crept up her spine as she watched her Hooded Demon staring at her from the corner of the tent. If this truly was the end, at least she would be free of that shadow, whatever it was. She took one final stroll around the yard as the Bondsmen started another day in the Pits. Doxies made their daily, muddy trudge to The Castle, like skeletons standing in line for the cemetery. Eva left her bowl with the Tigers and walked up to the large metal doors. Tarrying only for a moment on the threshold, she took a deep breath and stepped inside.

Darkness overwhelmed her senses. A slight heat permeated the main floor from the kitchens. The smell of cooking food filled her nostrils. Her muddy feet were warmed and dried on the stairwell. She scraped off the layers of dirt with her gown. Realizing that some patches of her dress were crusted with a dark liquid, she lifted it up and examined her wraps. Her heart skipped a beat. Blood stained her chest as well as the linens wrapping it. At first, she believed it was her own blood, but then she realized that it was Tiger blood from the day before.

Suddenly, footsteps rose from the floor below. Heart racing, she threw the gown over her torso and sprinted up the stairs. Yesterday she had wanted people to see her working, but not today. Today she was a ghost. It made slipping into McAvoy's quarters easier, and if no guard stood watch at his door, infiltration would be simpler still.

As luck would have it, the hallway on the top floor was empty for the moment. Just as Eva slipped through the closet door where her armor and weapons were stored, Dan McAvoy and six bodyguards marched past. His voice was sharp as he barked orders for the day. Pressing her ear against the wood, Eva listened closely as their footsteps echoed down the passageway.

"...And what of The Wanderer?" he asked. "No one has discovered her yet? I find that difficult to believe."

"No sir," a woman answered. "We have doubled our presence in the yard and every tower. Nothing suspicious to report."

"Then, clearly, all of you are imbeciles," he snapped. "Of course she would not draw attention to herself. Do you really believe that I'm looking for a simple, bumbling slave? *No*. This woman is significantly more intelligent than my Tigers, it seems. Triple your efforts. I want every woman questioned… *relentlessly*."

The group stopped right in front of the closet door. Eva placed her hand next to her ear. One of the male guards spoke. "My King. If I may ask, why do you care so much about *one* person? The Wanderer is just one woman against an entire army."

All of a sudden, the crack of fist on bone and the metal door shook violently as a body smashed against it. "My reasons for wanting her dead do not matter. *I* give orders. *You* perform them. *Without. Question.* Insubordination will cost you your rank. And you should be *grateful* it will not cost you more."

"Thank. You. Sir." The footsteps continued down the hallway until it was completely silent.

Everyone had left except the man who had been thrown against the door. Eva could hear him stagger to his feet, moaning and slurring his words. She opened the door slightly to find him hobbling towards the stairs, unsteady and stumbling against both walls. As he turned the corner to the stairwell, she heard a scream, and then a sound like someone had dropped a heavy bag down the stairs. Then there was a low moan followed by silence.

But Eva had little time to investigate. She quickly changed into her armor.

The thick leather tightened around her curves and seven knives wrapped around her thighs and chest, crisscrossing over her body. Finally, she strapped her gun, only second in importance to her blades, around her waist. It provided a feeling of safety and comfort. She no longer felt vulnerable. She was The Wanderer again.

Eva needed to bolster herself up. She repeated the phrases she told herself long ago, when she was the Mistress of the Serpents, "Play the game better than anyone. Better than *anyone*. Don't let anyone or anything stop you… I may not have my blades, but any weapon with Dan McAvoy's blood on it will suffice."

Her words were dark. Almost as dark as her demon. When she whispered the final phrase of murder, the Hooded Shadow completely dematerialized. *Why disappear now?* But she didn't have time to dwell on it. She focused herself on the next step, getting into The Chief's room. Eerie silence filled the corridor as she closed the closet door painstakingly slowly. On the other side, where she felt the jolt from the guard's body, were two dents. They were about the size and position of a human head and shoulder. A thick, crimson liquid near the top of the larger indentation dripped onto the floor.

Eva tiptoed down the hallway. With her back pressed against the wall, she peered around the corner. It was empty. The Chief's room was unguarded for the moment, but she was still wary. Everything had gone according to plan up to this point. She knew it was only a matter of time before her luck would shift. It always did. Whether her day ended with a gun to her face or a knife at her throat, things were going to change.

The door to McAvoy's chambers was unlocked.

Now, everything was starting to seem too easy. A pit formed in Eva's stomach. Either McAvoy was slipping, or she was being led right into a trap. Regardless, she had to continue. She closed the door behind her with a soft click and her eyes immediately locked onto her blades laying on the desk. The urge to take them was overpowering. *That will be the first thing he notices when he returns. It would be stupid of me to take them now. But when I confront him...*

Squeezing between the bookshelves directly next to his bed, she felt a shroud of invisibility encompass her. Lanternlight spilled over the walls and floor, leaving only her corner untouched, body swallowed in shadow. No one would be able to see her unless she stepped out. And only when she was ready to face McAvoy would she reveal herself. It would be hours before he returned and even longer before he was left alone for the evening. She knew from the moment Jake and Tommy had been dragged into the building, their father had discovered them. They would likely be held in a room near the Chief. Eva would use that to her advantage after striking down her enemy.

I hope they're close, she pleaded. *Maybe they'll be brought in here.*

The lack of planning stung. She scolded herself again and again—one detail, one stupid detail. Too much guessing. Not enough studying.

Was this it? The turning point?

Kill McAvoy in front of his sons. Lose the trust of Jake and Tommy, but finally taste the sickening sense of relief and revenge.

What if an alarm is triggered? The Tigers would be on her.

Or a thousand other endings.

Waiting for the Chief felt like a single breath, especially with her thoughts tangling in on themselves. He returned after completing his rounds, snapping his fingers and having servants tortured or executed. The sun was breaking through the window by midday and basked the room in a brilliant light. From where Eva was sitting against the wall, she studied every trinket and treasure hoarded in his room. And while McAvoy spent most of the day staring out his window, occasionally commanding his personal bodyguards, Eva examined his possessions. Scattered across his desk were a number of newspaper articles from the Old Times. Although she could not make out the headlines, she noticed their yellowed, brittle pages cracking under a periodic breeze. Directly across the bookshelves was a larger shelf. Upon it, dozens of knickknacks were arranged in two perfect lines, displayed like trophies. She immediately recognized the smaller figures on the top shelf. They were the same trinkets The Tigers had taken when they ransacked her home.

My things. So that's where they went. Years of collecting... all to be taken by this man. Funny, this isn't the first time he's stolen something from me.

Fatigue started wearing on Eva as the day went on. She nodded off a handful of times only to be awoken by the Chief yelling orders at another Tiger. It was a long wait. Finally, the room darkened with the sky. The guards took their leave for the evening, but not before receiving one final demand from their heartless leader.

The Wanderer's stomach shot to her throat.

"Retrieve my boys."

Day 3 – Jake and Tommy

Tommy was the only one that slept that night because he trusted that his brother would make the right decision. At first, when they had been thrown into separate rooms, they were terrified. Jake never believed his father would suggest something as heinous as killing his only family. He berated himself the entire night. *I should have trusted Eva when we first met.* She was right.

Their father *was* in a compound and he *was* dead. The parent Jake remembered no longer existed. This new life outside the Vault had changed them all. Jake had grown a lot and learned a lot. So did his brother.

But it also changed him. It must have. He stared out his window at the vast forest that separated the region. Right outside his window was freedom, seven stories down. No one would make it very far after jumping from that height. He looked around and found nothing to throw over the side and climb down either. It seemed like there was no way to avoid his father and his proposition, but Jake had already made his choice.

The sunrise was giving him a headache. Jake sat up in his cot and waited for a Tiger to unlock the door. Nobody came. Neither he nor Tommy would be working that day. They were given a day to ponder. Jake, about his choice. And Tommy, about his existence. His father was malicious in that way.

A bowl of food was slid through a crack in the door around midday before being locked tight. Both brothers ate their meals in silence.

While Jake was sulking in his room, Tommy got to work. He discovered a rusty old drill under an overturned chair that still worked. He started boring a hole into the stone wall. Paint chips broke away easily, but the concrete block was thick. He would have to be diligent to burrow a hole into Jake's room. All he wanted was to speak to his brother before being taken up to their father late in the evening.

It did not take long for Jake to hear the grinding. At first, he thought he was imagining things, but heard it getting louder. The sound came from the corner of the room where Tommy's room shared a wall. He had to move a few pieces of old furniture out of the way. Throwing a few things aside, he searched for an item to help his brother break through. Other than a handful of metal chair legs, he found nothing of use. Being forced to wait until Tommy made it through was maddening. It took hours. Eventually, he spotted a tiny patch of the brick giving way. It cracked and crumbled into small pieces of dust and rock. It grew in size until the drill pushed through and Tommy pulled it back in.

"Jake?" he called. "Are you there?"

"Yeah buddy." Jake sat next to the hole and peered through. "I'm here."

"Good," Tommy sighed. "I thought dad had taken you… maybe… trying to get you on his side."

Jake swallowed the lump in his throat. "No. Still stuck in my room."

His brother did not want to ask the obvious question. So he changed the subject. "Think Eva's still alive?"

"I saw her last night. When I was making runs. She was dressed like a Doxie. Really, Tommy. She cut her hair too."

"How did you know it was her?"

"At first, I didn't. But it *was*. And if I know that amazing woman, she's trying to break us out. *Both* of us."

There was a long pause. Jake stood up and pressed his ear to the hole, thinking he had missed something.

"Do you think she'll kill Dad?"

The thought had not crossed his mind. "Dunno. Maybe she knows that's the only way to save us. Now that he knows we're alive…if we escape, he will hunt us."

Both brothers felt their hearts stop when they heard a scream coming from the direction of the stairwell. It was followed by a crashing sound. And then, an unsettling silence.

"What was that?" Tommy grabbed his chest. "Sounded like someone…"

"Maybe Eva did it?"

"Or Dad… Hey Jake, was he always like this?"

No. He was a great father who took the time to teach me many things. "Yeah, but not this heartless. Always cold." Jake lied. He didn't want his brother to think he missed out on being fathered by a kind man.

"Are you scared?" Tommy's voice quivered.

"Terrified. You?"

"Remember the statue that Eva let me have? The one with the sitting man?"

"Yeah. Why?"

"When the Tigers took all of our things. They didn't notice that I had it in my hand. I held it so tightly. But then they left us… Every day since we've been here, we haven't been killed. Hurt, a little. But we're still alive. Maybe I'm not afraid because this gave me luck. I know Eva will save us… *Before* dad gets us."

Jake smiled and wiped his eyes. His brother, on the surface, sounded naive, but the meaning of his words carried wisdom far beyond his age. Even if they were to die today, they had no control over that fact. Oddly enough, that epiphany brought a strange feeling of peace over him.

Neither of the boys noticed that the sky had gone dark until the Tigers came. They stood at the doorway of each room and only said one thing, "Your father is ready for you." Both of the young men stood up and dusted off their ragged clothes. They were ready for whatever came next.

***

Eva had carefully positioned herself so she could see the front door of McAvoy's chambers. When it opened, her hand slipped over to the handle of a knife. Directly behind four guards were Jake and Tommy. She quietly gasped, but could not allow herself to be overwhelmed by emotion. For now, they were swept to the back of her mind. The Chief, with the flick of his wrist, ordered away his guards leaving only his sons in the room. He had no idea that The Wanderer also shared the same space.

"Welcome back." Dan McAvoy had already pulled out one of Eva's blades and stood between the desk and his sons. "I have two questions for you. One, I am sure you have been pondering the answer. The other, you may have forgotten by the severity of the first."

"Then ask us the latter." Jake tried to match his father's eloquence but not his lifeless tone. He felt the Chief's lifeless, blue eyes on him, tearing away at his courage.

"As I intended… What do *you* know of The Wanderer?"

His eldest son gave no pause. "Nothing aside from stories. We have answered this question bef-."

"*Have you?*" His anger surfaced only in his words, never his face. "And what if your answer does not please me?"

"Then you would have me lie to please you. I remember how highly you value the truth."

"As always, my eldest. You impress me with your responses… My absence has taught you well… Then what of my proposition? I have given you plenty of time to dwell on the implications."

"One day to make a decision to end my brother's life, by my hand, or you end both of ours?"

"Precisely."

Eva covered her mouth to muffle her shock. She had to move fast, but lingered just a few seconds longer. McAvoy had to take a few steps towards his sons so she could slink out of the shadows. Also, Jake seemed like he had crafted a plan of his own.

"Yes. I suppose I have made my decision."

"And?"

"I choose… *neither*."

McAvoy took a step back in confusion. Eva's brow furrowed in the darkness. Tommy's eyes widened in surprise. Then, The Chief laughed. It started as a silent snicker as he covered his face then exploded into laughter of pure rage. His stance straightened and words spewed out of him like lightning.

"*Laughable* to think that you have a third option, petulant boy." He started taking long strides toward them. He did not notice Eva creep out from between the bookshelves and grab her remaining blade, securing the sheaths to her back. This was the first time anyone had seen true madness in McAvoy's eyes. "You are just as *weak* as your brother. Foolish of me to believe that you were different. Shame. I admit that I was wrong about you. And in the rarest of events that I am wrong… I wipe out *everything* that reminds me of my mistake."

He had The Wanderer's other blade pressed against Jake's throat. Suddenly, The Chief felt another at his back. Both of his sons' gazes were fixated over his shoulder. And then, he recognized a familiar voice. "Your battle is with me, McAvoy. Or should I say, *Dan Avery*. As usual, *coward*, your anger is misplaced."

Dan McAvoy spun around so fast that his perfectly groomed hair fell out of place. Eva took a step back to dodge her other blade. She glanced at Jake and Tommy who both had looks of relief on their faces. She nodded at them and turned back to her opponent.

"I knew you would crawl out of the sewers eventually," he taunted. "You stand witness to all the power I hold and you have the audacity to call me a *coward*?"

"You have always been a *coward*," Eva mocked. They were circling each other in the middle of the room. "You were always the loudest of my men, and undoubtedly the laziest. Despite how methodical you claim to be, you're incredibly sloppy. And your hunger for power was only satisfied by mutiny. We both knew you were too weak to face me as Mistress… to strike me down like a warrior."

"I would have killed you-"

Eva cackled. Her tone matched his. "You *really* think your skills are superior to mine? No. You were definitely smarter back then because you *knew* you didn't stand a chance. And you *still* don't have a chance now. But you call your own sons weak. Pitting them against each other like animals? How far into insanity have you fallen?"

"Insanity? Ha! You would know all about that, wouldn't you? I know stories of the Shadow that haunts you. The nightmares that plague your every evening."

"And here I stand despite all of that. People across the region praise and fear my name, but *you* have nothing to show for your past. Only the Tigers know your name. You will *never* have my fame and the power it holds."

She could see the murder in her enemy's eyes. Despite his bubbling rage, he straightened his cloak and cleared his throat.

"We shall see cur. Let us be rid of our enemy. May the best warrior win."

"Oh, *I* intend to."

In a flash, Eva's opponent lunged towards her, blade outstretched. She parried, pushing her blade against his. He toppled towards one of the shelves of trinkets, knocking them over with an ear-shattering crash. Jake heard the guards outside and quickly locked the door. Tommy ran to the corner of the room and grabbed a chair, wedging it between the doorknob and the floor. Tigers began banging from the hallway, calling to their Chief. The Wanderer wasted no time slashing at his arm, missing by a hair. They traded sides and she was shoved against another bookshelf as the contents toppled onto her head. She shook it off just in time to dodge a punch aimed at her face.

Metal statues crashed to the floor as the two entwined in battle. Neither of them could gain an opening without the other changing their stance or parrying. Every slash was met with a side step. Each stab was met with the clang of blade on blade. McAvoy's lack of skill and Eva's exhaustion weakened both combatants. Still, they fought on.

Right outside the front door, they could hear the Tigers clawing at the entrance. Roars of concern rose over the sound of battle. Jake and Tommy remained propped against it, acting as extra wedge against the battering ram opposite the door.

"Leave her to me you imbeciles," he yelled out to them. His hair was falling in his face. Then he turned his eyes to his sons. "I will deal with you two later."

"You have to get back to your feet and face me first," Eva reminded. "Kill me if you can."

"With pleasure." An evil smile curled on his lips as he raced towards her again but crouched down at the last second, knocking Eva off her feet. She fell backwards onto the table, using her blade to block him. He lifted his weapon overhead and drew it down hard, using his weight against her shaking arms. She could see the bloodlust in his eyes tinged with lunacy. Cold metal almost pierced her forehead when she finally freed a leg and kicked him in the stomach. McAvoy staggered back. Tigers were still banging at the door, threatening to break it down. Jake and Tommy reinforced their makeshift barricade with more furniture.

Eva jumped back to her feet and sprinted at him, leaning forward and aiming at his waist. With all the strength she could muster, she lifted him in the air and shoved him against the wall. A picture fell from the wall and crashed over their heads, shattering glass everywhere. Eva felt him try to grab a shard. She screamed and forced his arm away. He was able to break free by rolling away.

They were both out of breath, but The Chief managed to let out another laugh. Eva's eyes widened as she reached down to where her gun was supposed to be holstered. It was no longer there. As she looked up, her heart dropped.

Jake.

Chapter 19

"Why the change of face, *Wanderer*?" Dan McAvoy had taken her gun in the scuffle. The barrel was now pressed against the head of his eldest son who was kneeling between them. Tommy was being held against the door by the edge of the Chief's blade. McAvoy's eyes were wild with rage. "I remember when you spoke to the Serpents about playing this game of survival. You claimed that you were the *best*. Maybe I believed it once upon a time, but it seems as though you've lost your touch. In my opinion, you lost it when you started caring for someone aside from yourself. And now. I have double the leverage."

"You care so little for your own sons that you would use them against me?" she tried to hide the panic from her face. "How disgusting."

Eva was screaming internally. She knew how unpredictable Dan McAvoy could be. There was no remorse in his face. His hunger for power and fame would make him pull that trigger and murder his eldest son. But that wasn't his only objective. To achieve his ultimate goal, he must slay the only person who could give him that ultimate power and fame, The Wanderer. If he was the one who paraded around with her head on a stake, his name would be known throughout the region. Finally, his dream was within his grasp.

"It is *you* who is on the wrong side of a gun this time," he smirked. "And you would question me?"

"And as I told you," Eva took two steps towards them but stopped when he pushed the barrel further into Jake's head. He did not notice that he had loosened his grip on Eva's blade at Tommy's throat. "I'm the one you want. Not Jake and not Tommy. *Let. Them. Go.*"

"This is not the circumstance to be making demands," he laughed. "You are no longer my Mistress. And you no longer have the upper hand."

"Chief!" Someone called from outside the door. "We can hear you in there. Please let us in."

"Shut up!" he yelled. "I have everything under control."

Everyone in the room stood in uncomfortable silence, waiting for what Chief McAvoy would do next. Eva brandished her blade, ready to strike. She noticed that when his Tigers called for him, he would get distracted for a moment. Each time, he would turn his head towards the door for a fraction of a second. That was her only chance, a shot in the dark. She would have to grab his gun with one hand and try to knock her blade from the other. If he pulled the trigger in the scuffle, Jake would be hit. But if he was disarmed, Eva had a clear shot to his torso. Jake was watching her very closely.

Whatever she's thinking, please let it work.

"Chief!"

Dan McAvoy turned towards the door.

Now.

Eva lunged. A shot rang off. It hit the ceiling, missing Eva's face by inches. When he dropped the blade, Tommy snatched it off the tile floor. The Wanderer and the brothers took action. Jake pinned his father's legs and right arm to the ground. Eva drove her knee onto the other limb hard, keeping the gun pinned to the floor. McAvoy's bones cracked under her weight. Flashes of red appeared in her field of vision as she raised her blade above her head, two hands grasping the hilt firmly. As she drove it downwards, the feeling of tearing flesh, muscle, and bone triggered something in her mind. Images and scenes from her days as a Mistress were starting to surface. Countless victims at the end of her gun and hundreds falling to her blades. She felt imaginary droplets of blood spatter across her face. Finally, the image of who she knew under the false identity of Dan Avery. The Chief looked up at her in horror. It was ultimately when the Tigers burst through the door that she was able to snap out of her trance.

Dan McAvoy clawed at the gaping hole in his ribcage, blood pumping hot between his fingers. Her aim hadn't been true enough for a fatal blow, but the damage was done. He would be dead within minutes. It had not been part of the plan, but watching his face contort to panic made her sickeningly euphoric.

Now, Eva, Jake, and Tommy had to focus on the horde of armed guards flooding into the room. She yanked the blade from her enemy's chest and grabbed the other from Tommy. The Wanderer shoved Jake away from the doorway. Her blades were going to be useless in the gun battle. She was able to take down three guards when she heard another, much louder gunshot. Tommy screamed her name.

"*Eva!*" he bawled over the commotion. "It's *Jake*. It's Jake. He's shot. Dad shot him in the arm. He's hurt. Come on! We gotta go."

Eva spun around to the spot where she had last seen her adversary. He was still lying there. The firearm in his grasp was still smoking. His only movement came from his heaving chest. Near the door, Jake and Tommy were motioning for her as more Tigers rushed in. Eva fired a few shots in the air with a gun nearby as a distraction. It was so chaotic that the guards were shooting at one another and did not notice the boys flattened against the wall. Their carelessness alone caused massive casualties. Without a moment to spare, Eva grabbed the boys and fought their way out of the room.

They rounded the hallway and sprinted down the stairs. Eva huffed, "To the second floor. A Doxie told me that where we entered has not been patched up yet. We get out. We find a place to hide and patch Jake up. Then we head South towards the city."

"But they'll follow us," Jake panted. He was compressing his arm so tightly, a trickle of blood found its way between his fingers and down his forearm. "We can't go back to the city. It won't be safe."

"You're right." Eva called back as they threw open the door to the main floor. Doxies and Bondsmen were filing in and out from the yard as the group shoved them aside. Some of them crashed against the wall, others fell to the floor, cursing at them as they ran past. Eva turned back to see a small group of Tigers approaching the front doors. They looked right at her and barreled through the crowd at them. Slaves pressed themselves against the sides of the corridor or were trampled.

"The Rovers and the Nomads can't fight an army." Tommy squeaked over the commotion. "Where do we go?"

Eva felt like a failure. Jake was injured, the entire Tiger Gang was after them, and they had nowhere to go that was safe. "We just keep going south." That was the only thing she could say. They could sense the defeat in her voice.

At least Dan McAvoy is dead, she thought. *And his sons are safe at the moment. Jake could have been hurt much worse.*

Something did not sit well with her. She did not get the satisfaction of watching her enemy take his final breath. A seed of doubt grew in her mind. *No.* She shook her head as they continued to race down the corridors. *I killed him. No one could survive that. It's over. He's done. I have my revenge.*

Jake pointed to a closet on the second floor with his good arm. They were almost free. As bullets whizzed past their heads, the three crowded inside the small room. Eva told them that she would go through the opening last. She slammed the door as Tommy scampered through the muddy opening to freedom. While Jake stepped up on the wooden box to lift himself up, The Wanderer sheathed her other blade and threw a metal shelf in front of the door as a barricade.

The Tigers continued shooting through the walls. One of them used the butt of his gun to smash the doorknob in an attempt to break through. Jake was almost through the exit as Eva forced his feet out as swiftly as she could. Her makeshift blockade was groaning under the weight from outside. She threw her arms over her head and hoisted her body through the cavity of crumbled brick. The leather in her armor acted as a buffer, keeping her stomach and legs from being torn to shreds. Jake and Tommy were already sprinting towards No Man's Land as she rose to her feet. Glancing behind her one last time, she heard the Tigers break through as she disappeared around The Castle.

Eva caught up to the brothers as they bolted into a nearby subdivision. Breathing in the fresh air for the first time in days felt refreshing but short-lived. Any minute, the Tigers would catch up to them. Even if they did not catch her, they would nominate a new Chief and he or she would send out a militia to hunt them. It may be years before the pursuit ended, if it ended at all. Jake's wound was not life-threatening, but it needed to be wrapped until they were safe. They hurried into the closest building, and she got to work.

"We have no clothes or weapons for this journey," Jake was trying to catch his breath. His lungs felt like they were going to explode.

Eva motioned to Tommy as she bound his brother's arm. "Go see if there are any clothes that will keep you two from getting sick. I have a few spare knives you can have for the time being. Because of your father, I no longer have my gun."

"We had no idea, Eva," Jake said. She did not look at him at first, so he grabbed her arm and forced her eyes to look into his. "*I* had no clue. He was never like this before. I'm so sorry Eva. I am so sorry."

"Please don't beat yourself up about this whole thing, Jake." Eva tightened the knot on his wrapping and rested a hand on his shoulder. "*None* of us could have predicted this. The most important thing right now is that we are all alive. And there *will* be someplace safe for us. We just have to find it… Either way, we need better medical attention for your arm."

Her voice cracked and she buried her chin in her jacket.

"Eva?"

"Yeah?"

"I've wanted to say something for a while. And if we don't make it..."

Jake reached up and wiped away a tear from Eva's face. She pulled him into an embrace and kissed him. He ran his fingers through her hair and danced his lips across hers.

"I love you Eva Calloway," he said. "Wholly and unapologetically. And thank you for saving us again. This will be the last time. I swear it."

She laid her forehead against his and chuckled, "I love you too, Jake. I sure hope so."

Tommy returned to the home with thick blankets and clothing. Eva let them dress as she scoured the desolate street for any sign of the Tigers. It wasn't long before she picked up the distant sounds of voices. Something dark moved out of the corner of her eye. When she turned, her eyes widened when she saw the figure. It was her demon. Until now, the face of it had been her own. This time, it had stolen the face of Dan McAvoy. At first, Eva thought he had caught up to them but remembered that she had driven a blade through his ribs. Her jump backwards was enough to alert Jake and Tommy.

"Are you okay?" Jake asked as he finished tying the laces to shoes that were far too large for him. His eyes slowly turned to the empty space where Eva had been staring.

"Fine." She lied. "We have to go. I can hear the Tigers coming up from the valley."

Eva handed them each a large knife and wrapped a blanket around her shoulders. They set off towards the south. As long as they continued moving, they could make it through the city and into unknown territory in two or three days. Unfamiliar lands frightened The Wanderer. Not once had she ventured so far south of the city. From the heights of the skyscrapers, the horizon had always been swallowed by wild green—ruins of the Old Times tangled in vines and forest. With no reason to leave her colony, she had let that distant wilderness remain only a thought, never a memory.

"You have no idea what's out there?" Jake asked.

"No." Eva replied. "But we'll find out."

Distant voices started closing in on them. Starlight was sparkling across the sky as the three escapees rushed out of the street towards the glowing lights of the Rover colony. Their route would take them past the town that Eva had lived and protected for years, only to be exiled. When they finally entered the labyrinth of streets in the city, they could put some distance between the hunters and the hunted. And after they left the skyscrapers behind, they would continue to travel South until they found somewhere safe.

Jake was injured. Tommy and Eva were exhausted and hungry. Every time they were forced to slow their pace, they would hear the distant war cries of the Tigers gaining on them. The only thing that kept them moving was the certainty of death if they stopped.

When the sounds of voices trailed off, they realized where they were. By the time the old roads turned into a long stretch of ancient highway, their field of vision started to shorten. A thick haze was forming from warmer air mixing with the winter chill. They realized that their journey had taken them miles closer to the Rover colony.

It was late the following morning when the city started coming into their view, just over the horizon. The fog was starting to clear but absorbed the noises all around them. The Gang could be closing in on them and they wouldn't know until it was too late. Eva couldn't hear anything, but she did not feel alone either. Someone was watching them. They started moving faster until they finally reached the northern outskirts of the city by the end of the second day.

They found a nearby stream and stopped to take a few drinks of water. Their mouths were dry, and they were extremely thirsty, so they each had their fill and kept moving.

"How's your arm?" Eva had not said anything to Jake for the entire day. Tommy had not made a sound either.

"It's okay." He winced in pain when she touched it. "Okay… it hurts. But I'll be okay for a while. You wrapped it up really well. Hunger is the thing I'm more worried about."

"We *should* make it to the other side of the city by the end of the night," said Eva. "What's beyond there… if we find a civilization… I promise we will beg for food if we have to. I don't want to risk searching for the Nomads and asking for food or stopping to scavenge. It will take too much time that we don't have."

"Thanks Eva." Jake nodded. "But I'm sure that begging won't be necessary."

Eva took a few steps ahead of him. "You never know."

Despite everything that happened, they were in good spirits. They were together again. Although not entirely safe, at least they were free. Eva had eliminated an old enemy. And though he was Jake and Tommy's father, they had come to know the truth before she ended his life.

The thin outline of the crumbling skyline began appearing through the mist. Eva took the lead again, winding between blocks, alleyways, and through buildings. Tigers could be tracking them, but only the Nomads knew the specific trail they journeyed. She escorted them into the very center of the city. Most Gang members would try taking the streets or alleyways to follow them, but these roads had become impassable from the destruction long ago.

"There they are!" Bullets pelted into a brick wall nearby. Eva and the McAvoy brothers ducked out of the way and started running again. The Tigers had caught up to them.

How did they find us?

Eva quickly led the boys further toward the southern outskirts. She guided them through a few small spaces, so the Tigers lost their trail again, but she lost the blanket wrapped around her in the process. The three of them pushed themselves to travel well into the night without food or rest. They were starving, tired, and freezing cold. As they journeyed on for hours, the city's high walls disappeared, and they found themselves standing at the edge of the region.

Overlooking an old neighborhood and seemingly endless wasteland, The Wanderer saw something. A haze of light in the distance. Fog had risen above their heads, transforming into opaque, low-hanging clouds. This mysterious light pressed its rays against the gray above, flickering like lightning. And yet, the glow was steady enough not to come from a thunderstorm. It was a civilization. It had to be.

"Is it a Gang?" Tommy asked.

"I-I don't know," Eva replied. They were being drawn to the light like bugs to a flame over the horizon. "We have to take the risk. It could be civilization."

That moment was when she fully realized how much these two siblings had changed her. Before, as the lonely Wanderer, death from starvation would have been a 'safer bet' than waltzing into an unknown town. They had softened her spirit, warmed her heart, and gave her hope. She still bore the skills, but no longer the stubbornness. She smiled at them and started down the street towards the glow in the distance. That was when Jake spotted the sign. It looked like it had been made only days before. The wet, blue paint was still bright against the freshly cut wood.

Rapture Welcomes The Wanderer

"Now if that isn't a *sign*," Jake put a heavy hand on Eva's shoulder, breathing heavily from exhaustion and pain. "I don't know what is."

"Under any other circumstances I would be hesitant." She looked back at the city. It looked desolate, but she knew that it was crawling with Tigers. "But death will come to us if we go back. Death will come if we do nothing. And to be honest, death may come if we follow this sign. But we have a better chance of living if we go with the third option."

Tommy nodded, looking back over his shoulder in worry. "Let's go."

About a mile now stood between them and the source of the light. Sudden waves of euphoria lifted their heels with each step closer. Thoughts of mouth-watering meals. Plates overflowing with meats, vegetables, and fruit. Kind, hospitable people showing them to warm beds near a crackling fire. A place to raise a family.

All of those images faded when they reached the foreboding walls.

This town called 'Rapture' bore an eerie resemblance to a Gang compound. Walls of white stone rose higher than anything Eva had ever seen. Still, no barbed wire crowned their tops, and the guard towers stood as if seldom used. Only a few small slits through the immense door acted as windows to the unknown. But when Eva peered through one of them, she was met with a pair of eyes staring right back at her. She jumped backwards.

"Who are you?" A male voice came from the other side. "State your names or move along."

"This is Jake and Tommy." Eva paused. Pondering how to address herself. The sign claimed she was 'welcomed' here. She bit her lip and answered truthfully. "And I am Eva. I am The Wanderer. We seek asylum here, if you would take us."

"Show me your blades," demanded the voice. "If you are who you say you are."

Eva took a step back. Jake and Tommy watched in anticipation as she reached up. Her hands caressed the leather and steel hilts, unchanged since she had first become their owner. Goosebumps prickled her arms as the metallic sound of unsheathing them reached her ears. She held one out at either side of her body, waiting for a reply. It was silent.

"Please," she said, looking over her shoulder to see whether she was being watched. "This man is injured, and we are being hunted by a Gang from the north. We saw your sign. Can you help us?"

They heard one pair of footsteps leave for a moment. Then, three or four pairs clicked on cobblestone back to the door. Eva could feel them watching her. She heard their whispers. Looking at her beloved Jake, shivering and becoming more pale with each passing moment, she felt her face get hot with frustration.

"Let us in," she demanded. Her voice became frantic and loud. "I will not have someone I love die in front of me while you continue to ponder who I am. Some know me as, *One who walks in shadow behind footprints of blood.* If you've heard this, then you should be well aware that I will stop at nothing to get care and food for us."

The massive metal doors swung wide, and a small group of armor-clad warriors stood to greet them. Eva nearly dropped her blades at the sight beyond. Jake and Tommy stood at either side, mouths agape. Rapture unveiled before her eyes. An entire civilization, vast and alive, greater than they had ever imagined could exist.

"Welcome *Wanderer*," said the guard with the most intricate armor. "No need for threats or pleas. We have been watching… and waiting for you to join us."

Eva looked at Jake and Tommy as they stepped inside. As the doors closed behind them, they took one last look at the life they had lived. Not one of them knew what Rapture had in store for them, but at least they would be together.

The Wanderer watched the massive gates shut and lock behind her. Just through the crack was her

Shadow. It flickered but did not disappear. She swallowed the lump in her throat as the face of McAvoy, stolen from this demon, revealed its pointed teeth in a terrifying smile. It mouthed the words "I'll be back," and dissolved from sight. But the feeling of unease lingered.

***

Some of the Tigers doubled back to the compound after losing sight of The Wanderer and McAvoy's sons. A high-rank member of the Gang marched up the stairs of The Castle to the Chief's chambers. Bondsmen and Doxies were cleaning up the battle and bodies were being dragged out of the room and down the hall to be buried. Bullet holes splintered the wood-paneled walls, and the floor was stained red. Only one remnant of The Wanderer remained, her gun. A guard tossed his slinged rifle over his shoulder and picked up the handgun. There was one round left in the chamber.

The Doxies remained silent as another set of footsteps entered the room. The man stood up with his back facing the doorway as his comrade entered. She was his equal of sorts, skilled not in taking lives, but saving them. He posed a question although hesitant to hear the answer.

"Will he make it?"

Her words were stern, but honest. "I'm not sure. But he's asking for you by name, Ian. *You* are next in line if he doesn't."

Ian nodded at the Healer who led him to the room across the hall. The sign that read *Wives* had been broken in the battle. While she opened the door, Ian wiped the blood from Eva's gun and stepped inside.

All of Chief McAvoy's wives were sitting in their beds, whispering to one another or weeping softly. The murmuring stopped when Ian entered the room but continued as he walked down the aisle between the rows of beds. At the far end were three more healers standing over a pale figure. His chest was wrapped in gauze and linen. When Ian, the next-highest ranked Tiger, stepped to the side of the Chief's bed, Dan McAvoy turned his head.

His irises were still icy blue, but his face had been drained of almost all its color. His complexion was white as a ghost and dark shadows formed under his swollen red eyes. Even though he was far too injured to sit up, he forced words out from his wounded lungs.

"I will *not* let her win," he coughed. "She and her tyranny will be vanquished. I refuse to die while she still breathes."

Ian nodded.

"Sir." The Tiger placed her gun on the bed near his hand. "Her gun. It has only one bullet left."

"How quaint," a weak, yet malicious smile crossed his lips. He wrapped his hand around the handle weakly. "Foreshadowing. Irony. To end The Wanderer's life with her own bullet. How great a story this will be."

www.ingramcontent.com/pod-product-compliance
Lightning Source LLC
Chambersburg PA
CBHW031241310726

48971CB00004B/1116